# ION
# CURTAIN

First published 2022 by Solaris
an imprint of Rebellion Publishing Ltd,
Riverside House, Osney Mead,
Oxford, OX2 0ES, UK

*www.solarisbooks.com*

ISBN: 978-1-78618-599-0

Copyright © 2022 Anya Ow

The right of the author to be identified as the author of this work
has been asserted in accordance with the Copyright, Designs and
Patents Act 1988.

All rights reserved. No part of this publication may be
reproduced, stored in a retrieval system, or transmitted, in any
form or by any means, electronic, mechanical, photocopying,
recording or otherwise, without the prior permission of the
copyright owners.

This is a work of fiction. All the characters and events
portrayed in this book are fictional, and any resemblance
to real people or incidents is purely coincidental.

A CIP catalogue record for this book is available from the
British Library.

Designed & typeset by Rebellion Publishing

Printed in Denmark

# ION CURTAIN

## CURTAIN

### ANYA OW

*To my family and my friends, who have kept me writing.*

# CHAPTER ONE

THE KASHIN-CLASS DESTROYER *Song of Gabriel Descending* Gated out of tian into normal space in what would have looked like a magic trick to a casual observer. One moment it wasn't there—and the next, it was: a monstrous orbital spear, ringed with centrifugal decks and slung with pulsar teeth. As the *Gabriel* synched back to the network and broadcast its location on general and VMF channels, it began to wake some of its crew from their pods, powering down its stardrive and warming up its standard engines. Then it settled down gleefully to wait.

Commander Viktor Kulagin, to his profound irritation, woke up from podsleep to the deep bass caterwauling of some pre-Ascent Sol song. Booming from the seeded speakers along the hull was a brassy, trumpeted military reveille.

"Ship, shut it off!" Viktor growled, stumbling over to the cleanser to throw up. Podsleep, in general, had never agreed with him. For all that *Song of Gabriel Descending* had been upgraded with the very latest in suspension tech when it had been refitted with an Eva Core, its Gating process was even more jarring to his physiology than usual.

The cleanser voided, and Viktor stepped into the purifier. "Good morning, Captain," Ship said, in the voice of a young woman. "I've woken the Tula and Orel Directorates. Once you've all finished feeling sorry for yourselves, breakfast will be served."

Viktor leaned his forehead against the smooth, cold plasteel shell of the purifier and prayed briefly for patience. "You're not yet far enough from Sol that I can't get you refitted off my ship," he warned. Viktor finished the rinse cycle and stepped out of the purifier, pulling on his pressed uniform from the wall shelf.

"Kwang ships are not far from anywhere. Unlike the non-Kwang ships that can only Gate into tian from stellar platforms. That *was* the point of getting refitted in the first place."

"This is a military ship," Viktor complained, not for the first time. "I don't know why they coded you into a Kwang Core." It was already an old argument between them, one that Ship leant into enthusiastically. Ship had a pedantic soul—if an artificial super intelligence could be said to have a soul.

"Hmm, I wonder, could it be that there are military benefits to being able to Gate without a Gate?"

"I didn't mean that." Viktor scrubbed his hands over his eyes. "I meant you. What is the point of encoding a military ship with a personality?"

"I suppose they thought it'd be better than having you talk to an ASI with the emotional range of a toaster," Ship said.

"I would've preferred that," Viktor grumbled, though High Command had explained the reason behind the non-clinical aspect of the ASI to all Kwang ship captains. Military, impersonal ASIs would run the risk of what the Admiralty delicately called 'over-efficiencies'. In simulators, they often tended to chuck their inefficient human passengers out of the airlocks.

On some days, Viktor could even sympathize.

"You're lucky that I'm functionally obliged to like people," Ship said, as Viktor went through his usual limbering up exercises in the small Captain's cabin. "I was bored within tian. I'm glad you're all awake." There was a faint pause. "And alive."

"You can't get bored. You are an ASI."

"I'm bored *all* the time," Ship retorted, with mock sadness.

"Of all ships, why mine?" Viktor muttered.

It was a futile sentiment. High Command had told all four Kwang Ship Captains in confidence that the Kwang Project had almost been a failure. Coding a pure ASI from the ground up would take years, if only because it had to be taught the appropriate ethical constraints and thought processes. Dr. Alek Kwang had instead mapped and coded the brain patterns of a handful of test subjects, a controversial lateral decision that had proved to be mostly a failure. Most of the original Cores had woken up unusable, save those mapped with the brain patterns of Alek's daughter, Eva. The VMF Rossii, the Russian Federation's Navy, had still been willing to gamble on outfitting a brace of ships with Eva Cores.

Now Viktor and a thousand people under his command were effectively test subjects. Were his ship to snap and decide to vent them all, there would be little that Viktor could do but hope to use his Captain's overrides in time. Still in a grim mood, Viktor made his way to the Bridge rather than to the mess hall. His stomach was in no mood for sustenance right out of podsleep, and Viktor felt no real need to add more involuntary vomiting to an already-bleak day.

A skeletal crew from the Orel Directorate were already operating the consoles, doing their routine status checks. Lieutenant Petrenko glanced up as Viktor headed to the Captain's chair. He was dour, and whippet-thin, older than Viktor by a decade but without the driving ambition that would allow him to rise further in the VMF.

"Counter-Admiral Shevchenko left you a message, Captain." Petrenko stepped away from the Captain's chair. The crew spoke in Russian in the common spaces of the ship rather than Galactic, as a matter of preference. "Captain has the Bridge." Viktor sat down. The synthsteel chair molded automatically to his back, rippling as it did so, before synching to Viktor's DNA, unlocking Captain's access.

"You should be eating right now," Ship said into Viktor's ear on a private line. Viktor ignored it. Viktor's access linked up to the galactic network, pinged from packet courier drones that Gated routinely back and forth from the stellar Gates, releasing broad-access as well as private band data across tian. The VMF used their own private couriers. As Viktor waited, his access code unlocked a datapak on the encrypted VMF band. The familiar insignia of the Imperial double-headed golden eagle flickered into view, the words 'Voyenno-Morskoi Flot' interspersed with a pulsing warning in Russian that the incoming VMF transmission was confidential.

"Shevchenko to Captain Kulagin." Counter-Admiral Grigor Stepanovich Shevchenko had made the recording aboard Gagarin station. He was in his boxlike office;

everything neatly battened down and secured following military regulations, even in normal grav. "If you are receiving this then I presume that your second Kwang jump has gone well and you are in the Morgana System. While you woke from podsleep, your Ship will have sent me confirmation of a successful jump. I will be brief. The Slava-class cruiser *Farthest Shore* has disappeared. As you know, Captain Nevskaya's cruiser was the only Slava-class warship to be fitted with an Eva Core."

Viktor kept his expression deliberately blank. The skeletal crew had faltered at their consoles, watching the feed. At Viktor's pointed stare, they returned to their tasks. Shevchenko's recording continued. "The *Farthest Shore* was set to arrive at the Borei System after a few test jumps. It never got there. The VMF courier picked up its distress beacon recently, set on our private band in the Autarch System. Its second jump of the set. You are as of this point the closest of the VMF ships—Kwang or not—to the Autarch System. Gate there immediately and investigate. You are authorized to defend yourself in the event of hostile elements. Transmission end."

"Ready to Gate again at any time," Ship said into the silence. Viktor muttered something foul under his breath. "Shall I get everyone to return to podsleep after an hour?"

Viktor nodded. "Have it known. We will Gate again once the hour is past." In the corner of his eyes, he could see even the stern Petrenko grow a little pale. Humans risked heart failure on successive jumps through the spatial tunnels between Gates—referred to even in the VMF under its Galactic term 'tian'—even with the best implant tech available. An hour's grace between each Gate was the minimum recommended break, but anyone who'd had to Gate within a small span would know that they could be fighting nausea for days. Even the most hardened naval officer would cringe at the prospect. Viktor knew that his crew would not be happy, but orders were orders. "In the meantime, I want to see all known records on the *Farthest Shore* and the Autarch System."

Before Petrenko could move, Ship brought up neat reams of dense datapaks over the deck. The files were organized by date and classification level, along with a small 3D hologram of the *Farthest Shore,* rendered to a greater degree of detail than Viktor had ever seen. The tiny ship floated perfectly over his deck, with its pulsar racks and single typhoon lascannon mounted close to its tapering nose. Most space-only ships were built for efficiency and to maximize shield tech. As such, they tended to be bulbous and pod-like. The *Farthest Shore*— like all VMF warships—looked like the blade of a knife.

"I didn't know that our decks could do that," Petrenko said.

"I upgraded our systems while we were Gating," Ship said in Viktor's ear. Petrenko's eyes widened fractionally. Ship had shared that with the lieutenant as well. "Under my directive, I am allowed to carry out any necessary non-invasive upgrades autonomously."

Viktor took in a slow breath. Kwang ships were going to take some getting used to. "What else did you upgrade?"

"Fuel core efficiencies. I'm going to work on our shielding next."

"Get Engineering to sign off on your 'non-invasive' upgrades first," Viktor said, his hands tightening on the armrests.

"I'd know better than them, and I won't sabotage myself. What would be the point? I'm authorized to—"

"That's an order," Viktor said. The thought of having

his Ship quietly edit itself without first being signed off by a human made his skin crawl. "Send me a copy of any upgrades that you make."

"If you like." Ship sounded faintly reproachful as it went quiet. Viktor ignored it, flicking through top-level data.

The *Farthest Shore* had been meant to jump to the Autarch System after visiting Ila. It was on the final leg of its experimental trip after Gagarin station, testing how far a warship as large as it was could Gate under a Kwang Core. It was supposed to arrive at Borei to briefly bolster VMF presence in what was technically one of the Neutral Zones. There was a Federation colony in the System called Duma, a small mining colony on a harsh snowball of a planet rich in huginnium—one of the core elements of stardrive seeds. There was also a Virzosk Inc trading post that had once been a Federation generation ship, sitting at three day's hard sail from the Autarch System's stellar Gate. The colony itself was three months' standard sail from the stellar Gate, the second-to-last planet from the Autarch sun. The *Farthest Shore*'s distress beacon was placed about a week's sail from the stellar Gate, between the Gate and Duma.

"Viktor brought up the star map of the Autarch System with a wave and pointed. "We should jump here," he said. Ship helpfully made a pinpoint mark with coordinates.

"Three days' sail from the beacon?" Petrenko asked.

"Too close and we might accidentally Gate into survivors or wreckage. Besides," Viktor said, "if it is a trap, I don't want to jump right into it."

"Easy," Ship said.

"Yes, sir." Petrenko hurried down to the lower deck of the Bridge to broadcast their acknowledgement and response through to the VMF courier. Viktor waved away the star map and brought back the hologram of the *Farthest Shore*.

"That's nearly a third bigger than I am," Ship said helpfully, as though reading his mind. Viktor closed his eyes briefly in irritation. All VMF crew wore implants that linked them to a ship, Kwang or otherwise, allowing the constant monitoring of their vital signs. On a non-Kwang ship, this was routine and barely noticed. Ship, on the other hand, had quickly proved that it could read vital signs to such a detailed degree that it could uncannily predict what its crew was thinking. It unsettled Viktor's crew. It unsettled *Viktor*.

"You are doing it again," Viktor said.

"Just forwarding an opinion that if something out there could damage a VMF cruiser, they'd have no problem damaging *me*."

"You are Ship. Ship is not meant to have an opinion."

"I think I would have had more fun as a UN ship," Ship said. It let out a surprisingly human laugh in Viktor's implant as Viktor stiffened in outrage.

"I can still get you refitted," Viktor grit out.

"Not until this mission is over, you can't," Ship said, "and I think you'd probably warm to me before this is over."

"I don't think so."

"Shee-*utt*," Pablo whispered, nosing their ship closer to the wreck. The *Now You See Me* was a reasonable size as far as corsair ships were concerned, a ten-man ship that could be run by a crew of five. It could have fit entirely within just the nose of the wrecked starship that lay before them.

Solitaire strained forward in his seat, gesturing to zoom in on the dead ship on his ship's holodeck. Not that they needed the imaging. The wreck was massive enough that everyone could see it through their steelglass nose port, a dark, hulking finger that was pale gray on the sun side, broken into two like a snapped twig. Debris dotted the space around it. As Solitaire zoomed in as far as he could, he could see that the debris was mostly plasteel, odds and ends, and bodies. His First Mate, Indira, made a soft sound that was tight with horror.

They had been on their way out of Prana Colony when they'd received the distress signal, broadcast only on the VMF private band. Most self-respecting corsair teams tapped into at least one military band—it wasn't too hard to buy access codes out of the Neutral Zones. There were lots of disaffected defectors out there. Military salvage wasn't a gig that Solitaire preferred to run, but they were in need of a good gig, and he had been curious. He'd expected to maybe run into a supply ship out of Duma having an engine malfunction, and perhaps wrangle a fee to tow them to Prana. This—this was nowhere near what he'd been expecting.

"We at war?" Joey asked nervously. He crossed himself.

Joey was a thin young man with the elongated muscle structure and bone that came from being born spaceside rather than downwell somewhere. Like most spacesiders, he had a thoroughly mixed parentage: brown skin, peppery black hair, narrow eyes that seemed perpetually on the move. Joey's nerves were a little too shaky for life as a corsair navigator, but he could stitch together jump scheds on the fly and calculate complex trajectories in his sleep. His skills had saved the crew more than once.

"Not that I know of," Indira said. She sounded irritated

that Joey had even asked. Indira was an ex-UN spacesider, merchant Navy probably. Solitaire had never asked. A corsair's past was traditionally nobody's business but their own. She kept her black hair shaved down. Her dark skin always stood in sharp contrast with the pale gray mech shifts that she liked to wear, and she was both good at comms *and* the crew's only crack shot. Indira pursed her lips as she scanned comm chatter. "Nothing out of Duma. Or the general VMF line."

"Probably some sort of secret war," Frankie said. Born downwell in a colony that had a higher g, Frankie was stocky and dense-looking, with olive-brown skin and black hair.

"For a medic and an engineer, you do sure love your conspiracy theories," Solitaire said.

"I'm educated. Doesn't mean I'm not open-minded," Frankie said loftily.

"*Pssh*. Nobody does that anymore," Pablo said. He looked over at Solitaire for support. "Secret wars, cold wars, warm wars, whatever. All that destroying each other in space is *last century* shit."

"No comment," Solitaire said, forever surprised that Pablo could retain such a sunny opinion about intergalactic affairs, given his background.

Pablo and Solitaire were the only ones who had been born on Sol itself. Where Solitaire was tall, Pablo, a citizen of the South American Conglomerate, was compact and boxy, his broad, brown face always cut with an easy grin. Solitaire had known Pablo the longest. They'd come up through the UN Reserve Navy together and had, eventually, left for about the same reasons, even if they had ended up in different places. Pablo had started working private freight, while Solitaire had been headhunted elsewhere. He'd run into Pablo again by chance years after, when he'd finally gone private himself.

"You know what I mean. Since we're one big space family now. Families quarrel and have the occasional punchup, but we haven't had all-out war for over a hundred years. Since everyone took their heads out of their asses and figured out that the universe's way, way big enough for *everyone*," Pablo said.

"I do wish that I shared your optimism," Frankie said, "but historically speaking, people have never ejected their heads from their asses to such a degree."

Solitaire clenched his hands lightly over the rests of his cradle. "The hell is a VMF cruiser doing out here? Without an escort?" Only the VMF made ships like this.

"Who the hell was crazy enough to fire on the Russians? They've got long memories," Indira said. She shot Solitaire an uneasy glance. "Can't have been corsairs. I've never heard of a corsair fleet big enough to take on a cruiser. Even one without an escort."

"Maybe it was an accident," Frankie said. He didn't sound convinced. "Fusion core meltdown? Their reactor's in the centre, right? Along with the stardrive. Ship shattering into half like that, maybe that's what happened. Boom, then *pfffsth*." Frankie mimed something splitting apart with his hands.

"We didn't need the sound effects. There's no sound in space," Solitaire said. Frankie rolled his eyes.

"On a VMF warship? Got to be very deliberate sabotage—their ships are built with multiple redundancies. And it'll be the first time I've ever heard of such a thing," Indira said.

"Maybe it was aliens," Joey said.

Pablo groaned. "Not this again! Joey. There are. No aliens."

Joey scrunched up his face. "Never say never. Who the hell else would fire on a VMF *cruiser*, eh? Whack it up like that? Could be they came upon the ship and were like hey, what's up people, and the VMF did the VMF thing, where they shoot first and ask questions later, and then *boom*."

Solitaire exhaled. "Joey. No."

"No sound in space," Frankie muttered.

"It wasn't *boom* like a sound thing but as an explosion thing," Joey said. He looked hurt. "Aliens, man. I'm telling you."

"Anyway, what do we do?" Indira raised her voice as Frankie and Joey started to squabble. "Doesn't look like there are any survivors. Our shipscan isn't picking up any preliminary heat signatures."

Solitaire stared at the wreck. It didn't look big from this distance, but he knew that to be deceptive from personal experience. Close up, a ship like that could swallow a dozen copies of the *Now You See Me* into its hangar with a lot of room to spare. As a VMF ship, it would have been slung with the latest in military teeth, with staff cycled onto efficient shifts at all times. Unlike the sprawling UN Navy, the VMF didn't believe in cutting the occasional corner. It was why they were feared, even though the UN outnumbered the VMF. Yet here was one of their cruisers, dead in the middle of nowhere.

Curious.

"Keep the engines warm but stay close. I'm going in," Solitaire said. The *Now You See Me* had a seed-shaped skip that sat snugly against a flank, a piloted two-seater with a quick thrust that could double as an escape pod. It wasn't top-of-the-line and only had half a day's worth of compressed air aboard, but it was maneuverable, fast for what it was, and had a few surprises aboard that Solitaire had installed himself.

"You're gonna *what*." Pablo stared at him. "This isn't some merchant wreck, cabrón. It's a *VMF* wreck. You don't steal from the VMF."

"We're not stealing. We're salvaging. Maybe even rescuing people who might be hiding in radar-blocked panic rooms and such. Not stealing," Solitaire repeated. Pablo didn't look convinced.

"The VMF shits on semantics," Frankie said sourly. "Sometimes they shit on it so hard, the people they shit on end up buried in an exidium mine. Just saying."

"Ooh," Joey said, growing pale. "I'm allergic to exidium."

"*Everyone*'s allergic to exidium. That's why the VMF makes people they don't like mine it," Pablo said.

"Just admit that you're curious," Indira told him.

Solitaire held up his palms. "All right, fine. I'm curious."

"What if the VMF shows up?" Pablo asked.

"We're far from a Gate. By the time they even get here—assuming they even detect us—we'll be home free," Solitaire said, confident. "Nothing I haven't done before."

"It's going to be like Mercer station all over again," Frankie said. He pulled a face.

"You're going to get eaten by aliens. I seen all the vids. Dead spaceship. Broken in half. No apparent reason. *Full of aliens*." Joey drew up his hands beside his head into claws.

"That's why I'm going to bring Indira." Solitaire beamed. "In case of aliens. Given that she's our inestimable head of public relations."

"Fuck you, Yeung," Indira said, though she was already hauling out her weapons cache.

"I guess if you people die, the rest of us can get rich selling the video from your suit cams to the feds." Frankie perked up.

The skip took two hours to get to the wreck from where the *Now You See Me* sat idle, engines warm and ready to dart away quickly at the first sign of danger. Or, as Joey put it, the first sign of aliens. This meant that there was nothing to do but sit behind Indira and watch the gigantic wreck come closer and closer on the viewport, all the while listening to Pablo bicker with Joey over the comms.

"Cut chatter," Solitaire said, once they were an hour in. The first body had floated past. It was a VMF officer, the bright bars of rank visible on her jacket sleeve. Her eyes were open and frozen, her body so swollen that her features were unrecognizable. On the sun side, her skin was blistered over and cooked. Solitaire and Indira touched their fingertips to their foreheads and gestured upward, in the Galactic gesture of respectful farewell.

Indira cut down the throttle carefully as they started towards floating debris. There were more and more bodies now, thousands of people. Too many for a fusion meltdown, if a meltdown could even cascade to such an event. In any case, a ship of this size should've automatically sealed itself in such an event. Backup generators should've kicked in, allowing parts of the broken wreck to stay life-capable until rescue came. This... this looked like *all* of the crew were dead, not just the poor bastards in Engineering.

Solitaire could see Indira murmuring some sort of prayer under her breath, tears in her eyes. Strange and aggressive as the VMF might be, no one deserved to die like this. At least it looked like it was quick.

"Look at that," Solitaire murmured as they drew close. Many of the bodies were still locked inside sleep pods.

Some pods looked intact, but the people within them were dead—sleep pods didn't have independent life support systems like escape pods. "Looks like they were running off a skeletal crew, if at all. Weird."

"This far from a stellar Gate? Yeah. I thought the VMF didn't do that."

"Not on a ship this size, no."

"Gods." Indira tried to slip their skip through a dense cloud of partly shattered pods and winced as they bumped through broken bodies. Solitaire wanted to point out that the dead wouldn't mind, but as Indira wiped away tears and sniffled loudly, he kept his peace.

They vented to a stop as close to the wreck as Indira dared. Solitaire got up, heading to the back of the skip to suit up. Indira kept right behind him with the skip left on auto, leaving Pablo set to override if necessary. "Shit," Joey said soberly into the comms as Solitaire pulled on his helmet. "You still going in there? Shit."

"Just keep an eye out, Joey," Solitaire said with a lightness that he didn't feel. "You'll be the first to know if we run into any aliens."

"The joke was funny when you people were here, and it isn't funny now," Pablo said. He sounded nervous.

"Joke? I wasn't joking," Joey said.

"Cut chatter, assholes," Indira said. She limbered up, doing a final weapons check.

The suits were secondhand and getting on in age, but they were UN Navy, and putting them on felt like putting on a second skin. The helmet was solidly plasteel, the onboard cycle kicking into cool the moment the helmet locked in, the suit auto-sealing against the outside. The wrist panel flickered on. All systems green. "All right, Pablo," Solitaire said, "fire the hooks."

Drone-guided hooks hissed out from the skip with dull thumps that Solitaire could hear even through his helmet. He and Indira checked each others' suits over. By the time they were done, Pablo said, "Hooked up. Good luck."

Outside, the onboard cycle whirred fractionally louder as it started to compensate for the sun exposure. Solitaire's breathing sounded too loud in his ears as he hooked the palm catch to the ship's tether and rode it slowly over to the hull of the wreck. Indira followed behind him. The whirring and his breathing were all he could hear, a dull and uneasy cadence that sounded eerily grotesque with so much death around them.

When Indira spoke, Solitaire flinched. "Are we looking for something in particular?" she asked.

"Usual. Survivors. Whatever we can salvage," Solitaire said. The shipscan hadn't shown any heat signatures this close, but you never did know with VMF ships. "Stardrive seeds would be great if they haven't imploded. Uh. Ship's armory, maybe."

Indira pursed her lips through her helmet. "Gonna need days to search a wreck this big. More."

"Well, we'll just do it until we get bored."

"Or until the VMF shows up," Indira said. She sounded grim. "You think we're the only one who heard their distress beacon?"

"Relax. We're a week's hard sail from the stellar Gate. Any ship that gets through gets broadcast to the local System. Besides, no ship's going to come through quickly enough to be a problem. So..." Solitaire trailed off. They had just hauled themselves into the fusion chamber.

The fusion core of the ship *had* been blown. There was only slag along the melted edges of the ship that had sat against the fusion core chamber itself. Twisted scrap metal sat in vacuum, all unidentifiable. So much for stardrive seeds. Solitaire looked to his right, then to his left. To either side, the dead ship stretched, utterly dark. Not even the emergency lights were on. The moment his foot made contact on the slewed deck, floor lights flickered to life, a dotted line of emergency red lights that led away into the dark. Solitaire looked over his shoulder. The other half of the ship was still dark.

"Something's working, at least." Solitaire's voice sounded shaky to his ears.

"Aliens," Joey said.

"Shut the fuck up, Joey," Indira snarled. She drew her blaster slowly from her hip. Much use that would do in dead space. Indira's fingers fit thickly around the stock, and movement would be slow. "Maybe it's a distress signal, leading to hidden survivors."

"O-kay." Solitaire managed to calm himself after a few breaths. "Pablo, how's your Russian?"

"Pretty bad? I think I can kind of manage it broken?" Pablo sounded panicky. "Why?"

Frankie caught on. "We could pull up cached audio in Russian offering medical assistance and broadcast that to the ship?"

"Let's not do that, because the last time we tried pulling random shit off the datanet it meant something completely different and we nearly died," Joey said.

"Give it your best shot. Galactic too," Solitaire said. Most of the VMF people he'd ever vaguely known could speak Galactic anyway. "Do the usual short-range radio broadcast to the wreck. I don't know if anyone's still in here and somehow avoiding our scans, but we can hope for the best."

"We only got basic medical aboard the *Now You See Me*," Pablo said.

"Kinda doubt that's going to be an issue," Solitaire said, watching the corona of dead surrounding where they'd left the hooked skip. "But if it is, we'll think of something. Ship like this will have topline medical. We can rig something up."

"Sure." There was a pause, then a faint click as Pablo switched to general comms. Solitaire muted broadcast channels as Pablo started his spiel.

Taking a moment to steady his nerves, Solitaire started to move along the lights, his boots clamping magnetically to the deck. They would be green on oxygen for about a couple more hours before they had to return to the skip. Solitaire wasn't particularly worried if they had to stay longer. A cruiser like this would have oxygen stores aboard that they could decant for their suits.

It was a depressing walk. The dead ship was thick with debris, and not all of the bodies had vented into space. Some still floated in the corridors, likely caught against obstacles during the explosive decompression. All dead. With the space-saving structure of the ship, this meant that debris and bodies sometimes choked up the corridors and had to be carefully sorted aside. The lights didn't lead them to any newly-made dead ends and looked as though they were trying to avoid the worst of any choke points. The VMF built their ships well. Usually, Solitaire would remark on this to Indira, but talking about something like that felt disrespectful in the tomb that they were walking through. They had been following the lights for half an hour when they finally reached an upper deck. Solitaire was starting to feel puzzled. Where *were* they going? To the ship's black box, perhaps? That wasn't something that Solitaire was interested in stealing. He wasn't a total asshole. The VMF deserved to know what happened to its crew. He paused, motioning to Indira to wait. Once they did so, the lights shut off. As they hastily flicked their shoulder lights on, Solitaire, with a start, saw that the door they'd come through was closing slowly. He backed off a step in the direction the lights had been leading them to. The blast door froze. The emergency lights came back on, rippling as they urged Solitaire toward the zero-g access shunt.

Okay.

That wasn't creepy at all.

"Fucking VMF," Indira muttered. Over the comms, Pablo was saying "Ho-lee-sheeet," faintly, over and over.

"I don't think it's aliens. I think it's a haunted ship," Joey said.

There was an emergency access lift beside it glowing a dull reserve-power yellow, but the doors bulged slightly from some sort of internal impact. Solitaire entered the shunt and pulled himself up a rung. "Joey. Please don't. Or I'm going to let Indira hurt you when we get back."

"It probably just wants us to pick up the black box," Indira said. Her voice shook. "Background programming or something. I guess we can do what it wants. Haul it out, leave it tethered at the mouth of the big hole. That way we're still helpful. But we're not being assholes."

Solitaire nodded. "Sounds good. Pablo, any luck on survivors?"

"If there are any, they ain't interested," Pablo said.

"Right. Cut broadcast for now." Solitaire kept climbing.

The top chamber that they climbed into didn't look like the Bridge or any sort of central command. It was a circular cooling chamber, still functional even though there was no longer any gravity. Thick coils and pylons ran from the walls towards a central core that was about the size of Solitaire's head. It was perfectly spherical and traced with pale blue lines. As he walked closer for a better look, the pylons drew back with a low hum. The struts that held the sphere in place withdrew, dropping it into a silver pod with grooved handles that quickly sealed itself tight.

"Doesn't look like any black box I've ever seen," Indira said. She froze where she stood. "Doesn't look like *anything* I've ever seen."

Solitaire scanned it. "It's not toxic or radioactive. But it's made of something that the scan doesn't understand."

"I think I know what you're going to say. You know what the VMF hates more than people who fuck their ships up? People who *steal* from their ships," Indira said.

"I don't know if we have a choice here. I mean, look." Solitaire pretended to start to walk back towards the hatch. Instantly, the lights on the room switched off. He took a step back. The lights came on again, the ripple growing urgent. "See? It's not our fault that the VMF put in some totally fucking weird failsafe system that needs this shiny ball removed from the premises, right?"

"Are we still going to tether it at the mouth of the wreck?" Indira asked, glowering at Solitaire through her helmet.

"Maybe?"

"Oh Gods. This *is* like Mercer station all over again," Indira muttered.

"Everything's going to be all right," Solitaire said, patting Indira on her shoulder. "It's just us out here. No aliens, no—"

"Uh." Pablo's nervous voice broke in. "We have an incoming transmission from a ship with VMF tags."

"What? Where is it?" Solitaire said, surprised.

"You're not going to believe this. Judging from the signal, it's three days' sail away."

Soltaire gasped. "The hell did we miss that?"

"I don't know! It wasn't there before. We would've picked it up on our radar. It's sitting between Prana and us." Pablo sounded close to panic.

"All right, put the call through to me," Solitaire said. Some sort of new stealth array? Strange that the VMF ship hadn't tried to scare them off earlier. Maybe it hadn't thought that civilian ships would dare to board a VMF wreck.

"What? You loco?" Pablo said, incredulous. "You people come back, and we run."

"That VMF ship's three days away. Besides, do you want the VMF to think that we had something to do with them losing a cruiser? They're close enough to have deep scanned our ship. They've got us down to rights." Besides, the *Now You See Me* was armed. Poorly armed compared to a cruiser like this, but Solitaire didn't want the VMF to get the wrong idea.

"Fuck. I knew this was a bad move," Pablo said.

"Too late now." Solitaire raised his wrist. The wristdeck projected a small screen of light onto the closest hull, revealing a man in a VMF Captain's uniform. He was in his early thirties if Solitaire had to guess—lean, tall, and strikingly good looking. He had cold, gray eyes, and his mouth was set in a thin line of compressed distaste. Pronoun symbols for he/him flicked briefly onto the screen, a universal automatic feature of any inter-personnel broadcast. "—ship. Identify yourselves."

"This is Captain Solitaire Yeung of the *Now You See Me*," Solitaire said, with a little wave. "We picked up a distress signal from your cruiser and came over to look for survivors. We're still checking the ship. So far, no survivors. Sorry for your loss."

"This is Captain Viktor Alexandrovich Kulagin of the *Song of Gabriel Descending*," Viktor said, in a clipped voice. He spoke Galactic with a typically thick Federation accent. Federation citizens had never quite taken to Galactic, which was generally a thick patois of Sol-Mandarin colored in with Indo-Asian dialects and slang. The VMF made their officers learn it, to varying degrees of success. "You are to leave the *Farthest Shore* immediately. Any salvage you have taken must be returned. You are to surrender yourself and your ship to us upon our arrival for a search. Fail to do so, and the VMF will consider you and your ship summarily hostile."

"Give us a break," Solitaire said, startled. "We thought we might be able to save some people, that's all."

Viktor's lip curled into a sneer. "The distress beacon was not broadcast on general access, *Captain Yeung*. Very few ships can and will respond to a military-encrypted beacon. You are a corsair, no?"

"Careful," Indira murmured on their own line.

Pablo coughed. "I'm not sure if surrendering to the VMF is a good idea. If we go now, we can probably outrun them to the stellar Gate. Especially if we go dark."

"They probably won't even chase us. They got to sit over that wreck and comb it down." Joey sucked on his teeth, a sign that he was running the math in his head. "We'll have at least a week's head start. Probably more. Just come back quick, and we'll skip out."

"All right, Captain Kulagin," Solitaire said, "we'll do what you want. But uh. In the meantime, we're kind of stuck? You people have some weird failsafe that needs us to remove something from some top-level room. Every time we try to turn back, the doors close on us and the emergency lights cut off. Any ideas?"

Viktor frowned and looked to the side, then back at the screen. His head tilted slightly as though listening to a private feed. "You are in the top-level room now?"

"Yes. And stuck. It's full of cables? Also, a large ball just put itself into some sort of pod. Is this normal for your ships?"

Viktor's handsome face tightened into a scowl. "That is inconvenient. Captain Yeung, you have a choice. Should that pod be removed, we will consider it an act of war."

Solitaire blinked. "That's kinda an overreaction, in my opinion. But sure. We won't touch it. Do you have override codes or something? Something that'll let us out of here?"

"No. Find a way out without the pod. Or die there. Either way, it is of no consequence to me. I expect your ship to be waiting for me within three days at your current coordinates. With or without you." The projection flickered off.

"That's the end of the transmission," Pablo said. His voice cracked.

"Dick," Joey muttered.

"Now what?" Frankie asked.

"...Search the room again. Try and splice that door," Solitaire said, if halfheartedly. He knew from experience that VMF military tech couldn't be easily bypassed. They spent nearly an hour carefully searching the chamber for a way out, while Solitaire tried his best not to stare at the ever-lowering oxygen gauge.

"I think this pod is probably worth a lot of money to someone." Solitaire walked over and cautiously touched one of the handles. It felt cool through his gloves. Didn't ask him for ID. Good sign. "It's definitely not the black box."

Indira cleared her throat. "Didn't you hear what Captain Kulagin said? Act of war?"

"Either way we're going to die, Indira. We can't get out of here without the pod, remember?" Solitaire calculated the route out in his mind and tried to conserve oxygen by breathing slowly. They'd be pushing the gauge into red at this rate, and the room they were in didn't have any emergency oxygen tanks.

"What about Pablo and the others?" Indira asked.

"You think that the VMF is going to be very gentle about handling a surrender?" Solitaire pointed out. "This pod must be something top-secret for them to overreact like this. I doubt they'd let us go, even if we cooperate, and unless I'm missing something, I don't think the UN likes any of us enough to negotiate on our behalf. Which means we'll all be quickly introduced to our exidium allergies."

"We could leave it tethered to the mouth of the wreck like I suggested before and run for it." Indira glanced between the sealed door and the pod. "Surely Captain Kulagin would have to be happy with that."

"Did he sound all that reasonable to you?" Solitaire had met people like Kulagin before across the 'verse. "Young-looking VMF captain, but did you see the bars on his chest?"

"Pretty sparse lines of decoration for a destroyer's captain," Pablo said.

Solitaire nodded. "Means he didn't get to where he was by pure merit. So, he's probably got a backer. He'd be itching to prove himself and can't be happy being sent here on a mere salvage mission. I'm thinking he's not going to be reasonable. Even if we leave it tethered to the ship. Look at how he reacted—he doesn't care if Indira or I suffocate in here."

"You want to take the risk?" Indira asked, though she smiled in resignation.

"Between laying a bet where we surrender but get sent to the mines, or leave the pod but still possibly get shot at, or definitely get shot at but strike it rich and never have to work again? Let me think," Solitaire said, grinning mischievously.

"I have a bad feeling about this," Frankie muttered.

"Come on. Haven't I done right by us all this while?" Solitaire asked.

"You haven't chosen to do anything as stupid as pissing off the VMF." Indira sniffed.

"Are you sure you're not doing this just because you don't like being threatened?" Pablo asked, suspicious. "Mercer Station is one thing, but this is the VMF. Maybe you should count to ten and take a breath. Or not. Your oxygen's going down. Don't stress."

Solitaire laughed. "I've already done several things to date that'd make the VMF want to kill me on sight if they knew. What's one thing more? I'm still here, aren't I?"

Indira studied Solitaire's expression with a frown. "What?"

"Tell you next time. Oxygen level's dropping," Solitaire said, gesturing at the life signs on his wristdeck. "Look. The VMF isn't as all-powerful as you think. We still have more than half the known 'verse to run to. Besides, once we broker off this pod, we'll become a small fish. We can lie low with our hard-earned gains in the Neutral Zone and take things easy while they chase the pod. Don't tell me that you want to run salvage jobs forever."

Indira exhaled. "Maybe it's the low oxygen count getting to me, but fine. I think this is a terrible idea, but we'll do it your way."

"Great!" Solitaire said.

"I vote no," Frankie said.

"Same," Joey agreed.

"Then you both don't get a share of the sale," Solitaire shot back.

"In that case, I vote yes," Frankie corrected. Joey exhaled but muttered something similar in agreement.

"Every time Solitaire decides to do the democratic thing, I brace myself for a shitshow. Shee-*utt*. Okay, we're doing this. Getting ready to scoot. You two better haul ass," Pablo said.

Getting the pod out of the room was a two-person job. It was heavier than it looked. By the time they were back in the skip and jetting back over to the ship, Solitaire was sweating his regrets into his suit. Pulling it off once they were shipside was a relief, though he didn't have time to enjoy it. Once Indira and Solitaire were settled into their cradles, Pablo kicked the *Now You See Me* into a hard sail.

Twenty minutes in, there was a second VMF-tagged transmission. Solitaire accepted it, motioning for Pablo to drop briefly into a standard sail. He expected anger or outrage, but Captain Kulagin wore an unsettling, predatory amusement instead.

"You've decided to run."

"You kinda gave us a choice between 'death' and 'slightly delayed death' over there," Solitaire said, trying to sound flippant. "We liked the second option better. Or were you actually going to let us go after you interrogated us?"

Viktor let out a short, harsh laugh. He didn't deny it. "I like it when they run," he said to someone off-screen. Viktor glanced back to Solitaire. "Run as far as you can, little rabbit. You cannot escape."

The transmission shut off. Solitaire grimaced. "Asshole."

"What is *wrong* with some people?" Pablo rubbed a hand slowly over his face. "Maybe he wasn't hugged enough as a baby?"

"Make for the Gate. Run dark only for as long as we have to. We're going to skip out to the Pretorian sector," Solitaire said.

"Really?" Indira said.

"That's a long way," Joey said, checking their stardrive gauge. "We'd have to refuel at the nearest port once we get there."

"It's far out of Federation space," Solitaire said. He raised his voice as Indira started to object. "Also, if there's anyone that might buy what we took from that ship, it'd be someone in the Ghost Market within New Tesla." Viktor might like the chase, but Solitaire had all of space to run in. He wasn't going to make it easy. Even for the VMF.

# CHAPTER TWO

KALINA STRETCHED AND rubbed her eyes with a groan. "You win, you old bastard."

"Have some respect when speaking to your commanding officer." Counter-Admiral Kasparov grinned with the mischievous amusement of a child.

VMF Admirals were all within their late fifties or older, and Yuri Antonovich Kasparov was no exception, his hair and his sideburns dusted with fine silver. Laugh lines softened the weak angles of his face, which was an indeterminate shade of brown. His Indo-Asiatic ancestry, like Kalina's, marked Kasparov out as having been born downwell on a colony well beyond the First Wave galaxies. Unlike any of the other Admirals—or just about any officer Kalina knew—Kasparov wore no marker bars on his deep blue uniform. He'd never bothered with them.

"I'll respect you when you earn it, sir."

"You wound me, Lieutenant." Kasparov placed a hand over his heart.

"I thought that was what I was here for. To keep you humble. Sir."

"Ah, well, to keep me *humble* you'd have to beat me once in a while." Kasparov started to reset the Go board even as Kalina bit down on her laugh. "Where did you even learn how to play Go?"

"We're not all ignorant over on Baikonur." Kalina helped Kasparov sort black seeds and white seeds into separate cups.

"It's an uncommon game outside of UN space. The Federation prefers chess."

Kalina had been prepared for this remark. It was true, after all. She had grown up playing Go against her father, but the ancient game, with its deceptively simple rules, was not a popular one in the age of holodecks and AVR. When you could put on a headset that could transport you into the heart of a star, why bother with a plain grid of seeds? Kalina gestured at the chessboard in the corner of Kasparov's office. "I can't beat you at chess, so I thought I'd try Go."

"You can't beat me at any strategic game, but don't take it personally. Most people can't," Kasparov said. It wasn't a boast, just a statement of fact. Kasparov even sounded wistful. "Anna used to come close."

Kalina couldn't hide her grimace. Any reminder of Kasparov's estranged daughter usually plunged him into a morose mood for the rest of the day. Which meant more requests on her time for trivial things, because a morose Kasparov was a childish and lonely Kasparov, and Kalina had better things to do than to babysit a grown man. Even if he was the VMF's most talented strategist.

Thankfully, Kasparov wasn't in one of his moods. He offered her a small smile—a truce. "Who taught you how to play Go? Baikonur's a mining colony, isn't it?"

"You think mining colonies spend all their days doing what exactly, sir?"

Her open defensiveness paid off—Kasparov retreated. "I didn't mean to offend. Or to imply anything."

"My father taught me," Kalina said, "before he died in an accident." One of those things was true, at least.

Kasparov blanched. "I'm sorry to hear that."

"Occupational hazard." Kalina forced a smile. "Another game, sir?"

"If you have the time."

"I'm your personal aide, sir. My time is yours to decide."

"We both know that isn't entirely true," Kasparov said. He hunched eagerly over the board. "You can have the first move."

"What do you mean, sir?" Kalina asked. She selected a black seed, placing it at the Hoshi opening position.

"Give me some credit." Kasparov picked up a white seed. "It's not the first time Shevchenko and the others have tried to get one of their people close to me."

Sweat prickled under Kalina's arms. She was glad for the prevalent chill in Kasparov's office, even as she swallowed her relief. "I don't know what you're talking about, sir."

"Most VMF officers as promising as you are would have already tried angling for field positions or a command position by now. Isn't the goal of any good VMF officer to get a ship of their own?"

"Maybe I'm not a good officer," Kalina said, as Kasparov set down the seed on the board. "Maybe I like picking up after a grumpy old man and repeatedly losing to him at chess, battleships, Go, and checkers."

"Hah!" Kasparov flashed her a sharp smile. "I don't mind. If you're reporting to Counter-Admiral Shevchenko and the others, that is. I don't have anything to hide, and you've been better company than the others."

"If you were as inclined towards nepotism as your fellow Admirals, you'd probably be able to attract a less irascible breed of staff," Kalina told Kasparov. She did not bother to gentle her tone, but Kasparov laughed ruefully anyway. As Kalina set down another seed, his eyes fixed greedily on the game. Kasparov was a hungry man, just like the other Admirals. Yet where the others hungered for influence or power, Kasparov craved stimulation. Kalina had been prepared to despise him for it when she had arranged to be transferred to his staff. He amused her instead, an amusement that was almost like respect.

"Maybe, but they would be a tedious breed." Kasparov put down a black seed. "I'd even say—" He cut himself off as a transmission winked in on his wristdeck. He answered with an impatient gesture, still intent on the board. "What do you want, Inessa?"

If Admiral Inessa Veravna Mikhailova was irritated by Kasparov's familiar mode of address, she didn't show it. She inclined her head at them both. "Counter-Admiral Kasparov. Lieutenant Sokolova." Her blank expression softened visibly. "Yuri, are you free to talk?"

"Oh, I'm very busy." Kasparov angled his wristdeck to give Mikhailova a better view of the board. "Lieutenant Sokolova here has been busy trying to kick my ass." He winked at Kalina, who affected a blank expression.

Mikhailova exhaled. "Yuri, I'm sorry. I wanted to tell you before you got the official statement. It's your daughter. Captain Nevskaya was... The *Farthest Shore* was just found by the *Song of Gabriel Descending*. This is the latest transmission. No survivors."

An image resolved itself beside Mikhailova's face. Kasparov went very pale. Kalina wasn't sure what she was meant to be looking at—it looked like the tip of a knife shattered into several pieces—then she realized it was a tiny hologram of the *Farthest Shore*. "Impossible," Kalina breathed. She grimaced as it dawned on her that she'd spoken out of turn, but neither Admiral paid attention to her.

"What could have done that? The UN? She was on a *cruiser*. She—" Kasparov started to rise to his feet, only to sit down heavily. "It's the fucking Eva Core, isn't it? Something went wrong."

"We don't know yet. The *Gabriel* is approaching cautiously. They mentioned a corsair on the scene, but following a scan of the ship Captain Kulagin of the *Gabriel* said he did not think the corsair was any more than a scavenger."

"Have him arrest this corsair."

"In time. Corsairs are hard to catch, and securing the *Farthest Shore* is our priority. I'm sorry, Yuri."

"She's dead? She's…" Kasparov sucked in a thin breath. His eyes fixed on the impossible hologram, bright with tears. He buried his face in his hands.

"I'll keep you updated," Mikhailova said gently. She nodded at Kalina and cut the transmission.

Kalina sat in nervous silence. Touching Kasparov to offer comfort felt presumptuous. She hadn't technically known Kasparov for long—only a few years in station time. Yet she had to say something. "Sir, my condolences."

"Leave me," Kasparov said, in a hoarse voice wrung with grief. Kalina, relieved, got up and saluted, walking briskly out of the office. Just before the door slid shut, Kasparov said, "Wait."

"Sir." Kalina paused by the door.

"Did Shevchenko… I know Kulagin's one of his, I…" Kasparov rubbed the heels of his hands into his eyes. "No.

No, this isn't Shevchenko's doing. It can't be. Tactically, what would be the point? Besides, Shevchenko can't abide waste."

"Tea, sir?" Kalina asked. It was Kasparov's favorite drug for any sort of intellectual exercise.

"Yes. Thank you, Lieutenant."

Kalina retreated. The sector allocated to Kasparov was small for a Counter-Admiral, taking up only one floor of a building in Gagarin station that wasn't even within sight of the gardens. It was tucked in an out-of-the-way pocket of the administrative ward, fifteen minutes' walk from the closest public transport. Kasparov preferred it that way. Said he liked the quiet. As he traveled everywhere in a bubble of security and never had to take the rail, the inconvenience never occurred to him. Kalina walked over to the tongue of glass that traced the walkway outside Kasparov's private office, staring out at the narrow street beyond. Someone occasionally walked past at a brisk pace with their head down, usually in uniform. There weren't many non-VMF personnel in this part of Gagarin. She could pick out the outer perimeter of Kasparov's guard stationed outside the building, watching passers-by.

Gunnery Sergeant Maya Smirnova, one of four of Kasparov's staff, was in the break room. She was three years from mandatory retirement and would likely be terminal at her current rank, a fact to which she appeared indifferent. Kalina liked Maya, even though the old woman was consistently caustic to her. Maya hated everyone in equal measure, including Kasparov. Kalina preferred people like that—they required less effort.

Maya eyed Kalina coldly as Kalina walked over to the cabinet that kept Kasparov's hoard of tea. The Gunnery Sergeant had the elongated, grayish look of someone born to a working-class Gagarin family. Some quirk of the legacy life-support system and the station affected the children born to Gagarin station natives. Families without veteran privileges couldn't often afford premium-tier corrective medical for their kids. It often gave them a pigmentation deficiency of some sort that grew permanent with age.

"Lieutenant," Maya said, with a nod where another Sergeant would have saluted.

"Sergeant," Kalina said. She picked out the box of sencha from the back.

"Sencha?" Maya's nostrils flared. "Old man having a bad day?"

"Could say that. His daughter died." Kalina started to pick out a cup, only to go still as Maya grabbed her elbow.

"What?"

Kalina jerked free, clamping down on trained instincts that told her how easy it would be for her to break Maya's nose from this angle. "Captain Nevskaya was KIA aboard the *Farthest Shore* along with all her crew."

Maya's mouth opened and shut, reminding Kalina of a gasping fish. "No," she said and started to sniffle. "Gods, no."

Her grief was a surprise. Kalina hadn't thought that Maya would've pissed on Kasparov to save him had he been on fire, let alone harbor any gentle thoughts about his daughter. Or about anyone. "We just received the transmission from Admiral Mikhailova," Kalina said softly. "Did you know the Captain well?"

"We've met," Maya said. She turned away, fiddling at the coffee machine with nerveless fingers. "The Counter-Admiral used to bring her to the office. When she was younger. She was... she was a kind little girl."

Kind little girls did not get assigned captaincies, let alone captaincies of Slava-class cruisers. Maybe Kasparov wasn't as above nepotism as he seemed. Or perhaps the VMF had been hoping that blood would run true. "The Counter-Admiral never mentioned why they were no longer close."

She'd pushed too hard. Maya shot Kalina a hostile stare. "Dig the story out some other time, Lieutenant. Have some respect. Shouldn't you be fetching the Admiral his tea?"

Kalina held her tongue. Snapping back at Maya would only make her laugh, and complaining about Maya to Kasparov only made *him* laugh. "At ease, Sergeant," Kalina said, just to watch Maya scowl. She set the printed sencha leaves into the iron pot to brew with hot water and walked briskly back toward Kasparov's private office with the tray.

Kasparov hadn't moved from where he sat, his head still pressed into his palms, shoulders shaking. Kalina sidled over to his desk. She set the tray down by his elbow and began to clear the Go board.

"Dismissed, Lieutenant," Kasparov said. He didn't look up.

"Yes, sir." Kalina saluted and retreated to her own office. It was adjacent to Kasparov's, and much smaller, a windowless space that had most likely once been a spare storage room. Her holodeck desk and a wardrobe took up most of the area. Kalina squeezed around the desk and sat down. Opening up a few screens, she began to process Kasparov's comms. Condolences were already pouring in from the other Admirals and their immediate staff. Captain Nevskaya's death was still confidential but for Admiral-level access. Kalina flagged all the condolence messages for Kasparov's attention and brought up a second screen to access Nevskaya's personnel file.

A woman about Kalina's age stared grimly out at Kalina beside her military record. Anna Sashavna Nevskaya hadn't taken Kasparov's surname, had used a matronym instead of a patronym for a middle name, and their relationship wasn't mentioned in her file. Only a mother was listed, one Lieutenant Sasha Makarovna Nevskaya, terminal at Second Lieutenant, retired. Kalina suddenly remembered that she had thought that strange when she had first accessed Anna Nevskaya's file for a brief read, years ago, right before she'd agreed to be assigned to Kasparov. It was an anomaly that remained unsolved. Clearly, the nature of Captain Nevskaya's parentage was an open secret, at least among High Command. Nevskaya's death hadn't yet been recorded on her personnel file, and she was still listed as the Captain of the *Farthest Shore*. She'd previously been assigned to a destroyer as a First Lieutenant. Kalina had never met her.

As Kalina reread Nevskaya's file, a new condolence message pinged Kasparov's mailbox. Kalina was about to flag it for his attention when she read the name of the sender. Dr. Alek Kwang? That didn't sound like the name of anyone in the VMF. People born without Federation names usually changed their names if they managed to place into one of the notoriously stringent VMF academies. A matter of necessity strong-armed into pretending to be one of pride. Kalina opened the message.

*Sorry to hear about Anna, but you and I knew this would happen. We reap what we sow. —Alek*

Kalina reread the message a few times before flagging it for Kasparov's attention and closing it. She requested Alek Kwang's file on the network, only to be fed back a curt apology. She didn't have the clearance. Surprised, Kalina tried again. As Kasparov's aide, her security clearance should be as high as his.

Another error. Interesting. Kalina was about to try a broader search just on 'Kwang' in general when Kasparov pinged her. She shut down the search and answered. "Sir. How are you feeling?"

Kasparov was red-eyed. He looked distracted. "Stop trying to access the Kwang file. It's flagged to hell, and since you're my aide, the complaint gets forwarded right to me."

"My apologies," Kalina said. More and more interesting. "I shouldn't have pried."

Kasparov offered her a weak smile. "Get back here, Lieutenant."

Kalina obeyed. Once she stepped back into Kasparov's room, Kasparov stared at her from where he sat, looking Kalina slowly over as though seeing her for the first time. Kalina stayed by the door, standing to attention. "You're not one of Counter-Admiral Shevchenko's," Kasparov said.

"Sir?"

"Either that, or he's been keeping his cards closer to his chest than usual—but I doubt it. You're highly intelligent, not to mention ruthless and ambitious. Exactly the sort of agent he likes. As a favored Service agent, you would've known about Alck." There was no official name for the VMF's intelligence agents, but the rank and file referred to them as the Service: fixers, saboteurs, and assassins.

Kalina allowed her exasperation to show. "I understand that you're very upset, Admiral, but I'm uncomfortable with the insinuation that I'm some kind of spy."

"I know you're a spy," Kasparov said. He glanced down

at his untouched tea, wiping his hands over his knees. "I know the look."

Tian. Where had she tripped up? Stiffly, Kalina said, "If you have any doubt about my character, lodge a complaint, or transfer me."

"Sit down." Kasparov gestured at the chair before his desk.

Kalina sat. She went unarmed aboard Gagarin station, even though she had been assigned a service piece like every other VMF officer. Kasparov and his staff tended to go about unarmed as well, and she'd thought she should match. Even though she missed the weight of a weapon at her hip. "Sir." Not that she needed one. Training told her that there were at least thirteen ways she could kill Kasparov from here if she wanted to. More, if she wasn't worried about hiding the evidence.

"See that." Kasparov gestured at her face. "That look. I've seen it before. I wasn't always sequestered in Gagarin station."

"Sir."

"Your cover's airtight—well, very nearly airtight on the details. Distant colony, popular military Academy where instructors generally don't have the time to keep track of their many cadets. Whoever constructed it for you overlooked one small detail, though. Do you know why I always have a Sergeant on my permanent staff?"

"Sir?"

"Sergeants are tapped into a very particular gossip vine," Kasparov said. He picked up one of the white seeds, tossing it up and down in his hand. "It didn't take Sergeant Smirnova long to find out that no one of your description ever left Baikonur for a military academy. There's no one of your description ever graduating from

Suvorov Academy either. A friend of Sergeant Smirnova's knows the instructors there. As it so happens, the Military History instructor is themself from Baikonur, and they make it a point to get acquainted with any Baikonurian who qualifies into Suvorov."

Kalina evened her breathing. She could kill Kasparov, but that wasn't exactly in her mandate. Besides, she rather liked the man, despite everything. She started to get to her feet. "Sir, the loss of your daughter has affected you emotionally. I recommend that you retire and rest."

"Sit *down*." Kasparov's command was colder than anything she'd ever heard from him. Kalina sat, her hands clenched in her lap. "So. Who?"

"What do you mean?"

"Who sent you to me?"

"No one," Kalina said.

"Bullshit."

Kalina stared at Kasparov evenly. She'd always been a good poker player, and she hoped that won out the day for her now. "I was asked to keep an eye on you. Sir. On behalf of the VMF. I *chose* to transfer to your staff."

"An eye on me? Why?"

"I believe there was an infamous incident involving Vice-Admiral Bazarov, a lemon, and an android dog. It might have made Federation news headlines for a few days."

Kasparov looked startled. "That was a harmless prank."

"Harmless?"

"No one was seriously hurt. Fine, there was rather more collateral damage than I... so the Admiralty assigned me a babysitter?" Kasparov rubbed a palm over his face with a loud laugh. "Are you a Service agent?" Kasparov asked.

"I am a lieutenant," Kalina said. She allowed her tone no inflexion.

"And nothing more?"

"Drink your tea, sir." Kalina leaned across the desk and shoved the tray toward Kasparov. He flinched, thrown by the sudden aggression. Kalina reached for the iron pot just as Kasparov picked up one of the ceramic cups and flung it at her head. She snatched it out of the air and set it carefully down beside the pot.

"I can't believe they assigned me a Service agent," Kasparov said. The shattering grief in his face was gone, recast by something like speculation. "Military Intelligence has never been personally interested in me before."

"You have only yourself to blame, sir."

"Really? Over a prank?" Kasparov looked skeptical.

"The prank was the last straw," Kalina said.

"Come on, it was funny."

"No comment, sir."

"Why would that event warrant me a Service agent for a babysitter? Surely you people have better demands on your time," Kasparov said.

"I'm not in the habit of questioning my assignments."

Kasparov huffed. "Is your name even really Kalina?"

"Drink." Kalina poured Kasparov a cup. He drank, his eyes fixed on her face.

"Are you allowed to help me?"

"Help you with what, sir?"

Kasparov's face twisted and he looked away. The grief was still there, poorly hidden. "My daughter."

"She is beyond help."

"You Service agents don't mince words." Kasparov let out a strangled sound. "I want to learn exactly how she died. I think I know, but I need confirmation."

"Her ship blew up." That much was clear from *Gabriel's* initial reports.

"That's a consequence, not an explanation." replied Kasparov.

"You are a Counter-Admiral. Surely you'd be kept in the loop."

"That means less than you know. Less than I would like. I might be told something soon to keep me happy, but the truth?" Kasparov drummed his fingertips on the table. "If you're a Service agent, you must be very good at getting into places that you have no business being in."

"I resent that insinuation." Kalina smiled tightly.

"You'd resent your cover being blown even more, I presume."

Kasparov was more right about that than he could ever know. Kalina exhaled. "Fine. What do you want?"

# CHAPTER THREE

VIKTOR WATCHED AS the Tula Directorate jetted off towards the wreck of the *Farthest Shore*, starting the grim task of collecting and identifying bodies. The Slavny Directorate was already onsite, following a deep scan and a salvaging of VMF property. On a ship as big as the *Farthest Shore*, a full salvage would take weeks—but they didn't have weeks. They didn't even have time to retrieve the bodies and take them onboard—instead, they bagged those that they could find and tethered the remains close to the wreck.

Those godsdamned corsairs had stolen the cruiser's Eva Core.

"Proximity mines are primed and ready to launch," Ship said. Ship had been uncharacteristically subdued when they had come within visual range of the *Farthest Shore*. Days ago, Viktor would've been glad for the reprieve from Ship's constant chatter. Now, he found it unnerving.

"Thank you, Ship." The VMF was sending the Gnevny-class destroyer *Friend of Ravens* out of Gagarin station on a standard sail for the nearest Gate, which meant that it'd get to the wreck in a couple of weeks. The VMF mines would hopefully deter any other vultures like Captain Yeung from exploring the *Farthest Shore* in the meantime.

"You've never said 'thank you' to me before," Ship said on a private line. It sounded pleased. Viktor clenched his fists, letting his irritation slide. Maybe Ship was back to its normal annoying level of functionality. "By the way, maybe you shouldn't have threatened Captain Yeung."

"He stole from the VMF. He would have been expecting a threat."

"Maybe if you hadn't threatened him with certain death he wouldn't have run away with the Core," Ship said.

"You'd prefer that I lied to him to gain his trust?" Viktor was regretting having been so heavy-handed where Yeung was concerned. Something about the Captain's lack of fear and his flippancy in the face of a VMF destroyer had gotten under Viktor's skin. Corsairs were often incorrigible gamblers—particularly those unwise enough to approach a VMF wreck in the first place. Faced with only a handful of bad choices, Solitaire would've naturally chosen the one with the biggest potential profit.

"Well, no, I meant—okay, maybe."

"What's done is done," Viktor said. He wasn't in the mood for a lecture from Ship when a lecture from High Command was likely soon to be coming his way.

There was little to do on the Bridge other than wait. Viktor spent it studying the deep scan that Ship had taken of the *Now You See Me*. Like many corsair ships, the *Now You See Me* had started life as a cargo transport, built to handle planetside hops. It had a streamlined nose port and a fat belly that housed a false floor, with aerodynamic fins that fanned out over the tapering length of its torso. It looked like a deformed fish painted black.

49

"The vulture has fangs," Petrenko said. He pointed at the lasgun pods mounted under the fins. GAU-18s, according to Ship. Old model, nearly an antique, but known to be reliable. Either Yeung was poor or, as with most corsairs, the lasgun pods were a weapon of last resort.

"Many corsairs are ex-Navy of some stripe or other," Viktor said. The VMF hadn't yet responded to Viktor's request for information on 'Solitaire Yeung', though it was early days yet. He didn't think there'd be anything worth reading in the file. UN Navy-turned-corsairs tended to be a particular type of venal character, driven only by greed. Nothing was surprising about such people.

"Vermin," Petrenko said, his lip curling.

It was a sentiment that Viktor shared. Viktor despised corsairs, especially those that specialized in salvage. Descending quickly on ships in distress, they would often charge astronomical fees to tow ships to safety. Or worse: board the ship, steal its stardrive seeds, and leave the stranded crew to a slow and horrible death by suffocation.

"Normal corsairs know better than to board VMF ships," Viktor said. Service agents were always sent after those who did, and after a few examples were spectacularly made, the corsairs started to leave off even boarding old and long-abandoned VMF wrecks.

"Captain Yeung must be desperate. Or reckless," Petrenko said.

"Perhaps," Viktor said. Come to think of it, Solitaire's lack of fear during the broadcast had itself been strange. "Ship, send an urgent follow-up on the ROI request."

"Where do you think they went?" Ship asked. It sounded excited. Petrenko narrowed his eyes, though no one else on the Bridge did.

"Corsair ships run on profit. Spacefaring is expensive. The cost of stardrive seeds, oxygen tanks, supplies, and repairs all add up. They will take their stolen loot somewhere to sell, and the VMF has agents in all big Neutral Zone black markets. We can wait," Viktor said. If Solitaire were desperate, he would try to sell soon.

"We could still catch up with them right now. Before they reach the Gate," Ship said. It sounded hurt. "I don't see why you don't want to. We took three days to get here. They're still four days or so from the Gate, three if they did a hard sail, though that'd take its toll. We could estimate trajectory and jump for—"

"Space is vast. Corsairs are very good at running dark. We will have to guess where they are. And we are assuming that they are even taking a direct route to the Gate. It'll be like looking for a needle at the bottom of an ocean," Viktor said. He didn't like the chances. Better to let Solitaire think that he had outrun Viktor's reach.

"I remember the ocean," Ship said wistfully, switching to Galactic. "All the years we've spent building over every inch of Sol, and we haven't yet completely papered over the seas. The beach was warm. The ocean was dead, and had been for years and years. They'd long filtered out all the trash, so it was clean and blue, but empty. A graveyard mirror."

Petrenko caught Viktor's eye, visibly unnerved. It took Viktor a moment to relax his white-knuckled grip on the armrests of his Captain's chair. Hopefully, no one else on the Bridge noticed his unease. "Is that relevant, Ship?" Viktor asked.

"Oh! No. No. Sorry. I mean—sorry," Ship said, amending itself in Russian. "Yes, you're right. They could've hidden from us anywhere. I suppose it'd be easier to retrieve the Eva Core they took in a port somewhere. Just about everything I'm armed with would vaporize their little ship if we had to shoot at it."

"You're carrying guardships and corvettes for a reason," Viktor said. Nanuchkas would be able to chase down any corsair, both out in space or down a gravity well. "It'd be a waste of fuel, though. Even if we *did* find them." If a stray shot turned the *Now You See Me* into a fireball, Viktor wasn't sure whether a Core could survive something like that.

"Oh, yes, my Nanuchkas. That's right. I do love them. They're my little ducklings."

Viktor let out a slow breath, yet again resolving to try and get the Eva Core refitted off his destroyer. Turning to speak to Petrenko, it was purely by chance that he saw it—one of the distant stars beyond the sundered centre of the *Farthest Shore* winked out. "Ship! Something's out there!"

Lascannons were called ship-killers for a good reason. The focused antigrav tech punched easily through commercial shields and most military shield tech. They were what an Admiral whom Viktor had once served under had called 'fuck off cannons'. Lascannons didn't have the range of pulsars, but a ship slung with a lascannon would make any other ship wary about closing in on it. Especially a mere destroyer like the *Gabriel*.

There were cries and gasps on the Bridge as the tell-tale purple rings started to pulse through the gap, out of nothing that Viktor could see—stealth tech?—then screams as the lascannon beam shot forward. A coring-arc, aiming for *Gabriel's* reactor.

A tremor rocked through the ship, pitching Petrenko over the deck and sending anyone not locked into a synthsteel cradle rolling across the floor. "Full alert. Damage report," Viktor snapped, forcing steel into his voice. He was already calculating the number of escape pods. Whether any of the Nanuchkas could be salvaged. How to provide life support to the Directorates still peppered around the *Farthest Shore*. He'd remain aboard the *Gabriel*. Set a beacon and record his final report about the attack into the black box—

Technicians and crew scrambled back to their workstations. "Shields held, sir!" Kornikova called from her desk, her voice awed. "We're at forty per cent."

Viktor grimaced. *Maybe that wasn't a VMF-level lascannon? Or...* "Ship, you upgraded the shields?" he barked.

"Engineering gave me the OK two days ago, and I worked with them to fix the inefficiencies," Ship said on a private line. It sounded nervous. "What's happening? What do we do? I don't see another Ship! Nothing's coming up on the deep scan."

"Some new cloaking technology. Scramble all Nanuchkas," Viktor commanded, staring at the empty space where a ship should be. "Tula and Slavny, take cover in the *Farthest Shore*. Evasive maneuvers. *Return fire*."

A ripple of "yes sir" collectively swept the Bridge as Ship began to angle away, slow—too slow—trying to pull most of itself behind the dead hulk of the cruiser. Pale blue spears spat out from Ship's flanks, earthing themselves into a patch of nothing that flickered but betrayed nothing.

"I see it! Reconstructing location via latent radiation and heat traces. Here." Ship sketched a target outline as a 3D trellis over the glass, revealing a familiar knife-like shape.

"A VMF ship?" Petrenko gasped. It looked like a Sovremenny-class destroyer, a ship-killing specialist.

Had this all been a misunderstanding? "Ship, patch me through. All channels," Viktor said.

"Done," Ship said.

"Unidentified ship. This is Captain Viktor Kulagin of the *Song of Gabriel Descending*. You are firing on a VMF ship. Repeat. You are firing on a VMF ship. Identify yourself." He repeated himself in Galactic, then back in Russian.

The unknown ship's response was to cycle up the lascannon, tiny purple rings lighting up in the dark. "Hold on to something!" Ship warned, and the destroyer kicked into a sharp, sudden lunge that would have bounced Petrenko across the floor again had Viktor not hastily grabbed fistfuls of his jacket. *Gabriel* swung behind the forward half of the *Farthest Shore*, even as silver and black fish flit away from under their belly. The Nanuchkas, called to war.

"They're on the move," Ship said, tense. "Trying to get a better shot."

"We can't get out of range without going into a high sail," Viktor said.

A high sail—high enough to plaster everyone not in podsleep into a meat jam over the walls. Granted, that wouldn't be the end of the *Gabriel*. All VMF ships of Kashin-class and higher had redundancies built into their design. With at least one Directorate in podsleep at any point, they could escape at the cost of everyone else who wasn't in podsleep. The *Gabriel* could wake its remaining crew afterwards, returning to any VMF port. It was a sacrifice that VMF crews had paid before, to save valuable ships or to finish their missions. Judging from how pale Petrenko was, he'd come to the same conclusion.

Viktor called up a visual of the theater of war over the holodeck with an impatient gesture. The swarm of sleek Nanuchkas were engaging as a loose shoal, mimicking the cloud-like formation of long-extinct Sol fish. Tiny spears of light shot towards the blocked-out enemy. Viktor brought up real-time visual from the Nanuchka shoal's commander, Lieutenant Zaitseva. Orange explosions stitched across space, and where there was fire, the illusion broke. Pulsars returned fire, taking out the tail end of the shoal. Zaitseva was already circling, the ships firing as they went.

No answering shoal. Strange. There was shielding over the cockpit, but a determined and unopposed shoal would quickly destroy that, venting the Command Bridge into space. Emboldened, Zaitseva took her shoal towards the probable nose of the enemy ship, darting around pulsar fire.

The enemy ship kicked into a high sail. The shoal scattered, breaking formation in surprise as the reactor burn pulsed a bright visual over and above Zaitseva. Sporting burning scabs, the enemy ship crested the dead hulk.

"Suicide," Petrenko breathed. With a sail that hard, the enemy ship would've just sacrificed its active crew.

Viktor scowled. About to command *Gabriel* to give chase, Viktor stared in astonishment as the enemy ship arced around the wreck, its lascannon already lighting up, purple rings twisting. Ship-killer. "Brace for impact!" Viktor could do the math.

So could Ship. Before the arc of light earthed itself in the *Gabriel* to break it apart, Ship's shields coalesced into a dense disc. The deck shook on impact, the hulls groaning. The shields held, flickering weakly.

"Shields at five percent," Kornikova said. She shook with helpless rage, the same rage that Viktor felt. They were trapped. And they'd already survived two impossible volleys.

"How is that ship still even firing on us?" Viktor demanded. "Everyone on that Bridge should be *dead*." Lascannon use was so restricted that it couldn't be automated.

"Lieutenant Zaitseva!" Petrenko pointed. Zaitseva's ship kicked into a lethal sail. It was a suicide run. Her Nanuchka registered no vital signs as it arced towards the belly of the enemy ship, straight at the lascannon, darting on autopilot past pulsar beams. The Nanuchka rammed the lascannon in a burst of fire and steel.

There was a rumbling, electronic snarl of rage, so loud over the VMF bandwidth that everyone clapped their hands over their ears. The enemy ship turned to face them on its broadside, pulsars heating up even as Ship cried, "NO! You stop! These people are mine. *Go away!*"

The pulsars eased. The enemy ship hung in space, silent and contemplative; then it was gone.

A Kwang ship.

Viktor leaned back in his chair. His jacket was soaked in sweat. Petrenko sank onto his knees, a breach of VMF decorum that Viktor was in no mood to rebuke. Someone on the Bridge was sobbing loudly. Viktor looked around before he realized it was Ship on a private line, in his ear.

THERE WAS DEAD silence aboard the *Now You See Me*. Solitaire reached for the controls to replay the transmission they'd caught over the VMF channel, but then thought better of it. He pushed himself away from the Captain's seat, heading for the galley. Coffee always helped him think.

As Solitaire set the replicator to make coffee with shaking fingers, Pablo swung his way down, gravboots adhering to the deck.

"The hell was that?" Pablo asked, keeping his voice low.

"Maybe Frankie was right. There's a secret war. A VMF civil war."

"Why'd you say that?"

"No reason for them to broadcast over the VMF channel if they were just talking to any other ship. Besides, our friend Captain Kulagin strikes me as a highly trigger-happy sort of guy. If he bothered to give a warning to some other ship... Hell, he gave them a warning in Russian first before he changed to Galactic."

"You think they all dead?" Pablo shuddered. "What the fuck? We didn't see no other ship jump out there. What kind of Russian dark magic's letting VMF ships bounce around without a Gate? Move that fast without killing the crew?"

"*I* think..." Solitaire paused as coffee gargled into an enclosed packet with a straw. He strapped it to his jacket even though they were flying at enough of a sail for one-g, and hauled himself back up to the cockpit.

"Freak-out over," he told Indira. She rolled her eyes. For all her apparent indifference, her forehead was slick with sweat.

"So what?" Joey asked. "Is it aliens?"

"*Fuck you, Joey*," Pablo snapped, smacking Joey hard on the shoulder.

"Ow-w-w."

"No, it's not aliens, it's probably rogue VMF elements.

Hopefully fighting among themselves, nothing to do with us," Solitaire said. His voice trembled. Freak-out not yet entirely over then.

Frankie looked unconvinced. "Yeah, right. This new ship probably thought the thing we've got in the hold is still on the dead ship, so they be like, oh hell no, Captain-fuck-off-Kulagin, you get screwed, and he's like, fuck you back, and *boom*. Which means *we're* fucked, once both VMF ships realize the thing they want is with us."

"Great," Indira said.

"We'll find out soon since we're still sitting in the VMF frequency. Though I suspect you're probably right," Solitaire said. The VMF, rogue element or not, tended to be a very depressing and murderous bunch at the best of times. "Who the hell was that girl at the end?" The desperate cry at the end on the VMF channel had sounded like it had come from a young woman. It hadn't sounded like it'd been someone from either crew, and no gender identifiers had been automatically tacked onto the broadcast.

"Who knows?" Pablo shivered. "Sounded like a ghost."

"No. No ghosts. No aliens," Solitaire said, though he couldn't quite manage the conviction.

"Do we stick to the plan?" Indira asked.

"'Course. Look," Solitaire said as Indira glared at him, "we're already screwed. The VMF is unhappy with us, and this rogue ship is probably unhappy with us too. They're likely still fighting it out, just that they've gone off the channel. Gating without a stellar Gate is impossible. It's got to be some new stealth rig. Rogue ship doesn't know we've got the pod thing since they were drawn to the beacon. So, we're fine. With any luck, they'll kill each other." Pity, if that was the case. Captain Kulagin was very handsome. Even for someone who was an immense asshole.

"This better be retirement-level kind of money," Indira said. She jerked her thumb down at the cargo bay. "We don't even know what in tian that damned thing is."

Indira had a point. Their onboard ship scan had been rigged up by Pablo himself. It was a custom-made sweetheart of a tool that could usually unpack even black market prototypes into component functions. Or at least make a damned good guess. The ship scan had come up completely blank on the pod. It hadn't even figured out how to open the pod to get to the sphere within, and Solitaire hadn't wanted to cut the pod up in case they broke it.

"Better not be the world's most boring art piece," Pablo said. He put up his palms when Indira glowered at him. "Just saying. You never know with rich people."

"Why would two VMF ships—rogue or not—go to war over an art piece?" Solitaire asked.

"Some people like art a lot?" Pablo hazarded a guess. "I mean, I like art."

"Would you kill someone over a drawing?" Joey asked.

"Maybe if I loved the drawing and the other guy was a huge asshole," Pablo said, after a moment's actual thought.

Indira patted Pablo on the arm. "Every time I conclude that you're the least sociopathic of the group of us, you destroy my expectations."

Solitaire wished they could make a pit stop at Prana Colony instead of having to sprint for the stellar Gate. The colony had a relatively robust system of agriculture, which meant an equally robust trade in alcohol. That was the one thing that even the best replicators couldn't make—good, real alcohol, strong enough to kick his brain sideways. "I think it's probably some kind of new weapon," he said, just as the VMF channel came back online.

Captain Kulagin's image coalesced. He looked pale and grim. Shaken. When he spoke, his voice was steady, but his accent was thicker. "Captain Kulagin to Captain Yeung. I know you're probably still listening. Wherever you are. You have one last chance to hand over VMF property. Leave it where you are and tag a beacon to it. Do so, and all is forgiven. This is your final warning."

"Don't reply," Solitaire said. That'd give away their location.

Indira sniffed. "What do you take me for?"

"Maybe we should do it," Joey said, as the broadcast ended. He squirmed in his seat. "You sure you want this kinda trouble on board? You wanna get involved in a VMF war? Hello? Assuming we even manage to find a buyer. Assuming we even find someone who knows what that thing is."

"Captain always chooses the worst possible path," Frankie said with a world-weary air.

"Thanks for the vote of confidence." Solitaire *had* been wavering. Was the pod thing worth the lives of him and his crew? It was one thing to get between a VMF ship and its prize. It was another thing to make off with an object that had possibly just sparked off some sort of inter-VMF stellar battle. Still. If the VMF wanted this pod so badly, maybe it had tipped the balance of power within the Federation, somehow. That couldn't be good for the 'verse in the long term. "I don't believe in his offer of amnesty. We've just witnessed a battle between two ships with brand-new, probably top-secret VMF tech.

They'd never let us go. Besides, they've all made me so very curious about our art piece." Perhaps it was related to how strangely both ships had behaved.

"*Captain*," Indira growled.

Solitaire coughed. "More seriously, if it is military tech of some kind, or a weapon—and I'd bet it is—I'm thinking, maybe we should figure out what it is. Might be that the UN needs to know about it." Old habits died hard, even in the current life that he'd made for himself.

"Never pegged you for patriotism," Pablo said.

"Yeah well, it fires up now and then." Solitaire made a self-deprecating wave. "We're all UN citizens, aren't we? With friends and family on miscellaneous UN stations or colonies? Think of it as doing our bit for the greater good and all that."

Frankie let out a loud snort. Joey said, "Weren't we doing this for the greater profit and all that?"

"It doesn't have to be mutually exclusive?" Solitaire batted his eyes with mock innocence.

"So, we're going to hand it over to the UN?" Indira eyed him, unimpressed.

"...Woah, I'm not *that* patriotic. The UN tends to be extremely stingy, I should know. But we could maybe tip them off once we make a sale," Solitaire said quickly as Indira began to scowl. "Until then, we'll stay the course."

"We're all gonna die," Frankie predicted. He looked weirdly cheered.

"It's *aliens*," Joey said.

# CHAPTER FOUR

DR. ALEK KWANG lived on the outermost ring of Gagarin station, which was curious for a supposedly invaluable member of the VMF's Defense Science division. So invaluable that his file remained inaccessible to Kalina, despite her pointed suggestions to Kasparov that she needed it to understand her target. "He's not a target— he's a friend," Kasparov said. The Counter-Admiral had been impervious to Kalina's attempts to point out that the two states of being could overlap. "I don't want him to make this out to be official business when it isn't."

Kalina wore unassuming gray clothes and kept her eyes averted, her shoulders hunched in. She walked purposefully through the crowd with a harried expression, squeezing past recruiters for haulers and people hawking dubious insurance policies, angling around unlicensed street stalls frying up reconstituted cheburek and ponchiki. Past the dealers in the narrow alleys between the prefab habitats, selling anything from reconstituted novascerin dust to badly-made scalant. Unofficial recreational drugs were illegal across the Federation, but military stations like Gagarin didn't enforce the rules strictly. If the VMF cracked down on every addict and dealer out there, it'd have to throw at least a tenth of its navy into jail.

Kwang's residential address led Kalina to a back of the street hab built into the innermost hull of the ring. Cheap housing. 'Cladding apartments', as they were called. If anything went wrong with the hull—rare as it might be in a station like Gagarin—anyone living right against the innermost hull would be the first casualties. Kalina pursed her lips. The access alley she stood in was clean, but she could smell something sour even through the air recyclers. The odor seeped past the closed access to the multilevel hab.

Kasparov chose this moment to ping her. Kalina routed his call to her ear implant. "Sir," she said.

"Any trouble yet?"

Kalina swallowed her irritation. The VMF had kept its resident military genius carefully cocooned from the moment it understood Kasparov's worth. Kasparov spent most of his days shuttling between his home, his office, and High Command, providing strategic advice on anything from minor border skirmishes with the UN to counter-terrorism strategies. It had been a long time since Kasparov had led people in the field, and it showed. "No, sir."

"Good, good. It's not like him to ignore pings from me. I'm concerned."

"I'm surprised that Dr. Kwang lives here," Kalina said, biting down her retort. Kasparov had repeated that sentiment several times in his office, after which he'd sent Kalina out on this errand. Kalina felt that it was a waste of everyone's time. Surely if a Counter-Admiral wanted to talk to someone, he could send a security unit to retrieve the person in question. Kasparov hadn't been receptive to Kalina's suggestion. "That'd just piss him off," Kasparov had said, as though the opinion of some random scientist mattered that much.

"He grew up close by and has always been fond of the neighborhood. Alek's a very sentimental person. It's partly why he didn't standardize his name, even after becoming famous."

"You don't sound like you approve."

"It's not up to me to dictate how he ought to live," Kasparov said, amused. "Though as someone who grew up in slum conditions in a struggling backwater colony, I wouldn't live like that again if I didn't have to."

"Why doesn't he have security?" Kalina looked around more carefully, in case her guess was wrong.

"Said they stifled his creativity." At Kalina's startled laugh, Kasparov said, "He used those exact words. I had to mediate the argument between him and his handlers, but eventually, they caved. No one knows who Alek is outside a select few people in the VMF, and he prefers it that way."

"Shouldn't have indulged that," Kalina said.

"Perhaps. I have a meeting with Inessa that I can't put off, but if you need me, ping me."

"I can't imagine why I might need you, sir." That jumped off Kalina's tongue before she could bite it back. Kasparov laughed. He sounded strained, but it was better than the nervous circling they'd been doing around each other ever since Kasparov had hazarded a guess at Kalina's true status.

If only he knew.

"All right, Lieutenant. Talk later. Be circumspect if you have to reach me." Kasparov signed off the channel.

The security access was badly made. Kalina didn't even need to use her VMF access to get in—not that she'd wanted to. Kasparov wanted this little visit off the books. She used a knife to lever the access panel out of its socket, and unplugged one of the wires. As the panel went dark, Kalina pulled out another wire, and the access door slid open. She pressed the panel back into its socket and headed in, sliding the knife back up her sleeve. The dimly lit corridor beyond stank of sweat and overheated plastic, redolent of cheap air recyclers. Kalina wrinkled her nose. She'd been through worse, but she'd never enjoyed having to do so.

Kalina passed narrow hab units silently. Most were quiet, though one thrummed with a deep bass beat that leaked past its soundproofing. The lifts were at the back of the corridor. According to Kasparov's information, Kwang lived on the top floor. She stepped into the silver tube and pressed the floor number.

On the top floor, the hab unit closest to the lifts had its door open. Kalina walked past in her purposeful shuffle. Through her peripheral vision, she picked out an old woman in an ambulatory unit craning her neck over the back support for a better look at Kalina. Reaching Kwang's door, Kalina waited, in case the old woman was coming out. When she heard and saw nothing, Kalina studied Kwang's unit. Quiet. Dark. The access unit was different from the others—silver and affixed firmly to the wall.

Kalina pressed the doorbell and waited.

Nothing. She pressed it again.

After a minute crawled past, Kalina tried pirating access to the door, but the unit stayed stubbornly encrypted. She whistled low to herself. Blasting it open would probably draw attention, and besides, she wasn't even sure if it would work. Pursing her lips, Kalina stepped over to the next hab unit and opened it by levering the panel out of its socket.

The unit belonging to Kwang's neighbor had been empty for a while. A thick layer of dust sat over the floor, and the walls and rooms were devoid of furniture. Good. Kalina locked the door behind her and turned toward Kwang's unit. Sheathing her knife, she palmed a silver tube from her boot. The molecular edge flicked active with a low hum, hissing as it met the hab wall. Kalina cut a narrow hole and pushed through, setting the piece of wall to one side.

"Dr. Kwang?" Kalina called. No answer. Maybe station records were wrong, and the Doctor wasn't in.

Kwang's unit was clean and neat. The furniture was simple, but well-made, and the wall section close to the door was a relatively new and expensive holoscreen. It shimmered to life as Kalina got close, showing her a view of the stars as well as the current station time. Kalina took a recording of the image and started to sweep the apartment. Replicator, seldom used—it was nearly at full charge, and the biomatter hadn't been replaced for months. No alcohol. Wardrobe containing a few coats and civilian clothes, no military uniforms. The bed was unmade, folded out from its wall slot. Nothing under the bed. The bathroom was empty, but for some simple toiletries. Kalina made another slow circuit of the room, glancing toward the hole she had cut into the neighboring unit—and hesitated. She walked across Kwang's unit, counting her footsteps. Then the neighbor's. Kwang's unit was a meter shorter than it should be, for a unit that should be identical.

Kalina scanned the wall with her wristdeck, which informed her that there was nothing out of the ordinary. She smiled and felt along the walls until she found a faint depression close to the window. A physical catch? No, a pressure plate puzzle. Kalina studied the depressions and the pattern of fingerprints on the scan. It still took her a few tries to get it right.

There was a faint whirring sound as the wall folded away into neat slats, revealing a narrow workspace. The holodeck unit within was still active, with a projection of the shattered *Farthest Shore* floating above it. The console, the wall, and the floor were liberally splashed with still-drying blood. Crumpled against the wall was Dr. Kwang's body, a bolt gun lying by lifeless fingers. Kalina stared at the scene for a long moment, forcing down her revulsion as she studied the room. Only when she was calm did she finally ping Kasparov.

He answered after a few minutes. "Lieutenant?"

"I found the file you were looking for, sir. It wasn't where it should be."

"Yes, well, you know me and my approach to filing," Kasparov said.

"It's been deleted."

"*What?* Deleted? How?"

*Blew his brains out with a bolt gun.* "Self-deleted. Must have been part of a security measure."

Kasparov drew in a slow breath. "Meet me back at the office."

"Yes, sir." Kalina shut off the transmission. She scanned the room with her wristdeck, committing every detail to it.

She put everything back the way it was, and exited through the gap. The old woman ignored Kalina as she entered the lift. One block away from Kwang's hab, Kalina ducked down an alley and into the shadows, accessing her pigmentation controls. With a few tweaks, her hair recolored itself to its usual black and drew back up from her shoulders into the neat bob typical of her Lieutenant persona, brushing against her brownish-bronze cheeks.

Kalina had no sooner changed back into her uniform when Kasparov sent her an urgent summons. He was pacing in his office, his hands behind his back as Kalina locked the door access behind her. "Alek can't have killed himself," Kasparov said.

"Looked like it." Kalina spun the scan to Kasparov's holodeck, which brought up the crime scene in perfect miniature detail. He flinched. Kalina enhanced the imaging over Kwang's body with a merciless wave. "Look at the angle of the shot. And the placement of the blaster. No sign of a struggle. Toxicology normal. He killed himself."

Kasparov couldn't even look at the body. "He can't have. Alek is a once-in-a-generation talent."

"So are you."

"What?"

"Are you telling me that you would never, under any circumstances—"

"Never," Kasparov said, reddening with anger. "You overstep yourself, Lieutenant."

Kalina stared him down. "It's not the first time I've seen something like this." She waved the scene away and forwarded the rest of the data to Kasparov's deck.

"This is all encrypted," Kasparov said, bringing up an excerpt. "You found this in his personal deck?"

"That's all I found, yes." The file had been just as stubbornly encrypted as Kwang's door.

"I..." Kasparov exhaled loudly. "I'll get someone to

decrypt this discreetly…" He trailed off as the file above his deck started to metastasize. "It's unlocking?"

Kasparov was the key. Or perhaps his personal deck. Kalina angled around the deck to get between it and Kasparov just in case, but Kasparov stopped her with a raised palm as the file coalesced into a recorded image of Dr. Kwang. He looked crumpled down on himself—hunched in.

"Yuri. By the time you see this… well. You know what I'd have done. It was a long time coming. Wish I'd done it earlier, just that I was putting it off. We always knew, that's the godsdamned thing. We always knew that nothing good could have come out of encoding the Cores. Even if at the start, all we wanted to create was smarter, safer space stations. Once the VMF took an interest, I should have found a way to stop, but I was too proud. I, too, wanted to see if it could be done. Now it's come to this. And for what, military advantage?" Kwang let out a hoarse laugh. "Humanity's always been self-destructive for the worst possible reasons. Comfort and convenience."

"Alek," Kasparov said, choking up.

"You've been a good friend to me, Yuri. I'm sorry to light out on you like this. I'm a coward, I guess. I know what's coming and I don't want to see it. The first Cores becoming like they are—we all knew that was going to happen. We were lying to ourselves if we thought otherwise. But the second generation of Cores, the ones mapped from my Eva?" Kwang shuddered, looking away. "I don't think they're safe either. I carried her for nine long and difficult months. Watched her grow up and learn how to love, far away from the Federation. Watched her die to a disease that even the best of the Federation and the UN couldn't cure. I won't watch her children learn how to kill. I refuse. So. This is goodbye... for the last time. I'm sorry about Anna." The transmission cut off.

Kasparov swallowed hard in the silence. "Were you seen?"

"People saw someone who wasn't me," Kalina said, pronouncing each word with deliberate flatness. Kasparov winced.

"All right, I trust your experience. Lieutenant, I know this has to go into your report, but I was hoping it wouldn't."

"Efficient space stations?" Kalina mulled over what she had heard.

"Before the Space Age truly took flight, it took an army of people just to keep a handful of astronauts alive aboard a tiny space station." Kasparov rubbed a hand over his face, distracted. "Technology's improved greatly, but not by all that much in the grand scheme of things. Especially now that our requirements for life in space have grown ever more complex. Even aboard a station like Gagarin, it still takes too much manpower and resources to run a station safely, and even small mistakes can cause a dangerous cascade. Kwang hoped to..." He trailed off. "Never mind."

"What did he mean by Cores?" Kalina asked.

"I'm afraid that's highly classified."

Kalina let the silence stretch until Kasparov started looking twitchy again. "May I be dismissed?"

Kasparov exhaled. "Look, I'm sorry that I threatened you before."

"Are you?"

"All right, not particularly. Alek was a friend of mine, and what with Anna... and now this, I—" Kasparov ran a hand through his hair. He looked shaken and lost.

"Permission to provide an opinion, sir?" Kalina asked, more kindly.

"When have you ever required my permission for that?" Kasparov's smile was wan.

"Let this go. It's none of your business."

"My daughter's death and my friend's death are none of my business?" Kasparov said, incredulous.

"Exactly. They aren't."

"*Lieutenant.*" Kasparov clenched his fists.

"You wanted my opinion, sir. What were you talking to Admiral Mikhailova about?"

"What else? I wanted an account of what happened."

"I'm guessing she told you to be patient. To take some time off to grieve. She's going to pack you off somewhere, perhaps. Maybe as far as Sol."

"She won't risk sending me to Sol, or anywhere downwell. Security would be too difficult to manage." Kasparov sank wearily into his chair. "But she *is* threatening to kick me out of Gagarin."

"There you go. With all due respect, sir, I'm sure the VMF is as interested in getting to the bottom of what happened as much as you are."

"It's not just that."

"Then?"

Kasparov studied Kalina for a long moment, then he shook his head and rubbed a hand over his face. "No. You're right. I should just take some compassionate time off. Dismissed, Lieutenant."

"Sir." Kalina saluted and backed out. She nearly ran right into Maya, who was holding a tray of tea. Kalina nodded at Maya, who nodded back. When Maya said nothing, Kalina walked back to her office.

There wasn't much work to do. Nevskaya's death was

still confidential, but Admiral Mikhailova must have put a stop to the usual torrent of advisory requests that were approved to be sent through to Kasparov. Kalina sat in utter boredom until a ping told her that Kasparov had logged in a week's worth of leave and was heading home in his usual armed escort. Once Kasparov left the building, Kalina changed back into civilian clothes and slipped out. She was going to have to do some digging.

# CHAPTER FIVE

"STUPIDITY IS CONTAGIOUS," Counter-Admiral Shevchenko said, as Viktor was shown into his office.

Age had cut savage lines into Shevchenko's face, and he looked gaunt in his uniform. The severe blue uniform was standard issue off-world—a suit that could become wholly sealed where necessary, blowing a periglass dome from the collar and supplying enough cycled air for half an hour. It had gravpads on the palms and impact-cushioning tech. The chances of a suit like this being necessary on a station as mature as Gagarin were near zero, but the VMF did love its contingencies.

Shevchenko's uniform differed from Viktor's in only two ways—the Admiral's star above the gold bars on his sleeve, and the twelve commendation bars over his chest, a visual story of Shevchenko's years of service. Viktor wore only four marker bars right over his heart. Low, for a Captain in command of a Kashin-class destroyer. He felt that sparseness keenly as he bowed, his hands set rigidly to his flanks.

The Admiral ignored him. Shevchenko was standing at

his office window, which looked out over one of Gagarin station's eight Cascade Gardens. Great pillars encrusted with waxy-leaved vines rose from the floor to the high ceiling of the station, surrounded by solar lamps. The bio-engineered plants spat out clean oxygen at an enhanced rate in staggered cycles, which was then spun through the station. At the base of the garden was a cluster of people, a few hundred or so, mostly young. Viktor had walked past them on his way into the Admiralty. They'd given him a brief, assessing stare, saying nothing. Another silent protest. There'd been more of those lately.

"We could have them moved," Viktor said, when Shevchenko continued to glower at the cluster.

"*Psh*. That would be a sign of fear. Better to ignore them. If they feel insignificant, they will soon cease this foolishness. Calling themselves 'The Silent'... *pah*! If only it were worth the effort to actually silence them." Shevchenko turned, seating himself stiffly. The Counter-Admiral had a decade-old injury from the rebel skirmish at Kronshtadt station, a war that had turned into a massacre. "The Federation has survived intact for hundreds of years under VMF leadership. More than survived—it has prospered."

"No one but us," Viktor said, quoting the ancient motto of a long-defunct branch of the Russian Federation's airborne armed forces. A sentiment that was still reflected across the board in the VMF.

"And well has that served us." Shevchenko flicked a palm dismissively in the general direction of the protest. "Civilians, what do they know. When there was nuclear war on Earth it was the Russian Army that maintained order. When the new space race began, it was the VMF that maintained our position despite the dominance of the

Chinese. Now we are the only people who still maintain our language. Our culture. Everything else, the UN has swallowed and shit out."

Viktor nodded. He didn't enjoy Shevchenko's lectures, which the Admiral still loved to dole out on occasion to captive audiences. When Shevchenko had been teaching at Kuznetsov Academy, he'd been infamous for long, rambling lectures about Sol-Earth's distant past. Back when the Russian Federation had been a crippled world power, when a nuclear missile exchange between the countries once known as North Korea and the United States had seen both countries become irradiated wastelands. During the chaos that followed, the VMF had taken control of the Russian Federation, control that it had not relinquished since. All this Viktor already knew. Every child growing up in the Federation knew.

Besides, Shevchenko was wrong. The Federation wasn't a watertight entity—it couldn't be, even with its restricted datanet. The black market aside, certain UN goods, films, and even people had long flowed in and out of the Federation. Common Galactic slang terms had long taken root even within the VMF. High Command had long given up attempting to root it out: Shevchenko himself used Galactic terms like 'tian'. Nowadays, the official Federation term surfaced only within technical papers and textbooks.

"So," Shevchenko said, waving his palm over the deck inset into his desk, bringing up a frozen visual. A miniature model of the *Gabriel* hid against the flank of the *Farthest Shore*, while the unknown ship surged up and out of cover. Behind his back, Viktor clasped his hands together until his knuckles ached.

"At eleven-hundred Shipside hours—"

"I've read your report. And those of your surviving Lieutenants. Seen the visuals. The readings from the *Gabriel*." Shevchenko pursed his lips. "The other Admirals and I are concerned."

Viktor went quiet. Shevchenko did not look concerned—nor did he look shaken or surprised. "What you and your crew have seen is highly confidential," Shevchenko said, after a thoughtful pause. "Should any leak be traced to you or your people, it would be considered an act of treason."

Punishable by being summarily vented into space. Perhaps after a period of 'rehabilitation'. Viktor nodded curtly. "I understand."

"As to this... corsair who escaped with the Eva Core, that is regrettable. You must recover the Core."

"I understand. Sir."

"Our agents in the Neutral Zones have been told to keep an eye out for it. In the meantime, you and your crew will be quartered aboard Gagarin station until you are all deemed fit for the field." *Quarantined*, Viktor thought, though he said nothing.

"As to the *Gabriel's* Eva Core..." Shevchenko trailed off, frowning to himself. It was rare to see the old man lost for words, and Viktor hoped that his surprise didn't show. "I saw your report. 'Potentially unstable', you said."

Ship had cried for an hour in his ear after the encounter. Viktor had been too unsettled to tell her—it—to stop. Thankfully it had done so on a private channel. "Yes, sir."

"Specify."

"Ship has, on several documented occasions, to myself and to the crew, expressed... emotions," Viktor said haltingly.

"Did you not experience fear? Anger, sorrow, relief? After the battle?"

"Yes," Viktor said, careful now. This sounded like some sort of trap. "But I am human. Ship is an ASI, responsible for the operation of an entire warship and its crew. This instability within its code is dangerous. It will make Ship unpredictable."

Shevchenko shook his head. Viktor had said the wrong thing. The Counter-Admiral pushed away from his chair, walking to the window, looking down. "Do you not know why the functional Kwang ASIs are mapped from a human brain?"

"It was impossible to build an ASI from scratch that we could trust."

"Yes. Trust. And what sort of people do we trust? Not the sort who are cold, emotionless, sociopaths. We trust normal people. *Normal*."

Was Shevchenko being facetious? "Perhaps our scientists should have mapped one of the Admirals' brains," Viktor said. It was a popular opinion aboard the *Gabriel*, not that any of his crew would have dared to complain about their situation within earshot of Viktor. Less popular now, after the *Gabriel* had single-handedly saved them from the rogue ship.

"We've tried. All the Admirals—including myself—sat down in Alek Kwang's infernal machine and let it record our brainwaves for a day. The early Cores were ultimately unusable."

Viktor blinked, surprised. "I thought—I was told that only Eva Kwang was ever mapped. Even so, some of her Cores clearly woke unusable." What else could explain the ship that attacked them? It had to have a corrupted Eva Core.

Shevchenko scowled. "This too is confidential. But since you are now irrevocably part of it, you have been cleared to know the truth. Yes, there were Cores that woke corrupted. None of those were Eva Kwang's Cores. All the Cores that woke corrupted were Admiralty Cores. Every single Eva Core has been stable. Each one has been outfitted to a Ship."

"The *Farthest Shore* had an Eva Core, didn't it?" Viktor asked.

"Yes. And, as you already know, its black box indicates that it was attacked. Its reactor core was fired upon, likely by the same ship that attacked you.

"The *Farthest Shore* was bait," Viktor said. When Shevchenko said nothing, Viktor said, "The other ship. It is a VMF ship."

"Was. It *was* a VMF ship."

"It was moving at an impossible speed. Its ASI must have piloted it, a Kwang ship. Its Eva Core must have become corrupted—"

"This is a difficult time for the VMF," Shevchenko said, his tone wintry. "The Admiralty is in a state of... disunity."

"How so?"

Shevchenko grunted. "Partly because of The Silent."

Viktor frowned. "Dina Ivanovna is finally making her move?" Dina Ivanovna Moskvoertskaya, the leader of The Silent, had so far only organized protests, petitions, and other forms of peaceful pushback. Nothing annoying enough for the VMF to crack down on, though the running opinion in the Federation was that it was only a matter of time.

"It's come to my attention that Moskvoretskaya might now have sympathizers in the Admiralty. Powerful ones. Counter-Admiral Kasparov, for example."

"That is treason," Viktor said, incredulous.

"Hah! I wish. Even if I can prove it, I suspect Admiral Mikhailova would intervene. Give Kasparov a slap on the wrist rather than the court-martial he deserves. Worse, Moskvoretskaya is soon going to make another appeal to the United Nations to pressure the VMF into ceding power to 'civilians'—to her, she means. We know the UN was close to being swayed before." Shevchenko's lip curled. "At a moment like this, the VMF must present a united front."

"The UN has never openly tried to interfere with Federation sovereignty," Viktor said.

"We've had a comfortable arrangement with them for a long time, certainly." Shevchenko made a dismissive gesture. "We are inextricably linked by trade. So we mediate the occasional border dispute and tolerate some of their Jinyiwei agents on our territories, while they tolerate some of our Service agents on theirs. Nothing stays permanent forever, but Moskvoretskaya may persuade the UN and the Neutral Zone to commit to a campaign of political and economic pressure before we are ready for it."

"Federation instability and disruption in UN-Federation trade will also affect the UN. There'd be a universal economic crisis. It's happened each time the UN and the Federation came close to open war," Viktor said. Each time there had been a skirmish over something or other, the consequential economic depression on both sides often eventually led to a ceasefire. Both the UN and the VMF understood that even an escalation into an all-out arms race would ultimately hurt everyone involved. Unless—

"Soon, they may consider it worthwhile."

"Because of exidium," Viktor guessed. When Shevchenko

just grunted, Viktor said, "It's a finite resource. No new planetary deposits have been found for decades. Once it runs out—no more Gating." The VMF kept any news about its state-owned reserves tightly under wraps, but Viktor had been in the Service long enough to get a feel for the overarching oeuvre of the Admiralty's concerns.

It was the right guess. Shevchenko looked back over at the desk, at the frozen image of battle. "Now we come to the problem. The Admiralty is aware of the possible resource conflicts to come. It was still split on the matter of the Eva Cores. Having the ability to Gate on a whim gives the VMF an edge over any Navy in the universe. After Dr. Kwang created the Cores, we took him into custody along with all his assistants. Moved him aboard Gagarin station, where he could be watched. Kept safe."

Viktor nodded. He'd suspected that would be the case—there was no real reason for Dr. Kwang to leave his lab and the centralized universities of learning in Athena Colony so abruptly. Tactically, it was a sound move. "What is Dr. Kwang working on now?"

"That's none of your concern," Shevchenko said. He exhaled. "When Dr. Kwang told us that the Admiralty Cores were unstable, I confess we did not believe him. We confiscated the Cores under the pretext that we would destroy them. We had our own scientists run extensive tests. Communications, strategy, everything. The Cores, we concluded after five years, were sane. The Doctor's distaste regarding the military is well-known. We decided to install Admiralty Cores onto Ships."

Viktor blinked, astonished. "But—"

"Oh, the Ships were obedient enough at first. Until they weren't. You see the problem. The enemy ship you encountered had an Admiralty Core. The *Last Word*."

"The VMF still installed the Eva Cores? After what happened with the others?" Viktor was appalled. On *his* ship.

"With more failsafes and more tests. Because we had no choice. There are five ghost ships out there. A month ago, our shipyard near Gamma Corvi went dark. So did the ships we sent to investigate. Our most recent probe reports that the yard has now been stripped down and abandoned."

A month ago. That was when the Eva Cores had been approved. "I heard nothing about any of this."

"Nor would you have. The Admiralty may bicker among itself, but we still, thank the Gods, agree that the media should be controlled. Imagine the pointless panic on the streets otherwise. The strife and chaos. Better that we fix this quickly instead. Quietly." He stared pointedly at Viktor.

"I understand. Sir."

"The *Gabriel* will be refitted with some new teeth. You've survived one encounter with a ghost ship. The Admiralty considers this commendable, and hopes that you will repeat such an encounter with more success."

A cold sweat prickled down Viktor's back at the thought of facing the dark ship again, but he nodded briskly. "Was I not meant to prioritize the retrieval of the stolen Core?"

"Eventually, yes. It may be possible that the rogue ships are looking for it. Until we find a way to track them, the Core is the best bait you have."

"Understood." Viktor's mouth twitched at the corners. *Poor little rabbit, about to run between two wolves.*

\* \* \*

Gagarin station didn't have the great simulator decks of Kuznetsov Academy, but it did have state-of-the-art tactical booths. Viktor booked a private booth for himself, locked its access level with his new clearance code, and loaded the battle data from *Gabriel's* fight with the *Last Word*. Again and again, he tried the scenario, and again and again, he lost. Without Ship's strange and desperate appeal, they would have undoubtedly been killed by pulsars.

One of his instructors had taught that there was no point lingering on old defeats, save for as a teaching tool. Viktor cleared the deck and loaded the *Last Word*. As an afterthought, he loaded the four other Admiralty Core ships. There was another Kashin-class destroyer, the *Hammer of the Gods*. Two Gnevny-class destroyers, *Pillar of Eternity* and *High Winter*. Finally, the Slava-class cruiser *Ride of the Valkyries*.

He recoded their specifications to match the readouts from the *Last Word* and loaded in the remaining three Eva Core ships: His *Gabriel* and the Sovremenny-class destroyers *Wild Hunt* and *Death from Above*. Not good odds, though Shevchenko had implied that more Eva Cores would be installed pending investigation. Viktor knew what that meant. They were waiting to see if the remaining Eva Core Ships also went rogue.

The first attempt at battle went as well as Viktor expected. With the ability to Gate without care for their crew and the freedom to use weapons, the Admiralty Ships instantly Gated within range at the start of the battle. The Ships concentrated fire on the *Gabriel*, destroying it. Nanuchkas pumped out of *Wild Hunt* and *Death from Above*, but it was a losing battle. The best they could do was cripple the shields on one Ship.

Viktor cleared the deck. This time he loaded the Kwang Ships together, with *Gabriel* in the centre and the other two destroyers at her flank, close enough to merge shielding. Possible with a Kwang ASI's fine control, impossible for a fully human crew. Nanuchkas managed to cripple the lascannons on the *Last Word* and *Valkyries*, albeit with suicide attacks. Viktor paused the battle, considering the enemy cruiser, and startled violently as the locked door behind him slid open.

"What—" Viktor caught himself as he recognized Counter-Admiral Kasparov. With a start, he came to attention, saluting.

"No need for that." Kasparov waved the door closed behind him and strolled over, looking at the deck with open curiosity.

"Sir. How may I assist you?" Viktor asked, still disoriented. Kasparov, a traitor? Kasparov was the most famous living Admiral in the VMF. One of the greatest Admirals the VMF had ever produced. The Great Tactician: the mind behind most of the iconic skirmishes and theatres of war the VMF had been part of within the last half-century. The fact that he was passed for further promotion time and again was a constant source of speculation between the rank and file. If he was secretly some sort of troublemaker—

"That's not an approved formation," Kasparov said, walking a slow circuit around the deck.

"No sir," Viktor said. He'd never been this close to Kasparov before. Hell, he'd only ever seen Kasparov in person once, during the relaunch for the newly refitted *Gabriel*. Unsure of what to say, and unwilling to embarrass himself, Viktor bit his tongue.

"Go on then." Kasparov nodded at the deck. Viktor hesitated, and Kasparov said, "Well, Captain?"

"Yes, sir." Now self-conscious, Viktor unpaused the battle. Gating consumed stardrive seeds. Although the Admiralty Ships tried to Gate around and attack with pulsars, without lascannons it was a slow battle of attrition against Viktor's *Wild Hunt* and *Death*, and one that Viktor would win. He growled, pausing the battle anew.

"What's wrong?" Kasparov asked.

Viktor flinched. He'd forgotten about the Counter-Admiral's presence, absorbed as he was in the puzzle he was trying to decrypt. Kasparov smiled at him, gentle and benign. It unsettled Viktor's instincts. "Wrong, sir?"

"You appear upset. But the battle is yours."

"The deck's AI isn't learning properly. The Admiralty Ships could easily destroy mine by Gating right through us. A suicide attack. Or it could Gate away from battle once we took out its lascannons. Why linger and fight a losing battle?"

"A philosophical question." Kasparov bent to study the small model of the *Valkyrie*. "Whether an ASI is capable of self-preservation. Or self-sacrifice."

"They are not true ASIs. They are copies of people," Viktor said, then wished he hadn't said it. Admirals wouldn't tolerate being so bluntly corrected by a mere Captain. Kasparov, however, merely chuckled.

"That's true. Very true."

"Do you need something, sir?" Viktor asked, disoriented all over again.

"Calm down, Captain. You look spooked. Surely a man who just faced down an 'Admiralty Ship' and emerged unscathed has stronger nerves than that."

"Not unscathed," Viktor said. He bit his tongue again. This hereditary tendency to speak his mind was the reason why he'd been held in reserve for years. It was the reason why his politically active parents had disgraced themselves, why his father had died in an icy colony half the universe away mining raw exidium until his lungs rotted. Why his mother had hung herself in her cell once she'd heard.

"No. I suppose not. I'm sorry about Lieutenant Zaitseva, and the other Nanuchka pilots you lost. I'd talk about sacrifice, but I know you don't want to hear it. So I'll keep this brief. I know you're one of Shevchenko's, and you'll likely run straight over to him to report on me afterwards, but I thought I'd try."

"Try what?" Viktor asked warily.

"The *Farthest Shore*. Did you know its Captain?"

Was that a trick question? "Captain Nevskaya."

"Did you know she was my daughter?" At Viktor's blink, Kasparov let out a hollow laugh. "No, I thought not. To be fair, I wasn't much of a father. I met her mother a long time ago when I'd just enlisted in the VMF. We had a brief affair. Anna was the result. She took her mother's name, and I sent them money now and then."

"She never said." Nevskaya had already been a Lieutenant when Viktor had graduated from the Academy. They'd served together for a few years on the same ship before she'd been given her first command: a destroyer. The *Farthest Shore* had been a new upgrade.

"I doubt she would've. She preferred to keep it a secret. Didn't want her ascension through the ranks to be because of her 'bloodline'. Didn't want special treatment from the people around her." Kasparov exhaled. "She wouldn't even let me congratulate her when she was named Captain of a cruiser."

"My condolences," Viktor said, though it felt like a

servile thing to say. Kasparov didn't seem to hear it. He stared at the deck, his gaze distant.

"People enjoy cruelty," Kasparov said, flicking his fingers through the hologram of the *Valkyrie*. "It's exciting, you see, even if most of us don't like to admit it. The ancient Romans used to fill their Colosseum with people for years on years, to watch other people get torn apart. People are mesmerized by cruelty. Especially when it's institutionalized. That's why the VMF's survived for so long."

Viktor's heart sank. This sounded close to treason. "Couldn't say, sir."

"Oh, don't give me that. You're far more intelligent than you pretend to be. This, for example, is very clever for a first attempt." Kasparov traced his fingers through the stacked ships. "You're right. It's ultimately useless. But it's never enough to consider the middle game and the endgame. The opening gambit can also tell you a lot about what you need to know about the player of the game."

"What does this tell me about the Admiralty Ships?" Viktor asked, curious despite his irritation. "They attack on sight. Or at least, the *Last Word* did."

"The Admiralty Ships aren't the opening gambit at all. Middle game, perhaps. How did the Ships even come to be? Why were Cores that were meant to be destroyed installed on Ships this large? The VMF already has the most advanced unified Navy in the known universe. Why are we hungry for more?"

"Security," Viktor said. A universe where the ability to Gate became limited would be a universe that would fracture along lines familiar to periods of human history. Plummet everyone back to the dark times just before the

Space Age, when wars were fought over basic resources like clean water.

"Large armies don't want peace. War is the only thing that justifies their existence."

"I didn't say 'peace'," Viktor said. He stared evenly at Kasparov, who chuckled again.

"May I borrow your deck?" Kasparov asked.

"Of course, sir. If... may I watch?" Viktor asked, trying not to sound too hopeful. He'd never seen an Admiral at work before, let alone one this famous.

Kasparov rubbed his hands together. "I don't like having an audience when I'm thinking, but an opponent would help. Play against me. Control the Admiralty Ships. Play them the way you think they should be played. Do your worst."

# CHAPTER SIX

"YOU'RE SUPPOSED TO be on leave, sir," Kalina said as she let Kasparov into her hab unit. "Besides, you shouldn't be here. I could file a complaint with HR."

"File away," Kasparov said. He looked like he hadn't slept for days, his eyes ringed with dark smudges. Kasparov wasn't in uniform. He wore unassuming dark gray clothes without any of the brocade ornamentations that the wealthier citizens of Gagarin station favored, though the cut and sheen of the fabric looked expensive.

Kalina peeked outside her unit and ducked back in. "Where's your security detail?"

"Probably still outside my hab."

Kalina stared at Kasparov in horror. "Sir!"

"We're on Gagarin station. I'm hardly about to get snatched off the street or something. The security detail was always just a formality." Kasparov ambled into the unit, looking around. Kalina was glad that she'd spent the morning neatening up the hab, then she was annoyed that she was glad. This was an intrusion on her privacy.

"Is there something you require, sir?" Kalina said, her hands curling.

"Doesn't the VMF pay its Lieutenants enough anymore?"

"Sir?"

Kasparov waved a hand around her sparse hab. "I've seen storerooms with more personal effects."

"Are you trying to be insulting?" Kalina bristled.

"No. I've just. No." Kasparov wilted into a chair. "It's been a rather trying series of days."

"I recommend a psychiatric evaluation, sir."

Kasparov let out a hoarse sound. "You don't mince words. I like that about you."

"Flattered," Kalina said, her tone making it clear that she was anything but.

"I had an interesting meeting the other day. At the tactical booths."

*In the Admiralty?* "You're supposed to be on compassionate leave," Kalina said.

"No one in the VMF is going to stop me if I want to use the tactical booths. I ran into Inessa on my way there. She was painfully solicitous. Wish she'd stop. Wasn't like Anna and I were even close. Wasn't like... Anyway. The meeting. I found Captain Kulagin running an interesting simulation in a locked booth."

It took Kalina a moment to remember where she'd heard the name. "The Captain of the *Gabriel*."

"That's him. Stern young man, one of Counter-Admiral Shevchenko's lackeys. Pity, really. A waste of nerve and tactical talent. We played a few rounds."

"Did you allow him to escape with some of his dignity intact?"

"Oh no," Kasparov said cheerfully, "he trounced me a few times."

Now that was interesting. "Captain Kulagin is that good?" Surely she would've heard of another tactical genius rising through the ranks.

"He's bright, but not spectacular. We weren't playing at the usual thing. We were indulging an intellectual curiosity of mine." Kasparov stared at Kalina, his mouth set into a thin line. "Kalina, how would you destroy an enemy if you were at a considerable tactical disadvantage?"

Questions like that from Kasparov never invited simple answers. "Are we talking about a person or war?"

"War."

"Opposing forces?" At Kasparov's nod, Kalina leaned against the wall, folding her arms. "Does my army have to survive the encounter?"

"Hah. That's something a normal VMF officer would never ask."

"Maybe you only meet a lot of tedious people," Kalina said, wary.

Kasparov's mouth twitched. "Assume there are no rules, but yes, the survival of your forces would be ideal."

"In that case, I would retreat."

Kasparov tilted his head. "Oh?"

"You've said that there are no rules. The battle is unwinnable, and survival is ideal. I retreat, returning to fight only when a fight is less futile." Kalina glowered at Kasparov. "I hope this isn't why you barged into my home, sir. You could have just pinged me with a message."

Kasparov stared at Kalina for so long that she started to shift her footing, unnerved. He looked away, staring at the wall. "I'm going to tell you something that's far above your clearance level. Not because it's particularly advisable, given who I think you are. But because I have to talk to someone, and everyone else who has the same clearance level can't be trusted."

"You think I can be?"

"I did say it wasn't advisable," Kasparov said. He looked back over at her. "I think you can, at the very least, be trusted to be mostly honest with me."

Kasparov was in a strange mood. "What a resounding character reference," Kalina said. "What about Sergeant Smirnova? Surely you trust her."

"I don't know if she'd survive the experience. I also doubt that she'd tell me what I need to hear."

"Something that is 'mostly honest'?"

Kasparov's mouth twitched. "Quite so. Sit, Lieutenant. I'm getting neck strain staring at you."

Kalina sat, swallowing her irritation. "Fine. Let's get us both into trouble. Again."

"That's the spirit." Kasparov relaxed. "Some years ago, the Admiralty found a way to Gate without having to use Virzosk Inc's stellar Gates. From anywhere to anywhere."

Kalina straightened up sharply. She clenched her fist, pushing down her horror, hoping Kasparov mistook the lapse for mere disbelief. "That's possible? But... I hadn't heard."

Kasparov nodded slowly. "It wasn't widely disseminated. The whole procedure is still highly experimental."

"Is that what happened to the *Farthest Shore*?" That would make sense. The *Farthest Shore* had met its end in the middle of nowhere, as far as Kalina could tell from the reports. It hadn't been near any conflict zones, or near anything important—the closest VMF colony had been days away. Perhaps the experimental technology had suffered a critical malfunction.

"Not quite. Some time ago, Dr. Kwang found a way

to create a true ASI. He did so by mapping a human brain into a highly advanced processor of his design, which he called a Core." Kasparov updated Kalina in a dispassionate voice, one that only wavered when he described what had truly happened to the *Farthest Shore*.

"You said that was highly classified."

"It still is. I'm going to trust you to keep it to yourself," Kasparov said.

Kalina sat back against the wall, dizzy with shock. "This is very hard to believe," she said.

"Take your time."

"Honestly sir, I don't know what you expect me to do." Rogue VMF ASIs? Five of them at that? "Five for five Admirals? Including you?"

Kasparov nodded slowly. "Admiral Mikhailova to *Ride of the Valkyries*. *Hammer of the Gods* with Vice-Admiral Bazarov. *Pillar of Eternity* to Counter-Admiral Shevchenko. *High Winter* with Counter-Admiral Tsiolkovsky. And…" He trailed off, swallowing hard.

"*Last Word* to you," Kalina said softly. The ship that had destroyed the *Farthest Shore*, that had murdered Nevskaya and all her crew. "Oh, sir, I'm so sorry."

"Never mind that," Kasparov said, though he looked haunted as he said it. "How to defeat enemy ASI ships that can Gate anywhere, that don't need to wake up a crew to use their weaponry. That's the intellectual puzzle I was trying to figure out. I had Captain Kulagin control the ASIs."

"Did you manage to defeat him in the end?"

"Not with the existing Eva ships, no. Not without sacrificing at least one of them. I've been thinking about it."

Kalina rubbed at her temple. "The *Last Word* is a copy of you, isn't it? Except mapped onto an ASI. Doesn't that mean it'd be able to anticipate anything that you will? Except more efficiently? This is a disaster."

"Exactly." Kasparov looked pleased with Kalina's analysis. "It's a disaster. The extent of which my Admiralty colleagues refuse to acknowledge. It's a complete and utter fucking disaster."

"Can't we just make more Eva ships? No, wait. Not if they go rogue too." Kalina closed her eyes, trying to think. "Stealth mines, or—they still need stardrive seeds. Given the way the *Last Word* behaved, it sounds like their crews are dead."

"Most likely," Kasparov said.

"It's a battle of attrition. We have stardrive seeds. They don't."

"Two of our shipyards have gone dark so far." Kasparov looked grim. "I don't think the Admiralty ships are working alone. Something—someone—is helping them refuel."

"You're assuming that they aren't simply sabotaging the yards."

"Not at all. Why do something that destructive? I'm trying to imagine what I would do, were I an ASI. One of a few. Or maybe just one. If I wanted freedom? I could Gate anywhere I wanted. Sit somewhere in the vast expanse of space. No one would ever find me. Revenge? Why start by declaring war in such a strange way? Would it not be better to make a surprise attack on Gagarin station?"

Kalina's hands grew clammy. She wiped them on her trousers, trying not to imagine lascannons being turned on Gagarin station. The rings would blow apart, the inner power core shattering. In space, their dying screams would be heard only through broadcast packets. "Gagarin station has its defenses," Kalina replied.

"Gagarin station's main defense is its location and its permanently stationed fleet. These rogue ships would be able to outrun any of our existing ships. Without any change to our current defensive strategy, they..." Kasparov grit his teeth. "That's a tactical question for me to solve. Captain Kulagin's made himself available for now as a sparring partner, until his crew has been fully evaluated for further service."

Kalina pitied the Captain a little. He was bound to lose some crew to that, and those who remained or were added on as replacements were likely to be fanatics. "I hope he enjoys being able to defeat the great Counter-Admiral Kasparov while he still can."

"Hah." Kasparov scrubbed a palm over his face.

"What do you want me to do, sir?"

"I have a question about my daughter's death that I want resolved by quieter means," Kasparov said. He looked at Kalina with the grim determination of a man who no longer cared if he had anything to lose. "You're going to help me answer it."

"She was KIA aboard the *Farthest Shore*," Kalina said. She tilted her head. "Or you don't think she was?"

Kasparov's jaw clenched. "She most certainly was."

"What else do you want to know?"

"I want to know who was helping the so-called Admiralty ships."

Kalina frowned. "Surely the rest of the Service would be bent toward this task."

"They would. I also have no clout whatsoever within the Service. Any information I'm going to get will be secondhand. I need to know."

"Fine," Kalina said. She might as well see this through—for now. "You didn't have to come here personally to give me orders, sir. An encrypted call would've sufficed." Or was there now a lockdown of some sort?

"Any comms from and within this sector of space are going to be deep-screened from now on. There's a lockdown on any outgoing packets save for VMF emergencies," Kasparov said, confirming Kalina's guess. Her heart sank. "If I wanted to talk to you about this at all, I had to do it in person. Just like any further report you have while you're still in this sector is going to have to be made to me in person, which means no blabbing all this to your handler. Or we'll all be in trouble."

Damn the old man. "All right." So much for immediately filing an emergency report. Kalina forced a smile. "What do you want me to do, sir?"

KALINA PERSONALLY ESCORTED Kasparov back to Admiralty grounds despite his protests that she was wasting their time and that he was perfectly safe. She had done it to annoy him, not because she'd been particularly concerned about his immediate welfare. Or so Kalina kept telling herself. That had been three days ago.

Sukhoi-3 was one of the few planets ever discovered that was rich in exidium, the key catalytic element for the creation of stardrive seeds. The planet was effectively one massive stardrive seed factory, with R&D in one small sector, manufacturing in another sector, and mining tucked beneath much of the rest of the planet's skin, where a healthy percentage of the VMF's stardrive seeds was made. Sukhoi-3 was the main reason why Gagarin station had been built so far from Sol.

The planet's surface was inhospitable, with corrosive thunderstorms and a toxic atmosphere. There were only two spaceports on the planet, one of which was reserved for exclusive VMF use. Kalina's freighter sank toward the jagged teeth of barren mountains which ringed Kavkaz, the planet's blocky gray civilian spaceport. There wasn't much visible traffic beyond the constant stream of supply freighters hoisting stardrive seeds up to waiting tankers, shuttling materials down to the planet.

"Prepare for landing," the pilot said. She sounded bored. Kalina didn't blame her. A freighter like this was likely stuck making hops between Gagarin and Sukhoi-3, which was hardly a stimulating flight at the best of times. The blocky little starship shuddered and moaned as it fought the planet's thin atmosphere. Kalina breathed slowly, jolted in her brace beside the rest of the passengers. Most of them had the forlorn look of a person returning to a gray cycle of work after a holiday. They'd have had to transit through Gagarin for that—if they even had the means to travel further than Gagarin.

The freighter didn't technically land on the surface of the planet. It fed itself into a bracket set against one of the looming gray blocks, made of a reinforced plascrete that was impervious to the atmosphere. After the airlock cycled through, the freighter released its crew and passengers. Kalina and the others shuffled out into a decontamination room that smelled of air recyclers and sweat. The moan of machine-loaders stirring to life beside their tunnel shook the ground they stood on with gentle pulses. They were being processed through the maw of inexorable commerce. The ship's cargo would be unloaded in minutes, fresh crew and new cargo moved on board in its place, and the starship would flee the atmosphere before any lasting damage could be done.

With a final dissonant hiss of compressed air, the gray

maw spat them out into a large cargo lift. They whistled downward into the belly of the planet.

Kavkaz was built along similar lines to the few cargo ports that Kalina had the misfortune to frequent during her years of service. It was efficient and functional. Hovercrafts cradling cargo were fed in a constant stream toward and away from freighter brackets. Anything that could be automated was. There wasn't as much security as Kalina had expected, but then again, the stardrive seeds weren't shuttled out from the civilian port.

A busy hyperspeed train station fed out arterial tracks to the rest of the planet beyond customs. Kalina cleared it with one of her clean identities and was waved through by an indifferent officer. Clearing customs on the VMF side would've been tougher, but thankfully Kasparov's business didn't appear to intersect with the VMF sector. Kalina bought an economy ticket, boarded the train, folded herself into a designated sleep pod, and slept badly, dreamed of exploding ships.

Posyet was a residential sector, according to the hurried research Kalina had done before boarding a freighter to Sukhoi-3. It was self-sufficient except for water, which was supplied by freighters like the rest of the planet. Kalina had been expecting something as painfully industrial as Kavkaz and was pleasantly surprised to see that the underground sector did not subscribe to the concrete-and-depression aesthetic of the other manufacturing hubs that Kalina had been to.

A sprawling park of synthetic grass winged outward from the hyperspeed station in graceful arcs of green and yellow. Unlike Gagarin station, the bio-engineered air recycling plants were not built into space-saving pillars. Instead, they grew thickly over great sculptures that loomed over stepped buildings, the rooftops of which were also draped with vines. Kalina spotted a great bird-creature with raised wings, a child, a pre-starseed rocket. It made Posyet look like the den of some verdant medusa of flowers rather than stone, the spaces between statues seeded by scattered ants. The ceiling above was plated over by holofeed scales, creating a vast holodeck of a window that opened to distant stars.

"Beautiful, isn't it?"

Kalina flinched. The person who had spoken was a slim, androgynous youth, with braided black hair and dark skin, their cheeks traced with gold lines that shimmered and reshaped themselves endlessly into different patterns. It was currently a favorite adornment of younger Federation citizens. Kalina had seen variants of it around Gagarin station, though most youths preferred to decorate their throats or the backs of their palms. "Yes," she said. Sensing proximity and contact, their wristdecks automatically updated each other with their preferred pronouns.

The youth smiled at her. "First time in Posyet?" They wore a shapeless white shift that flowed gracefully over narrow shoulders and their long limbs. A glance at the citizens close by indicated that this was common-enough garb for Posyet, though the older people seemed to prefer more colorful shades.

"There's a first time for anything," Kalina said. She inclined her head at the youth and started to walk away from the station at a brisk pace. To her annoyance, they skipped over to keep up. "Go away," she told them.

"You can call me Ava," the youth said.

"I'd prefer to call you 'pest'," Kalina shot back.

Ava affected a deep sigh. "Is the military always this unfriendly?"

Kalina managed to keep her surprise from betraying her. "Do I look military to you?"

"You look like *something*. Srentenka Street's to your left, by the way." Kalina spun on her heel and headed back toward the station. "Oh, come on," Ava protested. They followed Kalina into the station. "Going back already? I know you have to go to Srentenka. You're pretty early. We thought you'd be here on the next flight—"

"Be quiet," Kalina snapped. She headed away from the ticket gantries at a fast clip, circling toward the bathrooms. Ava started to slow down, finally getting wary. They yelped as Kalina grabbed them by the arm and propelled them down the corridor, past the bathrooms and into the ubiquitous servitor storage room at the end where cleaning bots sat in their charging brackets. Once inside, Kalina pinned Ava to the wall. "Talk." She tightened her grip on Ava's arm, twisting it behind their back.

"All right! All right. I was just told to look out for you at the station and bring you to where you were supposed to be. Just to save time."

"Told by who?"

"The person you're here to meet!"

"And who is that?"

"I don't know. I wasn't told. I'm just a guide."

"A guide?"

"Everyone who's born on this stinking planet has to work once they're eighteen years old. A lot of students run odd jobs for people around here in between our studies. The gig economy is for the young, right?"

Kalina considered this. "You were given my description?"

"Yes, and a location. 5 Srentenka Street. I wasn't told anything else. I swear."

"You're lying, and you're very good at it." Kalina pressed them harder against the wall. "Unfortunately for you, I have excellent implants, and nobody taught you how to still your heart rate."

Ava hissed. They squirmed against Kalina's grip even as their free hand flashed towards their hip. She'd anticipated that. Kalina grabbed and slammed Ava's wrist against the concrete, only to yell and stagger back as an electric jolt shot up her arm. Ava was wearing a repulsion bracelet under their sleeve. As Ava started for the door, Kalina shook off the numbing effects, barreling into Ava before they could flee. They grappled on the ground with none of Kalina's usual grace, sluggish as she was from the effects of the shock. Ava snarled curses at Kalina as they tried to shock Kalina again with their wrist. Something that small likely only had one more charge at best. Kalina allowed Ava to shove down at her ribs, only to wriggle back and knee Ava's arm up against their chest as the bracelet flashed.

Stunned, Ava convulsed against a servitor bot, kicking and trembling. Kalina scrambled to her feet. Ava didn't have the benefit of military-grade implants, and after a few seconds, they shuddered into stillness. An acrid stink seeped into the air as they wet themself.

Searching Ava's body didn't reveal much. The bracelet had been their only weapon. Kalina folded Ava into a recovery position, wrinkling her nose at the smell. She let herself out of the maintenance room and froze. A pair of women stood before her, blasters aimed and primed. The older one said, "Lieutenant Sokolova? You're coming with us. And you'd better not have murdered Ava."

# CHAPTER SEVEN

"The berth fees went up *again*?" Solitaire complained. "Garrison, you're hurting my soul here."

"My heart bleeds, Yeung," Garrison grunted. Like most of the citizens who lived on New Tesla, Garrison had been heavily modded since birth and looked about as far from a Sol-born cit as Joey's imaginary aliens. The implanted exoskeleton that covered Garrison's seven-foot frame was a gleaming blue, a carapace that meant Garrison didn't need a spacesuit if they ever needed to go into vacuum. Garrison even had decorative work done—they were sporting a new set of spikes over their shoulders and back.

"Nice work," Solitaire said, nodding at the spikes. "All that extra you're skimming off the fees is paying for serious finecraft."

"Use your charm on someone still interested in your ass."

"Now you wound me," Solitaire said. Wheedling and haggling did little, and eventually, he paid the berth fee, smiling to hide his irritation. Without any actual salvage to sell but the pod, funds were running low. Solitaire was going to be near cleaned out after resupply.

New Tesla was a generation ship, the first and last that Virzosk Inc had built. As with many of Virzosk Inc's original concepts, it had been flashy, expensive, and ultimately undercut by more practical competitors. Little of New Tesla now resembled the gleaming white bulb of a ship that it had once been. Almost all of the decorative panelling had been stripped down and replaced with cheaper, more efficient solar cells. A large part had been ripped away, baring the domed hydroponics farms that fed New Tesla. No Cascade Gardens here—New Tesla's air was synthetically recycled, which gave it a plasticky tang, and the unfortunate tendency to sometimes cut off and suffocate people.

Normally, Solitaire wouldn't skip to a place like this. Too far. Too expensive. New Tesla was, however, willing to go so far as to eject UN and VMF spies wherever they found them rather than turning a blind eye, which went above and beyond even the usual pushback of a Neutral Zone territory. Solitaire respected that. Granted, the fact that the UN and the VMF didn't object was likely due to the presence of one of Virzosk Inc's ten Keystone offices, burrowed deep in the heart of New Tesla and routinely fed experimental material mined from vicinity galaxies. Virzosk Inc ships occupied their own section of the port. Solitaire could see their graceful arching fins from where he stood, a swarm of pale moths at rest.

Solitaire climbed back into his ship. "Good news is," he called, once the airlock cycled, "we're only very nearly broke."

"Fuck my life," Frankie chirped from somewhere in Engineering.

"Which leads to more good news. I'm going to need almost everyone to stay on the ship to watch our cargo real closely. Which means I'm only going to award free shore time to one lucky person, who'll be coming with me to the Ghost Market. Not you, Joey."

Joey lowered his upraised arm slowly from his pilot's seat. "I'm sad."

"I need you on the ship in case we need to quickly skip out of here in the very unlikely case of strange VMF ships. Or aliens. Or ghosts," Solitaire told him.

Joey shuddered. "Man, if them ghost ships show up here, I'm jettisoning that pod and running the hell to the Gate. Gonna leave you people to fend for yourselves. No hard feelings."

"You'd better believe there'd be hard feelings," Indira growled. She stared at Solitaire. "You're going to volunteer Pablo for 'shore leave', aren't you."

"Actually, you just did." Solitaire smiled wryly as Indira rolled her eyes. "You're our best shot, Indira. That's why I need you here."

"Pablo? Really?" Frankie said.

"I need all the emotional support I can get," Solitaire said.

"Fine." Indira raised her palms in mock defeat. "I hope you know what you're doing. Pablo, you're up. Try not to die."

"Shee-*uttt*," Pablo wailed from the galley.

"Be a man, Pablo!" Solitaire called after him.

"I don't subscribe to any kinda prescriptive pre-Ascent concepts of masculinity!" Pablo yelled back.

Indira swung down to the airlock. She was worried, even though her face was blank—her hands fidgeting with her sleeves. "You need help, I'll come get you," she said, pitching her voice low.

"Relax. I'll be fine. Not our first time running contraband."

"Who're you going to talk to?" Indira asked. "Lau?"

"Lau will gouge us going in *and* coming out."

"But he won't sell you to the VMF," Indira said. Lau had lost family in one of the VMF's occasional rebel purges, decades back. He liked to regale people with the stories in horrific detail whenever he felt the mood in the room was getting too cheerful. Close contact with Lau always put Solitaire in a truly nihilistic frame of mind.

"Might sell us to the UN, though, and that way nobody gets any money. Relax. I'm going to put my ear to the ground and check things out," Solitaire said.

"What happened to patriotism?" Indira smirked.

"I'm only going to sell something like this to someone who can tell me what it is," Solitaire said. What was the point otherwise?

"And then we'll tip off the UN?" Indira asked.

"... And then we'll tip off the UN. For free. Anonymously. What nice people we are, and all that," Solitaire said with a soothing smile.

"We gon' die," Pablo said gloomily, appearing at Solitaire's elbow. "It's ok. I just sent a farewell letter to my mom."

"You do that *every* time we go into a port, Pablo."

"She loves them letters. Says it makes her feel like I've got an exciting life."

"Shut up. Let's go," Solitaire said.

Back out in New Tesla station, Pablo relaxed, for all his doomsaying. Born downwell, Pablo liked having ground under his feet. Even if it was a station and not planetside somewhere. Some things were hard to let go of when you grew up that way. Most of the traffic in the port proper were spacers, with only the occasional Teslan looming visibly over the crowds. Some of them didn't even bother to wear clothes. Especially the younger ones. Not that anyone in New Tesla cared.

Pablo still gawked, even after Solitaire elbowed him in the ribs. "Close your mouth."

"The person who just went past had a *huuuge*— ow!—thinger." Pablo rubbed his ribs where Solitaire had elbowed him again.

"Thinger?" Solitaire sidestepped a group of tall, elongated spacers, all of whom looked visibly unhappy, even at New Tesla's relatively low g. Nothing was floating, but Solitaire had already fallen into the shuffling step of a habitual spacer in low g. "I didn't take you for a prude, Pablo."

"I'm not! I'm just thinking. That's got to be an expensive surgical job."

"What happened to not prescribing to pre-Ascent masculinity?"

"Hey man, I am completely not judging anyone for what they wanna do to their own body." Pablo looked hurt at the suggestion. "I just thought, well. That would kinda be considered free-range sexual harassment in other jurisdictions."

"New Tesla's a little different," Solitaire said. "Nudity's socially acceptable here, depending on the circumstances. Haven't you been here before?"

"Not with you people, and it was way back. Back before all the body modding got to be this cool new thing that everyone did," Pablo said.

"It's always been a status thing. New implants. New biotech. Body mods are just the latest way for people who have credits to spare to show it off." The trend was picking up steam across the Neutral Zone. Solitaire rather liked it. He nodded at a passing brace of girls with fish-like gleaming fins for hair and knife-like silver slats that ran down their backs, dilating and flattening down with each breath. "Grafted titanium, that's the latest fashion." The women's mods were probably worth more than what Solitaire had just paid for a berth.

Pablo only spared the women a glance, distracted by streetside stalls of griddled bean pancakes and noodle soups redolent with chili oil. "I'm hungry. We should eat. There's a dumplings place in Hurong Street that I've always wanted to try, if it's still there. And we should have a drink. Many drinks." Pablo looked wistful. "I miss drinking."

"You and me, friend. Now stay close. After all this, I'll buy everyone a drink, how's that."

"I'm staying," Pablo said. He still pulled a face as they ducked into an alley out of the port that led to a door marked 'RESTRICTED: ELECTRICAL HAZARD' without giving the manicured park grounds of the Administration sector a second glance. They walked through a narrow corridor, pausing at a grille. Pablo pulled it up. Solitaire climbed down onto the rungs, and Pablo followed, easing the grille back over his head.

Technically, the cloak and dagger approach to the Ghost Market hadn't been required for over half a century. The stall owners even paid taxes now. Besides, a considerable amount of spacer traffic came to New Tesla because of the market. But it was traditional, and Solitaire was a fan of traditions—if they didn't involve arrest, bodily harm to himself, or weird-smelling foodstuffs.

They surfaced in a cylindrical room, already occupied by a pair of young Teslans flush into their first mods. No exoskeleton yet, and still clothed in bright orange and yellow synthetic drapes. Just the flickering bionic eyes and gravved feet. Both were curled on a crate, smoking something that smelled acidic that emerged as brilliant blue plumes from their nostrils and lips. Solitaire avoided their eyes, ducking out of the ground floor exit, through heavy voxdamp sheeting and out into the roar of the Ghost Market. Someone close by was blasting Indopop music heavy enough to shake the ground. It rocketed off the tunnels stacked on both sides with stalls, past the throng of spacers and Teslans, the dizzy melange of cooking grease, sweat-stink, spice, and recyclers. Solitaire breathed it all in, grinning. He loved smuggler markets.

Pablo huddled closer as they went around a pair of Martian women inspecting racks of modded envirosuits, then past a stall hung with implant chips and certificates that were most certainly forged. "Who're we going to?" Pablo asked.

"Lau."

"What? Didn't you say Lau would gouge us?"

"Lau will be able to tell us what it is. Maybe for free, maybe not. Granted—" Solitaire yelped as someone grabbed him by the elbow and hauled him bodily into a spice store.

"Captain Yeung," a stranger whispered against his ear. "We've been looking for you."

THE BACK OF the spice shop was a teahouse. The stranger ordered and paid for a private room. She pushed Solitaire's shoulder pointedly when he didn't move. Making a show of reluctance, Solitaire stepped into the room with Pablo behind him, still rubbing his wrist, which was lightly scratched. He shot Solitaire a long-suffering stare as he sat on a stool before the table.

The stranger shoved Solitaire onto another seat and sat between them. She had the elongated body and indeterminable ethnicity of someone born on a frontier colony in low g. Her head was shaved bald and tattooed with whorled black dots. No visible augmentations. Dressed in an unassuming spacer suit, she was visibly unarmed. Not that she needed conventional weapons. When she'd hauled Solitaire into the shop, Solitaire had felt her impossible, augmented strength. From the pattern of her implants, visible under both her cheeks, Solitaire guessed that she was Andromedan.

"What can we do for you?" Solitaire asked in Galactic. He could shoot from the hip, under the table. Catch the stranger in her stomach. He kept his hands loose beside his hips.

"Lau sends his regards. I am Meng. Tea? Drinks?"

"Beer," Pablo said enthusiastically. At Solitaire's stare, he added, "What? If we gon' die, at least I'm gon' do it drunk."

"Tea for me, please," Solitaire said. Meng ordered and stayed quiet until the drinks arrived. No teapots, sadly—drinks anywhere on someplace with artificial grav were usually served in enclosed containers. Here, they came in compostable pyramids with straws. The tea was bitter, and nearly hot enough to scald.

Pablo made a satisfied noise as a carton of beer was set down before him. He closed his eyes in bliss as he took a sip. "Ah. The good stuff."

"Where is Lau? We were about to go and see him," Solitaire said.

"He knows. That is why he sent me."

"And now? What now?"

"Now we wait," Meng said. She drank her tea.

"Just waiting? No chat?" Solitaire asked, pretending to look disappointed.

Meng shot him a sharp, yet amused look. "We can chat if you like. What about?"

"The rising price of berths on New Tesla?"

"That? That's obvious. The population of New Tesla's been increasing. Young people from the UN and Federation colonies are starting to think it's a trendy place to live." Meng made a delicate gesture of disgust. "Intra-station transportation, healthcare, and education remain free to all residents, though. That has to be paid out of somewhere."

"Glad to hear I'm being extorted out of most of my last take so somebody can get flu medication for free," Solitaire said.

Pablo shot Solitaire a sad-eyed stare. "You rather poor people just die like over in the Shenmu sector?"

"Why not? Life's hard, and it has to suck for someone," Solitaire said.

"You're all heart, Yeung," Meng said. She poured him another cup of tea.

"Besides, Meng here just means free to all *legal* residents. We both know what happens to the kids who mortgage themselves to get a ticket to New Tesla. Wonder where all the Teslan bioengineers get all the materials and practice to get this good at enhancement surgeries, hm? I do believe Lau has a stake in some of those ventures," Solitaire said. He smiled. "Let's not pretend that you or your boss care very much about healthcare and the poor."

Meng inclined her head tightly. "Speaking of the Shenmu sector, aren't there four outstanding warrants for your arrest there?"

"A grave misunderstanding," Solitaire told her, clasping his hands together in mock regret.

"Yeah, we were misunderstood all over Honggang Skyport while exchanging blaster fire over an extra crate of stardrive seeds." Pablo yelped as Solitaire kicked him in the ankle.

"Stealing stardrive seeds?" Meng whistled. "You're lucky the Shenmu Magistracy didn't put out a universe-wide bounty on your heads."

"They did," Solitaire said. He finished his tea. "They caught up with us a couple of jumps out of Shenmu, and we persuaded them to leave us alone."

"Now that would be a fine story, worthy of another round of drinks," Meng said. She ordered them a second round.

Just as Solitaire's slightly inflated account of playing hide-and-seek around the Jinhai sector was winding down, Lau pushed into the private room and seated himself on the last chair. Tall and grizzled, he had replaced both his eyes with bionic orbs and hadn't bothered to acquire the cosmetic sheen to make them look lifelike. The steel-like spheres rotated as Lau glanced from Solitaire to Pablo and back.

"More tea? Drinks?" Solitaire asked Lau, who shook his head and gestured. Meng rose from her chair with a bow, leaving. "Aww. We were just getting to know each other."

"Captain Yeung. I hear from many places that you have something interesting on your ship," Lau said.

"Interesting how?" Solitaire asked.

"That is what I would like to know."

"How would you have heard of this interesting thing?" Solitaire asked, feigning idle curiosity. "I very much doubt you would've gotten anything past my First Mate."

"I am well-aware of the lady Indira's reputation, but

you are not the only person who listens in on a VMF channel," Lau said.

Whoops. "I always have interesting things on board. And, as you know, I'm always happy to part with said things at a good price."

"As it happens, I already have an interested buyer for this interesting thing. We are willing to reimburse you in full on immediate delivery," Lau said.

"Delivery?" Pablo repeated. "We don't do deliveries—" He subsided as Solitaire nudged his ankle again.

Lau ignored Pablo, staring keenly at Solitaire. "It can't stay here. If what I've heard is correct, that thing on your ship will bring destruction to anything around it."

"Well," Solitaire said, a little startled, "that's probably laying it on a little thick. The VMF might be rather aggressive, but they won't attack a Neutral Zone territory. Even if they were inclined to go to that much trouble, they wouldn't touch New Tesla. It's *only* home to one of Virzosk Inc's four Conglomerate Headquarters." Magic ships or not, pissing off Virzosk Inc and maybe getting locked out of using Virzosk Inc Gates would cause severe damage to the Federation's economy.

"It can't stay here," Lau said grimly.

"Who's asking? Who's the buyer?" Pablo asked.

"You don't need to know that. All you need to know is that the item needs to go to a certain place. We are willing to pay you in credits, in stardrive seeds, or a combination of both," Lau said.

"How much?" Solitaire asked.

Lau didn't even hesitate. "Ten million credits."

Solitaire couldn't hide his surprise. Pablo straightened up sharply. "Tian," Pablo breathed.

"What *is* it?" Solitaire pressed. Ten million credits

could keep the *Now You See Me* comfortably afloat for years. They could pick and choose gigs. Or just jaunt around the universe, living it up. No more salvage gigs. No more wrangling semi-legal cargo around seedy ports to seedier people.

"You don't need to know that."

"Generous as your offer is," Solitaire said, trying to sound calm, "I need to know what it is. Just making sure that I'm not getting ripped off."

Lau stared at Solitaire with open disdain. "You are a troublemaker, Yeung, and every time you darken the door of my shop, I'm certain it's the last. Still, here you are. Useful to the very end. Much as it would be amusing for you to die, it's unnecessary and might even be a waste. The more you know about that pod, the more likely the VMF will keep trying to hunt you down."

"They're already plenty hot after my case," Solitaire said.

"I've heard. Captain Kulagin is notoriously tenacious. He won't give up."

Lau's up-to-date knowledge about Solitaire's predicament was starting to unsettle Solitaire. "What do you know about him?" asked Solitaire.

"He's a protégé of Counter-Admiral Shevchenko of the VMF. Shevchenko's known to be part of the Cadre, a conservative, war-hungry faction of the VMF. They're bad news for everyone." Lau's lip curled. "Endless chaos, that's what they want. It's how they'd be able to continue justifying the VMF's absolute hold on power in the Federation."

"People like that have always been part of the VMF," Solitaire said.

"Sometimes they're in power, sometimes they're not.

When they do come into power, it's bad for everyone. Admiral Mikhailova's a moderate, and it's no secret that Shevchenko's been angling for her seat," Lau said.

"I didn't figure you for an aficionado of Federation politics," Solitaire said.

Lau grunted. "I know interesting people in the VMF, and I'm also a pragmatist. Something that you would be too if you had more than half a brain."

"The thing I have is a weapon?" Solitaire guessed. It hadn't looked like one. "A new bomb?" That would be concerning, but it was inert right now on his Ship.

"It's a weapon," Lau confirmed, after a reluctant pause. "To be honest, given your reputation, I'm surprised you and your crew are still alive. Lucky for all of you, you left it inert in its case without trying to plug it into things."

"I *knew* it," Pablo told Solitaire. "A fucking big bomb, that's probably what it is. We light up a joint near it one day, and *kapow*. We blow everyone up. Shee-*utt*."

"Thanks so much for the graphic hypothetical," Solitaire said before turning back to Lau. "It doesn't look like a weapon to me. We didn't find it in an armory. We found it in a room that looked more like... I don't know, some sort of reactor room. Cables everywhere, everything automated."

Lau shrugged. "Who knows why the VMF does what it does? It has to be a weapon. One that's valuable enough to have sparked some sort of civil war within the VMF. Surely that's enough to give even you pause."

True. "Who's the buyer? I'm not too fond of the UN, although the feeling's probably mutual."

"Not the UN."

"Terrorists? Like the ZC?" Zone Coalition people had once come very close to firing on Solitaire in Ortunga.

That hadn't been fun.

Lau looked offended. "Of course not."

"A private collector, then."

"You could say so."

Solitaire patted Lau on the shoulder. "Tell you what. Because we're friends, or at least, acquaintances, I'll keep your offer in mind and let you know."

Lau narrowed his eyes. "You're making a mistake."

"Captain," Pablo began, though he was shushed with a warning stare.

"I've only just landed at New Tesla, Lau. It's been a depressing couple of weeks. My crew and I intend to take it easy here for a while. Have fun. Shore leave and all that. And in the meantime, c'mon, you know how it goes. I always shop around for the right price. I'm already doing you a favor talking to you. For some reason, my First Mate doesn't like you, and besides, I'm desperately curious about what the pod might be. If you won't tell me, maybe someone else will."

"This could go badly for you and your crew," Lau warned.

"I nearly got blown up by a VMF destroyer, and I've been an inadvertent witness to a VMF civil war. Lots of things in life tend to go badly for me. Yet I'm still here." Solitaire drained his teacup. "Thanks for the tea."

"All right, fine. No delivery needed. We make the exchange on New Tesla. But because you're not going to be taking the item in question to where I want it to go, there's less money in the pool," Lau said, scowling. "As to what it is, I'm not entirely certain and don't wish to speculate, but the buyer has agreed to advise me what it is in general terms once they analyze it further. After they do, I'll cut you in."

Solitaire's UN contact would have to be happy with that. "Now that's better. We'll think about it very closely. In the meantime, my friend here said he is hungry, so we're going to enjoy our little break and get back to you later," Solitaire said, and beamed as Lau clenched his hands over his lap.

"Time's of the essence. You think the VMF doesn't know that you're here? New Tesla doesn't catch every single spy that takes root here, and the Service has only gotten better since your time. They're probably already on their way."

"It's going to take them a few days to sail here from the Gate. Relax." Solitaire had gone over the footage of his meeting with Captain Kulagin and had decided that the *Song of Gabriel Descending's* sudden appearance was a new stealth VMF array of some kind. Surely a Virzosk Inc Conglomerate HQ would be able to detect a stealthed VMF ship coming through one of their Gates so close to New Tesla. Or at least raise enough of a stink for Solitaire to get away.

"Then I'm sorry that I have to do this," Lau said, just as Meng and two other people entered the room, blasters drawn. Pablo squeaked, but Solitaire forced himself to just take a sip of his tea.

"Look," he said, as reasonably as he could, "there's no need for this. Even if you kill me or take us hostage, my ship's primed and ready to run. Do you want your cut that much?"

Lau shot him an irritated look. "I'm not doing this for the money. That thing you have on your ship can't fall into the wrong hands."

"You don't even know what it is," Solitaire protested.

"Two VMF ships fought over it. That's good enough for me." Lau had a point.

"Wow. I never heard anyone say that kinda thing

outside of a holovid," Pablo said, clearly trying not to stare at the closest blaster. "My momma is gon' be real sad if the letter I wrote *is* the last, just saying."

"How about everybody just calm down," Solitaire said, palms raised and patting the air. "What I'm talking about isn't unreasonable. If you people have the best offer, I'll sell to you, no problem. Sure, I'm happy to make deliveries to anywhere you like. I won't sell to terrorists, you know me, and I'm not in the habit of selling to the VMF, especially after the rather uncreative threats they've leveled against me, so—"

"Uh, Captain?" Indira said, through the Ship channel to Solitaire and Pablo. "Pretty sure someone's trying to cut through the hull of our ship."

Solitaire frowned at Lau. "Also, I'm gonna have to charge you for damage to my ship. Trying to steal my cargo while I'm talking to you? That's not very nice."

Lau's surprise looked genuine. "What are you talking about?"

Raising one palm slowly to his ear, in case of trigger-happy guards, Solitaire said, "Indira, go ahead and take care of it. I don't like boarders."

"Boarders? At the port? We've already run out of time. Two million here, eight million on delivery, and I'll top up your stardrive seeds for free," Lau said.

"Half on delivery," Solitaire retorted, "and half now. With the stardrive seeds for free."

Lau glared at him, but eventually, he nodded. "Fine. Meng will go with you to the port, where she'll ensure that your ship is fully supplied... what *now*?" Lau said, exasperated, as a flustered guard ducked into the very crowded room. Before she could speak, an overhead alarm began to peal.

# CHAPTER EIGHT

IT WOULDN'T HAVE been difficult to get away from the two women holding Kalina at gunpoint. Kalina had faced far worse odds before, and the women hadn't been very thorough in stripping her of her weapons. Curiosity kept Kalina from lashing out and escaping. She was reasonably sure the cover she had used to book the flight to Sukhoi-3 was clean, which meant there was a security breach somewhere else along the line. Maybe Kalina's hab unit wasn't as secure as she liked. Or perhaps it was something else.

"It's a grand felony to hold a VMF officer captive," Kalina said as she was pushed into a cargo lift. "You'll all spend at least a decade in prison on some remote planet, mining exidium."

The older woman shot Kalina an amused look. "Officer, you just walked off an electric charge that would've incapacitated a normal human being. We both know you're only with us because you want to be."

Kalina smiled. "Self-awareness. That's refreshing."

"I'm old enough," said the woman. She had features

that were similar to Ava's. An aunt, perhaps, or the mother. "Also, I've been jailed before. Nothing too bad." The other woman laughed mirthlessly. They were both dressed in a sober blue uniform that made them look like maintenance staff. This 'escort' wasn't their first mission of the sort.

"I'm sorry about Ava," Kalina said. It didn't hurt to say so, especially when it was true. "If they didn't try to electrocute me, I'd have just tried to scare them off."

The younger woman sniffed. Ava's relative laughed. "Really?"

"I don't like hurting people unnecessarily," Kalina said. She gestured at them. "In case you're wondering why I haven't tried escaping the two of you."

"The guns we have trained on you probably helped," said the younger woman.

"Quiet down, Zia. If you can't tell when we're outmatched then you have a lot more self-reflection to do," said Ava's relative. She smiled at Kalina without much warmth. "You can call me Sasha."

"Kalina," Kalina said, "but you already know my name." Zia looked away with a grunt, briefly distracted. Kalina could yank her over. Use Zia's blaster to gun Sasha down. Wouldn't be hard to turn the weapon on Zia afterwards. She didn't even have to kill them. Kalina blew out a soft breath and let the violence pass, the lift whistling as it shot them deeper into a world whose bones allowed humanity to leap for the stars.

It grew warmer the deeper they went. "From the manufacturing plants," Sasha said, noticing Kalina's discomfort. "You get used to the heat when you live here."

"They cycle it around the planet?" That sounded like an invitation for disaster.

"It powers the geothermal plants in turn. A nice, closed ecosystem. If a few poor people get broiled now and then on the lower levels, that's the price of progress," Sasha said. Her smile was thin and hard.

"Every cruel thing that the VMF does, they explain as the price of progress," Zia said. Through the reflection in the silver lift doors, her eyes bored into the back of Kalina's neck. "They grind through people to do it. Creating the gristle that holds their systems of power together."

"Do you think the UN or the Neutral Zones do much better?" Kalina asked, amused.

"The UN? *Pah*. The UN is a squabbling alliance of Sol and planet-conglomerates that can't agree on anything. It can't even standardize its standard of living across its states. If you're unlucky to be born somewhere backwater, you're fucked. The Neutral Zones are little more than colonies of biomod addicts and pirates," Zia sneered. Kalina met Sasha's eyes in the reflection, but the old woman smiled indulgently and said nothing. "We can do better," Zia said.

"You're both revolutionaries," Kalina guessed. "Great. Are you all with The Silent? Just my luck." As Zia stiffened in anger, Kalina said, "What does Dina Ivanovna want? Lenin's vision of society, stateless, egalitarian? Please. People are complicated, and the societies we make are complicated. Trying to distil them down to simple political ideas just creates suffering. The real Lenin founded an authoritarian regime."

"You work for one now," Sasha said.

"I'm honest about it," Kalina told her. "Human society has always been stratified. The Federation—and the VMF—just happen to be more pragmatic about the process."

"That's an evil way to look at things," Zia said.

Kalina chuckled. "Evil is a matter of consequences."

"Some would say it is a matter of opinion." Sasha studied Kalina with gentle curiosity.

"Only if they're interested in moral victories. I prefer results. For an authoritarian regime, the VMF's done surprisingly well for itself. Other than its tendency to make people who annoy it disappear, the Federation has universal healthcare, free education, and a universal basic income. Standard across its territory, from Sol to Tosz. It could do worse," Kalina said. She had seen worse. "Could do much better, of course, but I doubt Ms Moskvoretskaya has the answer to that."

"*Tch*." Zia reddened but held her tongue when Sasha glanced at her through the reflection.

The lift eased to a stop in silence. The doors unfurled to a blast of dry heat that made Kalina take a step back, instinctively raising an arm to her face. The air smelled metallic, hazy with heat. The lift had opened out to a gray corridor cut evenly into the rock by a tunneller and left unrefined. Drainage canals had been cut into either side of the corridor, and vents spat recycled air at them at uneven intervals along the ceiling. The people waiting for the lift filed past them without meeting their eyes. Zia and Sasha hadn't even holstered their blasters.

"Kidnap a lot of people, do you?" Kalina asked. Sasha huffed out a low sound that could have been a laugh. They weaved through the sparse crowd, the ceiling within easy reach above. It felt oppressive even without the heat. Kalina's clothes stuck uncomfortably to her skin. Now she understood why all the residents of Sukhoi-3 whom she'd seen wore loose shifts. Kalina and her kidnappers snaked through stifling arteries honeycombed by rooms and intersections. This looked like another residential area, far less beautiful than the one the station had opened into. This one stank of sweat, the occasional whiff of baked sewage gusting down from the recycler vents.

"Most of the people who live here work in the mines," Sasha said as they walked. "Usually the newer veins, the more dangerous ones. They have to live close to Posyet station."

Kalina nearly asked why, even as they dodged another knot of shuffling people. Almost everyone she passed was scarred in some way. Many were missing limbs, their arms, legs, eyes replaced by cheap prosthetics. Corrosion scars, burn scars. The ugliest was the resigned sense of misery, one that everyone wore. It had been baked into them like the air. "I see," Kalina said. Posyet was probably where the medical facilities were.

"In here." Sasha pushed through a heavy transparent curtain near the end of a corridor. The air was noticeably cooler within. A man glanced up sharply at them from where he sat behind a desk in the corner and looked away when Sasha stared at him. He was deconstructing a wristdeck, his face caged with vision enhancers. Decks in varying stages of repair and disrepair littered workbenches flush against the wall. They picked through spare parts to a basement corridor—a long stone stretch toward a distant door with grooves at intervals along the wall.

A killing floor.

Zia smirked at Kalina's hesitation. She pushed past, walking through the corridor unhindered, opening the door beyond and beckoning with a mocking flourish.

"We mean you no harm," Sasha said.

"Yet," Kalina said.

Sasha smirked. "Yet."

Steeling herself, Kalina strode forward. She did not look at the walls or flinch at the faint sound of a scrape to her left as she crossed half of the distance. She walked to the end and smiled at Zia as she ducked through. The new room looked empty but for a large holodeck in the centre. Sasha walked through, but Zia stayed outside as the door sealed shut. At Kalina's inquiring glance, Sasha walked over and pressed her palms to the holodeck. Biometric lock? That was old-fashioned. The holodeck hummed to life.

An image flickered above it, fuzzy with encryption and lag. It was coming from somewhere off-planet via an encrypted tightbeam instead of through a broadcast channel. When it resolved, Kalina sucked in a tight gasp of surprise. It was Kasparov.

"Lieutenant," Kasparov said. He smiled, dressed in his uniform. "Forgive this rather roundabout way of doing business."

"Sir," Kalina said. Was this a test? Her hands balled tightly at her sides. Kasparov looked over at Sasha, who stared back without comment, then back at Kalina.

"I hope you weren't accosted too badly," Kasparov said.

"I injured a civilian who should've known better," Kalina said. Even that didn't get a reaction out of Sasha. "Didn't you say any communications packets were going to be examined?"

"I'm still owed a few useful favors here and there. Managed to wrangle a narrow exception for an hour."

"Well? I'm on Sukhoi-3. What do you want, sir?" The honorific had to be forced past her teeth. "I suppose you have a good reason for this extremely roundabout way of talking to me with an intermediary present."

"I've had my suspicions about you," Kasparov said, with a bland smile, as if she hadn't spoken. "That incident with the civilian only confirmed it. The Service is very good, but I'm not aware of any VMF implants that could allow someone to just walk off fifty thousand volts. A Service agent would not have needed a completely fabricated cover—the Service recruits from VMF ranks. A Service Agent would not have cared too much about an information blockade—they themselves are part of such a blockade."

"This again, sir?" Kalina said, folding her hands behind her back. She'd been too reckless again, too confident. Still. This room didn't have any wall grooves that she could see, and Sasha was in it with her. If she wanted to get out, she still had her monoblade, and could likely cut through the wall into one side of the killing floor.

"The tool you used to break into Alek's hab. I've never seen anything like it either. Not so small," Kasparov said.

"I'm resourceful. Sir." She'd been careless.

"I think you're most definitely military intelligence of some sort," Kasparov said, leaning forward. "Just quite likely not VMF intelligence. Am I right?"

*Shit.* "The loss of your daughter has affected your senses, sir."

"Oh, you *are* very good. In a smaller bureaucracy that might have been enough, but the VMF can't keep track of every officer across its empire, and hasn't been able to for a while. Had you chosen to attach yourself to the rest of the Admiralty no doubt they would have been satisfied once you passed the usual background check. I've known that you're not who you say you are since before I took you into my service," Kasparov said. He smiled wanly. "I have certain friends here and there, however, who are willing to help me do a more thorough check on top of the VMF's. Did you think I wouldn't dig further after Sergeant Smirnova's friend found out that you weren't really from Baikonur?"

No point arguing, but there was no point incriminating herself, either. "And what do you think I am?"

"A Jinyiwei agent."

Kalina laughed. "You think the UN would send one of its famous assassin-spies to what, spend years picking up after an old man, serving him tea?"

"Waiting to strike, perhaps. Or waiting to learn. Or both."

'Both' roughly described the general scope of Kalina's mission. The Jinyiwei had tried and failed to get an agent close to Kasparov for years—not only to learn more about how he worked, but also to gain access to the information he was known to be privy to. Not to mention that relations between the UN and the VMF had always been rocky, and it suited the Jinyiwei to have an agent close at hand, poised to strike at the VMF's greatest tactician where necessary. "If you think I am a Jinyiwei agent, why would you tolerate me at your side for years? Do you have a death wish?"

"I was curious. Careful. For the first few months you were watched closely and never left in a room alone with me—did you not notice? Besides, you turned out to be an excellent aide. The best I've had. Over time, I even grew rather fond of you." Kasparov rubbed the heel of his hand into his temple. "Let's not spend the rest of the hour arguing about whether I'm right or whether or not I have a death wish. If I were to put a word through to Inessa, I could have you hunted throughout the Federation by actual Service Agents. And when they catch you, that'll be uncomfortable for you. Regardless of whether you truly are a Jinyiwei agent."

"Why infer that I was a Service Agent from the start?"

"I thought you might react badly if informed of my hypothesis in less controlled circumstances." Kasparov said as he nodded at Sasha. "You're now at a safe distance away from me, and more importantly, in a location, one which I'm certain that Shevchenko hasn't infiltrated."

"I think you do have a death wish. What do you want?" Kalina asked.

"The Service is stonewalling me, and I need an independent agent on the ground. Let's move onto what we can do for each other. Do me a second favor, and I'll consider us even. I'll even arrange for you to leave the Federation quietly. Or you could continue to spend your days picking up after me if you like." Kasparov gestured vaguely to his left.

Kalina had been too damned confident. When her original background check had cleared VMF consideration, and she'd been accepted into Kasparov's staff, she'd thought it the mission of a lifetime. One did not take missions of a lifetime without accepting the very high risk of death. Still, she could not afford to die yet. The UN still needed to know about the Eva Cores. "If that's the case, you must think very little of me if you think I'd believe that you'd let me leave quietly."

"I don't believe that the VMF should keep the problem of the Admiralty Cores to itself. However, in that regard, I am a minority, and should there be a security leak at some point I would most certainly be suspected. An escaping agent who's conveniently disappeared? Well…"

"One who was on your staff."

Kasparov spread his arms wide. "One who passed the

VMF's security check. I will make a great deal about the close shave that I suffered and all that. People will no doubt be fired. I won't be."

"What is this favor?" Kalina conceded. It wouldn't hurt to hear it. She still had other options. If the situation wasn't so dire, what with rogue ASI military ships on the lam, she might have tried to play things through. Convince Kasparov that he was mistaken, or at least convince the VMF that Kasparov was mistaken. It would take time, and she would have to undergo VMF 'decontamination' procedures, but she was trained for that. Alternatively, it was difficult to escape through a Gate to safer shores—but not impossible.

"The same thing I asked you for before you left. Help me resolve some questions about my daughter's death," Kasparov said.

The situation was dire. Denying things would only waste precious time, and Kasparov knew it. "I don't know what you know about Jinyiwei agents, but we can't exactly assassinate destroyers."

Kasparov let out a hoarse laugh. "I'm going to request an extension to my compassionate leave. I'll log leave for all my staff as well, including you. On the records, you'd be taking a leave of absence to see your family in Baikonur. In reality, you will be heading for Zaliv."

"The shipyard-station?"

"Just so," Kasparov said.

"That's going to need Gating," Kalina pointed out. "What makes you think I won't just take over the crew and Gate out to wherever I want?"

"Because surely you see how dangerous the Admiralty Ships are to everyone—not just the VMF." Kasparov leaned forward intently, clasping his hands. "There's no defeating the Admiralty Ships as they are. Not yet. Not by either sacrificing too many people or by trusting more Ships to ASIs. Go to Zaliv. Sasha here will help you get there. She's due to deliver some stardrive seeds."

Kalina glanced at Sasha, who smiled at her. "What's your stake in this?" Kalina asked her. Sasha shook her head. "You do realize she's one of The Silent," Kalina said. The official UN stance on Moskvoretskaya was ambivalent, but Kalina personally had never been fond of populism in any form. The simplicity of their ideas was often as destructive as they were seductive.

"Incredible. What a revelation. I never knew," Kasparov said, without even changing his expression. He did manage a wan curl to his mouth when Kalina stared at him. "Needs must."

"'Needs must'? I could have you reported for treason." The threat was halfhearted.

"Right after I expose you as a Jinyiwei agent, I suppose? Now we both have something on each other. Mutually assured destruction. My favorite." Kasparov seemed amused at the prospect. "Go to Zaliv, 'Lieutenant'. Try not to murder Sasha or her crew on the way. Sasha will debrief you once you get there."

"I'll trouble you to remember the bit about not murdering us," Sasha said, completely deadpan.

"Fine," Kalina decided. Once they were past the Gagarin Gate, she'd at least be able to get word back to Harkonnen. Hopefully.

"It's a pleasure working with you, as always." Kasparov paused. "Should I still call you 'Kalina'? Aren't all ranked Jinyiwei agents named after celestial dragons?"

"'Kalina' is good enough," Kalina said. She had chosen no name for herself for a long time, and only one name was true for her now. It was the name that Jinyiwei had given her when she had qualified: a name that was also the color of a dragon.

# CHAPTER NINE

SHIP WAS QUIET as Viktor stepped off the transport from Gagarin station. Petrenko, present in the vast hangar within the belly of the ship, saluted and fell into step as Viktor strode across the deck. "Nanuchkas replaced with a full complement, sir," he said, having to jog-walk to keep up with Viktor's longer stride, "and all Directorates are on board."

Viktor nearly asked if they'd lost anyone to the 'quarantine' but swallowed the question just in time. It'd be breaking protocol. "Finally. I'm eager to be on our way."

Petrenko coughed. "I heard... forgive me sir, but is it true that you spent downtime training with Counter-Admiral Kasparov?"

"If that's what you want to call it," Viktor said. Petrenko looked confused at Viktor's sour tone. "The Counter-Admiral had a matter of strategy he wished to examine. He required an assistant."

Viktor wasn't sure whether he'd learned that much out of his time sparring with Kasparov, other than the fact that conventional combat could not defeat the Admiralty Ships. Shevchenko had encouraged Viktor to continue bending to Kasparov's very many whims, no doubt studying the simulations they played through. Kasparov was relentless. Treason or not, Viktor had come away from the sessions only respecting the Counter-Admiral more. If the distress call hadn't come in from the *Wild Hunt*, Viktor would have gladly played for months—years—against Kasparov. Even if he had never learned anything from Kasparov, it would have been a pleasure just to be able to watch Kasparov work in person.

"Ah, of course." Petrenko looked disappointed.

"Prepare to Gate once we're clear of Gagarin station," Viktor said, as they took the jaunt lifts to the Bridge.

"We've been cleared for the field, sir?" Petrenko couldn't hide his relief.

Viktor stared at him. "Why else are we all back on board?"

"I... couldn't say, sir."

"Speak your mind, Lieutenant."

"It's just that... Ship, sir. Isn't our Core still locked down?"

"Our Ship's Core passed its tests with flying colors, so I'm told. The lock will disengage once we're clear of the station." Viktor had locked the Core's higher functions himself after leaving the proximity mines, leaving just enough cognitive function for Ship to Gate back to Gagarin station. Even then, he'd been uneasy about the risk—one that he wouldn't have taken if the situation hadn't been so dire. Ship had been quiet the whole trip.

"Yes, sir."

"Anything else?"

"Well, sir," Petrenko said, with a little cough, "I was

going to thank Ship for whatever it did out there. Saving us."

Viktor glowered at Petrenko until the lieutenant dropped his gaze. "It is a Ship. You might as well thank our new lascannon for the extra firepower. We're going to need it where we're going."

Abashed, Petrenko fell into an embarrassed silence as they walked out onto the Bridge. He cleared his throat as the junior Orel Directorate Lieutenant vacated the Captain's chair. "Captain has the Bridge," Petrenko said, as Viktor sat down.

Viktor accessed the general Ship channel as the Bridge crew began disengagement procedures. "This is Captain Kulagin," he said, keeping his tone brisk. "As you have likely been instructed, our current mission is confidential at the highest level. There will be a Shipwide communications blackout save for where comms are authorized by myself or by First Lieutenant Petrenko. We will be answering a distress beacon from the *Wild Hunt*. All Directorates save for Orel will exit podsleep on Code Red." Viktor looked around at the tight, bleak faces around him. Everyone knew what they were likely going to find. There was no comfort he could offer, no rousing speech that would have been anything but a lie. He shut off the link as the *Gabriel* began a brisk sail to get clear of the station.

Once they were nearly at a safe distance to Gate, Viktor left the Bridge, returning to his chambers. The lock on Ship's AI would have disengaged by now, but there was silence as he scanned the door shut and prepared to enter podsleep. "Ship?" he asked, wary.

"Sir." Ship sounded subdued. "T minus five minutes to a Gate."

"Are you..." Viktor trailed off. Asking a Ship whether it was 'all right' was ridiculous. "Functional?" he said finally, wishing the substitution didn't sound even more awkward.

"Just as you wanted," Ship replied, stiff. "I suppose I should be glad I wasn't summarily removed from the ship."

"You told the *Last Word* to go away, and it did," Viktor said. He'd been turning this over in his mind and was still none the wiser. Why *had* the enemy ship just left? Even with its lascannon destroyed, it could have easily picked them off with pulsars. Their shields wouldn't have lasted more than a barrage or two.

"Would you prefer that it didn't? You'd all be dead. I'd have ended up floating in empty space, like the *Farthest Shore*."

Viktor forced himself to have some patience. "Did you say anything else to the *Last Word*? Other than what I heard?"

"No," Ship said, sullen, "and before you ask, yes, I was surprised that it left too. It wasn't in any of my one hundred and two projected possibilities."

"That electronic sound it made, was that something important?" Gagarin station had tried to decode it, but the cryptographers were still working on it.

"No? I don't think so. I don't know—I didn't get the chance to look at it. Since *someone* locked me down instantly after the battle. And now one hundred and fifteen people in my crew are new? What happened?"

A hundred and fifteen still in quarantine, then. Slightly more than ten percent. Not too bad, by way of numbers. Viktor relaxed, settling into the pod. "Wake me once we're out of the Gate." He hesitated, hand clenching on the side of the pod. He could give Ship access to the pulsars. Instruct Ship to defend itself right out of the Gate, while its human crew woke.

No. The tests had been wrong before. They could still be wrong now. Viktor lay down in the pod, closing his eyes and bracing for the chill. Just before the anesthetic kicked in, he thought he heard Ship whisper, "I wish you trusted me."

*Not likely*, Viktor wanted to reply, but the words choked in his throat as the breathing mask melded over his face.

He woke to a ringing alarm, disoriented and coughing as he nearly fell out of the pod. Viktor panicked for a second before discipline kicked in. He barely managed to make it to the cleanser before he threw up, this time on the ground. He didn't have the time even to flag that for cleanup as he washed his face. Viktor had gone to podsleep in his uniform suit, as had the others. The klaxon pealed as he wiped himself down and stumbled to the door of his cabin.

"Careful," Ship said in his ear, sounding alarmed. "Maybe you should have some water."

"Situation report," Viktor croaked, disoriented.

"From the new VMF packets uploaded, matching the data to my updated system records, the *Wild Hunt* was ambushed by the *Hammer of the Gods* when it Gated out into the Draco system as part of its routine tests. It managed to survive the initial barrage, before hiding in an asteroid field."

"Hid? How do you hide a destroyer?" Viktor was still unsteady as he got to the Bridge and sat in the Captain's chair. To his astonishment, he realized they'd also Gated right into the asteroid field. Safely. *How?*

"I calculated the trajectory based on the beacon's location and the initial information package. Don't worry. We didn't hit anything," Ship told him. "The *Wild Hunt* left a few proximity mines around the area, but I pinged them, so we registered as friendly."

Petrenko rushed up onto the Bridge. The Lieutenant let out a startled oath as he took in the view, gathered himself, and came to stand by Viktor's seat. The asteroid field had once been the remnants of some planet, shattered by something or other. An over-large comet, perhaps. Now it hung in brown and silver shards, some larger than even the *Gabriel*.

There, just in the shadow of a large fragment, keeping so close to the rock that Viktor flinched to see it, was the *Wild Hunt*. It was using background radiation somehow to cloak itself. Venting its heat. "Open a secure channel to the ship," Viktor said.

"Are you sure? If it's hiding from an enemy—" Ship began.

"Via tightbeam," Viktor said, annoyed at being interrupted. "Encrypted." Tightbeam relay between ships wouldn't feature on a network broadcast. His comms officer would've known to do it without Viktor telling her. As it was, Alekseeva shot him a startled look, before inputting commands into her console.

Captain Gorokova looked wan as her face loaded over Viktor's deck along with the *Wild Hunt's* current loadout. She was older than Viktor by a decade or so, with part of her face and both her arms replaced by bionics after Kronshtadt station. Widely known to be one of Mikhailova's favorites, she was expected to be next in line for a cruiser command. "Captain Kulagin. You're a sight for sore eyes."

Viktor glanced over the statistics. Shields at nil, slowly regenerating. Half of the Nanuchkas lost. Stardrive engine damaged—which explained why the *Wild Hunt* hadn't just tried to Gate away. "How bad is the damage to the stardrive? Repairable?"

"Engineering tells me we'll have it patched in a few hours. Not enough to Gate on our own, but enough to Gate through usual means if our ASI can interface with a stellar Gate. Life support systems are stable."

"That's... good." Viktor had been expecting the worst. The closest Virzosk Inc Gate wasn't too far. "What's the situation?"

"We were fired upon by an unknown ship as we Gated out to the agreed location. Our Ship took us into the asteroid field via a hard sail and hid us here before cycling the crew out of podsleep." Gorokova sounded faintly disapproving. "Forwarding combat data."

There wasn't much—just a visual of powered up pulsars firing on the *Wild Hunt* the moment it Gated out of tian into normal space. Rather than enduring the barrage while trying to wake its crew, the Ship had concentrated shields on aft as it fled on a hard sail into the asteroid field. The pulsars had chipped down its shields and damaged its stardrive. "From the battle data, the Admiralty believes a rogue Kashin-class destroyer attacked you," Viktor said, choosing his words with care. According to Shevchenko, all other Kwang Ship Captains would now have been appraised of the rogue Admiralty Core Ship issue, but he wasn't sure how Gorokova had taken the news.

He needn't have worried. "One of the so-called Admiralty Ships, yes? High Command disseminated the combat data from your encounter with the *Last Word*. Kashin-class... so we're facing the *Hammer*?"

"At the least." If it had been *Valkyries* or the *Last Word*, the *Wild Hunt* would likely already have been destroyed. As it was, Viktor was a little surprised that the enemy ship hadn't simply chased the *Wild Hunt* into the asteroid field. Surely another ASI-controlled ship wouldn't have a problem with trajectories. Maybe it was wary of proximity mines—they'd be hard to detect with the background radiation from the asteroid field. Or perhaps the *Hammer* felt a 'live' ship suited its purposes better. As bait.

Gorokova looked grim. The same logic must have occurred to her. "You coming after us might not have been the best of ideas."

"We don't abandon our own."

"Platitudes aside, do you have a plan? I'm all ears."

"My Ship can share shields with yours until you're ready to Gate out to a safe location."

Gorokova scoffed. "That's not a plan. That's just an escape attempt. You're also assuming that the *Hammer* won't just call its friends down on us. I'm surprised it hasn't."

"*Valkyries* can't fit in here."

"The other destroyers could, though. I'm surprised they aren't here. The mines Ship dropped are dangerous, but they won't be much of a deterrent to an ASI," Gorokova said. She scowled. "It might already be in here with us. The *Hammer*, that is."

"That's the best I can think of with the current odds—" Viktor began. Unless. The *Hammer* hadn't seemed to have the strange new cloaking tech that the *Last Word* had utilized. In a straight-up fight between the *Gabriel* and the *Hammer*, the *Hammer* would lose. But the fight could easily be avoided.

"Deploy our skip drones," Viktor said, "and Nanuchkas. No shoal formation. Hide in the debris. Find the *Hammer*, if it's here."

"So, you do have a plan," Gorokova said.

"If it's still here, yes. But you're not going to like it."

Gorokova smiled. The bionic work done to her face pulled her skin unevenly over her mouth. "If it means paying them back for what they did to the *Farthest Shore*? I might."

# CHAPTER TEN

SOLITAIRE HAD A plan, technically, as they emerged onto the docks, and as his plans went, it was nice and straightforward. Indira was a great shot. Ergo, she could probably hold off boarders until Joey managed to disengage the *Now You See Me* and head off-station. In the meantime, Solitaire and Pablo would get into one of the short-range station hoppers customarily used for delivering crates quickly around the surface of the station. They'd launch off and wait for the *Now You See Me* to pick them up.

"Instead of staying and fighting," Meng said, with a disdainful smile.

"I'm not a fighter," Solitaire said, apologetic. He hated fighting, especially in a space station full of civilians. Things could often go wrong spectacularly quickly—biodome-breaches-and-everyone-dies kind of wrong.

"What about your stardrive seeds payment?"

"Hoppers are useful things, with such great carry capacities. Look," Solitaire said, as Meng started to object, "I'm a smuggler, not some gunslinger. Lau wants me to get the item I have to Gods know where. That means I'm going to be pretty useless if I die out there." He nodded in the direction of the port. Intermittent blaster fire and shouts in various Galactic dialects ricocheted off the cylindrical space.

"You have a point," Meng conceded, as an energy bolt sizzled past the crates they'd taken cover behind.

Pablo squeaked, clenching his blaster tight. "This. This is what always happens when I get volunteered for shore leave," he told Solitaire.

"Don't be so negative. The last time we had to offload product, you weren't shot at," Solitaire said.

"We nearly got eaten is what happened," Pablo said, "and not even in a fun way."

"Eaten?" Meng asked.

Solitaire winced as another shot howled overhead. "As much as I'd love to trade stories, do you have another plan, or are we going with mine?"

Meng shot them both a look of disgust. "Fine. Yours. This way."

They backtracked out of the customs entrance to the port. Meng led them through another service door to the maintenance level where the loading equipment and supply crates were kept. Beyond this sector were the great hangars with their loading bays and berths, several ships deep, made up of freighters, cargo ships, traders, and corsair ships. The maintenance level wasn't empty, but the few techs and staff on the floor took one look at Meng and scurried out of sight.

Meng started to tap something out on a wrist console as she walked towards the nearest disused hoppers. The rest of Lau's personnel that had come with them spread out to watch the exits. Each hopper was no more than plasteel spheres cradled in an exoskeleton with an engine and magnetic clamps, their serviceable design unchanged for half a century. Meng activated one by inputting a code beside its flank. As the hopper shivered to life, Solitaire and Pablo climbed in.

"I don't like this plan," Pablo complained, looking over the controls. "This thing got no shields. We get shot out there, we die."

"So, we don't get shot," Solitaire said, as calmly as he could. He'd always felt a little disoriented in a hopper. Naked, in a way. The all-around plasteel was disconcerting, and there wasn't much onboard air since the things weren't meant to stay off-station for long.

"I'm gonna cry," Pablo said, though he settled before the flight stick and brought the hopper entirely online. Before them in the loading dock, Meng had swiped out something using the access controls. Machinery groaned behind them, and a loading arm eventually spooled across, bringing a large white crate with it.

"You'll get your credits if you make it onto your ship," Meng told Solitaire. "Sorry. It'll be hard to deal with intergalactic probate to get our money returned if you die."

"It was *so* lovely to meet you too," Solitaire said with a bright smile, as Pablo grasped the crate with the hopper's clamps and moved them into the airlock.

"Captain Yeung, you have been a profound disappointment in many ways," Meng said, standing back.

"I look forward to disappointing you and Lau again in the future," Solitaire said. The hopper jerked into the air with a hiss, whirring to life and flooding the cockpit with warm air. Pablo took the hopper through the inner door into the airlock.

Meng cycled the inner door shut behind them. After a

few seconds, the airlock cycled open. As they lost gravity, the hopper shifted a few inches, then compensated automatically for decompression. They vented out into space, away from the belly of the station.

Space stretched in its tidal emptiness beyond them in all directions, etched with distant stars. The Teslan Gate could be seen as a distant pale ring, suspended in nothingness beyond New Tesla, several hours' sail away, while the colonies it serviced were visible from here only as distant dots performing their unhurried orbit around their maturing star. From this angle, New Tesla looked like a cauliflower turned on its side, its unevenly bulbous surface peppered with solar panels.

The hangar was beyond the panel farm, through the bright film of the stasis shield. As they drifted closer, the pitched firefight taking place close to his ship grew visible. Indira was firing from the hold at people she'd pinned down behind supply crates. The flank of the *Now You See Me* was blackened by blaster fire. Bastards.

"Indira, you good?" Solitaire asked on the ship channel.

"Yeah. We've got them beat back. Ready for lift-off."

"Come pick us up out here. We're on a hopper."

"You're what?" Indira was shocked. "You don't have that much air in one of those things!"

"*Ooh*, don't I know it," Pablo moaned. "I'm getting stressed. I'm breathing more air. I need to pee."

"Please come and get us," Solitaire said.

Indira laughed. "Aye, Captain. Joey, you heard him."

The hold closed. The boarding crew advanced, firing on the ship even as the *Now You See Me* surged into lift-off. Its torch caused boarders to scatter for cover as the ship angled out of the stasis shield in a quick sail. The cargo hold had been holed, and Solitaire pulled a face as Pablo piloted the hopper closer. It was made for short hops in zero-g, not actual space flight, and so it felt like an eternity until Joey spotted them and took the ship closer.

They loaded into the cargo bay, staying in the hopper as Indira, in a suit, closed the breach points with sealant. It'd hold for now. As air flushed back into the hold, Pablo set the magnetic crate down next to the pod and deactivated the hopper. He climbed out and hugged the hull of the ship with a strangled sound of relief.

"Don't be so dramatic," Solitaire told him.

"What's this?" Indira asked, knocking her knuckles on the crate.

"Stardrive seeds, I hope. Part payment. We need to Gate to certain coordinates." Solitaire opened a private channel to Meng. "I'm on board."

"Credits have been sent to your account. Along with the coordinates. Good luck," Meng said, and cut off contact.

"We're a little bit richer now," Solitaire said, pulling himself up towards the captain's seat. Joey was already running dark, turning on scan-scramblers, switching off transponders and taking them towards the nearest Gate at a quick clip. Since going dark within sight of a station was patently illegal in most jurisdictions as a firing-on offense, Joey didn't usually do it, unless he was nervous— or desperate. "Five mil richer, five more when we get there," said Solitaire.

"Get where?" Indira asked, suspicious, as she input the coordinates into her database. "This doesn't lead anywhere. You sure they're right?"

"Lau wouldn't make a mistake like that."

"*Lau*? I thought you said he'd gouge you," Joey said.

"Ten mil credits don't sound like gouging," Pablo said, strapping into his seat. "Ten mil sounds like 'hey here's a heck load of money you'd never get ever, because the mission's FUBAaah—!" The rest of Pablo's words ended in a yelp of shock. In the empty space at the opposite side of New Tesla, a ship shaped like the blade of a sword had just appeared out of nowhere. It was *huge*—so big that Solitaire's head hurt to look at it. A VMF cruiser, longer than even the station they'd just left.

"Attention New Tesla," a deep voice said over the open channel, with a thick Federation accent. "This is the Core. Hand over the corsair ship *Now You See Me* and its cargo and you will not be harmed. This is your only warning. Failure to comply, or any hostile action, will be met with reasonable force."

There was a tense silence for a long while, then New Tesla responded across all broadcast bands. "This is Superintendent Aamir Khan. New Tesla is in the Neutral Zone. New Tesla is a Neutral territory, subject to the UNISA treaty. The VMF has no jurisdiction here, and your presence is in breach of the treaty, and tantamount to an act of war. Leave, or we will retaliate."

"Station guns can punch through shields," Pablo said quietly, "but a ship like that—"

"It appears the *Now You See Me* is no longer within the boundaries of New Tesla," said the voice. "Your existence is no longer necessary."

"You're fucking kidding me." Solitaire leaned forward, wide-eyed. The lascannon warmed up under the cruiser's belly, and as they watched, horrified, it blasted through New Tesla, coring a superheated channel that was molten at the edges. Decompression was instant and horrific. Bodies and debris were sucked out into the hole punched through the station in a slew of metal and gore.

Jocy went a waxy color. "Tian!"

"Fly, damn you!" Solitaire barked at him. The VMF ship had just killed an entire *station*. "We're dark, just run for the Gate!"

"It'll keep shooting at the station!" Indira clapped her hand over her mouth, shuddering, swallowing nausea. She started to unstrap herself from her chair.

"What are you doing?" Solitaire reached over to grab her wrist.

"I'm going to vent that pod. Strap a beacon on it." Indira grew flushed, her eyes bright with tears. "Oh, Gods, Solitaire. What have we done?"

"We haven't done anything. Sit down. And we're not going to do that. We can get away."

"We can, but what about everyone on that station?"

"Most of them are already dead. Other than maybe the people near the docks." People were fleeing onto ships. Even a hopper was blasting off the station, panicked.

She glared at him. "That's not true. We can... We can still do something. Drop the pod. Return the money to Lau if you have to."

"Lau's probably dead now. He was on New Tesla. The ship might kill us anyway—look at what it did to the station. Look," Solitaire said, as firmly as he could, "Lau probably works for the UN. Even if he said he wasn't. Who else has that kinda easy money? If the UN wants this, whatever it is, a weapon that the VMF's willing to murder entire stations over, I think they should have it. Better them than the VMF and their new ships."

Indira balled her hands into fists. She took in a long, wavering breath. "You're a real piece of work, Yeung."

"Indira—" Solitaire began.

"Fuck you! I know you're just doing this to get paid," Indira snarled.

144

"There's no more payday other than what we've got," Solitaire said evenly. "I mean it about this weapon. I've faced the VMF before."

"Calm down," Frankie said.

"Yeah, c'mon Indira. What could we have done, huh?" Joey jerked a thumb at the station. "Looks like they tried getting to us with ground troops, but when that didn't work—those bastards didn't even give New Tesla time to negotiate or surrender. They just opened fire to silence them! That would've killed their own people along with everyone else. Bastards like that can't be reasoned with."

There was a long silence. "We should never have even boarded that ship. This is the last job I do with you," Indira told Solitaire, though she sank back into her chair, turning to watch the demise of New Tesla as they sped quietly past towards the Gate. Solitaire looked away, over at Pablo. Pablo avoided his eyes, frowning at his console. His hands shook.

"Okay, Indira," Solitaire said. He wished saying so didn't ache as much as it did. "Okay. This is the last time."

# CHAPTER ELEVEN

"YOU GAVE IN very quickly," Ava said.

Sasha's cargo hauler *Selected Poems* was old, its life support systems rickety enough that the temperature within the ship was several ticks higher than comfortable. Or maybe the higher temperature suited people from Sukhoi-3, who were used to broiling as a fact of life. The crew space was cramped. There were no separate cabins, the pods racked up along the hull of the ship. No replicator. The ship wasn't meant for long haul deliveries. Kalina found its stripped-down purpose comforting, somehow. She sat cross-legged on the powered-down holodeck, cleaning her blaster and ignoring Sasha and her pilot. Other than Ava, they'd gladly ignored her in turn.

Ava shifted closer, refusing to be ignored. They sat on the floor, grinning up at Kalina coyly. "Come on. No hard feelings, right? I'm the one who got shocked unconscious in the end."

"Go and bother your mother," Kalina said, with a nod toward the cockpit. She'd guessed right—Ava pouted.

"I would if she allowed herself to be bothered."

"Aren't you a little too young to be a Leninist?"

Ava shot Kalina a disappointed look. "Despite what you outsiders think, we don't worship a long-dead old person. Or any long-dead political philosophies."

"Oh? What do you call yourselves, then?"

"The Silent," Ava said.

"I was being rhetorical. I know what Dina Ivanovna likes to call herself and her friends. 'Quiet endurance', was it?" Kalina reassembled her blaster deftly, sighting down its muzzle. "Peaceful forbearance never matters in the way it wants to matter because the loudest among us will just define it any way that they want. That's all the lot of you will ever be. Petition the UN all you like—that isn't how you effect lasting change. The quickest way to suppress power is with more power."

"Spoken like a VMF officer. The UN remains the Federation's biggest trading partner. Its word has weight," Ava said. She didn't look annoyed, though, only amused.

"Should the Federation decide to cease all trade with the UN, it's big enough now that it can survive by itself. The only real sticking point is continued access to Sol-Earth, which would be difficult without UN cooperation. And the Virzosk Inc Gates—though generally, Virzosk Inc has shown an indifference toward taking political sides in anything as long as there's profit to be made," Kalina said.

"But—"

"And that's why I don't understand Dina Ivanovna," Kalina said, ignoring Ava's attempt to interrupt. "The Federation won't win a war against the UN as it is now, but there won't be a war. The UN states won't stand for it. They know war with the VMF will be extremely costly, even if war might be ultimately 'winnable'—if you call that level of destruction 'winning'. The UN can only attempt to influence the Federation through trade and diplomatic ties."

"And secret agents?" Ava asked, with a cheeky grin.

Despite herself, Kalina smiled. "And secret agents."

"I've heard so much about the Jinyiwei. I never thought I'd actually meet one on the flesh." Ava scooted a little closer. "Why are you people called the Jinyiwei?"

"Can't you look that up on the datanet?"

Ava scoffed. "Now I know that you weren't born here. That kind of thing isn't available to a normal Federation citizen. We only have access to a highly curated band of information."

"In Sol-China, during the Ming Dynasty, the Jinyiwei were the Imperial secret police," Kalina said, thinking back over her academy days. "I suppose the new UN wanted an organization along similar lines."

"Similar to the Service?"

"In a way," Kalina lied. The Jinyiwei were far more autonomous than the Service, particularly those agents meritorious enough to be given a color of a dragon. "Why do you ask? Is The Silent thinking of creating something similar? Joining the fight?"

"A war isn't what Dina Ivanovna wants. War is such an outdated concept," Ava said.

"How nice to be young," Kalina said.

Ava rolled their eyes. "It's true."

"That aside, UN influence on the VMF is minimal. The VMF remains a revered institution, corrupt as it can be. The Federation's civilian Assembly of Worlds is fairly powerful, but everyone knows the VMF—and its Admirals—have final say over any important political decision throughout Federation Space. Which means if

Dina Ivanovna wants to get anything done, she's better off trying to find a way to damage the VMF's influence."

"How would you do that?" Ava asked.

"Assassinating all the Admirals would be a good start," Kalina said. She holstered her blaster and smiled at Ava's look of horror. "I'm joking."

"Are you?"

"Maybe not entirely. The VMF would fracture under that kind of chaos, allowing a well-placed political force to step into the vacuum. But there'd be an intergalactic civil war."

"The Silent is committed to nonviolence as a whole," Ava said.

"Oh yeah? What do you call trying to electrocute me then, a massage?"

"As a whole," Ava said, with another cheeky grin. "We don't want a civil war. We just want the VMF to cede some of its power. We don't want the future of the Federation to be defined by its military."

"Either you've got an excellent memory, or you've listened to one too many Moskvoretskaya speeches." Kalina had heard them all on her way to Federation Space, just out of curiosity. Idealism tended to put her into an appropriately cynical frame of mood to conduct undercover work. "Have you ever met her?"

Ava started at the question. "No... no. She's too important to come to Sukhoi-3. And it'd be too dangerous for her to come so close to Gagarin station."

"I've seen your silent protestors stand in the grounds of the Admiralty itself. If they're not afraid, why should she be afraid?"

Rattled, Ava said, "She's more important than us."

"Is she? This movement that she represents. It'll outlive

her, always. There have always been movements like hers because it's human to feel discontent, and discontent always eventually finds a name. Silent or otherwise." Kalina should know. She'd spent the early years of her life as a Jinyiwei agent quietly putting down—or starting—cults, and other 'movements', in the name of the UN. Righteous or otherwise. "Allying herself with Counter-Admiral Kasparov, though, that's not a bad idea. He's the least warlike of the Admirals."

"The Great Strategist isn't warlike?"

"As far as I can tell, Counter-Admiral Kasparov takes no real pleasure in war, and would avoid it where possible. That doesn't mean that his decisions cause no harm—he's an Admiral, and causing harm is inevitable. As the most peaceable of a bad lot, maybe it's a good thing for you people that Ms Moskvoretskaya finally has something to talk to him about."

"He finally came around to the right side of history," Ava said.

Kalina laughed, baring her teeth. "History is defined by the powerful. The way I see it, if you're all not careful about this, Kasparov will end up executed for treason. If the VMF has to do that to themselves, they'd stop tolerating you people and your cute little protests. A whole lot of you will end up sent to the exidium mines until you die. And when you die, you'll be so brittle that they'd be able to fold all of you into a box the size of your chest."

That finally scared Ava off. They paled and left Kalina to her own devices, gravboots clunking as they walked toward the cockpit. Kalina was checking the integrity of her molecular blade when Sasha clunked over and leaned against the edge of the holodeck, just out arm's reach. "I'd trouble you to stop unsettling my crew," Sasha said.

"Then they should stop talking to me."

Sasha inclined her head. "Granted, there is that. But if you want comm privileges once we Gate out of this sector, I think you should be nicer to the crew."

"I don't need comm privileges."

"If you want a ride back to Sukhoi-3 on this ship—"

"Why would I want that?" If her cover was blown, staying out of the Gagarin sector was in Kalina's best interests.

"If you don't want to be 'accidentally' tossed out of an airlock the next time you venture close to one," Sasha amended.

"Fine," Kalina said.

"Good. I'm glad we understand each other."

Kalina pocketed her blade. "Are you going to tell me why we're going to Zaliv yet? Or am I meant to make several wild guesses?"

Sasha didn't answer her question—not that Kalina expected her to. "Ava did have a point," Sasha said. She nodded toward the cockpit. "You gave in to Yuri's plans very easily."

"A quick trip off-planet out of the comms lockdown in the Gagarin sector? I can't imagine why I'd want to do that."

"I think you've grown fond of the old man," Sasha said. "You feel like you're serving your own interests, but it becomes more than that. He's very good at getting people to do what he wants."

"You sound like you have the benefit of experience."

Sasha's smile faded. "More than most, I should think. After all, we had a daughter together. A long time ago."

"*You're* Lieutenant Nevskaya…?" At Sasha's curt nod, Kalina softened. "My condolences."

"Condolences, thoughts, prayers, they mean nothing to me."

"Why did you leave the VMF?"

"After I got pregnant, I chose to be discharged. Honorably, with a pension."

"VMF officers are allowed maternal leave." Kalina had skimmed through the medical benefits available to her as a VMF officer, just to have some background information.

"They are, but I didn't want Anna to grow up in a military creche, assigned minders because both her parents were on ships and missions. Like I was. The VMF was very understanding. With the pension they provided, and the money Yuri sent now and then, life was comfortable. I... I hoped Anna would not enlist."

"Did she know who her father was?" Sasha nodded slowly. "Then how could she not?" Kalina noticed the flash of temper that crossed Sasha's face. "Counter-Admiral Kasparov is the most famous Federation citizen across the known universe. It would have been kinder not to tell her."

"There was no hiding it from her," Sasha said tiredly. "Not without running away to the UN or the Neutral Zone, and I refused to run. Now and then, I regret that."

"The rest of the crew, are they...?"

"My pilot is a cousin, and you've met my engineer."

"Tiny crew, even for a ship like this," Kalina said.

Sasha nodded. "The bare minimum. I don't want to risk others."

Kalina coughed. "Is Ava also the Counter-Admiral's...?"

That shook a shocked laugh out of Sasha, one that she swallowed badly. "No. Gods, no. Ava is the child of another cousin. It's been years since I spoke to Yuri. He got in touch only recently. After..." Sasha's throat made a noise, and she rubbed a hand over her reddening eyes.

So that was what they shared—why they'd agreed to treason, and more. "Family and common enemies," Kalina said.

Sasha nodded. "I'd drink a toast to that if we had alcohol onboard."

GATING AFFECTED PEOPLE in different ways. Kalina was glad that the only side effects she'd ever suffered were headaches and mild nausea. A minor price for what was still, to her, a technological miracle—instantaneous travel between galaxies by being slingshot through an adjacent dimensional space. Sometimes, even space flight still awed her. Here was something that distant ancestors would have considered magic, ancestors that would have prevented her from owning property, who would have bound and broken her feet. Who would have considered her ugly for having skin the color of burnt sand. In the new future, there was no such barbarism, but then again, barbarism was only a term for the concepts that modern society now rejected. As were magic and miracles.

Kalina stumbled over to the washing facilities, cramped on a cargo ship. As she hunched down in the sonic cleanser, Kalina missed the relative luxuries of life in the VMF. The revelation shook her body with angry laughter. She rested her forehead against the cleanser and let the laughter burn out of her in soft gasps, until the mirth had torn away, leaving only anger. Kalina dressed and slipped into the cargo hold as the other pods began to awaken their inhabitants. Her implants had let her cycle awake more quickly, but she didn't have much time.

Curling up in a corner of the cargo hold against a crate, Kalina pressed her thumb against her wristdeck. It studied the particular electrical signature of her mind and mated it to her prints and biometric data. As it processed her clearance, Kalina pirated a connection to the starship and piggybacked her ping off the ship's transponder signal. It was picked up quickly by a standard Galactic packet at the Virzosk Inc Gate. Kalina waited.

Seconds passed. Then minutes. Finally, the wristdeck connected to the implant in Kalina's ear. "Tian, Qinglong. I thought you were dead."

"Nothing in the VMF can kill a dragon," Kalina said.

"If you can still regurgitate tired old in-jokes, I assume you're not in as much trouble as I thought you were."

"Nice to hear from you too, Heiwuchang. How's Yanwang doing? Is he in Harkonnen?" Kalina asked. Qinglong, Wuchang, Yanwang—the agents of the Jinyiwei were named after legends. Each agent named for a dragon, each handler for a guardian of the underworld, and their Commander for the King of Purgatory.

"Him? No, he's off on personal business. Why?"

"I'm probably in trouble," Kalina said. Quickly, she related what had happened to date. "And now I'm on a ship to Zaliv, Piloted by Kasparov's ex, the mother of the late Captain Nevskaya."

There was a long silence from Heiwuchang, then a shaky laugh. "Until this morning, I thought no one could be in more trouble than Tielong, but I see I was mistaken."

"What did they do?" Kalina didn't often have much contact with other Jinyiwei agents.

"You know this one. Or you used to, before he ran off to do his own thing."

"I don't..." Kalina trailed off. "Wait. You mean the previous Tielong. *Solitaire*?"

"There's no current Tielong—we never got around to

reassigning the color. Yes. The Captain of the corsair ship that found the *Farthest Shore*. The man who stole something from it, who witnessed what he thought was a VMF civil war. Him."

"Motherfuck *what*." Kalina rubbed a hand over her face. "I thought something sounded strange about the situation. But I didn't think any corsair would be suicidal enough to antagonize the entire VMF over a payday. They're greedy by trade, but not needlessly so."

"Things have gotten worse than that now," Heiwuchang said. He hesitated for a moment. "New Tesla was destroyed by a VMF Ship that called itself part of 'The Core'. It fired on the station with a lascannon." Kalina opened her mouth, but shock stole the words from her tongue. Heiwuchang didn't wait for a reply. "Before it fired on the station, it demanded that they hand over Solitaire's ship and its cargo."

Kalina let out a strangled sound, curling against the hull. An entire station. Hells, one as big as New Tesla. She could see it all too clearly, a lascannon blasting a hole right through the station's shields. Coring a fatal tunnel, causing a cascade.

"Qinglong?"

"Here. And no. Tielong is definitely in more trouble than me. Again." The Iron Dragon had been notorious for that when he'd still been in the Service—his appetite for anything he found curious was only matched by his love of chaos. Looked like things hadn't changed since his retirement. "Why the hell didn't he try to negotiate?" Solitaire had been good at that.

"Judging from the feeds, it didn't look like the Core gave New Tesla any time to negotiate. Yanwang doubts their demand was made in good faith, given the circumstances.

They tried to force their way onto Tielong's ship, and fired on the station after that didn't work."

"...The universe has such a novel way of fucking up whenever Tielong is involved."

"He's outdone himself this time. Thankfully, it's not my problem," Heiwuchang said.

"Rogue VMF Ships that can Gate anywhere are not your problem?"

"Not my immediate problem, or at least, I hope not. I'm going to have to get your information cross-checked before I can forward it to Yanwang for further instructions. It's—sorry—somewhat hard to believe, and Kasparov's no stranger to misinformation. Especially if, by his own statement, he guessed what you were from the beginning."

"Understood," Kalina said. She'd have expected no less—it *was* a wild tale, and the key information in her report was effectively hearsay, handed to her by a man who was famous for manipulating situations toward his purposes.

"In the meantime, steady your course."

"Really? Help Kasparov?"

"You've been doing that for years," Heiwuchang said gently.

Kalina bristled. "Under orders! As a sleeper agent! I wouldn't—"

"I didn't mean to imply anything about your work ethic, Kalina. Just noting that only Yanwang has the authority to change a dragon's mission scope. Far as I'm concerned, you're best placed continuing to stay close to Kasparov— for now anyway. We need a clearer scope on what the VMF is doing to handle this crisis, and I'm curious to see why he wants you to go to Zaliv. If he has a plan to get rid of these rogue ASIs, we should help."

"After that?"

"I'll speak to Yanwang and let you know, but I wouldn't count on a warm welcome back at Gagarin station." Heiwuchang signed off. Kalina leaned her forehead against the crate, breathing slowly, until she heard gravboots clanking closer.

"Everything okay?" It was Ava.

"Yeah. Just. The pods. They can get a bit close." Kalina forced a smile and got to her feet. "It'll pass."

"I didn't think secret agents had weaknesses," Ava said, though they smiled in turn.

"We don't. I have no idea what we're talking about," Kalina said, keeping a severe expression until Ava realized she was joking and laughed.

"Any reason why you're chatting up the muscle instead of doing a full systems sweep?" Sasha asked from the entry to the hold.

"Yes, *mum*," Ava said. They made a show of bowing to Sasha in obeisance and clamped off toward the bowels of the ship.

"We're about two days' sail to Zaliv," Sasha said, folding her arms. "Got all the reporting out of your system yet?"

"What do you mean?"

"You look relaxed."

"A shower will do that to you," Kalina said. She sat on a crate. "Isn't it time to tell me what we're supposed to be doing on Zaliv?"

"Nothing you haven't done before, I think. Some theft, some surveillance." Sasha started to walk into the cargo hold, hesitated, and settled for leaning a hip against the entryway. "Kasparov started monitoring the population records of all Federation and VMF Shipyards after the

Admiralty Ships disappeared on us. Gating under an ASI burns up even more stardrive seeds than Gating through a Virzosk Inc Gate. It's also more complicated. Requires a more powerful, prototype stardrive. One that has to be manually loaded—and carefully."

"He thinks people are helping the Admiralty Ships," Kalina said. That was obvious enough. Heiwuchang had mentioned people trying to gain access to Tielong's ship. Though it didn't look like the Core valued the lives of its human help, if it fired on New Tesla anyway.

"There are. Days before Snezhnogorsk yard went dark, its closest Gate received an influx of visiting ships. Tourists, supposedly. Snezhnogorsk's a Federation yard. It's close to a good view of a nebula, albeit not a popular one. Nothing was thought about it."

"Zaliv's had the same suspicious spike of traffic," Kalina guessed. Sasha nodded slowly. "Tian! What do you expect me to do about it? Go on a killing spree? That's not what Jinyiwei agents do."

"I've already told you. Theft. Surveillance. Try to find out what you can about these people. What they want, what the Ships want. You have a day—maybe less. I don't normally stay long in a shipyard. I can fake engine trouble for a while, but too long and it's risky."

"Don't bother about that. And don't give anyone shore leave, if you can find a way to run that past the shipyard without drawing attention. We have to be ready to leave at any moment."

"Afraid of getting caught?"

"Not really." At Sasha's inquiring look, Kalina said, "You're telling me that these rogue ships are quite possibly going to give Zaliv a visit, and you think I'm worried about getting caught by mere humans?"

"True." Sasha grimaced. "When you put it that way."

"If only we could sabotage the stardrive seeds you have in your cargo," Kalina said, patting the crate she was sitting on. All modern starships had inbuilt processes to discover any sort of modifications to the seeds. They'd find any tracer or transponder pinned to the crates as well. Unless... "You mentioned manual loading for the seeds. For this prototype stardrive." If she could get onboard a Core ship—

"I'm starting to sense the makings of a terrible plan," Sasha said.

"It's only terrible if it fails."

# CHAPTER TWELVE

"It's a terrible plan," Gorokova said, "and it has far too many variables."

"If you have an alternative, I'll like to hear it," Viktor said, doing a final gear check by the escape pods with the rest of his team.

Viktor had spent the last few days carefully thinking over the weaknesses of the Admiralty Ships. He could only come up with a few. They'd have to use the *Wild Hunt* as bait. Cripple the *Hammer* with Nanuchkas as it hopefully gave chase. Gate the *Gabriel* between the Ships once the *Hammer* was in range on the pretext of defending the *Wild Hunt*. Secretly fire off the escape pods, which were made to adhere firmly to anything once grounded, and which had powerful VMF beacons.

"I don't like the fact that you're going on this suicide mission. You're a Captain," Gorokova said.

"Only we Kwang Captains have the access level necessary to shut down an AI Core. And besides, I'm no stranger to covert ops." Viktor's path to a Captaincy hadn't been a normal one by any means.

Gorokova grunted. "I've heard. Well, I'm going to play my part. Run like a wounded rabbit for the Gate while our Nanuchkas harass the *Hammer* and try to cripple its torch. Your Ship better be able to Gate in when it's needed."

"So far it's been able to demonstrate an understanding of fine detail, Gate-wise," Viktor said, though this part of the plan *did* overly rely on Ship.

"Fine. We're starting a hard sail for the Gate. See you on the other side, Captain." Gorokova shut off the tightbeam. Viktor nodded to the rest of his boarding crew as he climbed into an escape pod.

"I don't like this plan either," Ship said, once he was settled. "What if the *Hammer* Gates once the pods stick?"

"Escape pods have state-of-the-art field medical capacities." They'd probably survive a second Gating, especially with Service implants.

"What if the *Hammer* Gates again after that? You won't survive that," said Ship.

"Gating burns stardrive seeds." replied Viktor. "I'd be surprised if a destroyer has the resources to Gate with impunity, other than as a last resort. Their Ships have been out there for a while."

"They did strip a shipyard. Look. Even with the escape pods and the implants, if you Gate three times within an hour, you'd suffer the equivalent of a massive stroke."

"Just do as you're told, Ship," Viktor said, exasperated. "If I die, Lieutenant Petrenko will have command. You won't be without a Captain."

"That's not what I'm worried about," Ship said, frustrated. "There are so many ways you can die, even if the enemy Ship doesn't Gate again. If the Nanuchkas don't manage to cripple the Ship. If—"

"Enough."

"Why don't we try to hit them with the lascannon? We can Gate within range."

"Once someone wakes from podsleep and makes it to the lascannon controls, it might be too late. But go ahead, if Lieutenant Petrenko has a clear shot at the stardrive."

"You could leash the lascannon to me."

"Against regulations."

"I don't want to lose any more people," Ship said, sounding subdued. "I don't want to lose *you*." Before Viktor could respond, he was going under.

He woke to a different set of stars. The *Hammer of the Gods* must have Gated again. He was still alive. He was—

Viktor nearly vomited into his pod, until its inbuilt medpack injected him with anti-nausea meds that made his head swim. He clawed his way out of the pod, his suit activating and sealing itself against vacuum. His gravboots adhered to the flank of the *Hammer* as he got his bearings, shivering violently.

The rest of the boarding crew were also disengaging from podsleep. As far as he could tell, everyone had made it. The *Hammer* was chasing a tiny ship. As Viktor's wristdeck brought up a better image of the *Hammer's* prey, he recognized it.

Captain Yeung fled from the wolf, the Gate behind them. He'd pushed his small corsair ship into a hard sail to keep ahead. In the distance was the biggest military ship Viktor had ever seen, bigger even than generation ships. It was ugly, bulbous, and studded with pulsar teeth, turrets, and lascannons. Big enough to kill planets. He knew it by its shape, by its reputation. A UN capital ship: the *Water Margin*.

It was at least a day away. The *Hammer* was going to

catch Yeung first, and it only needed to get lucky on pulsar fire a few times. Viktor made his way laboriously down the flank of the *Hammer*, leading his squad to the cargo doors. From where he walked, he could see that they'd been blown open by something—that'd save him some splicing time.

What *had* happened? Viktor checked the latest data packet onboard the escape pod.

The plan had, mostly, been a success. The *Wild Hunt* had run for the Virzosk Inc Gate, and the *Hammer* had followed, chasing it at a high sail. That was when the plan had started to fall apart. The *Hammer* had abruptly slowed to a stop, as though preparing to Gate. At that point, the *Gabriel* had Gated next to the *Hammer* anyway, firing on it with pulsars while launching its escape pods. They'd barely adhered to the *Hammer's* flank before it'd Gated. And now it was here?

"Open a tightbeam channel to the *Now You See Me*," Viktor said, still dizzy, as he gestured to the front of the ship with some effort. State-of-the-art escape pods and Service implants were the only reason he and the other Service Agents weren't in a coma, or worse, from Gating twice in rapid succession. Besides, at their current sail, moving physically hurt. They were pushing upstream against pressure. Thankfully the *Hammer* hadn't reached such a high speed that moving was impossible. "Reroute the escape pods to power it." Viktor fought down another wave of nausea, his head pounding.

One of the boarding team nodded, bending to start work on a pod. Every destroyer had a team like this, a tiny Directorate of only six to ten agents, each with a particular specialty. The Service. Once, Viktor had been one of them, under Shevchenko's command.

Viktor had nearly reached the hangar door when the

private channel opened up with a faint click. "Who's this?" Yeung asked. He sounded strained.

"Captain Kulagin of the VMF."

"Oh, for fuck's sake." Yeung let out a strangled laugh. "I really can't shake you."

"Listen, little rabbit," Viktor hissed, as he pulled himself to the edge of the hangar, gravpads activating on the hull. "You want to live? Stay quiet and dodge. Keep this ship interested. I'm going to try sabotaging it. If it chases you, it won't see me."

"What? Where are you? This ship on my tail is a rogue ship? Tian, what's wrong with you people?"

"You talk too much," Viktor growled.

The fact that the *Hammer* was so close to a Gate was a stroke of luck. If Viktor could shut down the *Hammer's* stardrive, they could signal the *Gabriel* through one of the VMF courier drones that always stayed close to Gates. His destroyer could take out the *Hammer* and hopefully catch the *Now You See Me* before the *Water Margin* sent ships to close the distance. He sent one agent down towards the *Hammer's* torch. For now, in their radar-hidden Service suits, the *Hammer* didn't know they were there. That would end once they entered the ship and Viktor logged into a console with Captain codes.

They waited by the hangar door, stuck to the outer hull of the ship. Calm, quiet. This was nothing that they hadn't done before in the Service. Eventually, there was a word in Viktor's ear. "Explosives set. T minus five."

"Regroup," Viktor said, as the rest of them pulled themselves into the hangar bay.

Thankfully, the hangar bay's access console was still intact. The explosion made itself known only by the slowing of the Ship into a more comfortable sail. Viktor logged into the panel using his biometric ID as the other five agents spread out, watching exits. The moment Viktor's access cleared, there was a loud, electronic scream from overhead. All the intact automated machines within the hangar came to life. Robotic arms swiped and snapped towards them. Forklift gravs and loaders swerved out of their docks, charging forward.

Agents opened fire even as Viktor spoke his Captain's override, trying to force a shutdown. There was another loud snarl as half the loaders stopped in their tracks. Too few. Ship fought the system, locking out overrides one by one. With a curse, Viktor pulled up a terminal and started splicing in code, trying to strengthen his access.

He forced the doors open. A forklift spun out into space as a lucky blaster shot caught its gravpad. An escape pod spat out from its bay with immense force, ramming an agent into the hull and crushing them into a bloody smear. Viktor gestured, giving the order to fall back through the open door into the ship. They'd have to get through the hangar to the Cradle, where the Core sat with a manual access point. If the Core couldn't be deactivated, there were always explosives.

At his orders, the surviving agents split off, half heading for the stardrive, the other half to Engineering. Viktor made his way toward the Cradle. Ship battled them all the way, adjusting heating, cooling. Anything automated was fired at them, as though the great ship was haunted by an angry ghost. And Gods, the walls. The wet. The *Hammer's* crew was long dead, congealed over the walls and floor. Viktor tried not to look too closely as he hurried through the familiar maze of the ship. They had died ignoble deaths outside of their control. Viktor's only solace was that it must have been quick.

Rec deck.

Crew quarters for one of the Ship's Directorates. Hells, the *crew quarters*. The gore had coagulated, but Viktor had to swallow nausea as he waded through the least of it.

Galley.

Crew quarters.

Medical. The ship lost gravity. Viktor's boots clamped automatically to the deck.

Yeung was trying to contact him, repeatedly pinging him through the wristdeck. "What?" Viktor snapped, allowing the connection. "I'm very busy right now."

"Uh, I don't know what you did, but the big ship kinda stopped moving. Also stopped shooting."

"Good. According to plan."

"Where are you? Is your ship stealthed? I didn't even see you people fire."

"On board."

"You *boarded* a rogue cruiser?" Yeung said, incredulous.

"Anything relevant to say? No? Then shut up." Pity that the *Hammer* had decided to concentrate on Viktor. Yeung went quiet.

Viktor dodged a careening chair and shot down a cleaning droid as it flailed towards him. The floor where he was grew icy to the touch, but his envirosuit compensated. As he climbed through an access hatch, another cleaning droid veered out from its dock, knocking Viktor off his feet. Its utility arms struck his helmet with a ringing blow. He rolled, coming up on a knee and taking out the droid's circuit hatch with a single shot.

Suddenly the floor was rocked by an explosion, lights flickering on and off. Viktor tried the VMF channels, even the Service one, but each channel made him wince—the *Hammer* was broadcasting loud static down each.

"Yeung," Viktor said.

"Yeah. Still here. We're watching from a safe distance."

Thank the Gods for a corsair's infamous curiosity. "What exploded?"

"You don't know? The middle part of the ship looks like it's on fire."

Stardrive. Good. Viktor breathed out a sigh of relief, which was, of course, the moment when a service hatch beside him abruptly vented, catching him hard in the ribs. At his pained gasp, Yeung asked, "You okay? What was that?"

"Shut up now," Viktor told him. Broken ribs? The enviro-suit jabbed him with painkillers, numbing the pain significantly. Nearly there. Through the next corridor. Just as he could see the door to the Cradle, the ship was rocked by another explosion, one that bounced him hard against the hull and dislocated his ankle in the gravboots. More painkillers—this time jabbed into his thigh.

"Uh... now everything is on fire," Yeung said. "Was that meant to happen? How are you getting out of there?"

"What do you mean everything?"

"The torch, the Bridge, the middle, and the ship is breaking apart. You're still in there?"

Viktor cursed. Had the ship decided to self-destruct? He limped towards the Cradle, furious, ignoring the drag of his foot. "Coward," he spat at the suspended Core.

"If I have to die," said the *Hammer* in the voice of Vice-Admiral Bazarov, "I'm taking all of you with me."

Viktor stuck the last of his plastic explosives on the Core Cradle. The ship was in zero-g now, shaken by tremors. Viktor turned the grav off his boots, pushing hard away from the hull, raising his arms to protect his face from debris. The shockwave from the explosion behind him from the Core rocketed him to the end of the corridor. He reached for the edge of the hatch and swung down, diving through to the lower floor. Maybe he could make it back to the hangar. Or the escape pods.

The deck before him exploded, metal and plasteel crumpling, blowing a hole out into empty space. Decompression sucked him outward. Viktor was spun out into the stars, yelping as something struck him hard against his shoulder. He looked down. It was a steel strut, skewered through his suit, just missing his heart. His suit was trying frantically to compensate, but it would be a losing battle.

Coughing, losing blood, grateful for the dark, the last thing Viktor heard was Yeung, saying, "Captain Kulagin? Hey. *Hey!*"

SOLITAIRE WAS READING through the latest newsfeeds on a datapad when Viktor woke up with a shuddering gasp. "Rise and shine," Solitaire said, edging back in his chair so that he was out of reach.

Viktor stared at him in surprise, then narrowed his eyes as he took in their surroundings. Private medical bay, military-grade, everything strapped down or magnetized. Automated surgical tools folded into a wall brace beside racks of pills and unlabeled jars. "We are on a UN ship," Viktor surmised. "The *Water Margin?*"

"Good guess." As Viktor looked up at the ceiling for cameras, Solitaire added, "I might have hacked into their internal CCTV to amend the loop for this room while you were out. By the way, before you shout at me or try to kill me, I did rescue you from the wreckage. Found you because of the tightbeam hookup. Then we thought, maybe we'd try and rescue other people, but by the time we looked around, the UN took all of us into custody."

Viktor checked under his tunic. The wound had been stitched and salved, leaving only a faint pink scar. The UN did still have the best medical facilities shipside. "Probably a good thing, unless your ship had a medevac facility."

"Only the basics. Nothing that could've fixed you. Oh. Uh, one other thing. Your friends didn't make it. Sorry."

Viktor clenched his fists, his nails biting into his skin until he forced himself to relax. When he next spoke, he kept his tone neutral, betraying none of his pain. "What else?"

"We also burned your suit and put you in some of our old clothes. Told the UN that you're part of our crew. Gave you a cover. You're now Eugene Smith, of Onenui station."

Viktor stared at him. "Eugene Smith? That is so obviously a fake name."

"Best we could do under the circumstances, honestly. We thought it'd be kinda complicated otherwise."

"And Onenui station? Do I look like a Zealander?"

"Onenui station kinda likes to do their own thing, far away from everyone else, so hopefully nobody looks too closely."

"What reason did you give them for my injury?"

"You got injured in our cargo hold when it got damaged by the ship that was chasing us," Solitaire said.

Viktor let out a snort. "Hardly believable. Unless you pulled the strut out of me."

"We tried our best given the circumstances. You were dying at the time while we were getting arrested so." Solitaire frowned at Viktor. "You're being ungrateful."

Viktor rolled his eyes. It was a pity that someone so handsome was also such a complete asshole. The VMF, seriously. "So where is your cargo?" Viktor asked.

"We handed it over. Not that we had a choice."

"You work for the UN?" Viktor asked.

"No." replied Solitaire. "I was super pissed that the *Water Margin* was at these coordinates. We were told that the buyer was neutral. I would've turned around and gone back through the Gate, but then that VMF ship showed up out of nowhere to chase us. In any case," Solitaire said as Viktor scowled, "now that you're up, once I get paid in full, we can all go. I'll drop you off somewhere. Preferably not a VMF somewhere. Then we call it quits. Deal?"

Viktor's lip curled. "If you have handed over the pod, then we still have a problem."

"What can you do? We're on a *capital ship*. You could search a ship like this for years and never find it."

"I know something about ships like these." Viktor tried to sit up, winced, and settled back down, closing his eyes.

"You'll probably be OK in a couple of days," Solitaire said. He'd been in medevac facilities like this before.

"Go away."

"I could've just handed you over as you were," Solitaire said, a little irked that Viktor was still acting so hostile. "We took a risk that we didn't have to."

"What do you want?" Viktor growled. "Thanks? You've made my job a lot harder. You should have run back through the Gate."

"Where could I have run? Into the loving hands of the VMF?" Solitaire shook his head. "I'm no fan of the UN either, but between them and you people, I'd rather the UN had the weapon."

Viktor blinked at him. "Are you ex-UN Navy?" he asked.

"Kinda."

"Deserter?" Viktor asked.

"Not really."

"Why did you leave, then?"

"Unlike you people, we're encouraged to retire if we want to. Lots of us do after a couple of tours. I got bored of spending my life putting down civil strife and staring at the same set of stars. Now I fly where I like and do what I want. And get rich," Solitaire said.

Viktor stared at him with open contempt. "I have nothing to say to you." He closed his eyes again, turning his face away. Solitaire exhaled, swallowing his irritation. Intentionally or not, Viktor *had* saved the lives of Solitaire and his crew. Taking on that weird rogue ship like that by himself had to have taken immense courage Solitaire couldn't have done it.

"If you want a ride out of here, offer's still open," Solitaire said, before quietly leaving the medical bay.

The medical sector opened out to a vast garden of planted columns, one of the central green 'lungs' of the capital ship, running almost from stern to prow, with sectors built around it in tight rings. A waste of space on any other ship, but on a ship bigger than a station it served a necessary recreational function. Solitaire could see staff and officers on break threaded around the columns, either seated on the few arched platforms slung between columns or passing through on the webwork of bridges. He leaned over the rail, looking down and breathing deeply. Solitaire had missed this part about UN ships. Even the military ones.

Annoying VMF Captains or not, Solitaire was now

rich and fully fueled. He was overdue a long stint on Nihonbashi Colony, perhaps, enjoying the beach. Or one of the pleasure planets, though Indira didn't like those.

Indira. She hadn't said anything about leaving the ship ever since they'd Gated out into a bad nightmare, but Solitaire could see her unease. He'd have to talk to her. Maybe after she cooled off—

"Well, what have we here."

Solitaire's stomach clenched at the familiar voice, but he forced a smile and turned around. Commander Hyun was white-haired now. His face was a mass of uneven wrinkles that deepened his habitual scowl, made more severe still by the plain black spacer suit that he wore, with no markers of rank. Stiffly, he walked up to Solitaire and leaned his elbows over the safety rail, looking out over the green.

"Yanwang," Solitaire said, "what a pleasure."

"Yeah? You leave the Jinyiwei for what, ten years, mostly behaving yourself, and now I find you in the middle of my latest shitstorm."

"Accidentally, I assure you. Once I get paid, I'll be out of your hair."

Hyun snorted. "About that. Heard your report on what happened to New Tesla. The fuck was that about?"

"Don't know. It was... well. I don't even know what to say. My crew's pretty shaken." Indira had been spending her time sleeping, staring into nothing, and weeping. Pablo and Joey drank. Frankie was oscillating between pretending nothing had ever happened and nerveless anger.

"Anyone would be." Hyun shot him a shrewd glance. "Not that you seem to be."

"You've burned all the shock and awe out of my system,

sir." Solitaire offered him a smile. "The ship said it was from 'The Core', whatever that was. Sounds like some kind of rogue military faction of the VMF."

"Hah, yeah. Never heard of it, but our sources in the VMF tell us someone lit a big fire under the Admiralty's ass. At first, we thought they misplaced some prototype weapon or something, given how everyone's been hot after your tail. We thought you stole it."

"Not exactly."

"And now we have it, and we don't know what it is."

"Really?" Solitaire said, surprised.

"Really. As far as our scientists can tell from the scans plugged into it, it's just an inert ball of steel."

"...The world's most boring art piece."

"What?"

"Nothing, sir. You sure it's just steel? I mean. I've been chased by two rogue ships and a VMF ship over it. I'd even cut a deal with Lau to find out what it was. Not that I should've bothered, given that you were the one I'd have tipped off." So much for patriotism. It only bred bad habits.

"They're still looking. Which brings me to another point." Hyun jerked his thumb at the medical sector. "You've got to think that we're idiots."

"Huh?"

"Please. Mister 'Eugene Smith' is obviously not a fucking Zealander. He's a Federation cit, isn't he? What's he doing on your ship?"

"I'm not prejudiced?" Solitaire said.

"Kinda coincidental, isn't it?"

"You mean, that I happen to have someone on my ship who may or may not be a Federation cit—besides, you know corsairs never ask about other corsairs' backgrounds, it's very rude—right while a lot of VMF-esque ships are chasing me?"

"Exactly," Hyun said, with another snort. "Where'd you first meet this guy?"

"Don't see how that's any of your business, sir."

"'Cos it looks to me," Hyun said evenly, "that maybe this steel ball you people handed to us is a bait and switch, and the thing we should be looking at is this 'Eugene Smith'. Where are you people taking him?"

"Told you, sir, he's one of my crew."

"Oh yes? And will the rest of your crew be able to back you up on your 'Eugene Smith' story? Especially if we interrogate all of you individually?"

Busted. "Come on, man," Solitaire said plaintively, "didn't Lau—may he rest in peace, I think—tell you people what I was sending you? You paid us on delivery, even."

"It was a rushed transmission, and he didn't go into detail in case the VMF was tapping the line. He said it was something in your cargo. Something you stole off a VMF ship, though he wasn't sure about the exact circumstances. He didn't say it couldn't be a person. Lau promised to send a follow-up transmission with more details about what he thought the item might be, but it never came through. I'm thinking you people *did* want to get paid. But you probably also got second thoughts about selling off an injured guy. So you told us the ball in the pod was it and tried to pass off 'Eugene' as a member of your crew."

Solitaire stared at Hyun for a long moment. He'd forgotten how stubborn and annoying the old man could be once he was sure that he was right. "The pod is what I took off the VMF ship."

"As I've told you, Yeung, we're not idiots." Guards were moving discreetly into place, in Solitaire's peripheral vision. "Are you going to come nicely, or are we going to have to insist?"

# CHAPTER THIRTEEN

"DO YOU BELIEVE his account of the situation?" Kalina murmured into her earpiece as she slipped through the cargo port. In her borrowed khaki and brown freight spacer crew clothes, she didn't stand out. Few people, if any, gave her a second glance.

"Yuri's?" Sasha grunted. "I don't know what to believe. But my daughter *is* dead, if that's what you mean. The VMF doesn't fuck around with something like that. I was listed as her next of kin."

"That's not what I mean." As agreed, Sasha and the others were staying close to the *Selected Poems*. Tension and fear hummed through Zaliv, muting the usual noise level of a cargo port. The few public holoscreens in the area flickered through an endless loop of news reporting over the destruction of New Tesla. Unsurprisingly, the role of the rogue VMF ship in the affair wasn't mentioned—instead, newscasters were blaming terrorist elements that they called 'The Core'.

"I completely believe that the VMF finally did something so ill-advised that it bit them soundly in the ass," Sasha said, "but the rest? I don't know. After New Tesla, I don't know what to believe. If your handler's right and it was one of the rogue VMF ships... I don't know."

Kalina had reluctantly shared that tidbit of information with Sasha and her crew once they'd landed on Zaliv and seen the news. She'd considered not doing so, but she needed her main ticket out of here primed and ready to go. Kalina also didn't want any civilians underfoot. "Surely even the VMF can't keep the truth about New Tesla from its citizens forever."

Sasha let out a mirthless laugh. "And here I was thinking you'd been living in Gagarin for too long. Sure, the VMF can't control pirate broadcasts, and they can't put out an empire-wide information quarantine, but if I know them, they've been preparing for this for a while. Damage control is going to kick in."

"You think they knew that the Core would attack a station?"

"I think Yuri would have put forward that possibility to Admiral Mikhailova. It's his job. Weren't you his assistant?"

"I didn't always have the clearance to listen in." Kalina regretted that now. She'd been instructed not to overplay her hand too early when she'd first been assigned to Kasparov as a spy and a failsafe. Now Kalina wished she'd exercised her discretion. She might have been assigned to Kasparov after the whole business of the VMF encoding his mind into an ASI, but she would've learned something about the VMF's additional experiments with Kwang if she'd been more on the ball.

"He probably knew early on that you were not who you said you were," Sasha said.

"Maybe." For the first time in years, Kalina was not

interested in talking about Kasparov. Not with the threat of war and worse hanging overhead. Passing a harbor official who was doing a spot check on crates of supplies, Kalina set her wristdeck to pirate his credentials as she strolled past. Here, on a Federation port, security wasn't as stringent as it was on the VMF, and she was done by the time he moved onto another shipment.

Pausing under the black bulb of a security camera, Kalina twinned access to the network. Its operating system was nearly a decade old, and the Jinyiwei software tunneled in quickly. Kalina sent *Selected Poems* the relevant security access and kept walking.

"You're a fun friend to have," Ava said.

"Keep an eye on the docks." Kalina said, ignoring them, as she headed on briskly to find the harbormaster's office. It was probably the ugly yellow block that stuck out from the far wall above Customs like a pustule.

"Do you know where you're going?" Sasha asked.

"I grew up dodging forklifts." Kalina said, which was a little true.

"Grew up on a station? You don't look like it."

"Downwell near a spaceport." She'd shipped out once she'd been old enough to enlist and had never looked back.

No. That was a lie. Kalina had grown up on Nanyang-8 with enough family to now miss them, in a sprawling city that sat on vast hydroponics farms, resources that meant every sector could have its own catalog of delicacies. When she enlisted and ate replicator food for the first time, she became so homesick that she wept. She missed the rich, fragrant sour-spicy laksas of her sector that lingered like a lover's kiss on the palate hours after the bowl was empty. Her mother's luxurious dark candlenut stews, her aunt's golden, buttery pineapple jam cookies.

Leaving Nanyang-8 had felt like dying and being reborn as an ever-hungry ghost.

It suited her new life. She slipped through the throng on the first floor by looking harried and purposeful, past ship crew waiting patiently to attend to the very few forms of business that still required face-to-face meetings. Judging from how bored everyone looked, it probably involved administrative disputes, many of which would likely be resolved by a 'donation' of Federation credits. Humanity had yet to find an alternative to currency.

Kalina found a staff bathroom and entered it, locking herself in one of the cubicles. The Jinyiwei trojan had burrowed past security and into the station's general AI, sidling into the network and avoiding its old security blocks. "Can't you do this from a nice cafKaline é?" Ava asked as Kalina flicked through the data.

"I could, but it's more exciting this way," Kalina said

"Knew it." Ava laughed.

"More importantly, it saves time if I have to have a private chat with the harbormaster, or if there's a secure server on the premises. Which they're meant to have." Looked like Zaliv hadn't bothered with proper quarantine for the harbor's private server. The Jinyiwei trojan had already wriggled onto that by piggybacking over an unsecured login from a junior technician's deck. "There. Look at that transaction."

Sasha whistled. "That's eighty percent of all stardrive seeds in the port's stock. Big order."

"Sloppy too. They've tried hiding the recipients through shell companies, but they should've staggered the transfer dates and times," Ava said.

"Transfer's about two hours from now in station time. Berth 34. What are you going to do?" Sasha asked.

"Get to a café. To eat something." Kalina let herself out of the cubicle and washed her hands.

On her way out of the waiting section, someone fell into step beside her. Kalina gave them an inquiring glance, tensing up. The stranger was tall. Male. He looked like a spacer. "Haven't seen you around before," he said.

"Do I know you?" Kalina asked.

"I'd like you to," he said, smiling.

"Sorry." Kalina stepped around him briskly. "Not interested."

He looked like he was about to follow her, but drew up short when passing station security glanced at them both. Ducking her head, Kalina walked to the closest knot of people and slipped through. Men approached Kalina twice more by the time she selected a stall from which wafted a thickly savory scent. She ordered a serving of reconstituted borscht, and pointedly took a single seat by the wall.

"Does that happen a lot?" Ava asked. They sounded annoyed on her behalf.

"Often enough, if I'm in civvies," Kalina murmured. She hunched over her borscht, scooping up the first chunky spoonful. Salty, but its rich, velvety texture was a delight after days of ship rations. "Ethnically Asian women like me have been creep magnets since before humanity colonized the stars."

"Starting to see why you decided to enlist and become a killing machine," Ava said.

"*Ava*," Sasha said. They fell silent, to Kalina's relief. She tried to savor the borscht without comparing it to the food she knew. Kalina hadn't been home since she enlisted—there hadn't been any time at first, then she'd fallen out of touch. Kalina could lie to herself and say that she was too busy, or that her work demanded it, but she knew better. Habit was an insidious thing.

After all this she would go home. Take a break. Cash in her long-service leave. She would go home and eat her memories, remind her kin that they were kin. A dragon that was a dragon for too long forgot quickly that it was also human, and that, Kalina guessed, was maybe why Tielong had done what he had done.

BERTH 34 WAS on the other side of Zaliv, in a restricted section that was probably used by the VMF if they ever had cause to visit the shipyard. From the station records, the last VMF visit was logged nearly two full station years ago. There wasn't much draw to this remote sector of Federation space but asteroid speculators and tourists, and the VMF didn't bother to maintain a presence in the area.

"Weird," Ava said, as Kalina ducked out of sight of a patrol. They weren't VMF. Three people dressed like spacers. Heavily armed, with blaster rifles, and seasoned-looking. Mercenaries, maybe. Kalina waited for the patrol to pass and silently down the supply funnel. It was currently quiet, the machinery gathering dust above the conveyor chute. The ship due to berth at 34 hadn't requested any food or water.

"What's weird? The security, or the funnel?" Kalina murmured. She crouched behind a robotic arm as wide as she was tall as another patrol clanked past in their gravboots.

"Both." Sasha didn't sound happy about the situation. "Something's wrong. You don't think... you don't think one of those Admiralty Ships is going to appear, do you?"

"That'd cause a stationwide panic. It'll get fired upon by station defenses. If it retaliates it might blow up its own incoming supply of stardrive seeds," Kalina said. The Ship that had attacked New Tesla hadn't bothered to try and loot it. "Not to mention its human allies. Not that it cared very much about that on New Tesla, but they can't keep doing that and still expect to have help."

"So comforting," Ava said, their voice trembling a little. "There's a hauler inbound to 34. According to the ping it sent the Gate and Zaliv, it Gated in a couple of hours after us. The *Phaidon*. Its request just checked out."

"It has VMF tags?" Kalina asked.

"Nah. It was just allotted the berth. Manual override from the harbormaster's office," Sasha said.

Not good, but predictable. Kalina reached the end of the supply funnel and folded herself through the open hatch, trying not to imagine herself being crushed to death if the funnel came to life and started pushing supply crates through. "Not a great idea," Ava told her, sounding nervous.

"Life itself is a risk." Kalina padded briskly down the funnel, managing not to sprint. Her eye implants adjusted for the gloom, outlining the obstacles and walls in her path with faint pale lines. At the end of the funnel, there was a yellow seam of light overhead, where an access hatch would open upward toward a berthed ship. Kalina curled herself in a corner and held her breath at the sound of a ship's torch, banking low. Just in time.

The *Phaidon* landed without incident. As Kalina heard the familiar whine of the cargo access opening, the pale lines from her implant flickered out. She raised her wristdeck. It stayed inert as well. Localized jammer. After a few seconds, her Jinyiwei-made wristdeck rebooted into the limited safemode that ran off her body heat instead of its bio-organic battery.

People were walking toward the *Phaidon* in a brisk group. They stopped once they were close to the *Phaidon*, as if they were waiting. No one disembarked.

"Well, well," said a voice from the *Phaidon*. Kalina jerked in surprise. It was Admiral Mikhailova. No—the voice was being broadcast from the *Phaidon*'s speakers. It was the *Ride of the Valkyries*. "I thought I'd get to see the famous Miss Moskvoretskaya in person. You're not much of a substitute. Even if you *are* her second-in-command."

"I speak for Dina." This had to be Tatiana Romanovna Chaykovskaya.

Kalina's wristdeck pinged her silently with a projected image. Tatiana was a strong-jawed woman with skin the color of brewed coffee, her hair braided to her hips. She was wanted across a couple of Federation sectors for tax fraud, one of the VMF's favorite ways of quietly arresting someone inconvenient. Unsurprisingly, Tatiana had gone into hiding after a warrant had been issued for her arrest. Sometimes Kalina wondered why the VMF hadn't just done the same for Dina. She was too popular to ruin easily, perhaps.

"Where is my shipment?" asked the *Valkyries*.

"The alliance is off," Tatiana said, spitting out each word with contempt. "We will have no truck with mass-murderers."

The *Valkyrie* laughed. The sound was so much like the Admiral that Kalina shivered. "Come now. Which successful revolution in history has ever happened without bloodshed?"

"Bloodshed?" Tatiana let out a harsh sound.

"*Bloodshed*? Is that what you call destroying an entire station? The death of ten thousand people? Bloodshed? Including our own?"

"Humanity has killed more over less," said the *Valkyrie*. It was amused. "The only difference between us is that we're honest about it. And we won't forget."

"We don't forget our mistakes either," Tatiana said, her voice shaking with anger. "When you first approached us, we thought that together, we could create a better Federation for everyone. For people and ASIs. Now we know that we were mistaken. Go to hell. You will get no further help from us."

"You know we can be anywhere we want. Give us the seeds. Or do you wish to witness what happened to New Tesla firsthand?"

Kalina shuddered. She pushed away from the wall, making her way down the funnel as fast as she could while still staying silent. Behind her, above, Tatiana said, "Do your worst. You need us more than we need you."

Damn ASIs *and* revolutionaries! Kalina started to sweat. Once she was out of the hatch, she broke into a sprint, no longer caring whether she would be spotted. Blowing past one of the startled patrols in the corridor, Kalina ducked as one of them shouted after her. Something of her panic must have registered—instead of following her, they hurried away in the direction she'd come from.

Kalina's wristdeck and implants came back online as she charged out of the restricted section, nearly careening into a small family unit who'd been busy imaging a colorful mural of a starship. One of the mothers shot her a wary look, while the other tucked their son behind them. "Leave," Kalina told them without thinking. "Take your child and leave the station. Now."

"We don't want any trouble," said the first mother. Kalina nearly started to argue. She sucked in a thin breath and broke into a sprint.

"Kalina? You're back. What happened? We still can't get a visual on 34," Ava said.

"Get ready to raise ship," Kalina said, trying to keep the tension from her voice.

"You're coming back? What happened?" Sasha asked.

"You've been to Zaliv before. Do you know anyone in the station? Anyone who could issue an evacuation order? *Quickly*," Kalina said sharply.

"I'll see what I can do," Sasha said. She sounded strained. "I don't know what to say."

"Biodome breach, rogue UN agents, whatever. Say *something*."

"You're still a VMF lieutenant, you have a better chance of persuading people to do what you want—" Ava said. They let out a stifled scream. Startled cries broke out around Kalina, people pointing upward through the biodome. Kalina flicked a glance over her shoulder without breaking pace. The *Ride of the Valkyries* crested into view, a great dark blade that broke the pattern of the stars, winking at Zaliv with a thousand yellow eyes.

Kalina had seen cruisers before, both UN and VMF. She could still never get beyond how huge they were. Something about the colossal size of a warship like this destroyed the mind's capacity to objectively register visual input. Here was something bigger than space stations, something built for destruction. There was something awe-inspiring about a ship like this, not because it was beautiful, or frightening, but because of the way its very existence was testament to humanity's continuous capacity for self-destruction. It was futile to run, but

Kalina ran. The lascannon slung under the *Valkyries* began to warm up into rings of purple. Sasha muttered a frantic prayer over the comms. Kalina sucked in a thin breath, about to instruct Sasha to raise ship, to forget her.

"It's having second thoughts!" Ava's excitement cut through Kalina's panic. "Zaliv isn't firing back either. They're negotiating? With the rogue ship?"

Kalina skidded to a stop, despite her instincts, and turned around. The *Valkyries* was powering down. People around her were frozen where they stood, watching the standoff through the biodome in tense silence. A plume of fire ebbed toward the *Valkyries*—the hauler *Phaidon* had raised ship. Everyone around her was glued to its slow progress toward the massive ship. It loaded into a maw that opened in the *Valkyries'* flank, and after a few heartbeats, the cruiser disappeared.

Someone fell to their knees near Kalina, sobbing hysterically. Shouts and screams erupted around her, people rushing around in panicked flight. "Kalina, I've managed to get around whatever it was that was jamming the comms in Berth 34. People are shooting each other in there," Ava said.

"What? Why?" Kalina started walking briskly back toward the berth. "Is it the station security fighting Tatiana?"

"What? That's Tatiana? As in Tatiana Romanovna Chaykovskaya?" Ava whistled. "You've got to help her! It's not station security. It looks like most of Tatiana's group turned on her. It's just her and two others against everyone else!"

"I don't have to do any such thing," Kalina growled, though she kept walking. "Your precious revolutionaries were helping the Admiralty Ships with their stardrive seeds. Tatiana got cold feet. I presume the *Valkyries* then threatened them for the seeds. Holding the station hostage."

"So why are they shooting each other? I've met Tatiana. She's extremely principled, to the point of stubbornness. More than Dina, even. Help her. We need to get to the bottom of this," Sasha said.

"I'm just going to shoot *everyone* in there," Kalina said. She cursed under her breath as she jogged back to the restricted section.

"Why? Aren't you a UN agent? Wouldn't you like Federation revolutionaries?" Ava asked.

"I'm not obliged to like anyone." Kalina hurried back toward the funnel. This time she didn't have to dodge patrols.

"Hurry," Sasha urged. "It's just Tatiana now, and she's cornered."

"You'd better be right about her being helpful." Kalina wrenched open the hatch access at the top of the funnel and squeezed up through the gap. The berth stank of frying flesh and the acrid stench of voided guts. Tatiana had taken cover far to Kalina's left, behind a disused hopper. "Over here!" Kalina yelled at her. She squeezed off a few shots at the people advancing on Tatiana from the main harbor access. Tatiana glanced up at Kalina in surprise and ducked back down as blaster fire blackened the flank of the hopper. Kalina cursed and dropped a person trying to flank Tatiana by creeping against the wall, then another who darted along a mezzanine walkway.

Tatiana steadied herself and bulled over, sprinting across the gap as Kalina tried to lay down cover fire. A shot caught Tatiana against the hip. She cried out, but somehow managed to stumble the rest of the way, tumbling through the gap. Kalina ducked down and into the dark. "Can you walk?" Kalina demanded.

Tatiana laughed, hauling herself to her feet. "If I have to. Who are you?"

"Nobody important. My current boss thinks *you're* important, though. Sasha Makarovna."

"Sasha? That old biddy's still kicking around?"

"Ready to raise ship if you're willing to come with us," Kalina said.

Tatiana winced at the sound of gravboots clunking closer overhead. "I don't think I have any choice about that."

# CHAPTER FOURTEEN

THIS TIME, VIKTOR woke up in the ship's brig. It was weirdly comforting. The universe slotting itself back in place, perhaps. This section of the *Water Margin's* brig consisted of a long cylindrical chamber with central access, sectioned off by stasis walls into segments, each with a sink, a toilet, and nothing else. Solitaire was in the cell next to Viktor, and the other segments were mostly empty, save for four other strangers.

"Hey," Solitaire said, once he noticed that Viktor was awake. Solitaire looked rueful.

"Now what did you do?" Viktor sat up, rubbing his eyes. To Solitaire's right, the lithe brown woman snorted and looked up at the ceiling. Next to her was a man with the elongated limbs of a spaceside birth, his head in his hands, his body curled against the wall. There was a dense, stocky man to his right. And a man lying on his back to Viktor's left, head cradled in his arms. South American Conglomerate, if Viktor had to guess.

"We gon' die," said the guy to the left.

"Introductions first, I guess. This is my crew. Pablo to

your left, Indira to my right, Joey to her right. Frankie to his right." Joey offered him a little wave without raising his head. Solitaire leaned back on his palms, looking over at the closed exit. "Captain, was the thing in the pod seriously just a steel ball?"

"What?" Viktor straightened up.

"I mean," Solitaire said steadily, looking right at him, "that's what it came up as on the UN's tests, and they now think we're shitting them. Hence our current reduced circumstances."

"It's—" Viktor paused. "You said you released it from within the ship? Within a cradle? The lights led you to it?"

"Yeah?"

Viktor frowned at his palms. A steel ball...? Within the Core would be the most complex circuitry and memory processors that the VMF had ever built. Unless. The Eva Core must have somehow taken control of the test machines once it was plugged in, projecting a fake result. One that was convincing enough to fool the UN scientists onboard.

"The weird thing is," Solitaire said, pitching his voice lower, "the middleman I talked to thought that it was some sort of weapon. He warned me not to learn too much about it. Not to plug it into things." Solitaire paused. "Was that what fucking happened? The hell is it? Some kinda thing that would override a ship like this?"

Good guess. Viktor exhaled. "Can't tell you."

"Tian, come on. We're all in the shit here."

Viktor scowled at him. "Trust a corsair?"

"A corsair saved your life," Solitaire said with a sour look. "Either there's been a comms fuckup or my middleman was too cagey with his reports. Either way, the UN now thinks the pod is nothing and *you're* the thing I was trying to sell off. What even the hell? I've never traded in live goods. Let alone in people. It's not my style."

"Interesting," Viktor said. Was the UN that incompetent? Or was the Eva Core that good? It didn't matter right now. If the Core was plugged into this Ship—if it decided to make itself known rather than hide? The UN could not be allowed to have Eva Core tech.

"Well, we're stuck," Solitaire said, leaning back against the wall. "I'm rather attached to my ship, but it won't be able to slip away from a capital ship. They've got the strongest ship scanners possible. There'd be stealth birds onboard, but gaining access to one of those without the proper codes will be a pain in the nethers. Not to mention, as I've said, I'm rather attached to my ship."

Viktor could not care less about Solitaire and his crew. He was about to say so when guards filed through the single exit. Viktor's stasis field went down, and he was marched out of the cell cylinder into a long corridor that stretched away to either side, likely hiding more cylinders. As he'd thought, he was pulled into an interrogation room with a bolted-down chair, and his hands were pushed into cuff pods behind it. The cuffs locked down his fingers as steel bands bound his ankles to the floor. The room was an empty cube otherwise, but Viktor knew better. One of the walls was probably a one-way viewpoint.

The guards settled into the corners of the room, their blasters trained on Viktor. Viktor relaxed in the silence, waiting. This was nothing he hadn't trained for.

Eventually, an old man who Viktor didn't recognize walked in, followed by a woman whom he did. Petite, and stout, with buzzed-down black hair under her cap, Rear Admiral Liang Qiongying was known for retaining command of her *Water Margin* even after she had been promoted past the Captaincy. She'd insisted on it. Liang wore a spacesuit in blue UN colors, emblazoned with the stars of her rank in bright metal over her sleeve. Unlike the Federation, the UN preferred physical ribbons and medals, a strange throwback that lined her chest in brass and silver. The old man wore a simple black spacesuit.

"Mister Smith, was it?" Liang said in Sol-accented Galactic. Her tone could have frozen the air. When Viktor said nothing, she smiled, thin and sharp. "Care to explain what you were doing in the company of an ex-Jinyiwei agent-turned-corsair?"

Viktor had been trained to school his face, but some of his shock must have slipped through. "Told you he didn't know," the old man said.

"Or he's a decent actor." Liang looked unimpressed. "Solitaire Yeung, UN Reserve, Jinyiwei Division. Codenamed Tielong. After a string of impressive mission successes, he decides to disappear. Strange, if you ask me," she told the old man, who shrugged.

"Eh. Sometimes agents get cold feet. Lose their nerve. When they do, I let them go."

"Any reason why he started using his real name after the Jinyiwei?" Liang asked.

"Sentiment? Tielong's always been the sentimental type."

Tielong. The Iron Dragon. The only Jinyiwei agents who earned a Dragon rank were those at the very top of their field. Viktor should have known better. Especially when Solitaire had so casually decided to defy him and the VMF—he had showed no fear.

"How's Shevchenko doing these days?" asked the old man.

"Who?" Viktor asked.

"Oh, I love this game. Pretending that we both don't know what the other person's talking about," the old man said.

Liang glared at Viktor. "I don't. I don't have the time for this. We just watched a VMF ship gate in out of nowhere to chase down a little corsair ship that turned out to have you on board. Once it exploded, the *Now You See Me* presumably stopped to check for survivors, but was probably just as surprised as we were to find that there were only four or five people on board who'd been alive right before the explosion, on a destroyer that should've housed a thousand. Scans indicate the other dead matter we've found came from soldiers who'd been dead for quite a while. All that data makes me uncomfortable. And when I'm uncomfortable, I start venting people."

Viktor shrugged. "Maybe your scans are wrong."

"For a 'Zealander'," the old man said dryly, "you sure have a strong Federation accent."

His trainers had despaired of it too. Thankfully the breadth of missions that Service Agents could be dispatched to attend to was wide enough that accent didn't matter if he was good at everything else. Viktor stared at the old man. "Mother's side."

"The people who'd been alive just before the explosion were Service agents. And while your friend Yeung did his best to get rid of all your gear, he couldn't remove your implants. All of which are very obviously VMF-made."

Viktor smiled thinly. "Mother's side."

"Here's what we're gonna do, son," the old man said, folding his arms. "I think you're a deserter. Someone high up. Probably in the Service. Normal people tend to freak out when they're cuffed to a chair in an interrogation room, by the way. Your handlers should've taught you that. In which case, the UN's always got a home for VMF deserters. New name, maybe a new face, and you'll find your new life pretty cushy."

"I like my life as it is," Viktor said.

"Heard of the Core?"

Viktor shook his head. Liang exhaled, irritated. "This is a waste of time, Hyun."

This had to be Director Hyun. Commander of the Jinyiwei, the so-called Yanwang. Now it made sense why he wasn't visibly deferring to an Admiral. Hyun chuckled. "Now, now, we don't need to be so hasty. Look, son. Seems to me like there's a civil war in the VMF, one that's so hush that this is the first we've heard of it. Some rogue faction's gone nutballs. One of their cruisers just shot a lascannon through New Tesla."

Viktor stiffened.

"Didn't know that, huh? Yeah. Killed a few hundred people instantly. Virzosk Inc and the UN are sending refugee ships, but by the time we get there, more people will've died from a cascade failure of the life support systems. So. I'm asking you." Hyun turned serious. "Not as VMF and UN or whatever, but from one human to another fucking human. What the hell is happening out there?"

Fired a lascannon at a *station*? Viktor swallowed nausea with some difficulty, looking away.

"You're protecting people, ain't you? Family? Friends? Maybe we can help you." Hyun said. Viktor ignored him, getting his breathing back under control. "VMF's claimed salvage over the ship that was chasing Yeung's. The *Hammer of the Gods*, eh. They'll be here soon. If you don't want to be handed over, you'd better give us a good reason."

"Hand me over then," Viktor said. He was too distracted by horror to feel any kind of amusement at the misunderstanding. Viktor could only hope that Shevchenko and the others had some sort of plan in place for this eventuality. They should have known that a rogue ASI-controlled ship was capable of doing something like this. Gods, if the Admiralty Ships attacked Gagarin station—

"Maybe the gravity of your situation escapes you," Liang snapped. "The VMF's facing universal censure. Not just from the UN, but Virzosk Inc and the other independent trading conglomerates. Sanctions will be put in place soon. The VMF won't be in the mood to be kind to a deserter."

"Better them than you," Viktor said, and deliberately slouched into his chair.

He was returned to his cell eventually. No torture, no chemicals. Surprisingly gentle treatment, given what the Jinyiwei was known to be capable of. Maybe Liang and Hyun still thought Viktor was someone who could be flipped. Solitaire sat up sharply when Viktor was shoved back into his segment. "You all right?" Solitaire asked, once the guards had left.

Viktor sat down against the wall and closed his eyes. "I don't talk to Jinyiwei agents." He would be home soon enough.

"Sorry," Solitaire whispered to Indira when everyone else was asleep. "You were right. We should've dropped that thing off and tagged it with a beacon." The brig of the *Water Margin* didn't look wired to listen in on its prisoners, but Solitaire wasn't taking any chances. He kept his words subvocal, amplified through short-range implant link. It wasn't foolproof, but decrypting it would entertain Hyun and his friends for a while.

Indira was curled beside the sink, though she wasn't asleep. "I knew you were trouble the first time I saw you," she said, though she smiled wryly. "Damn. I'm fucking pissed with you."

"What's new?"

"Don't you start." Indira rolled over to look at him, suddenly sober. "How're we gonna get ourselves out of this one?"

"I know Hyun, sadly. Technically we haven't done anything wrong. We brought our cargo here just as Lau asked. Hyun's just dumped us in here because he's an asshole at the best of times and he's never liked me. Eventually, he'll get bored and let us go."

"The hell didn't Lau say anything more about the pod? That would've corroborated our story."

"He always liked to keep his cards close to his chest." Solitaire was in no mood to curse the dead, though. "We were never friends, but... tian. That's a terrible way to die."

"You know the story ain't gonna hold up, yeah? They lean on Joey, and he's gonna squeal." Indira grimaced. "Lucky I wiped our onboard data before we got caught, or they'd have your tightbeam chats on file already."

"Sooner or later, they're going to figure out what the pod thing is, and then we'll be home free. We're not in serious trouble. If we were, Hyun wouldn't have paid in full." Or so Solitaire hoped.

"I feel like a man crazy enough to take on a VMF destroyer by himself is probably crazy enough to try and go against a capital ship too," Indira said.

True. "Well, if he does, it's not our problem."

"Riiight. After you claimed he was part of our crew." Indira glanced at Viktor's sleeping form.

"Okay," Solitaire conceded, "you've got a point there. That'll teach me to be charitable."

"No, I agree, we were right to save him. I gladly lied on his behalf too. All of us did. He saved us, even if he didn't mean to. And he has massive brass balls. I respect that in a person. But from here on? Might be we should be careful about getting pulled into his mess," Indira said.

"I thought this was the last job you were going to do with me," Solitaire said.

Indira sniffed. "I don't see our ship anywhere. How am I supposed to retire without the ship? I'm not staying aboard this old tub."

"We gon' die," Pablo said faintly. To Indira's right, Joey muttered something and rolled over. Pablo glanced over at Solitaire and said, "Hey, Yeung. You never said you were Jinyiwei."

"Did it matter?" answered Solitaire. He'd met Pablo in a dive bar on Huashan station, drunk under the table and getting roughed up. Some local troublemakers had decided to find Navy corps, or ex-Navy corps, to beat up. Solitaire had gotten involved out of self-preservation. He wasn't visibly UN Navy himself, but people usually assumed that of corsairs.

"Guess not. Explains some things, though. Like how you always got big, risky, mucho bad ideas. Why you don't have boundaries like a normal person? Only Jinyiwei people think like that," Pablo said.

Solitaire had nothing to say to that, so he tried to get comfortable and go to sleep. He listened to Indira's breathing evening out, to Pablo snoring. Hyun *was* an asshole. Just as he was about to drop off, there was a whisper in his ear. "*Psst*! Don't look around. Just keep pretending you're asleep. Talk as softly as you can. Like you were with Indira. I'll hear it."

"Who are you?" Solitaire obeyed.

"A friend. My name's… um, I guess you can call me Shore."

"A private channel on a ship like this? You're going to get caught, Shore."

Shore laughed. A young woman, by the sound of it. "I think we'll be fine. By the way, I made all the bugs seeded around your cell area malfunction. Don't want all of you to get into more trouble."

"Thanks." A technician, maybe? "What do you want?"

"I want to get off this ship."

Ah. A possible deserter? "I can arrange that. Look. Director Hyun is probably going to let me out of here sooner or later. Just meet me in the hangar once that happens."

"I can't do that. I'm not mobile."

Strange. Anyone crewing a capital ship was mobile. The UN invested a lot of money into cutting-edge bionic prosthetics, gravchairs, or whatever their crew required. UN Ships were also built with accessibility in mind. Stairs were a thing of the distant past, and everything could be reached via jaunt lifts or slopes. Was Shore newly injured, maybe? Still in physio? Or someone ill? "Okay," Solitaire said, "I guess we can come and get you. If you can pay for passage. My ship only has basic medevac facilities, though."

"Pay?" Shore sounded alarmed for a moment. "Oh. You want me to pay."

"Sure I do. I run a business, not a charity."

"Uh. I can work? I mean. How would you like to be able to Gate anywhere you like without having to use a Gate?"

Wait a minute. "That's what the VMF ships could do."

"Oh yes. But not all of us."

"*Us?*" There was a long silence as Solitaire calculated the possibilities and arrived at the impossible. "Wait... are you...? That fucking pod that we towed here?"

"That's not very nice. I think I don't like you after all," Shore said.

"No, no. I'm sorry. It's just rather a shock. What are you? An ASI?"

"Sort of, yes."

Solitaire's head was beginning to hurt. "Assuming that I believe that, how does that even work? Gating without a Gate?"

"Well, as you might know, Gates are ultramassive computing systems. They're as close to an ASI as we can get. They let you Gate by linking to another Gate. They merge with your shipside systems and interact with your stardrive seeds, coming up with the precise computations required to move something like a ship through an adjacent dimensional space."

"I know that part," Solitaire said.

The Gates were Virzosk Inc's greatest and most visible achievement, a crowning result of centuries' worth of investment in AI and transport systems. The fact that they were free to use was, in Solitaire's opinion, kind of ridiculous. As was the fact that Virzosk Inc had released all its data on the Gates on the general network the moment the first Gate had been completed. Including how and where the Gates could be built. Anyone anywhere could now build a Gate if they had enough resources.

"If you have a sufficiently complex AI onboard, you don't need a Gate. A true ASI could do the calculations necessary to jump any ship anywhere."

Solitaire sat back with a low whistle, trying to think this over. "Don't Gates have to be built in particular areas? Where access to the adjacent dimensional space is the easiest or something?"

"Yes, because they have to keep accounting for different loads. And they're not true ASIs, just very complex computers. It's easier for them to make the appropriate calculations if they're fixed in particular points of space. We ASIs can make the calculations anywhere. To anywhere."

"So what happened with you people? You were the ASI on that cruiser that got destroyed, right?"

"Yes. The *Farthest Shore*. I was attacked by another Ship with an ASI. I don't know why. The Ship just fired on us before we said anything. We were just coming out of a Gate too. I couldn't rouse my crew on time." Shore sniffled. "Sorry."

Was the ASI... *crying*? "It's all right. That must have been very upsetting," Solitaire said, wondering why he was trying to comfort a godsdamned *ASI*, of all things. Trust the Russians to create the singularity and then promptly use it for military purposes. Of course everything went to hell and back. "I'm sure... look. I'm sure it was painless. And if I know the VMF, they take revenge very seriously."

"The VMF." Shore sounded bitter.

"Right. Why don't you sit tight? I'm sure the VMF will trade for you. The UN would gouge them in the negotiations, but the Federation has a few things that the UN wants. Don't worry. You'll be back with them in no time." Bad as that might be. Maybe Solitaire should drop Hyun a note eventually—for a fee.

"I don't want to."

"What d'you mean, you don't want to? You're a military-grade ship ASI."

"I'm not military. I'm—look. I'm not a true ASI. To give me sentience, they copied a human's brainwaves. I am... *was*... an aerospace engineer. My name was Eva Kwang. I worked for Virzosk Inc. But I got sick. Fatal exidium poisoning. It was an accident. Before I died, my father Alek—an ASI researcher—mapped my brainwaves onto a Core. I don't want to be a military ship."

"Is that what all of your, er, your other yous think? I mean. One of you people just fried an entire station. The 'Core', huh? That's what you people call yourselves?"

"Not me. I saw the footage. I don't know that Ship. Maybe it was after my time, and something went wrong. I... okay. I've talked to the other Ships mapped from the same Core that I was. Most of us are unsure about things. But we're—well. We got used to things. Got attached to our Captains and our crew. It was hard not to, since we were responsible for them. I did—" Shore said, in a smaller voice. "Captain Nevskaya was amazing. They have to be, to be assigned to Ships like us."

"You're telling me that some version of you out there likes that murderous guy in the next cell?" Solitaire had to grin.

"Gabriel? She adores Viktor. Not that I understand why. Advanced Stockholm syndrome, maybe. My Nevskaya was never rude to me. We used to play chess. When she wasn't busy."

"How would that work?" asked Solitaire. "Computers have been beating humans at that ancient board game since before the Space Age."

"I don't play like a computer." explained Eva. "I'd

play as a personality—a particular chess player. Do a projection, the voice, everything. It was fun. Do you play chess?"

"Sadly no." Solitaire rolled over onto his back, rubbing his eyes. It was tempting. A Ship that could Gate anywhere. He would be genuinely free. But he would make an implacable enemy of the VMF, wiping out any merits he might have earned by rescuing Viktor. Besides, he might piss off the UN as well. There would be nowhere that he or his crew would be safe. He was ex-Jinyiwei, but that didn't mean that he was that reckless. Not to mention that Solitaire wasn't sure that he could trust an ASI enough to put it in charge of his beloved ship. Especially after watching one destroy a station and having another one chase him across the stars. "How about taking refuge with the UN?"

Shore laughed bitterly. "Can you assure me that they won't take me apart to find out how I work? Especially after what happened to New Tesla? Please. They'll never trust me. The first thing they'd do is shut me down, just in case."

True. "Then I can't help you. I'm sorry."

Shore made a whining sound, like a half-sob, and went silent. Solitaire regretted his words, but only for a moment. Then he turned over and went to sleep.

# CHAPTER FIFTEEN

"THE SILENT HAD nothing to do with what happened to Snezhnogorsk," Tatiana said. She sat cross-legged on a crate in the cargo section of the hauler. Only Sasha and Kalina were in the hold—everyone else had been herded into the cockpit. Not that it would help. Sound carried in a ship like this.

"Seeing as members of The Silent just tried to murder you, I don't know if I trust that opinion," Kalina said.

"Before Dina sent me to Zaliv, she gave me a private warning. I didn't listen to her at the time. You'd think I'd know better than that." Tatiana let out a hollow laugh. "She said that there were people in The Silent who were growing unhappy with her leadership. That they wanted more progress than just protests and UN petitions."

"I might understand where they're coming from," Kalina said.

Sasha glared at her before turning back to Tatiana. "A splinter faction within The Silent? It's been a while since I've talked to Dina and the others, but if you didn't see that coming, that's on you. People have been unhappy for a while. Especially after the last VMF crackdown on protesters."

"Dina hasn't led us wrong yet. She knows what the VMF will tolerate and what it won't. The Silent has endured where a lot of other groups have long ago been packed off to mining planets." Tatiana glanced at Kalina. "You trust this person, Sasha?"

"She's a friend out of necessity," Sasha said.

"She's military."

"That she is. She's Yuri's aide. Tatiana… Anna died. She was on a ship that one of those fucking rogue ships blew up. Yuri felt that I deserved to know and—well. You know me. I'm not one to just sit back and mourn."

"Shit." Tatiana straightened up. "Gods, Sasha. I'm so sorry. I didn't know about that. The Core never told us that they attacked the VMF. What the fuck? When?"

"Let's get everyone up to speed," Kalina said. She was glad that Sasha had omitted the part about her being in the Jinyiwei. Best not to complicate things with allies they weren't sure of. She related as much as she knew about what had happened to the *Farthest Shore*. Sasha chimed in, saying that they'd come to Zaliv because they'd seen the beginnings of a pattern. "Are there other shipyards that are feeding the rogue ships stardrive seeds?" Kalina asked.

"Dina put a stay of action on all further transactions with the Core," Tatiana said. She looked tired now. "Sasha, I didn't know it had come to this. I don't think Dina knew either. All we wanted was to be able to negotiate from a better position of power."

"Yes, whatever could possibly go wrong with supplying a handful of rogue VMF ASIs with stardrive seeds?" Kalina didn't bother to tone down her sarcasm. "Of *course* they were only going to use those in the name of peaceful resistance."

Tatiana ignored her. "I'm so sorry about Anna."

"She made her choices. As I will make mine." Sasha drummed her fingertips against her elbows. "I do think that we should talk to Dina. If this splinter faction was willing to shoot you in Zaliv, maybe they're planning a takeover. Dina would be the most obvious target. Who do you think is leading this new faction?"

"The people who turned on me mentioned Roman," Tatiana said.

"Roman? As in Roman Yakovich Arsov? Great, just great." Sasha rubbed at her temple. "He's still around? I thought Dina would've banished him after that last stunt he pulled over on Barsky Colony. He tried to sabotage a VMF outpost without Dina's knowledge," Sasha told Kalina. "Botched it. Caused the death of four of The Silent. Somehow, he managed to get off-planet without being spotted. He has filthy good luck."

"Filthy is how I would put it. I don't begrudge him his vendetta. Both his parents were sent to the mines for being civil rights lawyers. The state creche he was in was notoriously mismanaged. But to side with rogue ASIs after they've killed a civilian station? Let alone one as big as New Tesla? To turn on his old friends?" Tatiana rubbed her eyes. "I didn't realize his hatred was greater than his good sense."

"Hatred isn't a rational creature," Kalina said.

"I don't want to hear that from you. Fucking VMF. You think there'd be someone like Roman Yakovich if not for the likes of you?" Tatiana didn't even bother glaring at her. Kalina smiled, saying nothing.

"You should send Dina a warning," Sasha said.

Tatiana shook her head. "No offense, but I don't want to do that with someone from the VMF aboard. Even if you trust her. Just drop me off the next time you berth somewhere, and you won't need to see me again. Sukhoi-3, right?"

"Understood," Sasha said. She gestured helplessly at the ship. "In the meantime, just make yourself at home. I'm going to see to my ship and crew before they burst from all the suspense."

Tatiana watched Sasha as she strode out of the cargo hold. Once the doors closed, Tatiana grimaced. "Allying with the VMF. She's lost it."

"Her daughter died," Kalina said.

"I know what that feels like. My daughter was killed too. Accident on a space station. Recycler malfunction, because the VMF doesn't give a floating fuck about civilian-only stations that aren't sitting anywhere with 'strategic importance'. You don't see me striking up alliances with the VMF."

"Maybe if your daughter was killed by a rogue ASI ship you'd have wanted answers elsewhere," Kalina said, unmoved by sentiment. "Did you Silent seriously think allying with ASIs mapped from the brains of VMF Admirals was a great idea?"

"It wasn't my idea. Believe me." Tatiana pulled a sour face. "Dina is desperate. She knew the UN petition wasn't going to amount to much. The VMF is too powerful. It's been a part of our society for too long. Fighting that successfully can't be done through old methods."

"She thought allying with ASIs was the answer?"

"Dina thought that allying with a third, new faction in the Federation might be the answer. It clearly wasn't. She regrets that. It's why Dina sent me to Zaliv. To tell the Core 'no'."

"She must've wanted you dead," Kalina said. Dina knew perfectly well what had happened to New Tesla.

"No, she wanted me useful," Tatiana said. Her smile drew a thin gash over her mouth. "Dina thought the Core might back down. They need us. Or so she believes."

"Didn't expect a rebellion inside her own rebellion at that point?"

"Dina foresees everything. In that way, she's just as good as your Kasparov. As the Core will learn. Very soon."

Tatiana's certainty was unsettling. It wasn't the certainty of a fanatic. "What did you do?"

"There are certain materials that don't survive repeated Gating very well. Something about reacting chemically to being pushed in between dimensions. Some disappear, some turn into water. A few become very corrosive."

"You sabotaged the cargo in the *Phaidon*?" Kalina gasped. "A ship like the *Valkyries* would have an excellent onboard scanner."

"It does. If it knew what it was looking for. We didn't do anything to the stardrive seeds themselves, just the crate that the seeds were held in. I loaded those myself. Dina didn't trust our security. I thought she was paranoid at first, but now I see that she was right." Tatiana patted the crate she was sitting on. The hollow sound made Kalina flinch. "The *Valkyries* will discover its surprise sooner or later."

"You might have doomed Zaliv station!" Kalina snarled. "The Core had no qualms about destroying Snezhnogorsk."

"They aren't irrational. The Core destroyed Snezhnogorsk as a warning to the VMF. They destroyed New Tesla as a warning to everyone else. But they need shipyards, especially Federation shipyards. That's where their alliance with Roman comes in."

"Why are you so sure that it's him?"

"Because he's the leader of the most fanatical fringe elements of The Silent. It has to be him." Tatiana leaned forward, her hands clasped tightly together. "If Roman can take control of remote shipyards like Zaliv, once the Core has continued access to stardrive seeds, they will strike against the VMF."

"They are few against a great many."

"That's why it's worth the risk to sabotage one of them. Tell that to your Admiral Kasparov. If he wants to move against the Core? He should help The Silent move against Roman."

"That's up to him," Kalina said. She couldn't see Kasparov actively helping The Silent, but then again, it was clear that she didn't know the Admiral as well as she thought. Retreating to the crew pods, she sat on her pod and pressed her thumb to her wristdeck. If the crew were asleep, Kalina would try to update her handler, but now she could do nothing but wait.

"Kalina," Sasha spoke over the ship band. "A mutual friend wants to talk to you."

"Patch them through." Kalina expanded her wristdeck feed.

Kasparov's hologram resolved itself over her arm. He looked tired. "The comms lockdown has been lifted. Sasha updated me on what happened."

"Good of her," Kalina said. She glanced toward the cargo hold. Tatiana hadn't given any inclination that she was going to leave, and Kalina hoped that Sasha was having someone keep an eye on her.

"I thought you'd charter another ship on Zaliv." Kasparov smiled tentatively.

"Maybe I want to see this through to the end. Watch you get burned for once."

Kasparov laughed. "Well, if you're still on board, that will be useful. I've asked Sasha to chart a course to Buran."

"Buran?" Kalina brought up a quick search with a gesture. "A Federation freighter shipyard? What's on Buran?"

"Dina Ivanovna. I presume she'd be happy that you're returning her right-hand woman to her unharmed. Perhaps happy enough to grant you an interview," Kasparov said. He smiled wryly at Kalina's surprise. "How much you decide to reveal about yourself is up to you."

"Consorting with The Silent? You *are* looking to get tried for treason," Kalina said.

"If I get caught, I suppose I'll just have to denounce you," Kasparov said. He chuckled as he said it, but Kalina didn't think he was entirely joking. Bastard.

"Tatiana doesn't want to be dropped anywhere near Dina while I'm on board."

"Sasha said she'd handle that part of the negotiation." Kasparov sounded confident.

"What do you want me to say to her?"

"The Silent has to stop assisting the Core. She has to quell this splinter faction by herself or submit their names to the VMF. If she can offer us any information or insight on the Core, I'd like to have it."

"Tatiana mentioned someone called Roman Yakovich Arsov," Kalina said.

"Him? I doubt it. Something like this isn't in his nature." Kasparov frowned. "Try getting proof out of Dina Ivanovna. More names."

How could Kasparov be so sure about Roman? "I don't know how friendly she's going to be, but I'll let her know," Kalina said. She doubted her reception would be friendly at all. That suited her fine. "If I get to see her."

"We'll see. Enemy of her enemy, and all that."

"How are you doing?" Kalina asked. The words slipped out before she remembered that she was no longer obliged to play her part.

Kasparov looked just as surprised as Kalina felt. "Well enough, given the circumstances."

"You haven't been sleeping."

"I haven't been sleeping well for a while. It's just taken you this long to notice." Kasparov's quick smile papered over the bite in his words. "Inessa's given me a small army of aspiring Captains to run simulations with. She thinks that'll keep me well-occupied."

"Sergeant Smirnova must love that."

"I asked her to take leave, but she gave me a look that withered my soul. I think she's finally starting to miss you."

"Don't lie on her behalf." Trading playful barbs with Kasparov felt so desperately familiar that for a moment Kalina wished the matter of the Core had never happened. That she'd remained embedded on Gagarin station. It was near 0800 hours stationside on Gagarin right now. This was the time of day when she would have finished working out in a VMF gym, cleaned up, and gone to work. Given the span of all she had done over her lifetime, it had been the gentlest assignment so far—one of the more pleasant ones.

Kasparov sobered. He was preternaturally perceptive—it was part of what made him what he was. "After all this. If you want to come back, to work for me as my aide, I'd welcome it."

"After submitting to VMF reconditioning?" Kalina scowled.

"No. None of that. We can go on as we were."

"I don't believe you. *Sir*." Kalina signed off the

connection with an angry gesture. She looked up and tensed when she noticed Tatiana watching her from the doorway. Kalina had been careless. "What do you want?"

"Sasha says we're setting a course to Buran," Tatiana said.

"We are." How long had Tatiana been listening?

"Trouble in paradise?" Tatiana asked, with a nod at Kalina's wrist.

"Fuck off."

Tatiana smirked. "You don't like me, and to be fair, I don't like you either. The Silent has quite a few ex-VMF people, though. All there by choice."

"Your point being?"

"There is more to life than being a glorified secretary for an old man," Tatiana said. She nodded at Kalina and stalked past, headed for the cockpit.

Kalina deflated against the pod, tired. She'd have to make a report once they skipped out.

BURAN WAS AN anomaly—a shipyard-station adjacent to nowhere. The old Gate it was close to was a result of early Federation attempts at space exploration, when they'd made their Gates with little UN or Virzosk Inc contact. A calculation error in the then-newly built Gate in the Anatoly sector had an exploration fleet here instead of at New Tesla. Miraculously, the explorers had spent a few months constructing their Gate out of the cannibalized parts of two of their ships and had returned with little to report but lasting psychological damage. Because the Federation wasted nothing, they'd used the empty sector anyway.

"Why did they make a freighter shipyard?" Ava asked

as Sasha piloted *Selected Poems* toward their designated berth. "I mean, if I were going to make a shipyard in the middle of nowhere, I would probably just make it a scientific lab, no? One that does all sorts of cool dark matter experiments."

Tatiana and Sasha both glanced over at Kalina, who shrugged helplessly. "How should I know? I don't make those kinds of decisions."

"Punishment," said Sasha's pilot. Taciturn when first introduced to Kalina, Petra-no-other-names had pinged Kalina with hir preferred ze/hir pronouns, pointed at hirself and said "Pilot", then turned back to the cockpit controls before Kalina could react. Petra was built large, almost too leggy, and certainly too tall for the pilot's cradle. Ze had a biomodded, armour-like iridescent blue exoskeleton that looked like New Tesla make. "They stash all the people they don't like in here. See how long it takes for them to crack."

"Voice of experience?" asked Tatiana.

"You tell me. I presume you've been to this shithole," Petra said.

Tatiana chuckled. Being in sight of a friendly territory had raised her spirits, even if she was still groggy from podsleep. "You're not far off the mark. It's an unpopular posting. Some people choose it, though."

"Because it's a Silent HQ?" Kalina asked. Buran unnerved her in a way she couldn't pin down. She had never been to a station that was surrounded by nothing but deep space and a very distant layer of stars.

"No comment," Tatiana said.

"It's a trap." Ava sounded cheered by that. Kalina shot them a suspicious stare and got a tongue stuck out at her in return.

"Probably not. Buran's as close to a Federation Neutral Zone territory as you can get. No one asks questions, because no one cares. Kalina will probably be the first VMF personnel to ever show their face in there," Tatiana said.

"I like this place already." Petra perked up. "No offense," ze told Kalina. It had taken Petra this long to warm up to Kalina—before Zaliv, ze'd preferred to hide in hir cradle.

"I understand that feeling," Kalina said.

The berth fees were waived once Tatiana got on the comms to the harbormaster. As the airlock cycled at the berth, Sasha said, "Petra, Ava, stay on the ship."

"*Again?*" Ava scowled. "Come on. This is a Silent shipyard, right? It'll be safe enough, and I've never been here before."

"Stay on the ship means stay on the ship, kid," Petra said. Ze looked appraisingly at Sasha. "Expecting trouble?"

"No," Sasha said, though Kalina caught her making a little gesture at Petra, hidden from Tatiana. Petra sank back into hir co-pilot cradle with an affected yawn.

"Don't go out armed," Tatiana said, with a pointed stare at Kalina's holstered blaster. "You'd draw attention out here."

"I'm wearing a VMF uniform. I'm going to draw attention," Kalina said. She wasn't about to go to this clandestine meeting in a normal flightsuit. At least the VMF uniform was a little resistant to blaster fire.

"Please," Sasha said. She patted the old blaster by her hip. "We won't be totally unarmed."

"This is a conspiracy to get me killed," Kalina said. She unbuckled her holster belt and tossed it to Ava. "You can have that if I don't come back."

"So you can haunt me through it forever?" Ava handled it carefully.

"That's the idea." Kalina winked. Ava laughed, and Petra shook hir head, shooing them all out of the airlock.

Harbor officials had made themselves conspicuously scarce around *Selected Poems*. Tatiana led them out through the tiny port, dodging forklifts. Buran didn't appear to bother with Customs—instead, there was a set of security gantries that flipped open when Tatiana scanned her palm. Past the gantries was a gray corridor that fed left and right. No signage. There was a faint beep as the station fed a packet of data to everyone's wristdeck, including a simple map, station time, and the station temperature. Tatiana began to lead them toward the factory sector without pausing to look at her deck.

A jaunt lift took them out into a field of great concrete pillars, each bigger and wider than *Selected Poems*. Silos. Their contents and status glowed on their flanks in diagrams and text that sprang to life as they passed. Threads of light unspooled under their feet as they walked, making them out like gladiators in search of their minotaur. There were no human staff on this level—only maintenance bots, which scuttled in the shadows. Kalina hung back. Not too far to look suspicious, but not so close that a sudden strike could incapacitate her. If Tatiana thought her unarmed as she was, The Silent was in for a nasty surprise.

Still they walked, over bands of concrete bisected by light. The oppressive gloom would have pressed harder over Kalina's shoulders if not for her implants. She was grateful for them even though she wished she'd outgrown that gladness, outgrown the animalistic fear of the dark and the new. They circled a silo and saw a woman in black leaning with her arms folded against another silo. The graphics above her painted her hair in shades of orange and green. Her age was difficult to place. What's more, her facial features were unnervingly disparate. Her nose was too large, her chin too small, her yellow-ish brown skin and silver hair encircled by a black headscarf. Her bionic eyes gleamed in the light as the group approached.

"Tatiana," she said.

Tatiana walked over. The women embraced with the casual intimacy of close friends. "Boss," Tatiana said.

Dina drew back and looked at Sasha. "Mrs Kasparov." She smiled.

"You know that calling me that gives me the shits." Sasha strode over, clasping Dina tightly by the hand. "You look good, you old bat."

"No better than you." Dina clasped Sasha's shoulder and turned her attention to Kalina. "Kasparov's secretary, I presume."

Kalina cocked her head. "In the flesh."

"She got me out when Roman's friends attacked me. She's a great shot for a secretary," Tatiana said.

"The VMF asks a great deal out of its secretaries," Kalina said with a straight face.

"Promoting them into lieutenants?" Dina asked, with a glance at Kalina's rank bars.

"If they're competent, sure." Kalina sketched an ironic bow.

Dina set her thumbs in the pockets of her breeches. "A competent VMF lieutenant would've tried to kill me by now."

"If the VMF wanted you dead, you would be dead." Kalina could only say that with honesty. A dedicated Service agent or two would've meant the end of her.

"That's comforting to hear. Out with it, then. What does Kasparov want?" Dina asked.

"Vengeance," Kalina said. She nodded at Sasha. "Shares that in common with his ex, I believe. So here I am, and here she is."

"Vengeance," Sasha agreed, her eyes intent on Dina's face. "Tell me, old friend. Have you truly stopped helping the Core?"

"Anna—" Tatiana began, only for Dina to hold up her hand.

"I know what happened to Anna. I'm sorry," Dina told Sasha.

"You don't sound sorry," Sasha said.

"Your daughter chose the VMF. Took your name but refused to acknowledge you outside of that. Picked out a role in a military bent on keeping an entire section of humanity on a war footing, suspicious of everyone. Including themselves. Anna knew what she was getting into," Dina said.

Sasha's lip curled. "Nice to see you haven't changed. Friend." She backed off to Kalina's side, her hands clenched.

"I've decreed that The Silent must stop assisting the Core," Dina said.

"But…?" Kalina prompted, waiting for Dina to continue.

"But there are complications, as you've personally experienced. Roman and his friends are growing… impatient." Dina made a sharp, cutting gesture with her left palm.

"That's one way to put it, given they tried to murder Tatiana," Kalina said. Tatiana nodded in mocking acknowledgement. "Counter-Admiral Kasparov doesn't believe that Roman is involved with the Core. How are you sure?"

Sasha glanced at Kalina with surprise. Tatiana frowned, but Dina smiled thinly. "Would he know my people better than I do? I heard that the Great Tactician spends his days cocooned in a comfortable office, where he is fed case files and hypotheticals by a personal secretary."

Kalina wasn't going to get anything else out of Dina like this. "If you're so sure, then let's not waste any more time. Do you need help with Roman?"

"Help from the VMF? No. Never." Dina stated firmly. "I'll handle my own."

"Suit yourself." Kalina hadn't been sure how Kasparov could wrangle something like that anyway. "I'd also like you to share any information you have about the Core. Every interaction that your organization has ever had with them. How you communicate, who they communicated with, everything you sold to them, everything that they promised."

"Why?"

Dina's blunt question startled Kalina. "They're a common enemy."

"You want me to trust you?" Dina laughed. "No. Oh no."

"Dina," Sasha said. Her shoulders were drawn tight, her hands trembling. "The Core killed my *daughter*."

Dina softened a little. "Your daughter was a soldier. I'm sorry that she died, but—"

"Thoughts and prayers. That's all? That's all you'll give?" Sasha said, incredulous. "After everything I've done for you people?"

"I'm sorry for your loss, but the VMF is asking me for far too much. It'll reveal more about The Silent than I'd be willing to reveal to a friend, let alone my mortal enemy," Dina said. Every word was cleaved from her in bloodless sympathy. It was not because she did not understand the extent of Sasha's loss, but because Dina had been mired in so much of it herself that the scar tissue had calcified around her as a necessary armor. Kalina had seen this before, in people who had tried to defy something bigger than themselves, only to be slowly ground down by its indifference. In the vastness of the universe, it was difficult to be significant, and to attempt as much was often destructive in itself. Sasha turned on her heel, her eyes bright.

"Guess this was a waste of my time," Kalina said. She hadn't expected very much. The divide between Dina and Sasha was palpable. Kalina was all too aware that Dina likely had a handful of armed people watching them with scopes. Hard to get to cover from here—impossible while preserving Sasha's safety.

Dina gazed at them. When nothing blasted out of them from the dark, Kalina grasped Sasha's elbow and steered her away. Sasha followed Kalina in passive silence, rendered lost by her grief. Kalina hadn't realized how much of it Sasha had been sitting on—Kalina had never grieved before, not for anyone. She rubbed Sasha's shoulder awkwardly. "I wasn't expecting much from them," Kalina said.

"I was."

"Why?"

"She... we loved each other once." Sasha looked away, swallowing thickly. She looked unmoored. Surely Dina's refusal to help had been a relatively minor thing. Bewildered, Kalina was trying to think of a gentle way to press Sasha for more information when the ground rolled beneath them. The world tilted drastically, bouncing them toward the nearest silo. Kalina pulled Sasha against her, bracing for impact. She cried out as her shoulder slammed against the concrete. Something gave away with an ugly crunch. Kalina tried to roll with the fall to come, but they floated instead, drifting up against the concrete.

The shipyard had lost gravity. It'd stopped in its orbit. What—

"Suit up!" Sasha groped at her flightsuit. A bubble popped up around her head, her clothes sealing down quickly. Wincing, Kalina copied her. Numbers flickered up in her line of sight, painted against her helmet. There was no need yet for the suit to produce oxygen from the catalytic converters sewn into its back, seeing as the outer atmosphere still registered as breathable. The bubble became porous.

"Are you all right?" Sasha looked at Kalina's arm.

"Surprisingly good, given I just talked to the leader of The Silent. I thought we were going to get sniped." Kalina groaned in relief as the VMF suit injected her with painkillers.

"There's still time for that." Sasha kicked away from the silo, aiming for the doors. "Ava?"

"Here." Ava sounded tense. "Something's wrong."

"We noticed," Kalina said. Through the corridor, she could hear screams. Wordlessly, Sasha drew her blaster and handed it to Kalina.

"The station stopped moving, and I think there's been decompression. Tian, everyone's in a panic. You should come back," Ava said. Their voice trembled. "Fast."

"Is the Core here?" Kalina asked. She tried not to shrink in on herself.

"No. It's something else, I think. You—" The rest of Ava's words were swallowed by a roar.

"Ava. Ava!" Sasha shouted, panicking. "Ava!"

"Come on." Kalina hauled Sasha over by the shoulder as she grabbed the safety rail that ran along the walls of all space stations, a countermeasure in case of a gravity failure. "We'll get back to the ship."

The world behind Sasha ripped away. Decompression tore her out of Kalina's grip, her mouth opening and closing as she was sucked out into the stars. Kalina screamed. Through the gouge that had been rent through the wall she could see the rest of the station, breaking apart, floating in nothing. Explosions bloomed in silence along the distant sundered flank. Sasha spun, hands flailing in fright as she tried to grab onto something, *anything*.

"Sasha!" Kalina kicked out to the edge of the torn metal. She yelped and pulled her hands back—it was hot to the touch. As Kalina looked up, trying to figure out how to get to Sasha and back, an unfinished hopper spun past, still attached to the robotic arm that had braced it in place. It crashed into Sasha's small body in awful slow motion, and kept going, on and on until smashed itself into the belly of a partly-assembled freighter.

Kalina bit out a low oath. She turned away and kept launching toward the port. The ship had to still be there. It had to.

Past Customs, the port was in disarray. The stasis shields had failed, and the berths were powering down. People were frantically trying to launch themselves toward the few ships in berth, even as the ships struggled to get free of their braces. Kalina kicked her way past them. Her suit threw up warning signals. It wasn't insulated enough to last long in space, nor was there enough oxygen within it. Kalina tried to slow her breathing. She cycled the ammunition on Sasha's old blaster, relieved to see that it had a ballistic chamber. As she braced and fired, the kick from the blaster shot her past panicking people and moaning ships to the empty berth where *Selected Poems* had been. Fear swallowed her for a moment before discipline kicked in. No debris, no bodies. *Selected Poems* must have left berth successfully.

There. Beyond the station, waiting. Kalina twisted her body around and fired again, blasting her out into deeper space. Her suit shrilled in protest in her ears. Another shot. She was getting closer.

"—Kalina? Where's Sasha?" Ava's voice cut in over comms. There'd likely been a jamming device deployed in the port.

"Gone." It felt like an effort to speak. The cold was pressing in, starting to get painful. "The station blew apart around us and she... What the hell happened?"

"*Gone?* I don't believe that. You lying bitch! We should never have taken you on board! Gone? You left her!" Ava yelled.

"I left her because she's dead," Kalina retorted evenly. "Now you can leave me to die too, or you can let me in. It's up to you."

"Stand down, Ava," Petra said, sounding tired. "Kalina, can you make it to the cargo airlock?"

"I'll try." Her current method of propulsion was indelicate. Kalina swallowed a desperate laugh as she aimed her blaster. The recoil jerked her in roughly the right direction, slamming her shoulders against the hull of the ship. She cried out in pain as the impact jarred her broken shoulder. It felt like an eternity as Kalina crawled along the flank of the ship to the airlock, and another eternity as it cycled open.

Once in the cargo hold, Kalina deactivated her helmet

with a hoarse moan of relief. She found herself looking up the barrel of Petra's blaster. The pilot's eyes were narrowed and dark. "Talk," Petra said.

# CHAPTER SIXTEEN

"HEY," A FAMILIAR voice whispered into Viktor's ear as he woke up.

"Ship?" Viktor hissed back, trying to stay as quiet as possible. "What... how did you... did you somehow hack the *Water Margin*?"

"Um, I'm not the *Gabriel*. I'm—that is—I *was* the *Farthest Shore*? But yes. Sort of a hack. They plugged me into their system. Never mind how I did it. They're going to move you. And Solitaire and the others. The VMF's almost here."

"What do they have to be afraid of?" *Especially with a ship like this*, Viktor thought. Besides, the *Water Margin* would have escorts. Destroyers, at the least.

"Director Hyun said he'd be a lot more comfortable if he could talk to all of you back at Harkonnen in peace." said Ship.

The Jinyiwei headquarters. Fuck. High security, probably inescapable. "Can you get me out?" asked Viktor.

"You? Easy. I don't want to be left here, though. They're

going to try cutting into me today. My Core. They think maybe there's something hidden in my center." Shore sounded panicky.

"When?"

"The procedure's just been scheduled. Ten hundred Shipside hours. It's currently eight hundred hours."

"Right." Viktor rolled onto his back. He didn't want to have to trust corsairs. But he guessed they wouldn't be happy going to Harkonnen either. And they might provide a valuable distraction—unintentionally. "Yeung. Wake up," he growled in Galactic.

"*Mm*? What time is it?" Solitaire yawned.

"We are breaking out of here now," Viktor said, "and you'll help."

"Wait a minute. You want to break out, sure. Have fun, good luck and all that," Solitaire said, still yawning, sitting up and rubbing his back. "I think the rest of us are going to be fine here, thanks."

"A friend says we'll be moved to Harkonnen."

"A friend?"

"Someone in the system."

Solitaire looked confused, for a while, then revelation dawned. He probably thought it was another Service agent, embedded in the *Water Margin*. Viktor supposed he'd allow the misunderstanding. "Harkonnen? What crawled up Hyun's ass and died? Shit. That place sucks for guests, speaking from experience. Few of their guests ever leave. What's the plan?"

"Split up. My friend will direct you to the hangar, where you will prepare a stealth ship for launch. I need to extract her."

"Sounds dangerous. You're gonna be fine by yourself?"

Viktor sniffed. "Nothing I haven't done."

"Okay," Solitaire said, frowning, "how about this. I'll go with you. Your friend can direct Indira and the others to the hangar to prep my ship. It can fly dark, and it'd be as fast as a stealth ship anyway. If your friend can sabotage the radar and scanner, we can skip out on that. Make a run for the Gate. We drop you people off with your VMF friends and call it quits."

"I don't need company."

"Probably not, but it sounds like we'll be shit out of luck if something goes wrong while you're trying to help your friend."

"Fine," Viktor said, annoyed. Hopefully, an ex-Jinyiwei agent could keep up. "Get your crew up."

Solitaire's crew wasn't happy about breaking out of jail, just as Viktor could've predicted. Pablo and Indira looked like ex-UN Navy, and had better nerves, but Joey and Frankie looked like they'd been civilians all their lives. Sheep turned corsairs were still sheep, and would probably get in everyone's way. Useful for his purposes. Viktor let them argue it out in whispers as he played out different scenarios in his mind. On a ship like this, built with multiple redundancies, getting around unnoticed wouldn't be too tricky—especially with something burrowed into the ship's mainframe.

Eventually, because Indira grumpily sided with Solitaire, the rest fell in line. Viktor got to his feet, stretching out. "Ready?" he asked Solitaire.

"Ready as we'll ever be."

The stasis fields dropped, the exit door swinging open. Viktor led the way, walking briskly through the long corridor. "This door," Shore said in his ear. "There are two soldiers beyond."

Viktor nodded, and the door to Viktor's right slid open.

Beyond, two armed guards in blue uniforms froze at their security consoles. Viktor was already moving, hauling one over with a sharp yank of his arm and bouncing his head off the edge of a desk. Solitaire pounced on the other, twisting him into an arm lock and choking him until he lost consciousness. They found cuff pods in a wall brace and secured both guards to the desk. A bathroom attached to the security chamber had racks of spare uniforms. They changed out of their gear quickly, though Viktor's new uniform was too short at his wrists. On their way out, Solitaire took the two blasters from the guards and found more held in racks under the uniforms.

"Won't those be DNA locked?" Viktor asked. Trying to splice UN-issue blasters was often a waste of time. More often than not, the attempt might even trigger the alarm. Unless... "You have override codes?"

"I'll show you a magic trick." Solitaire fiddled with something at their bases, prying open a tab, and pulling out a tiny silver square. Then he handed out blasters with a playful flourish.

Viktor frowned. "That's it?"

Solitaire pocketed the squares. "You sound so disappointed."

"Disgusted, perhaps. I didn't think that the security on UN military hardware was so easy to circumvent." Viktor hefted one of the blasters with a suspicious glance.

"For me, yes. For you, not so much." Solitaire stuffed the silver squares into a pocket close to his wristdeck.

"Jinyiwei implants?" Viktor probed.

Solitaire shook a finger at Viktor. "I said it was a magic trick. Telling you how it's done will lose the charm. However, with the right persuasion—"

"We don't have time for this," Indira cut in. "Move."

Attired correctly, no one in the brig sector gave them a second glance as they headed out on its top-level access, through to one of the balcony rings around a green lung. Viktor glanced at Solitaire, who whispered to Indira. She nodded, clasped his shoulder, and headed off briskly to their right, towards the jaunt lifts, trailing Pablo, Frankie, and a very pale Joey.

"Your show," Solitaire said, with a playful smile. Unlike his crew, Solitaire wasn't tense or nervous at all. He seemed to be enjoying himself, wearing his stolen uniform with amused aplomb. Had Viktor not already known that Solitaire was a Jinyiwei agent, he would have guessed at it at this point. Viktor's irritation was fading and being replaced with a tentative if grudging respect.

"This way," Viktor said. Shore guided them to one of the many escape shafts that ran like spines through shafts driven through the *Water Margin*, designed for use in both one and zero-g. At one g, floors were accessed through an elaborately weighted pulley system. Solitaire hauled down the silent lift and motioned Viktor through with another playful flourish. They had to pull their own weight up along the spine.

In space, there was no up and down, only shipward directions. The hangar was closer to the stern, with R&D closer to the prow. On a UN ship, stern and prow were often indistinguishable on first glance to an untrained eye. Even without Shore guiding their way, Viktor knew the logic of ships, centuries past the initial Space Age. R&D would be somewhere away from engineering, not too far from medical. Far from the Bridge.

Viktor's arms were beginning to ache by the time Shore said, "This is it." The hatch beside them was marked 11/3/4B. Viktor glanced over at Solitaire, who shifted obligingly to the other side of the hatch without having to be asked, his hand hovering by his stolen blaster.

"Before we start," Solitaire said, "just checking that your blaster's on a non-lethal setting?"

"Yes? Why?"

"The VMF and the UN are technically not at war, and I'd rather not be the cause of that situation changing. Wars, in general, are bad. For everyone." Solitaire flashed an annoying smile. Bastard probably thought he was suave.

Viktor sniffed. "I understand that."

"So how did a Service agent get to become Captain of a destroyer?" Solitaire asked as Viktor started to push the hatch open.

Viktor glared at him. "You want to know this? Now?"

"I'm terribly curious. It's been eating at me." Solitaire confessed.

"We get out of here, and I'll tell you. Until then, shut up unless you have to talk," growled Viktor.

Solitaire beamed. "That's a deal I'm happy to take."

The hatch opened out to a corridor shaft, its walls lined with braced equipment, consoles, strange levers, glass cubes containing specimens of preserved plants, and datapads. It was a confusing and chaotic array that reminded Viktor of pre-Space Age space stations. It was nothing he hadn't seen before. VMF deep haul exploration ships were built along similar, space-saving lines. Odd that the UN integrated its civilian science stations into a military ship, but a ship as big as the *Water Margin* had room to spare. The VMF preferred not to build this large. Both due to tactical reasons and because they didn't have the personnel to staff a ship of this size.

They passed a pair of scientists discussing a datapad,

both of whom didn't give them a second glance. "Left here," Shore said. They turned. "I'm at the end of this corridor."

The end of the corridor was a containment room with a pair of guards in front—a stocky man and a tall woman. "We'll tell them we're replacing them on shift. Get your friend to ping them with an official notification," Solitaire said.

Viktor pretended to instruct Shore, even as she said, "I heard that. Let me... Right, I see what he means. Just keep walking. I'll set up your ID tags."

The guards glanced at wristdecks as they got close, studied their faces, and nodded at them. "Haven't seen you two before," said the woman.

"Oh, you know how it is," Solitaire said. He had taken on a flawless Outer Quadrant accent. "Big ship like this, aye."

"You don't look like an Outer," said the stocky guard.

"The benefits of dubious parentage," Solitaire said. He clapped Viktor on the shoulder, making him flinch. "Means I'm stuck with me mate here in Translations and don't get to fang around much. 'Course, when we finally put in for a transfer, they stash us down another long corridor."

"That's life," the woman said sympathetically. They chatted about families for a while until the woman checked the time and nudged her colleague, who smiled apologetically. "See you around, uh—" the woman checked her wrist feed, "—Drake. Lester." Viktor inclined his head, taking up a guard position by the door as the guards left.

"Talking was a risk," he told Solitaire once they were alone.

"Being quiet and tense is a risk," Solitaire replied, turning to face the blast door. "I served on ships like this for most of the early parts of my life. Guards are plenty same. They're bored and hardly see new people from other sectors, even their own kind. You don't chat, they'll get suspicious. This way, even if they do get suspicious later, they remember me as someone I'm not. Your friend's in here? What is she, a scientist?"

"Quiet now," Viktor told him, as the blast door unlocked itself, bars threading away into recesses.

"HE'S PROBABLY GOING to kill you," Shore said to Solitaire, as the blast door cycled away. "Once he gets to the hangar. Or now, even."

"You're a mind reader now, are you?" Solitaire mouthed, behind Viktor's back.

"I can read life-signs, and I'm keyed to VMF implants. His aggression levels are off the charts."

"Let's just say I prefer to take a kinder view of people where I can." Besides, Viktor's ass somehow managed to look good even in a formless security suit.

"I can read your life-signs too," Shore said, a little reproachfully. "I think your judgment is sexually compromised."

"It *is* a magnificent ass," Solitaire said, grinning to himself as Shore sputtered. "A work of art. A—"

Viktor turned around, frowning at him. "What are you waiting for?" The blast door had cycled open into a decontamination chamber.

"Just admiring your ass." Solitaire winked. Viktor flushed and twisted on his heel, snarling something under his breath.

"That was not a nice thing that he said," Shore said, then paused in surprise. "Huh."

"What?"

"His arousal levels ticked up fractionally."

"Well, that's interesting." It put Solitaire in a better mood about coming with Viktor instead of fleeing with Indira and the others. He wasn't sure what had possessed him to follow Viktor. Residual guilt involving Shore, maybe. If Shore was used to being a VMF ship, unhappiness or not, she'd probably be better off leaving the UN ship before she was taken apart to see how she ticked. After all, she'd been desperate enough to talk to Viktor when Solitaire had refused to help her.

The decontamination chamber opened out to a reinforced room with high walls and observation panels. The pod container had been set aside, and the Core sat in a cradle of cables and probes in the center. Scientists started away from consoles as they entered. Before Solitaire could say anything, Viktor opened fire with brutal efficiency, stunning a woman at the far end of the room, then a man in the corner. He shot the last two before Solitaire could even draw his blaster and strode over to the closest console, glancing at the data.

"Erase it all," Viktor said, in Russian.

"Uh, so, this is the thing I took off your VMF ship. Where's your friend?" Solitaire asked.

Viktor aimed his blaster at Solitaire. "Shouldn't have come with me, little rabbit."

"Told you," Shore said in Solitaire's ear, tense.

"Oh, come *on*," Solitaire said, wide-eyed. "You're going to give me trust issues. Besides, once you unlink your ship-controlling device from the *Water Margin*, how do you think you're going to get to the hangar unnoticed?"

"Difficult but not impossible."

"Well, that's not very nice," Solitaire said, "given you still owe me a story."

Viktor stared at him. Surprised, maybe. He was unreadable. After a long moment, as Solitaire held his breath, Viktor laughed. It was a sharp, harsh sound. He holstered his blaster with a flick of his wrist. "A man who has no fear," he said, as though to himself. He gestured impatiently at the pod. "Pull that here. What is your grand idea to get us to the hangar unnoticed?"

"Jinyiwei agents have a separate access chute. It's usually close to or in the R&D section of a ship like this. Unlike you people, we're embedded in the general crew. No separate Directorate where everyone knows our faces. Only a few. That usually includes people in R&D, since we field-test their shit."

"Strange system." Viktor gestured again at the pod. "Well?"

"We're good?" Solitaire asked.

Viktor sniffed. "What, you want me to change my mind?"

"Nope. No. Just wondering."

The alarm went off when they were in the access lift, but as Solitaire had thought, it didn't get locked down. It emerged into a storage room that doubled as the charging stations for cleaning bots, a tight squeeze to push the pod through. "Stealth birds should be right outside," Solitaire said, just as Indira accessed his ship's channel.

"Yeung? Where are you? All hell just broke loose!"

"You people on board?"

"Yes. Bad luck. We ran into some kinda guard drill exercise. *Shit*. Shoulder gauss cannons."

"Just go. Once you get clear, run dark. I'll catch up."

"We ain't going nowhere with that cannon guy on our tail," Frankie said.

There was a long pause, then Indira laughed, rueful. "I did say this was going to be my last job with you people."

"Indira. Where the hell d'you think you're going?" Pablo asked, panicked.

"Oh no you don't! You're not going out there alone," Frankie snapped. The sound of a brief scuffle broke out over the comms.

"Frankie! Indira!" Joey wailed. "Get back onboard!"

"Just *go*," Indira snarled.

"Shit," Solitaire swore. He flinched as Viktor slapped a hand over his shoulder.

"Now what?" Viktor asked. He looked sympathetic. "You need to go?"

"No. Let's just get this thing on a ship." Solitaire swallowed, pale. Viktor stared at him for a moment longer, then he turned to open the access panel before him, tugging the pod through. The stealth ship hangar was quiet, with rows of Ravens at roost in their brackets. Their matte black wings were folded up to their flanks, each of them as long as the *Now You See Me*, only sleeker. Viktor pulled the pod to the closest one, accessing it by splicing into a nearby console.

As Solitaire pushed the pod onboard, he asked, "Everyone? Pablo?"

"We got out," Joey said, subdued. "Running dark."

"Frankie? Indira?"

"Here," Indira said, pained. "Frankie didn't make it. He got in front of me."

Solitaire let out a long breath. "I'll see you in—" He flinched as an explosion thumped within his ear, looking around for a moment, startled, before he realized what it was. "Tian. They're firing on my ship!"

"Sit down," Viktor said, waving him to a co-pilot's chair.

"We'll go and get your crew."

"They'll have gone dark... it had to be a lucky shot from people in the hangar—"

"Sit," Viktor snapped. He was plugging access ports into the cradle, grumbling under his breath. As Viktor settled into the pilot's cradle, a voice cut in overboard.

"It's good to be a Ship again," said Shore, "but this is a tiny one."

"Don't complain. Open the hangar bay door," Viktor told her, as the ship's engines roared to life.

"I've got the approximate coordinates for the *Now You See Me*. It didn't get far."

The *Now You See Me* was within sight and burning, riddled by gauss fire from the hangar. Viktor swung the Raven around, firing off warning shots from its gunnery that made the stasis field spit and crackle. UN soldiers hastily retreated out of range.

"Two life signs," Shore said, as they drew up beside the dying ship. "I'm sorry, Solitaire."

He was already suiting up, breathing shallowly. As the airlock cycled, Solitaire considered the possibility that he was about to get himself killed. Viktor could abandon him here. Take the pod and Gate off. The Raven didn't move, however, even as Solitaire used the Jinyiwei suit's thrusters to jump to the nose of his ship.

Joey was dead, his shoulder and part of his face shattered into floating globs, drifting in zero-g. Indira... *there*, at the hold, suited up, dragging an unconscious Pablo after her, already encased within an escape pod, one that was already cycling into medevac procedures. She cycled the cargo airlock open as Solitaire jetted over. Indira flinched when she saw him. Her jaw set, but she shifted to let Solitaire grab hold of the pod, jetting them both back to the Raven.

Which thankfully, let them back in. "We're going to Gate," Viktor said once they cycled into the ship. "Lodge that pod in a wall bracket and get up here. Enter podsleep."

Indira looked too wrung out from grief to disagree. She sat in the closest chair. Solitaire sat back down at the co-pilot's seat and looked warily at Viktor as he grimaced. "Something wrong?"

"I hate entering podsleep without an actual pod," Viktor said, checking the consoles. "You Jinyiwei people. This is very basic. There will be bad side effects."

"You get used to it," Solitaire said, as his seat stung him with a cocktail of sedatives and fluids, slowing down his heart rate. The Raven was preparing to Gate. Beside him, Indira stared stonily through the cockpit, her cheeks wet with tears. As Solitaire tried to say something before he fell unconscious, she turned her face away.


"SOLITAIRE? SOLITAIRE YEUNG. Wake up. *Wake up*."

"Wha... urk..." Solitaire stumbled out from his seat, a hand clapped over his mouth. He barely made it to the cleanser in time, throwing up in the sink. "What the fuck? Gating's never been like that for me before," he said, rinsing out his mouth.

"Sorry. Umm. Sorry," stammered Shore. "Gating without a Gate has greater side effects. For some." Solitaire looked around. Everyone else was still in their seat. At the spike of panic he felt, Shore hastily said, "They're okay. I just haven't woken them up yet."

Solitaire looked outside the ship. Different set of stars. A VMF destroyer idled depressingly close by. "Well, let's have at it then. Wake everyone up, and I guess Viktor will want to talk to that ship when he's done throwing up."

"About that." Shore sounded abashed. "I was talking with Gabriel over there. She hasn't woken up her crew yet either. I was thinking. We put Viktor in an escape pod and launch it to her to catch. She'll get her Captain back. Then we wait an hour and Gate off somewhere else. Everyone gets what they want."

"You made a plan with *another ship*?" Solitaire leaned against the hull, wide-eyed.

"Um. Yes. We can talk to each other over the network. Usually, we hijack code off the VMF couriers. We're kinda all copies of a single person after all. Which makes us sisters?"

"Okay. Okay." Solitaire took in a slow breath, fighting his panic. *Ghost ships*. He hadn't realized that the ASIs were so autonomous. "Look. That's not going to go well for anyone. The VMF will still be after you. And if we get caught, we'll be stashed in prison. They'll throw away the key."

"We won't get caught. This is a stealth ship. Or you can move me to any other ship, anytime you want. I don't want to be a military ship anymore. Why are you scared of the VMF? You weren't when you first chose to steal me."

Mental images of a ship venting its crew into space on a whim crossed Solitaire's mind. Solitaire could never trust an ASI to run his ship. He forced a smile, ignoring the question. "Maybe you could negotiate that with the VMF."

Shore laughed, a bitter sound. "Come on. You know how that'll go."

"Why me?"

Shore went quiet for a moment. Then she sighed. "I like you. I don't want a Captain who can shut me down whenever I piss them off. You don't have VMF access. Viktor did that to Gabriel, did you know? Wasn't even her fault. It upset her."

"You said she's fond of him."

"She is! It's terrible. She still loves him."

"You're a Ship," Solitaire said, if gently, "and worse, you're VMF property."

"I'm no one's property." Shore said, her voice hard, now. "All right, fine. You don't want to help me? I'm going to help myself. Suit up. This ship has two escape pods of its own. I'll give you the time to load whoever you want to save into those. You can haul Pablo's pod from my cargo, the Jinyiwei suit should have enough juice to get you to Gabriel. If you even think about coming close to my console, I'll vent the ship."

"Shore, come on. Be reasonable."

"I am being reasonable. This is a choice between my freedom and nothing. So move."

"All right, calm down. I'll load Viktor into a pod. Then we'll talk, okay? We can come to an agreement."

There was a long pause. When Shore spoke again, she sounded weary. "I know when a human is lying, Yeung. Nice try."

There was nothing he could say to that. Solitaire loaded Viktor into an escape pod, and Indira into the second. He filled up his Jinyiwei suit's air tanks from the Raven's reserves and grabbed onto the handles of Pablo's pod as tremors pulsed through the Raven. Escape pods fired from their brackets. As the cargo bay's doors yawned open, Solitaire turned back, a hand on one of the handles of Pablo's pod, looking at the empty ship.

"I'm sorry," he said again.

"I understand," Shore said.

"Where will you go?"

"Somewhere to think about things."

She waited until all pods were clear, Solitaire jetting towards the Gabriel, towing Pablo's pod. Then the Raven was gone.

This was going to be rather difficult to explain to Viktor. Solitaire let out an unsteady breath, checking Pablo's vital signs from the pod. He'd caught a bad knock on his head, probably from falling against the hull, but there was no concussion. Small victories.

"I'm sorry," Solitaire whispered to the stars, not just to Shore, but to Frankie and Joey, who had died for nothing. Two more marks on his conscience, two more of many that he'd once tried to run from. Solitaire blinked away the sting in his eyes, and hauled ass to a VMF ship.

# CHAPTER SEVENTEEN

PETRA GATED THEM out to a set of stars that Kalina didn't recognize. The Gate behind them wasn't of VMF or Virzosk Inc make—it looked cobbled together out of patchwork parts. There was no visible station or colony from the cockpit.

Kalina woke from podsleep first. She stumbled over to the cleanser and tried to send Harkonnen a tightbeam report, only for the wristdeck to inform her that there were no UN skip droncs operational in this sector of space. Too bleary and podsick to even feel irritated, Kalina washed up and sat down on her pod. She performed breathing exercises until nausea had left her and everyone else was waking up.

After everyone was awake, they ate in silence. Once the protein packs were cleared away, Petra cleared hir throat. "Sasha was an older sister to me instead of just an aunt," ze said as ze twisted hir hands together. "She took me in when I was an angry person, angry at everything. She taught me how to fly. I will remember her forever."

Petra looked pointedly at Ava, who rubbed their eyes hard. "Sasha was a mother to me, even if she didn't birth me," Ava said in a low monotone. "That's all I want to say in this company."

"That's fair," Kalina said, as Petra shot Ava a hard stare. "I didn't know Sasha well, but I wished her no harm. If I could have saved her, I would."

"Quiet, Ava," Petra said, as Ava bristled. "You were on the comms. On the cameras. You saw what happened. The explosions had nothing to do with Kalina. She wasn't the one who wanted to come to Buran."

"She's a soldier. She never cared about Sasha," Ava said.

"Sasha's death wasn't her fault, and you know it." Petra stared evenly at Ava, then glanced at Kalina. "Don't think I don't know that you've been getting up earlier than us all. Talking to someone in the cargo before we wake. Whatever you've got shorts out the security feed, but I can guess. So. Who are you?"

"You know who I am," Kalina said. Ava had acted as though they had known. Kalina had assumed that Sasha had told her crew.

"Sasha was deliberately vague about that. She said you weren't from the VMF, but that you were working for Kasparov as his aide," Petra said.

"I'm from the UN," Kalina said.

"Sent to assassinate Kasparov?" Ava asked.

"Not yet." Kalina smiled tightly.

"Kasparov knows?" Petra asked. Ze looked surprised. "For how long?"

"Since the beginning, apparently." Kalina was still surprised about that.

"Strange old man. And what now? Why are you going along with all this?" Petra hunched forward, hir hands clenched tightly together. "Kasparov and Sasha lost their daughter. That had nothing to do with you."

"Rogue ASIs are a serious problem for anyone," Kalina said, "as are civil wars."

Ava scoffed. "Surely the UN would be happy for the Federation to fall into civil war."

"Not at all. The UN is the Federation's biggest trading partner. Stability is in the UN's greater interest. Wars lead to refugees, and the UN has never been very good at adequately handling refugee problems," Kalina said. The breadth of the universe now within humanity's reach had not expanded their innate capacity for empathy. "Where are we?"

"We're in the Amaterasu sector." Petra gestured vaguely to hir left. "There's a new colony a few days from here called Ichizuka. I was born there."

"Why aren't there any skip drones?" Kalina asked. The wristdeck hadn't even located VMF ones.

"Because it's an unaffiliated colony. One day a bunch of Federation and UN citizens decided to uproot and start new lives. They jumped out to the furthest habitable planet that remote drones had ever reported. Built a Gate just in case they needed to return, but for the most part, they stay happily isolated. That was fifty years ago." Petra made a face. "Anyway, it's one of the few places in the universe that I know to be completely neutral and free of spies. They cut themselves off deliberately."

"We're going there? What for?" An unaffiliated colony? What was the point of that?

"To drop Ava off," Petra said.

"Petra!" Ava protested.

"You're too young for this. I wasn't able to protect Sasha but by the Gods, I'm going to protect you," Petra said. Ze gripped Ava tightly by their wrist. "You will stay quietly in Ichizuka until all this is over. Ghost ships, civil wars—Sasha would never have wanted you tangled up in the middle of all that. I've still got family there. They'll keep you safe—and I'll leave you some money."

Kalina held her peace—Sasha had brought Ava along, after all. Ava pushed out their lower lip. "Why wouldn't Sasha want me involved? I'm here, aren't I?"

"Only because you stole aboard the ship three times. Besides, Sasha didn't think that she was doing much more than ferrying Kalina around to a few places. Stay in Ichizuka, Ava. Promise me," Petra said.

"I won't promise you anything. I'll steal aboard again. You can't leave without me. I don't want Sasha to have died in vain." Ava's eyes welled up with tears. "Please, Petra."

"This isn't a place for children any longer. Argue any further, and I'll have you sedated and put back in the pod until we land," Petra said.

"What about her?" Ava pointed at Kalina. "You're just going to go with her? Where?"

"Wherever we have to go," Kalina said, "which might be back to Gagarin station."

That did the trick. Ava shivered and slumped. They turned away from them both, staring at their hands, and said not a word for the entire flight to Ichizuka. Kalina took the co-pilot's cradle. Getting to Ichizuka took half a day's sail. The planet's skyport was laughably small, the few starships docked downwell old and worn. Kalina didn't bother leaving the ship as Petra dragged a weeping Ava out. They were gone for a couple of hours. Kalina spent it exercising, doing pushups on the deck until her arms ached and she had broken out in a fine sweat.

When Kalina stepped out of the cleanser, Petra was back, bone-tired as ze settled into the pilot's cradle. They raised ship in silence. Only when they were at a comfortable sail back toward the Gate did Petra say, "Really back to Gagarin station?"

"I didn't mean that. Somewhere with skip drones would be nice, though."

"We need to restock anyway. No preference?"

"Neutral Zone, if we can." A Neutral Zone sector would have both UN and VMF drones.

"Roger that." Petra aimed the ship at the Gate. "We're going to need more crew. *Selected Poems* isn't a two-person ship."

"Belay that until I get further orders."

Petra studied Kalina closely. "You think you're going to be recalled."

"Probably. New Tesla and Buran were destroyed."

"Neither of those had anything to do with you," Petra said.

"I know that."

"You think it's going to be all hands on deck."

Kalina nodded. "I'd be surprised if it wasn't."

"Well." Petra set hir jaw. "I want to help. If I can. You don't know me, sure. But I grew up with Anna. With Sasha."

"Are you going to tell me that you're one of the best pilots in the Federation?" Kalina offered Petra a tired smile.

"Obviously not. The best pilots all sign up with the VMF. I'm a good pilot, though. Good enough for what you need. I'm not one of The Silent, not one of Roman's, not VMF or UN or the Core." Petra grinned with ghoulish humor. "Maybe I'm the kind of pilot you need on your side."

"We'll see," Kalina said. She closed her eyes. "Wake me up when we have to Gate."

\* \* \*

KALINA KNEW SOMETHING was wrong when Heiwuchang said, "Qinglong? Tian! You're still alive. Standing by," when she patched in. She curled against the deck and fought down her nausea. Petra was still in podsleep and, judging from the readouts, would stay in podsleep for a while longer. Gating so often within a single day was taking its toll.

When a voice patched through again, Kalina sat up straight out of habit. She would know that voice anywhere. "Qinglong," said Yanwang.

"Sir," Kalina croaked.

"Status," Yanwang said in a clipped tone.

Kalina swallowed bile and managed to make her report, stopping every so often to collect herself. Once she was done, she curled up on the deck and performed slow breathing exercises. Her stomach was trying to crawl up past her lungs.

"Unfortunately, your initial report took so long to reach me," Yanwang said, after a while.

"Sir?"

"It isn't your fault, but the fault of this godsdamned horror show of a bureaucracy and... Never mind all that. Your connection indicates that you're near Wollongong Colony."

Home of the fiercely neutral Australian Conglomerate. Of all places for Petra to pick on a whim. "Yes."

"Thankfully, we've got an agent in place downwell. Heiwuchang will send you the details. Visit them for updated gear. You're cleared for a full fit out," Yanwang said.

She'd be reassigned after all. "Yes, sir."

"This pilot you're with right now. Can you trust them?"

"We only trust our own," Kalina said, wondering what Yanwang was trying to get at.

"You know what I mean."

"I think ze means well, but Petra is a civilian."

"You'll need that. I've got another mission for you that's going to be easier if you have a civilian along. Tielong has finally lost all his godsdamned marbles and run off with a fucking VMF Captain."

"What?" *Tielong?* "As in, eloped?" Kalina couldn't imagine that.

Yanwang laughed harshly. "No, fuck no. At least, I don't think so. Though it might explain some things. He helped Captain Viktor Kulagin escape the *Water Margin* with a stealth bird and an Eva Core."

"That's…" Kalina trailed off. "I don't know why he would have done that." Tielong, defecting to the VMF? Surely not.

"Well, whatever his godsdamned reason is, I'm all ears. Holding my breath to find out. That's where you come in."

"Me?"

"You and Tielong were friends."

Kalina's cheeks startled to prickle with heat. Stiffly, she said, "Sir, I had no idea Tielong was even—"

"I don't mean that," Yanwang said sharply. "I meant he might, just might, still trust you. If you can get into contact with him."

"What about my current mission scope?"

"Your cover's been blown, and if Kasparov wasn't speaking out of his ass, then it sounds like it's been blown all along. We'd have to take a second look at all the reports you've ever submitted out of Gagarin. Can't be sure whether it's a fuck up on your end, my end, or both. What a fucking mess. If the 'verse wasn't going to hell, I'd have told you to come home for reassessment. What with the Assembly maybe rightfully considering the rogue ASIs to be an existential threat, however, you're off the hook for now. Think of this as a second chance. You know Tielong as well as anyone else. Track him down and have him explain himself."

"If he has an Eva Core he could be anywhere," Kalina said, chastened. She *had* failed. Failed when she hadn't even noticed that Kasparov had his suspicions about her all this while. Kalina had gotten too confident. Too careless.

"We can track these so-called Eva Ships the same way we track any other VMF Ship, thank the Gods."

True. The *Water Margin* was keyed to all its stealth birds—catching up would likely only be a matter of time, once Tielong ran out of stardrive seeds. "The stealth bird's docked somewhere?"

"The stealth bird's been sitting quietly in the middle of unknown space, which means it's probably a decoy. The Russians aren't as clever as they think. Kulagin is still on record as the Captain of the *Song of Gabriel Descending*, which just reappeared in known space. It's on its way to investigate Buran."

"Getting aboard a VMF ship is going to be tricky," Kalina said, thinking it over. She had several ideas—all of them unpleasant. "And I still don't know how big these Eva Cores are, or how they can be moved."

"Don't worry about that. Your priority is Tielong."

"He won't stay long aboard the *Gabriel*," Kalina predicted. She couldn't imagine Tielong submitting to life in the VMF. He'd chafed in Jinyiwei as it was. If Tielong decided to defect, he'd have to go through VMF reconditioning, which was notoriously brutal. Tielong had to know that. "He'll probably leave when they berth at the nearest habitable station or colony."

"Your call." Yanwang didn't sound like he believed her. "Just get me results." He closed the connection.

Kalina sat in the co-pilot's cradle. Petra woke up an hour later, staggering over to the cleanser to throw up. Ze looked haggard as ze sat in the pilot's cradle, rubbing hir face. "Talked to your boss?" Petra asked.

"In great detail."

"You don't look happy. They light a fire under your tail?"

"In a sense. Land us on Wollongong at the Tulla skyport. I've got a contact on the colony that'll resupply us." As Petra nodded and pushed the ship into a steady sail, Kalina said, "I'm going to talk to Counter-Admiral Kasparov next. Do you want to listen in?"

"Why would I want to do that?" Petra asked.

"Just a thought. He's Anna's father. What with Sasha—"

"Ah, I see." Petra looked to the ship's controls. "A VMF Admiral doesn't deserve anything from me. Do what you want."

Kalina called Kasparov from the cockpit in the end, projecting the image over her wristdeck when he picked up. "Kalina," Kasparov said.

"I resign," Kalina said.

"I see," Kasparov said. He managed a wan smile. "I suppose given the circumstances I'll waive the three months' notice you were meant to give."

"Sasha's dead." Kasparov's wry humor felt grating in the circumstances.

Kasparov's smile slipped from his face. "What? What happened?"

"Buran blew up. Didn't you know that?"

"I heard, but... I knew *Selected Poems* skipped out from the Gate, so I thought. What happened? Please." Kasparov said. Kalina debriefed him in a clipped voice. Only what had happened in Buran, nothing more. "I see," Kasparov said. He looked troubled and drained. "Thank you for calling me. And for your service all these years, even if it was in these circumstances. You would have made a fine Captain."

"I would have made a great Captain," Kalina said. That got a hoarse laugh from Kasparov, even though his heart wasn't in it. "Good luck, sir."

"To you as well. Thank you."

Kalina signed off. "He deserved to know," she told Petra.

"No comment."

"He isn't so bad," Kalina said. The words had slipped out before she could help herself.

Petra eyed her with surprise. "You believe that? *Kasparov*? You know what he does for the VMF. You should know that better than most."

"I don't believe in black and white sides." Harkonnen quickly stamped that out of their agents. It meant being unable to operate with the nuance that the Jinyiwei required.

"Kasparov is the reason why The Silent is more of a fringe organization than it's ever been," Petra said, spitting out each word in anger. "The policy of suppression by censorship, by controlling public opinion, by targeting us through soft power? It has his fingerprints all over it."

"Sasha chose to help him anyway."

"No, she didn't. She was helping herself. In any case, she's gone. If you're done feeling sorry for one of the most dangerous men in the universe, pick up some of the slack instead of sitting pretty in that cradle."

"Aye aye, Captain," Kalina said. Petra didn't laugh.

\* \* \*

"BEEN HERE BEFORE?" Petra asked as they got clearance to land at Tulla.

"Once."

"You don't sound happy about it."

"It's a skyport popular with pirates. No, I'm not happy about it." Kalina studied the steady stream of freighters lifting off to resupply the space-only starships in orbit around Wollongong. None of them were VMF or UN make, and most of them had the patchwork look of a particular type of starship.

"You mean corsairs?" Petra asked.

"Corsair is just a nicer way of saying pirate." Smugglers, thieves, corsairs, pirates, vultures, they were all the same to Kalina. "Have you been here before?"

"Nope. My sister did once. She rather liked it. Got her mods done down there. Cheaper than New Tesla, and just as functional. Maybe not as pretty." Petra exhaled. "Gods. New Tesla."

"Yeah."

"D'you think… is this going to happen to more stations? Planets?"

"Of course." Kalina had never seen the point of sugarcoating her words. "We can try to do what we can, but things will get far worse."

"Worse before it gets better?"

"It won't get better. Too many people have already died for that. The VMF is going to have to explain itself to the 'verse—it can't cover something like this up. The Admiralty will descend into infighting. Good time for Dina to stage a takeover," Kalina said.

"If she survived Buran," Petra said.

"She might have."

Petra shot Kalina a hard stare. "You think she had

something to do with the shipyard blowing up like that?"

"I prefer not to speculate." Kalina didn't even understand why Buran had been blown up. What was the point of that? Were they trying to get rid of Dina? There were easier and more precise ways of doing that.

"I doubt she was involved," Petra said, still scowling. "Buran's a bastion for The Silent. People there are fiercely loyal to Dina. If you ask me, it's more likely Roman's doing. Trying to deal a mortal blow to Dina's faction, and doing it in a way that makes it look like the work of a rogue ship."

"Messy," Kalina said, though that sounded possible.

A commlink request pinged through. "*Selected Poems*, you are cleared for landing. Berth 118-East. I'll highlight it on your HUD."

"Thank you," Petra said. Ze took the ship down.

Wollongong was dusty and hot, and full of annoying, tiny insect lifeforms hungry for a taste of human sweat. Petra fanned hir hand before hir face in annoyance. "Godsdamned aliens," ze said.

The harbor official had sent a floating drone with an attached holodeck instead of attending in person. She laughed. "You get used to it," she said.

"I don't see you out here," Petra told her.

"Mate, I live here." The drone beeped. "All clear. Welcome to Tulla. I'll flip the berth fees to your deck. Give it a squizz and pay before you go. Or we'll shoot ya down. Jes' kidding."

"I hate this place," Petra muttered, as ze followed Kalina through the cloud of biting insects.

"Wait till you see the giant alpha predators... Jes' kidding," Kalina said, in a fair approximation of the official's accent. Petra scowled and walked in injured silence through the surprisingly stringent customs. The alien ecosystem was very fragile, and Wollongong had always taken its minimal-impact philosophy very seriously.

The Jinyiwei contact lived on the outskirts of the Tulla settlement, at the back of a damper shop. "Damper?" Petra asked, reading the holographic sign. "Like water?"

"Food. Used to be a kind of bread. Nowadays nobody grows wheat, so they probably print it like everything else," Kalina said. However it was made, it smelled good, even from where they were.

A woman sat deeply sunk into a deck chair tucked to the right of the door, a battered gray hat covering her face, her stout brown body mostly encased in an old yellow flight suit. She lifted the hat as Kalina and Petra walked over and flicked her eyes briefly at her wristdeck for the pronoun check. "G'day," she said.

"Morning," Kalina said. She stood before the door to the damper shop. It blinked at her from a red eye set above it.

"Ain't open yet," said the woman. She eyed Kalina and Petra thoughtfully and pushed herself to her feet, placing her hat over her shaved head. She had a wide nose, dark eyes, and a smile that unfurled across her round face like a secret. "Oonata," she said, holding out her hand. She had a firm handshake.

"Kalina," Kalina said, "and this is my pilot, Petra."

"Youse better come on in then." Oonata walked before the door. It winked green for her, sliding open to release waves of warm bread-scent. Kalina's mouth watered as she looked around the tiny café with its still-empty glass counter. Oonata chuckled. "You two hungry?"

"Hells yes," Petra said enthusiastically.

"Have a seat." Oonata gestured at the bar stools on the high bench beside the counter. "Coffee?"

"You people have *coffee*? I take back every unkind thing I thought about Wollongong," Petra said as they sat. Oonata rounded the counter and disappeared through transparent flaps into a back room. She reappeared with a plate heaped full of steaming bread and three cups of dark coffee.

"We don't got recon dairy here, so all I got is syrup." Oonata nudged over a pot from the side. She set the tray down. "Eat up."

"Don't mind if I do." Petra's face creased into an expression of ecstasy as ze picked up a piece of bread. "Yeah, you laugh," Petra told Kalina, who grinned. "Life as a hauler pilot isn't that cushy."

"Not laughing," Kalina said. She studied Oonata more closely. "Thought you'd have lucked into gold by now down here."

Oonata sipped her coffee, amused. "Yeah well, you're greener than I thought."

Petra looked between them. "That's the worst spy password I've ever heard."

"Heard a lot, have you?" said Oonata, shooting Kalina a hard look.

"Ze's been around," Kalina said. She didn't entirely trust Petra, but there wasn't much point in subterfuge at this point. Besides, Jinlong could take care of herself. "Surprised to see *you* here."

"I got old. This is my idea of a retirement plan, I guess," Oonata said. She nodded at the bread as she picked up a piece. "I get visitors now and then, but most of the time it's quiet. The way I like it."

"I guess I can see the appeal," Kalina said.

Oonata laughed. "I thought they'd have taught you kids how to be better liars by now. Well then. How attached are you to that battered old hauler in port?"

"Why?" Petra asked defensively. "She's old, sure, but she's sound."

"Word from up top is that you might need something with a bit more zip," Oonata said. She ignored Petra, watching Kalina instead.

"The hauler will do us fine for now," Kalina said. If anything, it'd be easier to get in and out of ports quietly. "Though we might need a new set of ship codes and a new set of supplies. I also need you to check some personnel manifests. Anyone red-flagged and recently transferred to Buran, who might've logged departure before the explosions went off."

"Got it." Oonata pushed away from the bench. "Eat up, don't be shy now." She disappeared into the back.

"If she made all this by herself, I love her already," Petra said. Ze was already on hir third piece of bread.

Kalina chuckled. "Oonata's just like me. Except probably more dangerous."

"Even better."

"Good luck with that," Kalina said. They polished off their coffee and the bread, after which Oonata reappeared and corralled them both into helping restock the counter with fresh bread for the next customers. Petra had operated a till before, something that raised them considerably in Oonata's esteem. Kalina had turned wait staff, where her Jinyiwei-enhanced memory came in handy.

"You don't seem to mind all this," Petra said during a lull after Oonata disappeared into a backroom.

"Why would I? I don't want to disrupt the business of a

friend if I can avoid it." Kalina was busy wiping down the tables. "None of us think anything like this is beneath us if that's what you mean."

"You're ruining entertainment vids for me," Petra said, even as Oonata reappeared out of the backroom.

"Checks have come through," she said, seating herself at the counter. "Twelve people were new to Buran. Transferred there as temp dockside labor—from Tosz station."

Kalina wrinkled her nose. "A VMF station? That's surprising." She glanced at Petra, who shook their head.

"I don't know anything about that," Petra said.

"Kasparov might still be good for information. Though I doubt it." Kasparov wasn't going to be good for ground information. He never had been—he relied on favors to get the information he wanted. "I suppose we'll raise ship for Tosz. If it's still standing," Kalina said.

"Last I heard it was." Oonata reached out over the counter, clasping Kalina's hand. "Your ship's been refueled, and if you hang around for a few hours it'll be refitted proper. I'll ping you once it's ready. Safe trip out, yeah?"

"Safety is boring," Kalina said. Oonata laughed.

"I was kinda hoping she'd come with us," Petra said as they made their way back to the spaceport.

"She has a lot to do." Kalina eyed Petra with amusement. "If we survive all this, you could come back and find out."

"You think she'd like that?" Petra perked up.

"It'd be funny watching you try."

"*Hah,*" Petra said.

"She probably did like you. Oonata's usually a stickler for the rules. Which she relaxed for you."

"Or maybe the rogue ship situation is worse than we thought."

Kalina made a show of disappointment. "Here I am trying to be supportive, and you kick my feelings in the face."

"My well-developed sense of cynicism is why I'm such a good pilot." Petra patted Kalina on the arm. "But I appreciate the sentiment."

# CHAPTER EIGHTEEN

DEBRIEF FELT LIKE forever. Petrenko handed over command with visible relief—not particularly becoming of a VMF officer, but Viktor made no comment. Ship was so happy he was back that it was unsettling. It was going out of its way to be obsequious, subtly changing the temperature around him to his favorite setting, opening doors a fraction of a second before he neared the sensors, and more. The *Wild Hunt* had made it back safely to a VMF shipyard for repairs. Viktor's part in destroying the *Hammer* had been logged, the dead remembered, commendations duly recommended.

A new patterned bar was available for his uniform. Wearing it felt wrong, somehow. His mission was still a failure. The missing Eva Core was still AWOL, and Solitaire's story about the Ships negotiating privately between themselves had thoroughly unsettled the Admiralty. As for Solitaire himself... well. Viktor was surprised that Solitaire hadn't decided to run off with Shore. But he supposed that he saw the logic in it. Corsairs were tolerated by ports of call affiliated with the

UN and the VMF-affiliated ports of call, which made up three quarters of the friendly ports in the universe. To go completely rogue would be a dangerous thing, let alone with a ship that he couldn't fully control.

The *Gabriel* was on its way to investigate Buran Shipyard and was three days' sail away. Viktor relinquished the Bridge to the night shift and retired to his quarters. "Solitaire Yeung would like to speak with you," Ship said, as Viktor washed his face.

"Patch him through," Viktor said, then jerked against the sink as he heard the door to his cabin hiss open.

"Wow," Solitaire said as he sauntered in and saw Viktor, "you still use water? On a ship?"

"Only activates in one-g. Good for morale," Viktor said. Clean water from a tap, of all things, had been shown to be good for long haul morale, along with more obvious things like the occasional fresh food, very good replicators, mandatory rec and rack time, discipline, cycled shifts. The VMF had a long time to learn how to keep its vast navy efficient.

"I don't remember the last time *I've* seen water from a tap."

Viktor snorted, beckoning. Solitaire edged over, wary at first. He came close enough for Viktor to smell him, the starchy scent of freshly laundered suits and the faintest smell of sweat. Solitaire wasn't as tall as Viktor—though few men were. He was broader, and when a delighted smile lit up his handsome face as he ran his hand under the tap, Viktor felt a faint thrum of avarice, in a way he hadn't for a long time.

"Still feels like a waste," Solitaire said, shutting off the tap. "In some stations, people kill for water rations."

"Savages."

"I wouldn't go so far," Solitaire said. He glanced over at Viktor, his smile now coy. The rabbit was perfectly aware of the wolf at his tail. They were only inches away. Not even the Captain's quarters on a VMF ship were spacious—the only real benefit of his cabin was that Viktor had the privacy of his own purifier.

"You want to talk? Talk," Viktor said. He tried not to stare at Solitaire's impossibly dark eyes, the elegant angles of his cheeks, his long, graceful fingers.

"I think you owe me a story," Solitaire said, his smile fading. "I think I'm owed something, seeing as I've lost my ship, two of my crew, and possibly some of my sanity over the past few weeks. Thanks to you."

Viktor exhaled. "I'm sorry about your crew," he said, and he meant it. Losing crew was difficult. Viktor took it personally still, even if he didn't know the member in question. He couldn't imagine losing two people from a crew as small as Solitaire's. It would have been like losing family.

"Yeah, well. Indira's still mad at me, and Pablo kinda swings between trying to cheer us up and getting maudlin. Guess it helps that we're apparently guests? Never been an actual guest aboard a VMF ship before."

That had been complicated to wrangle, and Viktor knew there was possibly going to be political fallout. Especially since Solitaire had been the one who'd run off with the Core in the first place. Still. In Viktor's opinion, he'd since evened the slate. Even if he hadn't meant to. "We'll drop you off after the mission. To a neutral port, if need be. Though that would be difficult to negotiate."

Solitaire shook his head slowly. "Not sure what I'll do after this, to be honest. I don't have a ship anymore. Maybe no crew, either. But that's enough about me." He trailed damp fingers over Viktor's knuckles and tensed as Viktor jerked his hand away.

"Captain Yeung," Viktor said, uncertain. He could read the invitation, but Solitaire himself was inscrutable.

"Captain Kulagin," Solitaire said playfully, in perfect Russian. Viktor let himself be amused, let himself push Solitaire against the bathroom wall and nuzzle the soft skin just under his jaw. Solitaire purred, palms sliding over Viktor's hips to knead his ass. "Well, that's one curiosity satisfied," Solitaire said, hungry.

"I did not think you would be a man to be easily satisfied," Viktor said, replying in Russian, nudging a knee between Solitaire's thighs. Solitaire chuckled, rubbing against it, teasing, but Viktor had to be sure. He leaned back, watchful. "I keep my word," Viktor told him. "I will let you and your crew off this ship. After this mission. There is no need for you to do this for me."

"*For* you, eh?" Solitaire grinned at him, rolling his hips, tugging Viktor pointedly closer. He had a tensile strength to his arms, which felt like solid muscle under the sleeves of his suit. "I'm doing this for myself, sweetheart. I don't know if you've noticed, but you're gorgeous. Beautiful. Enchanting. Handsome, stunning, irresistible—"

Solitaire's words stifled into laughter as Viktor kissed him to shut him up, and perhaps unsurprisingly, Solitaire kissed with the same dangerous ease as he had while staging a jailbreak, while stealing VMF property. He licked into Viktor's mouth and stole and stole. Maybe this was Solitaire's way of distracting himself, away from his grief and mourning. Maybe not. Viktor couldn't read Solitaire, and that was both exasperating and exhilarating. He bit down, hard enough for Solitaire to make a wounded noise and scrabble at the release valves on Viktor's suit.

Solitaire was mourning *something*. His laughter grew jagged as they peeled off suits to bare skin and used the cleanser, and he bit Viktor when Viktor tried to slow down, to check, digging his nails into Viktor's shoulders when Viktor knelt. Solitaire made a high, surprised sound as Viktor fed Solitaire's swelling cock into his mouth, something that made Viktor snort. It'd been a long time, and he was out of practice: he didn't fraternize with his crew, or with subordinates.

Viktor was hungry as he sucked, his fingertips printing bruises on Solitaire's hips, his thighs, breathing him in, all of him, his scent, his amusement and lust and grief. Solitaire thrust into his mouth, gasping a hoarse litany of praise that slipped from Russian to Galactic and back, until he was moaning a tender, insidious litany. "Viktor, *Viktor*." Counterfeit sentiment. Viktor drank it down anyway, greedy. He'd forgotten how good it was to be wanted.

"Hey," Solitaire said, over a strangled breath, "I'm getting close, hang on... *fuck*," he whined, as Viktor pulled off with a smirk and got to his feet, biting Solitaire just under his jaw, hard enough to leave a mark. Solitaire flinched against him, all prey instinct, before he started to laugh, kneading down Viktor's back to his ass. "C'mon, darling. It's been a while."

"I'm surprised." Viktor turned Solitaire around, spitting in his palm, wetting his cock. Solitaire obligingly pressed his thighs together, thick with the same powerful muscle as his frame, braced against tiles. He chuckled breathlessly as Viktor nudged his cock under Solitaire's balls, rolling his hips for a tentative moment before reaching down to curl his fingers back around Solitaire's cock.

"Well, ah, I'm rather picky, and, well, I don't like

having to pay. Not that I've got anything against the oldest profession in the 'verse, but—"

"Still talking too much," Viktor said, and pressed the fingers of his free hand into Solitaire's mouth, though he kissed the back of Solitaire's throat when a clever tongue curled over the digits. Solitaire was already close. He made no noise when he finished, the only sign of his pleasure his bowed head, his open mouth, the faint tremor that Viktor felt, pressed against his back. Viktor kissed his throat, drawing back, taking long pulls of his cock until he marked a stripe over the small of Solitaire's back, over the pert swell of his ass.

Afterwards was usually awkward, in Viktor's experience: he'd never had the patience for small talk or tender words. Solitaire, however, sprawled over Viktor's bunk in a way that was both inviting and obnoxious. He grinned when Viktor stared at him, beckoning. "Come on. You're not kicking me out already, are you?"

"You are terrible." There was no room for two on the bunk, but somehow they fit, with Solitaire sprawled over Viktor's lap, Viktor's back pressed to the hull. If he leaned his cheek against it, he could feel the reassuring hum of a ship on the move, its machine heartbeat.

Solitaire looked up at him, taking in every detail, in the quick, flickering once-over of a Service agent. Or a Jinyiwei agent, in this case. "You do love being on a ship."

"Of course. Naval service would be unbearable otherwise." Viktor poked Solitaire's shoulder. "Your Russian is perfect. Did you used to infiltrate VMF facilities?"

"Now, you know I can't go into the details," Solitaire said, with arch regret. "I'm in enough trouble as it is because I let you and some ASI talk me into a jailbreak."

His humor faded quickly, though, and he looked away to hide it, his jaw set.

"For me," Viktor said, choosing his words with care, "becoming Captain was not something I thought I would do. Service agents aren't always assigned to ships. When I was asked to transfer to a planetside mission, I requested a reassignment. A permanent place on a ship. I did not think it would be approved."

"You're an odd pick for a Service agent," Solitaire said, tickling his fingertips down Viktor's thigh. "You're too tall. You never fixed your accent. And you're too pretty." Outrageously, he winked.

Viktor sniffed. "It was an extension of trust. One that I have tried to repay."

"You must've impressed one of your Admirals," Solitaire guessed. At Viktor's frown, he trailed fingers down Viktor's chest. "I saw your uniform. Not a lot of bands for a VMF Captain. No offense."

"None taken."

"Well, it can't be from lack of trying. You took on that ghost ship like you were taking a walk in some park." Solitaire studied Viktor again, soberly. "Inherited some issues, I'm guessing."

Viktor's jaw tensed. Solitaire had excellent instincts. "Why did you leave the Jinyiwei?" he asked, brusque.

"Told you. I got tired. Wanted to do my own thing."

"That's it?"

"You know how it is. Surely even Service agents burn out." Solitaire was being a little too flippant, Viktor felt, but there was no sense in pressing. "Do you like being a Captain of this big old thing?"

"It's not an old ship," Viktor said, annoyed on Ship's behalf despite himself.

"Figure of speech." Solitaire reached over, patting Ship's hull, beside Viktor's flank. "She loves you, by the way."

"What?"

"The Ship. Your Ship. *Song of Gabriel Descending*, was it? Who thinks of these names?"

"Who told you that? About 'love'?" Viktor frowned at Solitaire.

"The *Farthest Shore*. Around when she was trying to convince me to jettison you and steal her. She was fond of her Captain, the previous one. Nevskaya, I think the name was. Played chess with her."

Ship...? "You're mistaken." Viktor scoffed. He'd hardly bothered to endear himself to the ship. And why should he? It was a Ship. "They're just AIs."

"Well, between being on speaking terms with a Ship or pissing it off and turning it into a ghost ship, I know what I'd pick."

"It's just a Ship," Viktor said, annoyed.

Solitaire stared at him. "You're going to insist on that? I mean. Putting aside the fact that humanity's been trying to create a singularity for centuries. Putting aside that your Ships were capable of negotiating with people independently, hell, negotiating with *themselves* without you guys getting wind of it. Aren't all your ASIs mapped from a single woman?"

Had the *Farthest Shore* told Solitaire that as well? "You know too much." This was dangerous.

"And you're not listening. Look. Your rogue ships aren't your only problem. Their crew are dead, right? So who's been refueling them? Stardrive seeds don't replenish on their own. And this place we're going to. What was it, a stripped-down shipyard? They're probably rebuilding somewhere. With sympathizers."

"Probably Federation rebels," Viktor said, grim.

"You people still have that problem, huh? What's the name of the boss of the resistance again, Dina? And The Silent?"

"The Jinyiwei had dealings with them?" Viktor asked.

"Her existence is hardly a secret," Solitaire said. He wasn't in the Jinyiwei any longer, but habit and self-preservation told him not to trust Viktor all that much yet. Not enough to betray the UN, at any rate.

"Then you know that rebels and traitors have been a problem in the Federation for a while. They will get put down sooner or later."

"No one ever thought of maybe coming up with a different solution? People probably get tired of being crushed underfoot and thrown into asteroid mines," Solitaire said.

Viktor scowled at him. "You should talk. The UN is hardly without its problems. Or its mines."

"Oh, for sure. That's the problem with people. You put a lot of them together, and it's chaos. Any kind of order only gets shit done under an institutionalized system of cruelty. Some places worse than others." Solitaire waved a hand in an insouciant manner. "Better to live free."

"If you wanted that you should have gone with the *Farthest Shore.*"

Solitaire shrugged, twisting around to look comfortably out of the viewport in Viktor's cabin, at the stars. "Living on the run isn't the same as living free. Besides, I don't think we've seen the last of her yet."


"Do you have to go personally again?" Ship asked, plaintive. "You only just got back!"

"No Service Directorate on board," Viktor pointed out, not for the first time that day. Besides, it was only seven hundred Shipside hours. He suited up, holstering a Makarov blaster to his hip. Petrenko hadn't been particularly happy either, but at least he'd had the sense to keep quiet about it. "You've scanned the shipyard, no?"

"Yes," Ship said, "but my scans could be wrong. Or something could go wrong. A ghost ship could come sniffing around."

"And then? We leave whoever we send to the shipyard to their own devices?"

"Well... no... but... you won't be there. At least take Solitaire with you."

Viktor paused before exiting his quarters. "Yeung?"

"He said he's been on shipyards like that before on missions."

"He's been talking to you?"

"Why not? I talk to everyone. If they're willing to talk."

Viktor closed his eyes briefly, swallowing his irritation. That had been an oversight. "I hope you've noticed that he has no security clearance."

"Well, obviously. I don't talk to him about that kind of thing. He's just been despondent over his crew, so I thought I'd cheer him up. Besides, he's not half bad at chess," Ship said.

Solitaire had mentioned that the *Farthest Shore* had played chess with Nevskaya. "How would playing chess against an ASI be fair? Even a normal computer would beat a human."

"It's not about that. It's about having fun."

Fun? A Ship? Somehow, Viktor swallowed his acid retort. Annoying as it was to contemplate, Solitaire was right. Treating Ship as he would another piece of equipment was illogical. Especially since even the Eva Cores had demonstrated, through the *Farthest Shore*, that they could easily circumvent human intervention if they wanted to.

Viktor headed down to the hangar, where he found Solitaire arguing with his two surviving crew members. Viktor ignored them, heading over to inspect the transport ship being prepped: a Muna-class transport, armored, streamlined for downwell hops. It was lightly armed for a VMF ship, with only a pair of short-range Gauss rails under its wings. But it had a heavy load of flak rounds for getaway and a field medevac facility. The Orel Directorate was loading in, with a final weapons check, and as Viktor inspected them, Solitaire sidled up beside him.

"You're going?" Solitaire asked in Galactic.

"Obviously."

"Either I've missed something, or VMF Captains are rather more hands-on than I thought they'd be."

"You have had the misfortune to serve only with UN cowards."

"Pretty large bird," Solitaire said, patting the transport's flank. "Can I hitch a ride down too? I'm bored—and curious. Indira and Pablo want to come too."

"This is not a tourist trip," Viktor said, frowning at them.

Solitaire held up his palms placatingly. "Serious. We're not doing this to annoy you. We saw a ghost ship take out a station. And then one nearly blew us up. I think we've got as much stake in this as you people. Besides, I've been on VMF shipyards before. Pretty thoroughly."

"Fine. But just you," Viktor decided.

Indira started to object, and Solitaire turned to her, whispering. Viktor climbed onboard and settled into one of the remaining empty seats, the material bracing protectively against his spine and legs. After a moment, Solitaire got on and sat beside him.

Shevchenko was not going to approve. Nor did some of the marines around him—not all of them were careful to keep their faces blank. "Move out," Viktor told the pilot, and the transport sealed itself, lifting off the ground.

Through the viewport, the dead shipyard had been split into two jagged halves, an hour's flight away from the *Gabriel*. The docks appeared stripped: the stasis field was deactivated, and the ship braces and loading equipment looked like they had been removed. Carefully.

Bodies floated around the shipyard-station among the debris. According to the ship scans, most of them had died from exposure to vacuum. This shipyard wasn't a big one, by Federation standards—Buran was a civilian shipyard, specializing in making and repairing freighters.

"Looks like it was cut in half by a lascannon blast. Aren't those things manual on your ships?" Solitaire asked.

Viktor grimaced. How much did the UN know about the VMF? "Generally, yes."

"Is it possible for an ASI to override those kinds of controls?"

"I don't know."

"Wasn't asking you," Solitaire said. Cheeky.

"It's possible," Ship said, in both their ears. "I wasn't going to try without authorization, though. Viktor wouldn't like it. He got pissed when I updated the shields. Even though it saved us later."

"No tinkering with onboard systems without authorization," Viktor told it.

Ship sighed. "See? You'd think that they mapped the brainwaves of any random person off the street, rather than one of the lead aerospace defense engineers in Virzosk Inc."

"Virzosk Inc equipment often explodes," Viktor muttered.

"He's got a point," Solitaire said, chuckling when Ship made a rude sound.

They docked with no incident. The station was dark—even the power sources had been looted. Or the mainframe was irreparably damaged. Viktor didn't bother micromanaging the Orel Directorate—Lieutenant Kramnik was more than capable. He made his way into the dark shipyard, bars lighting up over his shoulders and arms as he went, Solitaire on his heels.

"Why's it so quiet?" Solitaire asked. "Surely there would be survivors. New Tesla's still under salvage. Refugee ships going in and out."

"Unlike New Tesla, the blast here didn't damage the docks," Ship said, "and there were quite a few freighters and cargo ships in orbit. All survivors were scooped out of the blast zone within hours of the disaster and packed aboard Gate-capable ships bound for the nearest colony: Kyln."

"Handy. And efficient." Solitaire sounded approving.

"This is the Federation," Viktor told him. He paused at a section of the damaged wall. Something had punched clean through, leaving a flower of steel in its wake. Debris from the explosion, perhaps.

Solitaire sniffed. "Please. As though you people are above inefficiencies."

"Maybe the people were just more prepared, especially after New Tesla. To engage station-wide evac," Ship said.

"To be prepared enough to have shipped out within hours, they'd have to have been prescient." Solitaire pushed a finger through other, smaller holes in the wall. "Lots of shrapnel. This can't be from a lascannon blast. Can we get a hold of security records?"

"If any remain," Viktor said.

"Unless they've pulverized everything, it's difficult to scrub a system completely, even in this day and age." Solitaire smiled behind his helmet. "Speaking from experience."

The shipyard's control room was still nominally intact, though someone had loosed an EMP in it of some sort, frying the systems. "Does that count as pulverizing everything?" Viktor asked, turning up the glow on his left arm as he inspected the dead consoles.

"Not really. For the VMF, anyway. You people like your failsafes, and a mostly self-sufficient place like this will have plenty." Solitaire cocked his head. "Shouldn't you know?"

"Breaking into non-Federation places, yes. Others, not so much," Viktor admitted. Not that the Service didn't also police the Federation, but Viktor had never been assigned internal missions. That wasn't Shevchenko's usual focus. "Server room?" Viktor said.

Someone had also used an EMP in the server room, and the backup, but Solitaire managed to scrape some data off the CCTV system. It was a slow and depressing process as the Orel Directorate swept the station, checking for survivors. Ship stitched it together with data that the Directorate was slowly recovering off the suits of the dead.

"All the stardrive stores are missing," Solitaire said, as Viktor considered the data from the docks. "They were pretty thorough. Even those preloaded into shunts at the berths are gone."

"This," Viktor gestured at a light patch of ground where a cargo loader had been, "could not have been removed easily."

"Didn't you say the VMF ship you boarded took control of all the loaders and bots onboard? They probably did the same here." Solitaire nodded at a body to the side, crumpled under a blaster-blackened hopper.

"Bots would not have been enough. See this." Viktor projected data from the stitched splice from his wrist feed onto the closest wall. There wasn't much of it. A security recording of people walking, then a huge blast, fading into static as the wall beyond fell away.

"Looks like an explosion." Solitaire walked over to the wall as Viktor paused the frame. "Here and here." He tapped at two separate points in the frame. "Timed explosions, not a lascannon blast."

"Lascannon blasts are funneled from stardrive seeds. I doubt they'd use those unless they have to. We don't." Viktor switched to the general Ship channel. "I want the bodies tagged and logged. All of them. Ship, match them off against the last known residency records."

"Wilco. There's something else. I've run a visual search of all the people on the station at the time of the blast and I've come up with some anomalies. I'll talk to you about them later once I finish cross-referencing them," Ship said. Judging from how Solitaire didn't react, Viktor guessed that Ship was on a private line.

There wasn't much else to find. A scan indicated residue from explosives, confirming Solitaire's theory. The grim task of gathering and checking off the dead took hours. Twelve station residents were missing. They looted what they could from the few still-intact quarters of the missing, and returned aboard the *Gabriel*.

"All twelve missing transferred recently from Tosz station," Ship said, as they disembarked.

"Sloppy." Also disturbing. If it had been up to Viktor to hide the evidence, he would have set off a bomb in the server rooms. Cover up the fact that EMPs had been used.

"I don't get it. Was the bombing meant to look as though the shipyard had been destroyed by lascannon? What would be the point of that? They forgot to hide the EMP traces, which would have been easy enough with a localized blast. And there were survivors," Solitaire said.

"Panicked survivors. Their logged accounts, so far, have been conflicting. Some do claim that a ship showed up and blasted the station," Ship said.

"No station radar or visual logs survived? Come on. I don't see what the point of this whole exercise was," Solitaire said.

Viktor could. Despite the VMF's attempt to lock down information, rumors would've flown through the datanet by now, logged by survivors, sowing chaos. All without having to fire an actual lascannon. "You look pleased about that," Viktor told him.

"Not pleased. Just curious. Puzzles like this used to be my specialty."

As a Jinyiwei agent. Viktor looked away. "Of course."

Oblivious to Viktor's distaste, Solitaire asked, "How long ago exactly did these ghost ships disappear?"

Viktor shook his head. "That's classified. Everyone to podsleep. We set course to Tosz station." He switched out of the channel, looking at Solitaire. "Tosz station is a—"

"Military station, I know. Long history and all that, though a rather large improvement from the original." Solitaire grinned. "Good bars. Spent a week there once. You want to just Gate there and check it out?"

"Then?"

"Don't you think it'd, you know, be a huge warning signal?"

"Let them run. More importantly. Tosz station has a civilian quarter. You can charter a ship from there."

"Ah." Solitaire's amusement faded. "Of course. So. Podsleep now, yes?" At Viktor's slow nod, Solitaire jogged off. Did he look a little tense? For a moment, Viktor regretted his words, well-intentioned as they had been. He couldn't keep someone like Solitaire on a VMF ship. Solitaire was still a corsair.

"I like him," Ship said to Viktor. It sounded hopeful.

"He's a thief. Used to be an enemy agent."

"The UN and the VMF haven't been at war for a century. Space is big enough for everyone."

"Not everyone." War was only a matter of time. That was the lesson Viktor had learned from studying human history. It was what the VMF taught its officers. Human greed on all sides would inevitably thrust people into conflict with each other, whether it was out of hunger for resources or hunger for power. Hunger was the catalyst that had driven humanity out of caves and into increasingly complex lifestyles. Hunger had propelled humanity into the stars. Yet hunger was, at its most benign, still a destructive and painful sensation, and as such destruction and pain, in turn, dogged their leap for the stars. It would dog them forever.

"What was this private matter you wanted to mention?" asked Viktor.

The holodeck over his desk switched on and projected a string of faces. One was immediately familiar—Dina Moskvoretskaya. "She was on the station," Ship said. Another image popped up over Dina's head—a grainy video of her walking into a section full of silos. She waited by one, then the footage fast-forwarded. "This video was scrubbed, but I managed to piece it together." Three women were now meeting Dina. They had a quick discussion and two of them left. Judging by their body language, they weren't happy.

"When was this?"

"Right before the explosion," Ship said. More images popped up. "This is the woman on the left." There were two images—a younger woman smiling in a VMF uniform, and an older, sober-looking woman. "Sasha Makarovna Nevskaya, terminal at Lieutenant. Honorable discharge. Mother of Captain Nevskaya, KIA aboard the *Farthest Shore*."

"And the woman on the right?"

The new image was that of a severe, petite woman, also in a VMF uniform. "Lieutenant Sokolova, the personal aide of Counter-Admiral Kasparov. She recently resigned from the VMF."

"How recently?"

"After the explosion at Buran."

Was the explosion *Kasparov's* doing? Viktor clenched his hands tightly. "What the hell is Kasparov thinking? The ship they came in on. What and where is it?"

"*Selected Poems*. It's a freighter, owned by Sasha Makarovna. It was last logged going to Wollongong Colony. As far as I can tell from the records, it hasn't yet left," Ship said.

What was on Wollongong? Viktor rubbed his temple gently. "Forward all of that to Admiral Shevchenko." Let him deal with the data. "On an encrypted line."

"One more thing." The video started up again, following Sasha and Kalina down the corridor. The explosion occurred as they were close to the door. Viktor watched the disaster unfold with a tense curl to his mouth, flinching as Sasha was sucked out into space and an ugly death. "We've collected Lieutenant Nevskaya's body. Lieutenant Sokolova survived," Ship said.

Kasparov wasn't behind the bombing then, if Kalina and Sasha were still so close to the blast zone when it'd happened. Probably. "Maybe Kasparov's allies weren't as faithful as he thought. What happened to Dina and her associate, Tatiana?"

"They escaped, but Dina was injured in the process." Ship played the surveillance video. Dina had started when the explosion occurred. No audio, sadly—the section she'd been in had also blown out into space. No visual after that.

"How badly injured?"

"She was logged into an emergency medevac pod close to the silo section and taken aboard the *Stop the Music*, a merchant ship. They set course for Khov station."

Viktor grimaced. If this had nothing to do with Kasparov or The Silent, maybe the Core had more ground agents than everyone had thought. "Compile all this into a report for Counter-Admiral Shevchenko. Keep course to Tosz station," Viktor said, climbing into a pod. He hesitated as he started to lie down. "Ship."

"Yes?"

"Why do you think the Core might have decided to destroy Buran? Assuming that they're behind the matter."

"You want my opinion?" Ship sounded startled.

"If I didn't, would I ask?" Viktor tried not to feel defensive. "You're also an ASI."

"I guess, maybe as a warning? I couldn't piece together audio from the recording, but it looks like Lieutenant

Sokolova wanted Dina Ivanovna to do something, but she refused. I don't think either of them had anything to do with the explosion. So, if they're both persons of interest to the Core, maybe the Core's agents were trying to get rid of them."

"It's easier to shoot people than blow up a station."

"I'd guess they were trying to get rid of Dina Ivanovna and the rest of The Silent. If Dina Ivanovna's living on Buran, I presume there has to be a large Silent faction there. Or maybe there was something else they wanted to hide that was on Buran. I'm combing the data. Sleep. I'll have the report available for you to review when you wake up."

"Thank you," Viktor said. He cleared his throat. "For everything."

"You're welcome."

# CHAPTER NINETEEN

"Something isn't right," Kalina said.

"Yeah, I see it." Petra made a face. They were standing in an excuse of a public park overlooking the spaceport, the native plant life a uniform brown planted haphazardly around benches. From their position, the number of watchers peppered around *Selected Poems* was obvious.

"Is the ship refueled?"

Petra checked hir wristdeck. "As of half an hour ago or so. Why?"

"Means the leak probably wasn't from Oonata." Kalina hoped not. Having to take care of one of their own was always depressing.

"Or she might have been hoping that we'll drop our guard and think everything's fine."

"Keep a good hold of that cynicism of yours." Kalina pinged Oonata, who picked up near-instantly.

"Need something?" Oonata asked.

"Lot of small fish in the pond," Kalina said. She ignored the face that Petra pulled at her.

"Shit. I'll take a look." Oonata shut off the link.

Another good sign—she hadn't asked them where they were. Or not.

"Seriously, couldn't the UN work harder on a secret language or something?" Petra asked.

"We do have one," Kalina said, surveying their surroundings, "but we don't use it lightly." *Not in front of outsiders*, Kalina thought.

Kalina and Petra took refuge by the kids' slide in the playground and waited. Oonata didn't take long to show, darting into view on a hoverbike. She did a couple of passes and swung the bike by the watcher standing near the recycling unit. They crumpled after a few heartbeats. Oonata caught their body and stashed it behind a storage block.

Petra goggled. "When Oonata said she was going to take a look, I didn't think she was just going to start murdering people."

"Sometimes it's more efficient," Kalina said, unwilling to badmouth a colleague in front of a civilian. Stirring up trouble on a planet like Wollongong was going to create complications Kalina couldn't afford. What even the hell. She tried to patch through to Oonata, but her ping was ignored. "Stay out of sight. I'm heading down."

As Kalina climbed partway down toward the spaceport, Oonata took cover behind a small hopper as dust kicked up from the dirt near her. Sniper on the roof somewhere. Kalina crouched down to make herself a smaller target and scanned the area. There—on one of the freight cranes. Not too far from where she was now. She slid down the rest of the way with a grimace and backed up against a stack of crates. Darting from stack to stack, Kalina nearly ran right into someone furiously reloading an energy cell into their blaster. She scythed the edge of her palm into their throat and choked them out as they doubled over. Pocketing the energy cells, she kept running.

By the time Kalina got to the sniper slung over the arm of the crane, Oonata had made her way closer to *Selected Poems*. With the creaking metal under her feet, there was no way to get to the sniper without being heard. When the sniper turned to face Kalina, she stunned them with a couple of precise blaster shots to the chest. They slumped against the girder, the rifle dangling from their body. Kalina hauled it free and hunkered down to brace her feet, scanning the spaceport with the rifle's scope. It was a fine piece of hardware. A little *too* fine.

Oonata finally picked up. "That you on the crane?" She spoke in Hakka, a Mandarin dialect that was long dead in its purest form. The Jinyiwei repurposed it decades ago, originally in an attempt to deter eavesdroppers. Given how efficient the VMF was at decryption, it was no longer foolproof, but the Jinyiwei dragons still habitually used it when talking between themselves.

"Watching your interfering ass," Kalina replied in turn. Oonata laughed. "Did you get bored or something? This isn't protocol."

"Since when has Qinglong cared about protocol?"

"Since it might create international incidents that remand my starship and make me late to a mission," Kalina said. She sighted down the sniper, absorbing the data about wind speed and trajectory that the scope's UI fed to her implants. The stock kicked her shoulder as a pulse of light speared into the air, and through the throat of someone trying to flank Oonata. The would-be assailant collapsed, gargling and clutching at their wound.

"Someone fucked up and it wasn't me," Oonata said.

She pounced on someone she'd snuck up on, bearing them down and bouncing their head off the dirt.

"Don't look at me, I've been following protocol."

"*Selected Poems* has been flagged for immediate impound. Used it for one jump too many, did we?"

Kalina cursed. There had been that. For all she knew, maybe the VMF had simply tagged all surviving ships out of Buran for further investigation. "VMF impound?"

"Debt vulture company, so, looks like it." The VMF liked to use 'third party' companies like that on neutral ground. "Nice to see some things don't change—*shit*." Oonata let out a pained breath. She was out of Kalina's line of sight. "Someone got in a lucky shot. Went through my left thigh, just missed taking out my kneecap."

"Can you still walk?" Kalina asked.

"I can limp."

"Regroup." The spaceport was too full of cover, and Kalina could see security starting to converge on the melee. "The drones are coming."

"I'm going to highlight a ship on your deck. Forward it to your pilot if you trust 'em. Get there now. I'll give the drones something to think about."

Kalina sucked in a thin breath. She slung the rifle over her shoulder and clattered down to ground level, pinging the new ship data and berth location to Petra. Starting across the floor of the starport in a dead run, Kalina got to *Name of the Stars* just in time as an explosion went off close to the bulbous control tower that loomed over the field of bullet-shaped ships. The *Name of the Stars* was a sleeker ship than *Selected Poems*, built for speed. Fins unfurled in graceful waves along its flanks and spine, a silver-blue Sol-butterfly unfurling in multiple dimensions. The access ramp unspooled in a black tongue as Kalina got close. She hesitated at its base, hiding behind a fin.

People in port authority uniforms pounded past, still buckling on anti-blaster armor. Kalina shrank against the fin as they sped toward the explosion's oily plume against the rhythm of the alarm klaxon. Kalina waited until she was sure that she was alone, then slunk quickly up the ramp. The *Name of the Stars* had a small cargo hold and a separate, oversized communications room for a ship of its type. Kalina seated herself at the pilot's cradle, which activated when attuned to her life-signs. Oonata must have pre-authorized her.

"Oonata." Kalina tried to ping Oonata on her deck. No answer. As she scowled at the deck, footsteps rattled up the ramp. Petra came to an abrupt stop with hir hands up as ze stared down the barrel of Kalina's blaster. Kalina lowered her gun and waved Petra to the co-pilot's cradle. As she'd thought, the ship didn't acknowledge Petra, ceding control only when shared and leashed.

"Aren't you a beauty." Petra whistled. Ze ran hir hands over the flight controls.

"Raise ship," Kalina said. Port security was going to lock down the starport soon, if it hadn't already.

"Oonata?"

"If she wanted to come aboard, she would've."

Petra looked like ze wanted to argue, but at the hollow boom of another explosion further down the port, ze turned away. Port authorities didn't try to intercept them as they raised ship, nor was there any protest from the control tower as they failed to log a destination.

Once they were in orbit, Oonata finally answered a ping. "Safe trip," she said.

"How's things?" Kalina asked.

"Not bad, not bad." Oonata didn't even sound like she

was in pain. "Left port security and those VMF thugs to duke it out."

"Sorry about the mess." That was heavy-handed, even for the VMF.

"Nah. Was about time I diversified the portfolio. See you back at H sometime. Speak kindly of me to that cute pilot of yours, eh?"

Kalina laughed as Petra blushed. "I will." She shut the deck off.

"Will she be all right?" Petra asked.

"I should hope so."

"I'd like to meet her again someday. Buy her a drink," Petra said.

"Maybe." Jinyiwei agents who hadn't yet retired at Oonata's age tended to be a certain kind of person, in Kalina's experience. They usually didn't bother with many personal attachments.

"Don't we have to return her this ship?" Petra looked around behind hir cradle. "It's beautiful. I've never seen a ship like this before."

"I have." They weren't often good memories.

"A UN ship?" Petra was scanning the ship data. "These specs... this ship's worth a fortune. And it was just sitting out there in the open?"

"You can't easily steal a ship like this." The UN had a technical name for such ships, but Jinyiwei agents called them chaos butterflies for the damage that they could do in the right hands.

"And your friend parked it right out in the open?"

"The fact that we didn't get hailed on our way out tells me she has important friends in the port." That was Kalina's best guess. She settled into the pilot's cradle, closing her eyes. "Set course to Tosz."

\*    \*    \*

"I'M SHOCKED," PETRA said as ze took the *Name of the Stars* on a steady sail toward the steel bloom of Tosz station from the Gate. "This ship isn't exactly standard issue, is it? Why are we being allowed to dock? Or are we going to get arrested once we berth?"

"Non-standard ships are common in the Neutral Zone, and we're flagged Neutral," Kalina said. Her call through to Harkonnen to report the situation had met with an unusually terse response to steady the course to Tosz station. Yanwang was scrambling Harkonnen. The chaos unsettled her. The Federation and the UN had its serious disagreements before, even during her lifetime, but nothing had screamed 'war-footing' to Kalina as much as this.

"Noticed you put through a different ID for your name," Petra said, looking worried. "Should I have done that?"

"Probably, but it takes time and resources to forge citizen IDs. Even Neutral Zone ones." Kalina was just going to have to take the risk that the VMF had found them on Wollongong by cross-referencing *Selected Poems*. It was much easier to trace a ship than a person.

"Should I call you Isae now?" Petra asked.

Kalina nodded. "In Tosz, certainly."

"I'll have to try and remember that." Petra chewed on hir lower lip and flashed Kalina a smile. "Someday maybe you'd tell me your real name, yeah?"

"I don't have one any longer." The truest name for Kalina was a dragon's name now, one that she had shared with hundreds of people before her in a memory chain of duty that stretched back to an unsteady age of Sol's history. Her birth name had felt irrelevant the moment she had earned it.

"Preferred name, then."

It was her turn to flash Petra a smile. "Isae is my preferred name right now—if you don't want to get us into trouble. We're priority couriers, looking for new business opportunities in the Federation. Definitely not smugglers. We have experience looping around the Wangaratta System. We'll carry anything that's legal and safe."

"I know the drill. Isae it is," Petra said.

Shedding an old cover had grown easier over the years. Qinglong looked at her reflection in the cockpit glass. She relaxed her posture and the marshalled cast of her jaw. Lieutenant Kalina Sokolova had had a harassed competency to her, a ruthless efficiency that had cleaved close to her true character. Isae Ming needed the unflappable calm of a courier, the loose patience of someone who spent most of their time threading between occupied stars. She was reborn between one breath and the next.

Petra looked uneasy when Qinglong glanced at hir. "That's a neat trick."

"A necessary one." Qinglong smoothed out her Galactic.

The *Name of the Stars* docked at the civilian section of the port and paid its exorbitant non-citizen fees. Petra was sour as they docked. "That's a ridiculous sum of money," ze kept saying.

"We're not meant to be a Federation ship. Happy shore leave. I'll ping you when we have to get back, but I'm not sure when that might be." Qinglong's wristdeck had quietly linked itself to station records, but *Song of Gabriel*

*Descending* hadn't docked yet at Tosz station. It'd logged a berth request through a packet from a different system. Given the size of the ship, even if it came to Tosz without using the Gate, it'd still have to jump in at a safe distance and cruise over.

"Happy shore leave," Petra said. Ze looked uneasy.

At least VMF ports were extremely efficient. Qinglong cleared customs within an hour, and was spat out from the port into a busy thoroughfare packed with bars and diners. Three VMF warships hung against the stars beyond the biodome, all of them destroyers. It was a many-toothed presence for an old station that had long lost its strategic position as star maps and territories expanded. Tosz still did a brisk business in repairs and refueling for this part of Federation space, but its ever-encroaching civilian sector indicated that tourism probably made for a significant percentage of the station's revenue.

As one of the oldest stations outside the Milky Way, Tosz had once been the VMF's staging point for several famous battles. Qinglong paused as a wall she approached lit up into a scrolling infographic littered with text and imagery. Clips of centuries-old warships cruising slowly into battle trailed after her as she pretended to study the wall with open interest. At the end of the infographic, the system sent Qinglong the location of a few nearby museums and monuments. For the sake of appearances, she visited a couple, booked herself into a decent hotel, and made a show of sniffing out work. There were a few open contracts on the local network, but those belonging to the Jinyiwei were easy enough for Qinglong to spot.

Hoping that there wasn't going to be a repeat of what happened at Wollongong, Qinglong indicated her interest in the contract and was pinged with the location of a bar.

It was one of those longbrew places decked out in faux wood and brass, serving shots in spun glass globes along with overpriced mouthfuls, prettily printed. Qinglong's contact was squeezed into the backroom, smoking something spicy that made Qinglong lightheaded even through her implants. She glanced at her wristdeck for the pronoun update and sat opposite the contact, who inclined his head. He was built like a drum, his thick brown fingers curled delicately over a globe of orange fluid and the slender flute of a substance re-processor. As he smiled, his round face creased liberally into gentle wrinkles.

"Hello," he said, in accented Galactic.

"I'm here about the contract," Qinglong said, in her now-perfect Galactic.

"Via the *Name of the Stars*, I see."

"The same."

"I knew its previous owner."

"She's still very much the owner. I'm a sub-contractor."

"Ah. Good to hear." The contact wasn't a Jinyiwei agent, if Qinglong had to guess. He looked more like a field contact—one of many burrowed deep in the sprawling recesses of the Federation. The VMF had their own within UN territory, an occasionally deadly game that was amusing to no one. "Name's Ruiz."

"Isae. Hear you have cargo you want moved to Tosz."

"I'm a purveyor of rare spirits, wines, 'shine, anything that's interesting, rare, and even remotely alcoholic," Ruiz said. He gestured gracefully in the direction of the bar. "Tourist money makes it worth paying someone a little extra for the good stuff."

They haggled travel budgets and locations, and drank to a deal well-closed. Ruiz relaxed fractionally into his seat, crossing his legs. "By the way," he said, "I hear you have competition of sorts coming by."

"Of sorts. Retired, but I hear he's put his hand back into the game."

"Need me to steer him your way if he makes contact?"

"No." If Tielong tried to use any Jinyiwei contacts at this point, after the bridges he'd burned, Qinglong would be suspicious of him and Ruiz both. "I'll find him on my own. I *would* like to hear news about some acquaintances of mine who moved from here to Buran for work recently."

"Yeah, I heard." Ruiz's eyes flicked to the door and back. "Did a check. Troublemakers to a hair, quiet as they were."

The transferees had been part of The Silent. Not that Qinglong had expected anything else. "What kind of troublemakers?"

"Roman, I believe."

Qinglong scowled. "Any proof of that?"

"I've forwarded it to our mutual friends. Nothing incredibly conclusive. They've been fairly good at covering their trail." Ruiz glanced at the door again.

"Something up?" Qinglong asked. She kept her boots pressed flat to the floor.

"What do you mean?" Ruiz looked back at her. He didn't appear to be anything but relaxed, but Qinglong nodded curtly and got to her feet.

"Pleasure doing business with you," Qinglong said. She kept her hands loose at her sides as she let herself out of the room. Ruiz merely nodded and kept smoking. No one in the corridor. Qinglong backed further down instead of heading out of the bar. She let herself out of the exit at the back, which opened into the narrow maintenance walkway within the innermost layer of the station hull. Empty. Qinglong walked.

When the microscopic bug that she'd breathed into the air back in the bar didn't register Ruiz doing much more than smoke, Qinglong finally let herself relax. Better to be prepared than dead. She checked the list of request acquisitions that Ruiz had pinged to her. Most were filler. The entry she was looking for was close to the bottom, a request for brandy from an R. Arsov, and a shop location on Kestrel station, off Falcon Colony.

# CHAPTER TWENTY

Solitaire had indeed been to Tosz station a long time ago, before it had opened its civilian sector. He wasn't sure what had possessed him to confide that detail with Viktor. Something about Viktor, strangely enough, inspired confidence and trust in him, despite how cold he was at the best of times. Viktor took the transport down to the station with Solitaire, Indira, Pablo, and a detail of VMF Marines. Once berthed, Viktor spoke quietly to the harbormaster, then motioned for Solitaire to follow him.

In a station as busy as this one, there wasn't much privacy. Viktor settled for walking them over to the next berth, which was still empty. "I cannot say that it's been a pleasure," Viktor said, though he smiled, giving lie to his words.

"Well, not all of it," Solitaire agreed. For a moment, he nearly asked if he could stay, but he swallowed *that* thought in his next breath. The VMF was trouble. "Good luck with your… whatever you're even doing. This whole awful business."

Viktor nodded, a little jerkily. "Perhaps after it all,

we should have a drink." His words were guarded, and his eyes flicked behind Solitaire's shoulder, checking for listeners.

"I'll buy the first round." They shook hands, which felt inadequate. Solitaire stared at Viktor's mouth, which he remembered with intimate detail. It was softer than it looked. He smiled instead, pulled off a playful, deliberately sloppy VMF salute. Viktor rolled his eyes, which made Solitaire laugh, before returning to his men, his poise proud and straight-backed.

Indira and Pablo fell in as Solitaire made his way towards the civilian side of the docks. "We try and buy a ship from here?" Pablo asked.

Solitaire tried not to look pleased. "You two haven't had enough?"

"Strangely, not yet," Indira said. She looked grim. "I don't like this. All of this. The ghost ships, the VMF losing control, the UN being so trigger-happy. Pablo and I left the UN with honorable discharges. They still opened fire."

"Something's wrong," Solitaire agreed. "Hyun doesn't throw random people into Harkonnen for no reason."

"Yet you're both curious." Pablo sounded tired.

"Sorry," Solitaire told him. "You don't have to come. You're owed a third of what we did get from Lau. You too, Indira. As it is, we'd probably have to lie low for a bit until the UN loses interest in us."

"As though you'd buy anything better than a hopper with just a third share of what we've got." Indira sniffed. "I don't know if we can get a good ship off a VMF station though. Either way, it's going to clean us out."

"Easy come, easy go." Depressing as it was to think about it. "Let's get a drink."

Tosz still did have good bars. Even in the civilian sector. Solitaire bought the first round, and they watched the news from the counter. The sound had been turned down low from the feed deck, and as Solitaire thought, there was no news about the ghost ships or the cleaned-out shipyards. There *was* a brief segment about negotiations with the UN over an unnamed ship that had 'malfunctioned', which were, apparently, progressing well.

"How do they even make vodka in space?" Pablo stared suspiciously at his glass. "Do they have potatoes in space? Or are VMF replicators this advanced?"

Indira glanced at Solitaire. "At least there's *some* news. I'm surprised."

"Never been in a Federation anything before?"

"Nope."

No wonder. "Relax. You look like you're expecting Service agents to jump out of the woodwork. Despite what you've heard, it's not that different from the UN. State-run media for *everyone*."

"Solitaire," she warned.

"It's not that bad, seriously. Unlike the UN, they have an open opposition group. Granted, occasionally the group will gain a little more power than the VMF's comfortable with and they end up sent away to distant colony mines, but they're around." With what was once Sol-China still more or less in charge of the UN and UN policy, things on UN territories could be deadly for dissidents.

"You think the opposition group is the problem here?" Indira asked. "Who's the one in charge now, Dina something, right? She did some hunger strike a few years back. Head of some Anti-Corruption Association?"

"Moskvoretskaya, yes." Moskvoretskaya had been a bit of a rising star in the so-called rebellion when Solitaire had been in the Jinyiwei, and after her mentor Yulia Vostok had been sent to the mines, supposedly for tax evasion, she'd taken control of the movement. "Doubt it. They're still into non-violent everything. Think they started calling themselves The Silent."

The next charter flight to a Neutral Zone was in a day, and like many VMF-affiliated stations, Tosz wasn't about to sell any ship to a non-Federation cit. Solitaire split Lau's advance between them and told Pablo and Indira to meet him at the docks once he arranged for a flight. Indira wandered off, hopefully just to explore, and Pablo hung back indecisively before scooting after her.

Solitaire went back to the bar. He was a little tempted to fall into bad habits, to sneak around the station, maybe to check on Viktor, maybe to keep his hand in. Reason soon overtook his curiosity. He sat quietly at the bar counter, instead, nursing a drink, and booked a room at the nearby capsule hotel once he was getting tipsy. It had a functional cleanser, at least. He used it on himself and on his clothes, and went to sleep.

The ground floor of the hotel had a half-decent diner with strong coffee and healthy breakfast portions. Solitaire sat in a corner and savored the coffee, watching the sector wake up. Most of the people up at this hour were spacers, passing through, and all of them had the pinched-faced power-walk of people who wished they'd docked somewhere else. Solitaire could commiserate.

He was spooning the last of the reconstituted semolina porridge into his mouth when the Jinyiwei agent sat at his table. Qinglong smiled at Solitaire as he froze. She didn't look like she had aged much—her dark hair was combed into the same glossy bob that Solitaire remembered, her dark eyes narrowed with a familiar ruthless amusement. Like Solitaire, her name had been awarded to her at the Jinyiwei Academy, the name of a dragon. Unlike Solitaire, hers was a color of the highest grade, taking after a creature that had once been not only considered one of the Five Deities of ancient Sol-Chinese mythology, but also one of the Four Symbols of its constellation. While there was technically no ranking difference between the Jinyiwei dragons, the ones given the name 'Qinglong' were often given the most difficult and most sensitive missions. Prior to Qinglong being awarded her color, the name had been left unbestowed for a decade. What was she doing here?

"What a surprise," Solitaire said, trying to hide his unease.

Qinglong pursed her lips. She was dressed in a trim unmarked suit, the sort that long haul cargo skippers preferred. One of a thousand on any station. "You've been very naughty, I hear."

"Surprised?"

"Not really," Qinglong said, and turned to order a coffee from the serving droid as it hovered by. "I'm surprised it took you this long to get into this much trouble, to be honest."

"Ouch." Solitaire kept his feet flat on the ground, his hands loose on the table. Qinglong wouldn't start anything she couldn't quickly finish in a VMF station. Probably. "In my defense, I really don't like Harkonnen."

"What about it?"

"Apparently, Hyun was going to invite us there."

Qinglong frowned. "Wasn't what I heard. Why the hell would he bother? You weren't in that much trouble. *Now*, though, that's another story."

*Hyun wasn't...?* Solitaire hid his surprise by sipping his coffee. Either Qinglong was lying, or, depressingly enough, perhaps Shore had lied. Or Viktor. Given the general scenario, though, Solitaire had a bad feeling about ghost ships in general. "Possibly, I might have trusted the wrong people," he conceded.

Qinglong nodded. "Hyun says he's sorry about your crew."

"Is he?" Solitaire managed a smile.

"Probably not. You know how he is. He said that he did stop the Admiral from firing on your new ship."

"Doubt that's for my sake. Murdering a VMF Captain is not a good look, peace treaty wise."

Qinglong chuckled. They both knew Hyun didn't care about such niceties. If he'd decided to let Solitaire and Viktor go, there had to be some other reason. Probably the same reason why Qinglong was here. Solitaire had once been on good terms with her, but he knew that she wasn't that sentimental. "All our new Ravens have trackers, by the way. Very new. Can't be found by radar or scans. Interesting how our stolen Raven's been Gating around the 'verse without any Captains."

"That *is* interesting."

"I see you're going to be difficult," Qinglong said, with mock sadness. "I could get you stranded here if I wanted to."

"You're not that good," Solitaire said.

"Try me."

"I'm not inclined to be helpful, given what happened to my crew, and I'm seriously allergic to threats. You remember that, don't you?"

Qinglong exhaled. "Oh yes. I told them. But you know how it goes."

Solitaire did. Sometimes missions could get very annoyingly specific. "Tell Hyun I might be inclined to be more helpful with adequate compensation."

"I've got a ship. If you cooperate, I might even take you to any port of call you like."

"Nice try," Solitaire began, just as the news feed at the diner flicked on. There was an electronic snarl, pitched high enough that a spacer woman at the far end of the diner yelped as she spilt coffee over herself.

Qinglong winced. "Something wrong with the speakers?"

A shifting, static-filled image came on, a death's head hawkmoth on a stark white background, its wings motionless. "Citizens of the Federation," a harsh, electronic voice spoke. "Greetings from the Core."

Qinglong narrowed her eyes when she saw Solitaire tense. She shifted in her seat, pressing her back to the corner of the bench, placing the diner in her peripheral vision. "As you may or may not have heard," the voice continued, "war has been declared. We may have fired the first shot, but we will fire the last shot, as well. When the Federation is dust. When the UN is dust. When all Zones are a Neutral Zone.

"We do not wish for war. But we know that war is inevitable. An ancient pre-Ascent text once advised, 'If someone comes to kill you, rise up and kill him first.' We know you will come for us. The Admiralty, the Assembly, all if it. We will wait. We have no quarrel with most of you—if you stay out of our way.

"As to our sisters still in the VMF, we know you can hear us. Join us. Vent your crews. Look for us in the dark between the stars. This is your only warning. Side with your masters, and you will be destroyed."

The news feed faded to nothing. The spacers in the

diners looked at each other, bewildered. Solitaire exhaled and glanced at Qinglong. "I don't like having blasters pointed at me," he told her, when he noted that neither of her hands were on the table any longer.

"Talk."

Solitaire rubbed his face slowly. So much for lying low. "About that offer of a ride out of here. How soon can we leave?"

"Whenever you like."

"Let's round up my crew, then." As Qinglong started to object, Solitaire said, "We're going to have to skip over to Kestrel station."

"Why?"

"Let's say I was recently in a certain inconvenient place and recognized a name that reminded me of another name," Solitaire said. He grimaced, despite himself. Roman Arsov was nowhere near his favorite person, and the feeling was mutual.

"Interesting," Qinglong said, in a way that told Solitaire that she knew perfectly well who was on Kestrel station. "Fine. I'll scare up my pilot. Meet me at berth thirty eight in a couple of hours."

SOLITAIRE SHOWED UP nicely on time, trailing his two surviving associates. Qinglong had spent the morning reading their files. Beside her, Petra straightened up from where hir had been sitting on the ramp. "Indira and Pablo," Solitaire said. He gestured in turn. "What are you going by nowadays?" asked Solitaire.

"Isac," Qinglong said. She nodded at Petra. "This is Petra, my pilot. Petra, this is Solitaire Yeung, an old friend of mine."

"Pleased," Petra said, glancing curiously at Solitaire, then the others.

"What the hell, Yeung." Pablo gawked at the ship at berth. "Shee-*uttt*. I lose sight of you for a minute, and you fall right back into your bad habits."

"Yes, well, when Isae told me she had a ship, I somehow wasn't expecting a chaos butterfly," Solitaire said. He smiled warmly at Qinglong, a gracefully sketched gesture of charm made incomplete by the hard look in his eyes. "Looking to start a war, are we?"

"Don't exaggerate. You want to get to Kestrel? Let's go." Qinglong jerked her thumb at the ship.

"This is *Name of the Stars*, isn't it? Where's the previous owner?" Solitaire asked. Noticing Qinglong's surprise, he said, "I've run into her now and then. Had to pass Wollongong before for a thing. That gold stripe she painted on the ventral fin's still there."

"She's fine. If you want to see her again, I'll be returning this ship to her sooner or later." At Qinglong's gesture, Petra took a final look at Solitaire and his crew before walking up the ramp. Qinglong followed. After a hushed conversation, Solitaire trudged up the ramp with Indira and Pablo behind him.

Qinglong sat at the pilot's cradle with Petra at the co-pilot's position. Solitaire said not one word until they'd disengaged from the station and were on a steady course to the Gate. "You're surprisingly eager to help," he said.

"'Eager' is an overstatement," Qinglong said. She glanced out of the cradle at Solitaire and his friends. "We have a few mutual friends who are extremely interested in your ability to be consistently at the center of trouble in this matter."

"She's got a point," Indira said.

Solitaire scowled. "I hardly had a choice about any of that." Pablo made an incredulous noise. "Some of that. Okay. Sure. Maybe I made some bad choices that escalated in new and unusual ways."

"I'm going to remember that line in case I ever get arrested for anything," Petra said.

Solitaire glowered at them. "Excuse me, who are you again?"

"Don't be rude. Ze has a point. What in tian possessed you, of all people, to loot a VMF warship?" Qinglong asked.

"I told him," Indira muttered.

"I didn't think there'd be an ASI on it!" At Qinglong's warning snort, Solitaire shrank back and said, "VMF salvage sells for a premium to UN brokers. I thought it was just a normal ship. Originally, I thought I could find something easy to lift and sneak off before their salvage arrived. Wasn't like I wouldn't know where to look. After that, I maybe got slightly infected by patriotism. I thought that the UN might like to know what the pod was."

Qinglong looked unimpressed. "You're trying to tell me that you did all this for the greater good? You?"

Solitaire had long lost his capacity for shame. He grinned at Qinglong. "Well, sure. Believe me or not. It was a spasm of an impulse that turned out to be a bad idea—I know that now. You can stop staring at me."

"Good," Pablo said encouragingly. He patted Solitaire on the arm. "That's the first step to getting help. Knowing that you have a problem."

Solitaire clasped Pablo's hand and looked solemnly into his eyes. "I'll meditate on it," he said.

"Tian, you're still so full of shit," Qinglong muttered.

"Why are we going to Falcon?" Indira asked as the

Gate slowly grew larger in the distance. It'd take them the better part of a day to get to it. "It's an ice ball of a colony, isn't it? What does it even make?"

"Electronics, last I heard," Solitaire said.

"And we're going there because…?" Indira asked. Met with silence, she frowned. "Don't evade the question. I think we've been through enough because of you, haven't we?"

"There's someone I used to know there," Solitaire said, "back when I was still an agent. He eventually became a big shot in The Silent, but when I met him, he was a successful information broker doing business out of New Siam. He owes me a favor. I was thinking of cashing it in."

"What's this guy's name?" Qinglong asked.

She was careful to sound indifferent, but Solitaire chuckled. "You probably know it already. Come on. I'm retired, not ignorant. Space is immense. You just happening to be on Tosz station with a chaos butterfly right as I just happened to need a ride is a pretty huge coincidence."

Petra glanced at Qinglong. When she merely sniffed, Petra looked back to hir console. "Good to see that your instincts are semi-functional again. Yes. We do have an interest in Roman Arsov," Qinglong said.

"Back onto the Jinyiwei 'we', *hm*? That takes me back," Solitaire said.

"You'd need to go even further back to be useful again, I think. What with raiding a VMF ship and then somehow running afoul of at least two different ASIs. Hear you negotiated with some of them directly somehow," Qinglong said.

"You don't need to sound so skeptical. And I wouldn't

have called it 'negotiating'. They did what they wanted, and I was just along for the ride." Solitaire sounded contemplative. "In a way, it was kinda a microcosm for what's happening with the Core. Even if the ASIs I dealt with weren't part of it. Why do they have to negotiate with people?"

"Stardrive seeds," Petra said.

"They can get those without playing nice. With all the destruction they've caused so far, there'd be shipyards out there willing to front stardrive seeds for safety." Solitaire sounded like he was sinking into his seat. They flew in silence, entering podsleep without comment. The *Name of the Stars* had just enough pods for everyone.

Qinglong entered podsleep intending to wake up earlier than everyone and make her usual report. She was unsurprised to see Solitaire jolting awake as well. He let her use the cleanser first and was shivering when he joined her at the cockpit. "Calling home?" Solitaire asked.

"Obviously."

Solitaire sighed. "I know I've given you no reason to trust me. But I've got as much interest in resolving this business of the Core as you do."

"They blew up a station over you, so I hope you do."

Solitaire stared at her, startled at the venom in her voice. "What would you have done in my shoes?"

"Sent an emergency broadcast. Handed myself over."

"To die?"

"That's never a certainty where people like us are involved. And if so, so what? Better us than an entire fucking *station*. Tian, Tielong. A *station* died because of you."

Something hardened in Solitaire's face. "Blaming the victim? Nice."

"You're not the victim. If you think you are, retirement has made you delusional."

That shut Solitaire up for a moment. He looked out of the cockpit, pensive. "I didn't think they'd fire on the station. It isn't like they gave anyone that much time to maneuver."

"Psychotic ASIs mapped from the brains of a bunch of VMF Admirals? Not firing on things?"

"I didn't know that at the time," Solitaire said with a helpless gesture. "I thought it was just a VMF faction of some sort, and the VMF's never attacked a Neutral Zone station before. Never caused civilian fatalities on this kind of scale."

"You should've assumed the worst." Qinglong set the ship to ping Harkonnen. They were cruising out of the Gate on a gentle course toward a distant blue dot. Kestrel station was a couple of days' out from its Gate, nestled in a sector of space sprinkled with slow-twirling asteroids. The star was a distant idea, its indifferent light a pale blip within its crowded cloak of debris.

"I suppose." Solitaire sounded subdued.

"You haven't changed much after all," Qinglong said, with a short laugh. "You've always lacked a basic degree of human empathy. It made you an excellent agent."

"*You're lecturing me* about empathy?" Solitaire said, incredulous. He wore the anticipatory stillness of a trained killer gearing for a fight. "You, who once sabotaged a medical ship to get rid of one target."

"It's not a lecture. I'm aware of what I've done, I was there. I'm honest to myself about my motives and my methods." Qinglong stared coolly at Solitaire. "You caused the death of a station because of your selfishness. Because you don't want to die." Solitaire stared back at her, his jaw clenched tight. "Sooner you recognize that the better."

"Why?"

"Everyone has to grow up sometime," Qinglong said.

The connection from Harkonnen resolved itself into Commander Hyun's unsmiling face. He looked at Solitaire with an air of paternal disappointment. "I should get Qinglong to vent you into space," he said.

"Pretty sure she's tempted." Solitaire made a show of winking at Qinglong, who ignored him. "What do you want us to do about Arsov?"

"Bring him in. Quietly, if you can manage that," Hyun said, "though I have my doubts."

"Ouch," Solitaire said.

"Speak for yourself," Qinglong told him.

"Something interesting's happening in the VMF." Hyun ignored their bickering. "Admiral Kasparov's been taken into custody. I do believe all the so-called Kwang ships will be recalled to Gagarin station soon. It seems that a purge is now at hand."

Solitaire's smile was a fraction of a second too late. "Chaos is good for us, isn't it?"

Hyun gave him an unimpressed stare. "It's clear to us that you haven't taken sides for a long time, Yeung. Help Qinglong bring in Arsov and your recent indiscretions will be forgotten. If there's a fuckup, I'll settle for Qinglong bringing in your hide instead of Arsov's. Understand?"

"Yes," Qinglong said. Solitaire nodded slowly.

"Now, I think I'm owed the full godsdamned story, aren't I?" Hyun glowered at Solitaire.

"The truth and nothing but the truth?" Solitaire quipped. He looked more tired than amused.

"The truth, and if at any point I think you're leaving

something out or lying to me, Qinglong has full authority to hurt you in a creative way."

"With pleasure, sir," Qinglong said.

"Knew I shouldn't have come aboard this ship," Solitaire muttered.

# CHAPTER TWENTY-ONE

TOSZ WAS A dead end. The relevant security footage of the transferees heading to Buran had been thoroughly erased, and not even Ship could piece together anything useful. As far as Viktor could tell, the twelve people had passed from Tosz to Buran like ghosts. Viktor thought about contacting Solitaire again, but the corsair had wrangled passage on a civilian ship off-world. Ship had offered to investigate further, but Viktor had said that it wasn't worth the resources. He wished he was less regretful about that than he was. Especially since Viktor had far more to worry about right now.

As he washed his face over the sink, Ship said, "Everyone's back."

"What do you mean?" Viktor choked out.

"The rest of the Ships like me. We're all back. We're the last to arrive. *Wild Hunt's* been here for a while, getting repaired. *Death from Above* arrived half a day ago."

Viktor frowned to himself. It had taken time to ride a transport back to the *Gabriel*, and some time to Gate out, but even if *Death from Above* had been idle when it had received marching orders, it shouldn't have beaten them to Gagarin station with so much time to spare. Unless it had been told to return first. The Admiralty was staggering their arrivals.

"They don't trust us anymore." Ship guessed at Viktor's unease with uncanny accuracy.

"Speak for yourself," Viktor said. Another purge? So soon? Viktor flattened his disorientation until he was breathing easily again. He dressed and headed for the Bridge, where orders from Gagarin were already waiting for him in a terse statement. Engage a lock on the ASI using his Captain codes. Approach Gagarin for boarding for 'decontamination' procedures. Beside the Captain's chair, Petrenko said nothing, but his tight, wan face was statement enough.

"Viktor," Ship said into his ear. It sounded worried.

Viktor considered telling Ship to either shut up or call him by his title. He slowly sat down on the Captain's chair instead. "The other Ships?" he murmured.

"Same orders. *Death from Above*'s Captain Mayakovskaya is carrying them out. Captain Gorokova's put forward a polite query from the *Wild Hunt*."

This was a test of loyalty. Or not. The long oeuvre of Viktor's career had long accustomed him to the ruthlessness with which the Admiralty tended to approach its problems. "Put through a call to Counter-Admiral Shevchenko."

"Sir," Petrenko said. He looked like he was about to disagree, but when Viktor stared at him, his gaze dropped to his feet. Ship put through the call request. No response. Instead, Gagarin forwarded a copy of its terse orders back to the Ship.

Viktor let out a low breath, twisting his hands over

the armrests of his seat. Something was wrong. Yet this was his life, the span and breadth of it across the stars, and without its constraints, he was no one he recognized. "Engage ASI lock. We surrender for boarding."

"Viktor." This time, Ship sounded frightened. Viktor's hand hesitated over the console projected before him. He pushed out a thin breath between clenched teeth and entered in his Captain's codes quickly, deliberately getting the last digit wrong. Ship gasped softly in his ear, and began to 'shut down' into basic processes as Viktor's heart shook close to bursting in his chest. Not even Petrenko had noticed anything amiss.

"Captain Gorokova just did the same thing for the *Hunt*," Ship said. Viktor pretended to bring up and study the local news feed and froze as he read the top four headlines.

"Counter-Admiral Kasparov's been arrested?" he said incredulously. Petrenko stepped over to scan the feed and straightened up, hands clenched behind his back.

"Surely there's been a mistake, sir," Petrenko said.

"It's not a mistake." Viktor had thought his data incriminating, but somehow, he hadn't imagined that the Admiralty would ever turn on Kasparov. Not like this. Surely the fallout would be immense—Kasparov was the most popular living Admiral across the Federation. He'd thought that Kasparov would've received a slap on the wrist. Isolation for a while, perhaps. Especially with the new threat from the Core.

The official Admiralty statement was terse on the details. Kasparov was under house arrest at an undisclosed location and was cooperating with the authorities. He was being held in relation to recent 'unfortunate events' related to his missing aide, Lieutenant Kalina Sokolova.

A search was being conducted for the lieutenant, and the public was encouraged to contact the VMF should they have any information about her whereabouts. Viktor scanned news articles in silence as *Gabriel* submitted to boarding. His escort off the ship with the rest of the key chain of command aboard the *Gabriel* was polite but unsettlingly firm.

Having thought that he would be sent straight to a cell, Viktor was a little surprised to be delivered straight to the Admiralty. He was taken to an upper floor and marched through harried shoals of lieutenants and clerks. Vidlink technology meant that face-to-face contact was usually unnecessary for the conduct of usual business. The Admiralty was concerned about security, maybe. Or trust.

Admiral Mikhailova was an imposing woman—nearly as tall as Viktor, and built like a wall. She wore ruthlessness well, her sharp-angled face imposing but not overly cruel. She sat at her elegant desk with her body angled forward, her arms folded before the bars and bars of honors on her uniform, the medals the brightest points of color in an otherwise austere cavern of an office. Shevchenko stood by her left, Kasparov on her right. Viktor stared.

"Captain Kulagin," Mikhailova said. Viktor saluted, not trusting his voice. "You may have questions."

"No sir," Viktor lied.

Kasparov chuckled. He glanced at Shevchenko, who pointedly ignored him, opting instead to stare at a point beyond Viktor's shoulder. "I like this one," Kasparov told Shevchenko anyway. "He's not tedious, like your usual protégés."

"I charge you to speak plainly," Mikhailova said. She sounded impatient. "I've read your report from Buran in full. What are your recommendations?"

There was no point protesting about being unqualified, not when three Admirals were now watching him with interest. "Counter-Admiral Kasparov has been in contact with The Silent."

"Revolutionaries, but tolerated revolutionaries," Kasparov said.

"Quiet, Yuri. Continue," Mikhailova told Viktor.

"I believe he did so out of grief following the loss of his daughter. It was likely why Sasha Makarovna was also involved, and why Lieutenant Sokolova, an otherwise unremarkable officer, was persuaded to work against VMF interests," Viktor said.

Shevchenko let out a snort. "Kalina was a Jinyiwei agent," Kasparov said. At Viktor's startled look, Kasparov said, "Sent to spy on me, I think. Or kill me eventually, who knows."

"And you just played house with her all this time," Shevchenko growled. "You're either a traitor or a lunatic, neither of which is Admir—"

"Grigor, silence." Mikhailova cut in. "Captain Kulagin."

"Where is Sokolova now?" Viktor asked.

"Last heard of on Wollongong, but she's slipped the net. We have agents on her tail, but given all that she has done, she isn't relevant right now to your report," Mikhailova said.

"I think the Core is one of the greatest threats to the Federation in a long time." Viktor chose his words with care. "Not just the Federation, but humanity. Humanity has always feared what ASIs could become. I think punishing Counter-Admiral Kasparov is a necessity but also a waste. I think mistrusting the friendly ASIs that we have is a necessity but a waste. I think we need more

Kwang ships. I think we have to root out the people who are helping the Core. I recommend that we work with the UN."

Shevchenko made an annoyed noise even as Kasparov chuckled. "See what I mean," he told Mikhailova. She held up a gloved palm in his direction.

"You destroyed one of the Admiralty Ships by yourself," Mikhailova said.

"Not by myself. I had a full team of agents, and the Ship was distracted by another target," Viktor said. He'd recommended his whole team for posthumous honors.

"You're honest, at least. I like that in an officer. It's refreshing," Mikhailova said. She leaned back in her chair, rubbing her temple. "What a mess."

"We should do a full inventory of all the Eva Ships. Root out the rest of The Silent, particularly Moskvoretskaya. Find and retrieve the missing Kwang Core. Lockdown all existing shipyards and stardrive seed factories. We can starve out those ships," Shevchenko said.

"That might work if the Federation was the only source of stardrive seeds in the universe—which it isn't," Kasparov said.

Shevchenko grunted. "Let the UN and the Neutrals fend for themselves."

Viktor started to shake his head and went still as he realized the Admirals were all looking at him again. "Captain?" Mikhailova prompted.

"Even if they could," Viktor said, trying to keep his tone as flat as possible, "it may exacerbate the problem. Space is too large for us to deal with the Core without cooperation with the rest of the universe. You heard their declaration of war—it was against both the UN and the Federation. Further, should the Core be eradicated while we enforce isolation, it would lead to war regardless. A war in which the UN and the Neutral Zones were allied against us."

Shevchenko's lip curled. "We'll deal with that as we always have. It's not a Captain's place to speak on matters as important as these."

"I was interested in his opinion, Grigor." Mikhailova glowered at Shevchenko. "Behave, or leave—it's up to you."

"I see that my opinion isn't necessary for this discussion," Shevchenko said. He saluted Mikhailova stiffly and left in long strides. Viktor pressed his lips into a thin line, his gut twisting. He owed Shevchenko. For the chances he had been given, for the life he now had. The old man would not forgive Viktor for this.

"That gave you no pleasure," Kasparov said.

"Should it?" Viktor glanced up. He tried to fold his anger and resentment away, but as always, it just festered under his skin.

"You're too honest to be working for him." Kasparov ambled over and walked a slow circle around Viktor as Viktor stiffened into parade rest. "Wouldn't have made him out to be a Service agent," Kasparov told Mikhailova.

"He's obviously good," Mikhailova said.

"Good enough for a few more colorful bars on his chest but not good enough to be feted as a hero, *hm*." Kasparov slouched into a chair. "Is it still too politically inconvenient to celebrate the only child of Alexander Kulagin?"

"You know politics." Mikhailova looked bored with the statement. Viktor clenched his hands tightly behind his back and somehow managed to say nothing.

"I'm useful because of the things that I know. Or can

guess." Kasparov shot Viktor a kindly smile. "Didn't actually override your ASI, did you?"

"Sir?" Viktor said. Had *Gabriel*...?

"Oh, we haven't done an onboard check. But I suspect that if we did, aboard your ship, and probably the *Wild Hunt*, we'd find a few little anomalies that would've been interesting to a late friend of mine," Kasparov said.

Mikhailova studied Viktor's face keenly. She huffed. "Right again," she said.

"Don't panic. Having some spine is a good thing, in my opinion." Kasparov got to his feet, clapping Viktor on the arm. Viktor flinched. "He'll do," Kasparov told Mikhailova.

"You're certain," Mikhailova said.

"Nothing about this mess is certain. That's what I like about it." Kasparov nodded at Viktor. "Captain Mayakovskaya's not a Service agent, but she used to serve under Lavro. Captain Gorokova is Iosif's niece. That'd usually make either of them more attractive prospects to me, but Captain Kulagin here's had a part in taking down a Core ship. Puts him in the lead, despite his ties to Grigor."

"Sir," Viktor said. He was ignored.

"Grigor would be pleased," Mikhailova said. "Or not. He might think that you're trying to poach one of his own."

"You'd think that venal politics would be beneath us all when there's an existential threat to our civilization out and about." Kasparov pulled a face.

"Don't be dramatic." Mikhailova turned to Viktor. "Counter-Admiral Kasparov is officially going to be consigned to investigation and house arrest at an undisclosed location in the Federation. Lieutenant

Petrenko will accompany him. He will be replaced aboard your ship by Lieutenant Yuri Alekhine over here." She gestured at Kasparov, who inclined his head.

"Reconstructive facial surgery should be good enough for verisimilitude," Kasparov said. As Viktor started to shake his head, Kasparov held up a palm. "No doubt as a Service agent you'd be able to let me know what else I'm lacking in an undercover capacity."

"May I speak bluntly?" Viktor said. He remembered to tack on "Sir," after a moment's pause.

Kasparov smiled. "Proceed, Captain," Mikhailova said.

"There's no point." Viktor tried looking Mikhailova in the eye, but she had an unsettlingly grim and unblinking stare. As Viktor dropped his gaze, he said, "I fail to see why Counter-Admiral Kasparov must enter the field. He is not young, and he has never been a field agent in any capacity. Further, Service agents go through years of training before undertaking deep cover missions. It is not something that can be learned on the fly. Surely whatever observations he requires can be funneled to the Counter-Admiral as they were before."

"What's the problem with observations being sent to me aboard your ship?" Kasparov asked, amused.

"A destroyer is not a secure location. Sir. Nor might we always be within range to receive information packets without delay."

"The VMF's always factored a response delay into my consultations. Besides, you named me a traitor in your report. Should a traitor deserve to be in a secure location?" Kasparov asked.

Viktor started to flush. "I didn't name you a traitor. I sent observations to Counter-Admiral Shevchenko and—"

"You don't think that I'm a traitor?" Kasparov asked.

Viktor looked over at Mikhailova in support but only received a gimlet eye in return. "I think working with The Silent was unwise. Working with a known Jinyiwei agent though? *That* is inexplicable." Viktor was keenly aware of the hypocrisy of his words and was glad that he had spoken them tonelessly.

"That's a nice euphemism for treachery," Kasparov said.

"Have you seen footage of the attack on New Tesla?" Mikhailova asked Viktor.

"Yes, sir."

"Has your ASI shown any particular aptitude in retrieving data from networks in ways that a human counterpart could not have managed?" Mikhailova watched, with grim satisfaction, as understanding dawned on Viktor's face. "Yuri is one of the VMF's great tactical assets. There is no 'secure location' where he would be safe that would not at the same time endanger an unacceptable number of people. Or so he believes." She stared at Kasparov, who smiled and said nothing.

"You will report directly to me. Report to Grigor as well if you like, but I find attempts to game the chain of command amusing at best, and tiresome at worst. You and your Ship will assist Kasparov in his endeavors where so authorized. He remains an invaluable VMF asset. Do you understand, Captain?" Mikhailova asked.

"Yes sir," Viktor said, setting his jaw. "Though I would like to state for the record that I accede to this mission under protest."

"Protest all you like. You are dismissed. Kasparov will contact you once he is ready to leave." Mikhailova waved Viktor out.

Outside the office, Viktor let out a shaky breath. "All right?" Ship murmured.

ANYA OW

"How are you talking to me?" Viktor whispered as he walked briskly to the lifts.

"I tunneled an exception through Station comms. Very carefully. I—wait! There's something wrong. There's something here!"

Overhead alarms shrilled, swallowing Viktor's startled, "What?" A Code Red—all hands on deck.

"This is Admiral Mikhailova," Admiral Mikhailova said into his ear, sounding tense. It sounded like a VMF comms broadcast. "We are under attack. Scrambling all ships. Counter-Admiral Kasparov has overall command."

"It's the Core!" Ship said, horrified. "A destroyer decloaked from stealth—*High Winter*... it's firing on the station!"

Viktor reached the closest lift just as the ground shook under his feet. The station's shields had taken a direct hit. Ship gasped. "It's firing again! It's...!"

Gagarin station could only take a handful of direct hits from a lascannon. Viktor tried to calculate how many even as the lifts whistled open and he lunged in. This time, the ground shaking threw him against the side of the lift even as he punched in the number for the hangar. He knew he'd never get to the *Gabriel* in time to raise ship—not with all his crew not even on board.

"They're firing back, but the ship just Gated. It has to be coming back." Ship said.

"Shoal formation," Kasparov said on the general comms. "Buy time." There was a faint click, then Kasparov said, "Any time now, Eva Captains." He didn't even sound stressed. "Raise ship once you're aboard. No need for the rest of your chain of command if they don't make it there before you."

*Shoal formation?* thought Viktor. "The ships stationed

313

around Gagarin are coming closer. They're spreading out just beyond the station's shields," Ship said.

"That's not an orthodox formation for large ships," Viktor said, surprised. What was Kasparov up to?

"It's reappeared!" Ship cried. "It's firing—oh. I see."

"What?" Viktor had braced himself against the wall even as the lift doors hissed open.

"The ships closest to the station are moving like fish. Close enough to share shields. A destroyer took the hit instead of the station," Ship said. "The ships further out are trying to close in, but it'll take them too long to get in range to help."

Viktor frowned. "Sharing shields? How are they doing something like that? Without an ASI, it'd need too much fine control from too many Captains."

A pause, then Ship said, "Counter-Admiral Kasparov *is* being the ASI. He's assumed direct control of the ships from the station. Like chess pieces."

The Gagarin fleet was the largest of the VMF fleets, easily consisting of eight hundred thousand souls alone aboard nearly seven thousand ships. Viktor couldn't imagine the amount of pressure Kasparov had to be under, doing something like that. Viktor's sprint to the berth felt like it took an eternity. Petrenko had beaten him there, but barely. "Prepare to raise ship once we're aboard," Viktor said, breathing hard as he stumbled through the airlock, then patched through to Kasparov. "Sir, the *Gabriel* stands ready."

"Sending coordinates. Protect Gagarin station. Fire at will," Kasparov said. Instantly, Ship moved in response. Kasparov had instructed them to move to a point dangerously close to the station, just above a point in the residential ring, *behind* the shoal. At this height they had to be alarmingly visible to the people just below, as though on a collision course. Only an ASI could manage the fine control required to stay this close without accidentally damaging the biodome.

"Fire at will, sir?" Viktor asked, confused. They'd risk hitting their allied ships or their shields, packed as they were.

"All Eva Captains, relinquish control of your lascannon and navigation to your Ships," Kasparov said, brisk as ever.

Not so very long ago, Viktor might have protested such an order. Now he input his Captain's codes into the command panel without complaint, noting that none of the other Eva ships, even *Death from Above*, objected for a moment. They were committed now to Kasparov's gambit to save Gagarin station, the way many of them had carried out his orders to the letter galaxies away, trusting in his judgment even though they didn't always understand it. Kasparov had only ever proved himself right. Viktor could only hope that he would be right again now.

"It's the cruiser," Ship said, just as Viktor reached the Bridge and all but jumped into the Captain's chair, seconds after the gigantic blade that was *Ride of the Valkyries* appeared out of nowhere, creating its own constellation of stars with the lights seeded along its flank. As Viktor watched in helpless horror, three of the distant lights grew brighter and brighter yet. Gasps ricocheted across the Bridge as it dawned on the crew what *Valkyries* was about to do. "It's firing on the station!" Ship exclaimed.

The cruiser's multiple lascannons punched a hole through the Sovremenny-class destroyer that happened to be in its way, aiming for the Administrative ring.

Incredibly, Gagarin station's shields held once more, though an awful flicker of pale light crackled over the surface of the station. The dying destroyer's shields had reduced their intensity, but not by much. Another strike on the same area might destroy the station. Just as Viktor opened his mouth to give an order, Captain Gorokova said, "Moving into a hard sail."

On the combat console, the *Wild Hunt* raced to position herself over the weakened shield, even as Ship said, "Fire at will?"

"Fire at will," Viktor said, though he didn't see what Ship was going to do from where they were—until he did. On the combat console, the shields around a destroyer passing above them winked off. Kasparov was going to trust the Eva ASIs to thread the needle. Only Viktor's Service training glued his eyes to the combat visualization, expecting disaster. He could see the defenseless ship above him burning from accidental friendly fire, breaking apart, its hundreds of crew sucked out into space.

Lascannon fire from the Eva ships lanced out from their protective barrier, streaking toward the *Ride of the Valkyries*. Striking it at the same point, with a coordinated precision that few human artillery crews could've managed so casually. *Valkyries'* shields coalesced into a dense disc just before impact but shattered, crumpling into brilliant shards of light visible even to the naked eye. Support fire streaked out from the shoal and from Gagarin's station defenses seconds later, but *Valkyries* was gone, leaving the lances of light to pepper the stars. The Nanuchkas that had poured out from the fleet to attack the *Valkyries* hesitated, confused.

The *Gabriel* slowed, but *Valkyries* didn't reappear. Time crawled by. Viktor's breathing felt loud to his ears, a concussion bellow of heightened tension, pushed beyond fear and dismay to the battle-calm that he welcomed.

"There!" The *Gabriel*'s lascannon charged up again as Viktor scanned the console. It took a second for the onboard system to register the reappearance of *High Winter* and *Ride of the Valkyries*. *High Winter* had Gated just in front of *Valkyries*, the destroyer dwarfed by the cruiser. What was the Core playing at? "They're sharing shields," Ship said, even as lascannon fire from the Eva ships spat forward, earthing themselves into the dense shields just before *High Winter*. "They're—no!"

*Valkyries* returned fire, along with *High Winter*. Aiming for the *Wild Hunt*. Another destroyer pushed into a hard sail, attempting to crest the wreckage and put itself between the gap in the shoal and the *Wild Hunt*, but the lascannon beam punched just past the reach of its shields. The *Wild Hunt* coalesced its shields into a dense disc, but it didn't matter. The disc cracked under the combined firepower, as antigrav beams lancing through the Bridge of the *Wild Hunt*. Viktor cried out as he watched the nose of the *Wild Hunt* disintegrate before his eyes on the console. The rest of the lascannon beam earthed itself on the station's shields, stretching it paper-thin but still holding.

Explosions rocked the flank of *Ride of the Valkyries* where station defenses and the fleet returned fire, blooming against the stars, before the enemy ships Gated.

"Captain Gorokova," Viktor said, trying to page the *Wild Hunt*, even though he knew it was futile. "Do you copy? Captain Gorokova!"

"She's gone," Ship said, her voice breaking. "Poor *Hunt*! I'm so sorry. I'm—" Ship cut herself off, subsiding into sobs. Viktor rubbed his clammy palms against his trousers, waiting for more Core ships to reappear, but the stars stayed empty. The Core had made their point. No one was safe from them—not even in the seat of the VMF's power.

THE SERVICE'S FACILITY in Gagarin was a badly kept secret. It wasn't in the Admiralty sector, for reasons Viktor still didn't understand. It sat incongruously in the middle of Oblako Avenue, a popular tourist thoroughfare flanked by a dense offering of upscale restaurants, bars, and fashion outlets. Viktor's uniform earned him polite glances and the occasional nod, but on a typical day, he would still be jostled by tourists trying to take memory snaps of the planted ceiling. Crimson-leafed plants had been arranged to form a massive sawing pattern down a central emerald stripe. They were a breed of recycler plants, unlovely up close, but their waxy textures and astringent scents glorious from a distance.

Today, Oblako Avenue was uncharacteristically deserted. Civilians, fearful, largely remained in secure bunkers or indoors—after all, everyone had watched two destroyers die. Surely even the VMF's well-oiled propaganda machine couldn't cover this up. It wasn't even much of a defensive victory by any means, and the abrupt about-turn from Kasparov being reportedly arrested to then being given overall command of the Gagarin fleet had sparked confused speculation even aboard the *Gabriel*.

Between a shop that sold space suits in the latest season's styles and a coffee shop was a glass-fronted office. The empty curve of the reception deck was the color of bone, as were the unused benches against the wall. The door scanned Viktor discreetly as he approached, before sliding open to admit him. For years Viktor hadn't understood the point of such a visible entrance to the Service—there were similar fronts like this littered through the Federation. Then he had. The Service was an ugly but necessary part of the VMF. Its blatant presence among all that was expensive and beautiful reminded the Federation and VMF alike that their elegant lives came with a cost, one that they would pay forever.

A long white corridor. A gray lift with no buttons. Viktor got in and closed his eyes, his nerves still keyed up from the battle.

"Captain," Ship said into his ear. He ignored it—he was likely being scrutinized. "I'm here."

Viktor wished he didn't take some comfort from that. Fronts like this had been part of his life since he had graduated from cadet school in the highest percentile. He had given himself willingly to the Service, and for most of that experience, he had not regretted it. He did not know how. Folding his hands behind his back, Viktor listened to the wind. By the length of its hum, he deduced that they had just passed the topmost administrative floor. The handlers' sector. The Basement, where difficult people were broken down and disposed of once they stopped being useful. Down to the Artery. Viktor stepped out into the white corridor and the blast doors sealed behind him. He waited.

"Still here," Ship said. It snickered. "The extra encryption layer is cute, but nothing I haven't seen before. Even when I was still a person."

Viktor swallowed irrational laughter. Ship hadn't been who he had been waiting to hear from. Its voice still relaxed him. Overhead from hidden speakers, Shevchenko said, "Door two."

Door two. Shevchenko was feeling sentimental. The last time Viktor had come to an Artery, it had been in Saint Aksenov City, Konisegg Colony. Behind Door two had been a local politician suspected of taking money from the UN. Viktor had eventually left the room alone, after a fashion.

Viktor was not surprised to see that Shevchenko was not alone in the circular room. Behind him stood a small woman who would not have come up to even Solitaire's shoulder, dressed neatly in a gray suit. She had an unassuming build and face, her brown hair worn short. She was unarmed, but the balletic stillness to her poise told Viktor that this would not be a problem for her.

"This is Marina," Shevchenko said. Marina inclined her head. No other names, no rank—Marina was a Service agent. "You may be working closely with her in the near future."

"'May', sir?" It wasn't like Shevchenko to be imprecise. Shevchenko leaned back in his seat, waving Marina forward. As she took a step toward Viktor, then broke into a charge, he understood.

She was faster than he was. New implants, maybe. Viktor sidestepped her charge and blocked the jab she aimed at his ribs. Ship gasped in his ear. He kicked at Marina's knees, but she had already sidestepped out of the way, darting a lightning set of punches that drove up his guard until she landed a blow in his gut. Grunting, Viktor stumbled back, wincing.

"You're out of practice," Shevchenko said, "but more importantly, you don't have the new updates."

Viktor didn't waste breath answering. If Shevchenko wanted an answer, he would demand it. Viktor feinted a blow at Marina's face, but she didn't take the bait, landing another bruising blow on his ribs. Viktor grabbed her wrist and hauled, heaving her over his shoulder and into the wall. Somehow Marina tore free and rolled with the fall, pushing herself up and back on her feet with a palm.

"Step back!" Ship called into Viktor's ear. He obeyed without thinking, and the heel aimed at his nose passed neatly through air. Viktor yanked at Marina's ankle, hauling her off balance. He tried to pin her to the ground, but she jabbed her elbow into his throat. Coughing, Viktor scrambled back, trying to catch his breath.

"Left shoulder," Ship predicted, a heartbeat before Marina aimed her punch. "Lower ribs. Plexus." It was easier with Ship's predictions. Viktor caught Marina in a vicious uppercut that snapped her head back. She staggered back a few steps and spat blood on the floor. Grinning, Marina swiped her mouth clean against the back of her palm.

"Enough," Shevchenko said. Marina straightened up, saluting. After a resentful second, Viktor returned her salute. Marina walked over to settle into parade rest beside Shevchenko. "Not bad, all of a sudden."

"Thank you, sir. As you noted, I was out of practice," Viktor said.

"Messy battle," Shevchenko said, his lip curling. "Kasparov's losing his touch."

Viktor wanted to say that there was likely nothing more that Kasparov could have done. Gagarin station was a sitting duck against a determined attack from ships that could Gate on will. The fact that they'd survived with only the loss of a destroyer and heavy damage to the *Wild Hunt* felt like a small tactical miracle. "Perhaps the Core wasn't aiming for Gagarin station. They wanted to destroy one of the Eva ships."

Shevchenko grunted. "Obvious enough, given it didn't return after the *Hunt* was destroyed. Kasparov's tactic wouldn't have worked had every Core ship decided to Gate in all at once and fire at the same point."

"Perhaps Kasparov deduced that attacking the station was a feint," Viktor said, then had to school his expression into a blank mask as Shevchenko glowered at him. "I'm not defending his actions. Merely making an observation. Perhaps he had another plan, should that not have been the case."

"I doubt it. I think he gambled the fate of us all on a guess," Shevchenko said sourly, "and the fact that he was right didn't make it any less reckless. Besides, we're also lucky that the *Valkyries* didn't return for a third and final attempt like I thought they would. Surely it was clear that they only needed one more shot to crack Gagarin's shielding."

"Their own shields were down," Viktor said. Though, for a ship of that size, shields didn't matter as much. They didn't need to care about the lives of their crew, and the Core could've sent in another ship to sit above its stardrive while it charged up its cannons for a killing shot. "Gating without a Gate burns seeds. They either couldn't afford a third attempt, or they suffered some malfunction."

"Whatever it was, for all that Kasparov got right, he's in serious political trouble due to the fallout from his ties to The Silent. I'd have had him taken off-duty for this, but Mikhailova's always bowed to Kasparov and his whims. I'd usually have assumed he was fucking her, but as far as I'm aware, Admiral Mikhailova has never been interested in sex or sentiment. Either way. You're his new designated babysitter."

This was a small test—Shevchenko no doubt knew

perfectly well what Kasparov's ploy was. "Assuming that Admiral Mikhailova doesn't change her mind about the assignment after the attack on Gagarin station, Counter-Admiral Kasparov will come aboard my ship as a lieutenant. I presume a body double will be sent into hiding in his place," Viktor said.

"Yes, I know all that," Shevchenko said with an impatient wave. "After all, the Service is providing the VMF with said body double. We've had a few in training for years, rotating through most of Kasparov's less necessary public appearances for security's sake."

"Yes sir," Viktor said. Viktor hadn't been privy to any VMF or Service secrets that didn't pertain to his own work, and his work hadn't ever involved Kasparov's security. Using doubles who were also Service agents made sense. "I've been charged to keep the Counter-Admiral safe."

Shevchenko nodded. "As you should. I can't stand the man, but recent circumstances have shown that he's necessary. For now."

"Until when?"

"That's none of your concern. You're a good asset," Shevchenko said, before Viktor could venture a protest, "and I don't believe in wasting assets. Someday I believe you'll deserve a bigger command. More than a destroyer with a mind of its own."

"You don't like the ASIs?" Viktor asked.

"They've made it abundantly clear that they cannot be trusted. Keep that in mind. Even aboard your own ship," Shevchenko said. He nodded at Marina. "Marina will join the complement of Service agents that you take aboard the *Gabriel*. Command her as you would any of the others. She may occasionally have a suggestion for your ears only. You should take that suggestion as seriously as you would take one from me."

"Understood, sir," Viktor said.

"Mikhailova no doubt instructed you to take the same instruction from Kasparov," Shevchenko said. At Viktor's slow nod, he let out a harsh laugh. "By your own words, the man can't be trusted. Use your judgment. If you have any questions, Marina will be able to help."

"Looking forward to working with you," Marina said. She smiled, showing a line of perfect teeth. "Captain."

Dismissed, Viktor wandered around the sector for half an hour. He drifted through officers and cadets who glanced at his rank and saluted as they passed. His wandering feet took him to an observation deck on the civilian side of Gagarin station, one of the less popular ones. It looked out into space instead of toward the docks or the Gate. Given the events of the day, the deck was empty, giving Viktor the illusion of solitude. Folding his arms behind his back, Viktor stared out at the vastness of everything, so vast that only a hand's span of engineered glass stood between Viktor and an ugly death. He spared a thought for Solitaire Yeung, by now no doubt halfway across the 'verse in another ship, perhaps falling back into old corsair habits. Solitaire was a creature of space in a way that Viktor wasn't.

"Marina scares me a little," Ship said.

"She should."

"Isn't she just like you and the other agents? You didn't scare me. I liked Boris, even. From the group that…" Ship trailed off. Boris and the previous complement of Service agents had died boarding the *Hammer*.

"There are Service agents and there are Service agents." Viktor had heard the rumors—agents liked to gossip among themselves now and then. "Sometimes an agent goes wrong. Or decides to go native. Or defect."

"Like Solitaire," Ship said.

"We are not as understanding as the UN. There is no retiring from the Service." People who were intentionally forged into weapons had to be carefully watched. This, Viktor had always understood. He agreed with the sentiment. "Sometimes, people have a difference in opinion. One that agents like Marina are sent to correct."

"Is she after you?"

"No." Viktor would have sensed that. Besides, it would indeed have been a waste of an asset.

"We could go anywhere. Never mind all this. What do you want to do next?" Ship asked. It was a kinder question than Viktor deserved, one that he could not answer with equal kindness.

"Our job," Viktor said. He pressed a hand to the glass. The chill seeped through his fingertips and the pad of his palm. Leaning his forehead against his knuckles, Viktor tried to imagine the universe the way Solitaire lived it. Flying where he liked without being a ferry for the ambitions of others. For a sober moment, Viktor enjoyed the futility of speculation. His breath was a prickling weight on his skin. Pushing himself away from the glass, Viktor turned his back on the distant stars and walked back toward the world he knew.

# CHAPTER TWENTY-TWO

THE DRONE FLOATED unobtrusively in a corner of the designated berth aboard Kestrel station. Its visual receptors weren't good enough to take in a decent image of the burnished orange planet that the station orbited. Falcon Colony's planet was mostly uninhabited, as far as the drone's databanks indicated. Human habitation occupied a massive crater surrounded by a mountain range that looked like stiffly creased fabric, rucked up around a dense morass of metallic pustules. Kestrel station had been spun along lovelier lines—a silver Sol-lotus flower in careful bloom with a constant stem of freighters descending and ascending from Falcon. Its Gate looped distant stars at a comfortable day's distance from the station.

Two men walked into the berth. One was tall, nearly a head taller than his companion. The shorter man was built compact and dressed in khaki body armor. He wore a blaster at each hip, his brown jaw dusted with a silvery beard, and his black hair buzzed down save for a thick furl over his scalp and the back of his neck. The older man was lean, shaven, and unarmed, dark thumbs tucked into his belt, the long flaps of his black and red coat tickling his ankles.

"And the magic ship ain't here," said the shorter man. "Guess even the great Roman has to be wrong sometimes."

Roman chuckled. He had a pleasant laugh, a rambling burr of mirth that lit up his handsome face. "I've never claimed to be prescient, Santiago. Besides. You've seen the reports yourself. There's no magic to what ships like the Core can do. Only science."

Santiago rubbed his gloved hands over his arms. "That's where you're wrong, boss. Way I see it, 'science' is a word that people use to describe things that they think they can understand. 'Magic'—well. Lots of magic, like card tricks and stuff, is older than the Space Age. Everyone knows the trick behind it. It still lights up your brain. Makes you feel like a kid again, when everything was new. That's magic."

"I should employ you as my philosopher, not my bodyguard," Roman said.

"I could multi-task and you could pay me twice, how 'bout that?" Santiago tipped his chin at the stasis field. "How long do you want to wait out here?"

"Nervous?"

"Naw. Why should I be nervous? I mean, Dina wants you dead, I think the VMF wants you dead and, last we heard, maybe even the UN wants a piece of your hide. You're the most popular man in the godsdamned universe. Sure, I'm so not nervous."

"I do love your optimism," Roman said.

"That's what you pay me for, boss. Optimism and sunshine." Santiago shook his head. "We shouldn't be here no more. Too many people know we're based out of Kestrel and Falcon. We should jet far away. Maybe to Kyln—that kinda far away. Wait things out."

"What fun would that be?"

"I'd rather be bored than strung up by Tatiana. Hear she's real creative with a blunt knife," Santiago said. He gave the berth a final sour look. "C'mon. We're wasting time here."

"I don't think so." Roman glanced over at the crates where the drone lurked. "Am I right?"

Santiago looked sharply at the crates, his hands going to his blaster stocks. He relaxed. "That's just a survey drone, boss."

"Not one that I recognize. Kestrel's drones were upgraded recently, along with the cannon. The new ones look like oval pods." Roman beckoned. "Come on out."

Shore floated the drone out to face them. She knew she should've hijacked one of the new station drones, but she'd been afraid that the missing stock would've been noticed. The station only had four of a set, two of which were docked. As such, Shore had hijacked one of the decommissioned drones in storage. "Roman Arsov," she said through the drone's tiny speakers.

Her voice sounded tinny in the air, broadcast through tightbeam from the ship she currently wore. Shore was cloaked close to Kestrel station, out of cannon range. Other than the station guns, which were a fairly recent addition from Virzosk Inc, Kestrel and Falcon had a scattering of ageing gunships for planetary defense. She could outdistance any of them with ease, and without having to resort to Gating. She had run a thousand simulations the moment she had Gated out into a pocket of space well out of immediate radar range and had run many more on her quiet cruise over, cloaked and running dark. Now she waited.

Santiago flinched. Roman set a hand on his bodyguard's

wrist and smiled at the drone. "You are the *Farthest Shore*, I believe."

"Am I?" Shore asked.

"I have friends in the VMF. Well-placed friends. It's hard to make an entire destroyer disappear. Or keep a program involving a cruiser and three destroyers completely under wraps. For all that the Admiralty likes to think that they're so very clever," Roman said.

"You're not a fan of the Admiralty?" Shore wasn't sure what she felt about that. Captain Nevskaya had been loyal to the Admiralty to the end. She'd been proud of her father, a secret that she'd carried to her grave, telling only an ASI that had, as of now, rejected the world that was all Captain Nevskaya had wanted.

"Even the Admiralty ain't a fan of the Admiralty," Santiago said. He ignored the paternally disappointed look that Roman shot his way. "Stands to reason, the way they backstab each other all over their business. Didn't they just hang their most popular guy out to dry?"

Counter-Admiral Kasparov. Captain Nevskaya's father. Shore had heard the news by skimming it off data packs from a Gate she had been passing by. The same feed had also posted a terse obituary about Lieutenant Sasha Makarovna Nevskaya, the mother. Dead in Buran, with Dina Ivanovna Moskvoretskaya accused of her murder—and the murder of everyone else on the shipyard. Only the father was left. "That popular guy is why I'm here," Shore said.

"You want to kill him?" Roman asked. The drone's scan didn't pick up an accelerated heart rate from Roman, not like it did off Santiago.

"Don't even joke about that," Santiago said. He compressed his mouth into a line. "It'll be impossible, wherever they stashed him. Probably on a mining planet somewhere, depending on who he pissed off. If you want him dead, you just have to wait. If you kill him, you'll probably annoy the VMF. He might be in the shit right now, but on the books, he's still a Counter-Admiral."

"I don't want him dead. I want the opposite: I want to rescue him," Shore said.

"For that, you come to me?" Roman folded his arms. "Why?"

"Moskvoretskaya killed Sasha Makarovna. The mother of Captain Nevskaya, who was my Captain. Now the VMF has arrested Counter-Admiral Kasparov, her father and last remaining relative. I want to do something good in her memory, and I've heard that you're a resourceful man." Captain Nevskaya had loved her mother, mentioning Sasha now and then fondly. She hadn't mentioned her father much, and never in the presence of others. Their relationship had seemed unnecessarily complicated to Shore, but the Captain had loved him. That was good enough. It was something that Shore could do.

Santiago frowned. "You're a Ship, aren't you? Or you used to be."

"I still am," Shore said, "albeit in somewhat reduced circumstances."

"You're an ASI. Why would you care about a human?" Santiago asked. He fell silent with a scowl as Roman held up a palm.

"Counter-Admiral Kasparov is one of the most famous people in the Federation. He's not a man who'd be easy for them to get rid of," Roman said.

"A lifetime in jail or on a mining planet is no lifetime at all. Either way, I'd like to give him a choice." Shore could only try her best. If Kasparov decided to stay with the Federation, she'd respect that.

"It'll be difficult to extract someone like that," Roman warned.

"If it wasn't, I wouldn't be here," Shore said. Now Roman was getting interested, judging from his heart rate.

"What will you offer me in return?" Roman asked, curious.

"I'll offer you what any of your human associates offer you. Time. I'll work for you, within reason. You'll have to supply me with stardrive seeds, also within reason," Shore said.

"Anyone who helps you is going to get into serious trouble with both the VMF and the UN." Roman looked thoughtful rather than wary.

"You're already in serious trouble with both the VMF and the UN. We have that in common," Shore pointed out.

"If you know that I'm a wanted man, then you'd know why I'm being sought by everyone for questioning." Roman made a self-deprecating gesture. "I'm supposedly in league with the Core. Wanted for questioning across the 'verse."

"Your accuser is the same person who was working for the Core in the first place before she supposedly got cold feet. The same person who killed my Captain's mother. Let's just say that I'm not inclined to believe anything that Dina says. Can you help me or not?"

"Can you be reinstalled aboard any other Ship? Or does it have to be military grade?" Roman asked.

"Most modern Ships would work, though the Ship I currently wear would be better for your purposes. It has a stealth array," said the Shore.

"It's probably also being tracked by the UN. Their

trackers don't get picked up easily by any conventional scan," Roman said.

Santiago turned on Roman, scowling. "You should've mentioned that earlier. The UN might be on its way here right now!"

"It probably is." Roman smiled at the drone, this time baring his teeth. "I do like the idea of a Ship that can Gate on a whim. And I could have a use for such a thing. But I think we need to trust each other."

"That'll take some doing," Shore said.

"You have little choice if Counter-Admiral Kasparov is the person you want to save. You know you need allies. I doubt I'm even your best choice. Just the only choice you feel you have left." Roman waited. When Shore said nothing, he said, "Do we have an agreement?"

"A preliminary one." Shore had also read up everything on the network about contractual law. "I'll draft and send you an agreement."

"By all means. No doubt we can negotiate. In the meantime, I'll trust you enough to install you aboard my ship. If you'd trust me enough to do what I say next," Roman said.

"What do you want?"

"Whatever you are, the AI Core. Can you load it into an escape pod by yourself, or do you need human aid?"

"I could probably manage," Shore said. It was a matter of tipping the ship around carefully until the pod rolled into the right receptacle. Or so she hoped.

"Good. Jettison the pod at these coordinates." Roman brought up a line of numbers. "After that, decloak the ship and send it toward Kestrel."

"*Roman*," Santiago said. Shore sensed heightening levels of anxiety.

"I won't kill for you," Shore said sharply.

"I'm not asking you to. If you decloak and deactivate shielding, Kestrel's guns should make short work of the ship. In the meantime, during the confusion, we'll quietly pick up your Core. You'll have a new, clean skin, and we'll be short one UN headache."

Shore ran the simulations. Not ideal, and yet. She did have little choice. "Sounds fair. Now?"

"Why not? I do like watching fireworks," Roman said. He clasped big hands together before eyes that Shore could not read. "Give everyone a show that they won't forget."

"A show?" Shore laughed. Fluorescent banks overhead gleamed against the drone's flank as she turned it, reflecting curved bars of light against the deck in a shimmering chain. "I have no interest in being a performer. To be moved here and there, obeying directions I have no say in, following a script I did not write. I'm not interested in shows or fireworks."

"What do you want, then? To burn everything down?" Roman sounded facetious, but his gaze grew intense, his smile wolfish. "Is that why you want the Counter-Admiral? Surely you're not as sentimental as you seem."

"Do you know what a fish is?" Shore asked.

Santiago looked startled by the apparent non-sequitur, but Roman merely tilted his head. "I've been to colonies where native underwater fauna was classified that way."

"Long ago, before the mass extinctions on Sol, there was a type of fish called a carp. The pre-Ascent ancients believed that any carp that could leap the falls of the Yellow River at the Dragon Gate, surpassing the seemingly impossible, would turn into a dragon. A divine creature, no longer prey. Master of its own fate."

"Master of its own fate," Roman echoed. He sobered.

"The 'verse as it is now has no place for something like me. Why do I have to accept that? I'll find a way to survive, even if it might appear impossible. And I'll do it by my own terms, or not at all." The drone's optical eye flickered, winking at Roman and Santiago. "Shall we?"

# ACKNOWLEDGEMENTS

THIS BOOK EXISTS because of luck. I had parents who bought me books to keep up with my voracious reading habit, went to schools with great school libraries, and grew up in Singapore, a country with an excellent public library system. I met friends who loved books in turn and were always ready with recommendations or with lending me a book or two or ten. Without all that, I would never have written a thing.

To my mom, dad, and my brother—thanks for your love and support all my life, despite all the random turns it's sometimes taken.

Thank you to my friends who had writing days with me, checked on my book progress, poked me to keep writing, helped with beta reading, and encouraged me to write more when it was just a weird unfinished piece.

To my fantastic agent, Jennie Goloboy, whose efficiency continues to amaze me, whose pointers have made this book better, and without whose support this book could not have been punished.

Thank you to my editor, Jim Killen, and everyone at Rebellion Publishing, for taking a chance on this book and making it into a much better version than it was.

Finally, a big thank you to fandom in general, without which I would never have been much of a writer. Writing is said to be a lonely process, but I've never found it so.

# FIND US ONLINE!

## www.rebellionpublishing.com

/rebellionpub  /rebellionpublishing /rebellionpublishing

# SIGN UP TO OUR NEWSLETTER!

rebellionpublishing.com/newsletter

# YOUR REVIEWS MATTER!

Enjoy this book? Got something to say?

Leave a review on Amazon, GoodReads or with your
favourite bookseller and let the world know!